. . . MIDNIGHT ON THE STATEN ISLAND FERRY . . .

Paul gazed down at Gwen a moment and smiled. "You know," he said, "You're not the only one who has built defenses. During my life with Verna, I've built some pretty solid ones of my own. But the first time I saw you, they all came tumbling down. You're the kind of woman most men can only dream about —intelligent, perceptive, sensitive—and beautiful, too. Don't hold yourself back from me."

For a second, her old fear flashed through her, and Gwen started to move away. "Please, Paul . . ." she whispered. But he put his hands on her shoulders and prevented her from moving.

And this time, she didn't shrink beneath his gentle touch.

Other Avon books by
Barbara Brett

BETWEEN TWO ETERNITIES

Love After Hours

BARBARA BRETT

AVON
PUBLISHERS OF BARD, CAMELOT AND DISCUS BOOKS

LOVE AFTER HOURS is an original publication of Avon Books. This work has never before appeared in book form.

AVON BOOKS
A division of
The Hearst Corporation
959 Eighth Avenue
New York, New York 10019

Copyright © 1981 by Barbara Brett
Published by arrangement with the author
Library of Congress Catalog Card Number: 80-68416
ISBN: 0-380-76257-9

All rights reserved, which includes the right
to reproduce this book or portions thereof in
any form whatsoever. For information address
McIntosh & Otis, Inc., 475 Fifth Avenue,
New York, New York 10017

First Avon Printing, January, 1981

AVON TRADEMARK REG. U.S. PAT. OFF. AND IN OTHER COUNTRIES, MARCA REGISTRADA, HECHO EN U.S.A.

Printed in the U.S.A.

To Hy, who has always believed in me—even when I haven't believed in myself.

... "Come then, Sorrow!
   Sweetest Sorrow!
Like an own babe I nurse thee on my breast:
   I thought to leave thee
   And deceive thee,
But now of all the world I love thee best.

   "There is not one,
   No, no, not one
But thee to comfort a poor lonely maid:
   Thou art her mother
   And her brother
Her playmate, and her wooer in the shade."

JOHN KEATS
Endymion

Chapter One

There is an unwritten law in Manhattan offices that the person who has been dismissed be shunned, but that the person who leaves of his own will, having neither need nor desire for moral or alcoholic support, be feted by his associates at a gala luncheon. It was in observance of the latter rite that a group of men and women met in the lobby of the Waterford Building promptly at noon on a cloudy Friday in May 1970. The guest of honor was Nadine Osgood, departing editor of *True Affairs*, and the destination was the Gold Rail Restaurant.

Ordinarily, when such an exalted personage as the editor of one of the magazines in the Waterford chain left, he was wined and dined at Sardi's, but the circumstances surrounding Nadine Osgood's departure were not ordinary. Unlike her predecessors, Nadine was not leaving the company for an executive slot in a public-relations firm, or for an executive position on a magazine different from any Waterford published, one devoted to a newly discovered vital interest of the American public—macramé, transcendental meditation, Japanese flower arrangements. Nadine was going over to *Intimate Experiences*, *True Affairs*' biggest competitor, where she would be paid a very handsome salary to use her thorough knowledge of her former magazine to knock it off the newsstands.

In short, Nadine Osgood was a Judas. But the rituals of a publishing office being more rigid than the loyalty and tractability of its personnel, even a Judas must be taken to lunch. Certain lines were drawn, however: The memo that had been circulated as an invitation specified that the luncheon was to

be an "intimate" one—a rather unfortunate choice of words
—meaning that only a few persons were being asked because
the company would frown upon Nadine's being given a rous-
ing send-off; Jason Bart, Waterford's editorial director, who
always represented The Company at such events, let it be
known that he had a long-standing previous engagement for
root-canal therapy; and the Gold Rail, a good restaurant, but
one of a chain of many like it, was substituted for Sardi's,
which is unique, not to mention much more expensive.

The party included the five members of Nadine Osgood's
editorial staff, the beauty editor of Waterford's women's
magazines, and the editors-in-chief of *Virile, Real, Modern
Movies* and *American Health Ways*. The editors of the company's paperback-book divisions—too exalted—and minor
magazines—not exalted enough—had not been asked.

There were some in attendance who might have cast a
cloud over the festivities: Terri Ainsworth, an associate editor on *True Affairs*, who resented having been passed over
for promotion in the general upheaval that resulted in the
wake of Nadine's departure; Neil Mennen, editor of *Modern
Movies*, who had been kicking himself lately for having
turned down an offer similar to Nadine's less than a year
before; and Cameron Eckhart, editor of *Real* and the current
fair-haired boy of Waterford Publications, who always took
it upon himself to assume the outlook of The Company on
matters of employee loyalty. They didn't stand a chance.
Their reservation melted under the magic of the martinis,
and, like the others in the group, they soon found themselves
eager to make the most of an excuse to enjoy a three-hour
lunch. Besides, the genuine good spirits that Nadine Osgood
and Gwendolyn Hadley, her successor to the editorship of
True Affairs, so obviously felt about the turn of events that
had brought them both good fortune seemed almost contagious.

As usual at any gathering attended by Bill Saxon, *Virile's*
vigorous editor, laughter bounced around the table. By the
time the happy group was ready to head back to the office at
three-fifteen, Terri Ainsworth had flirted coquettishly with all
males present (including the waiter), and Nolan West, editor
of *American Health Ways*, true to form, was thoroughly

sloshed. As for the others, all faces were flushed, and all eyes were bright.

As they waited for the elevator in the lobby of the Waterford Building, Nolan put an unsteady arm around Nadine and gave her a resounding kiss.

"I can't remember when I've had so much fun," he slurred. "You must come back and leave us again soon."

Nadine joined in the general laughter as all present heartily agreed.

Two telephone messages awaited Gwendolyn Hadley when she returned to her desk. The first read: "1:30. Your father called. Please stop at the store on your way home." The second: "1:35. Your mother called. Don't bother to stop at the store."

Gwen balled them up and tossed them into her wastebasket. It was an old story to her—the daily battle royal her folks had about her father's drinking—and she refused to let it penetrate the heady glow of excitement she was feeling.

Propping her feet on an open drawer, she settled down to the pile of manuscripts on her desk. The little crease between her eyebrows deepened as she tried to force herself to concentrate. Though her height was only an inch or two more than that of the average woman, her long, shapely legs and slender body gave her the appearance of being much taller. Her auburn hair, worn in a short, fluffy bob, offset the angularity of her straight nose, high cheekbones, and slightly pointed chin. The sharp contours of her face had deprived her of any aura of prettiness in girlhood, only to bestow upon her a much more lasting gift in maturity; the severe-looking girl of twenty had matured into an extremely attractive woman of thirty-one.

Betsy, Nadine Osgood's teen-aged secretary, popped her shaggy, frost-tipped blond head into Gwen's office. "Boss lady wants to see you."

Shuddering at the thought that Betsy would now start applying colorful appellations to *her*, Gwen approached the sacred cubicle, larger than all the others in the department, that was the sanctuary of The Editor. She had never coveted the extra space and extra window, but now they were to be hers. It struck her, as she pushed open the door, that she and Nadine Osgood were finally professional equals—no longer boss and employee, but editor and editor.

True Affairs not being as lucrative a property as *Real*, the editor was deprived of a carpet and drapes. Aside from the extra window and space, the sole mark of prestige in the room was the executive desk, which was approximately six inches longer and wider than those issued to the other members of the magazine's staff. Nadine was seated behind this expanse of gray steel as Gwen entered, and, as usual, because of her petite figure, gave the impression of a child play-acting in her father's office. It was a fleeting impression, however; no one could come in contact with Nadine Osgood without being struck by her intelligence and competence, without being left a little shaken by the calculating pale-blue eyes that gave the impression that the whole world paraded naked before them.

Nadine had already cleared her desk of her personal belongings, and her pocketbook stood on its vast, empty expanse like a lonely sentinel. "I hate leave-takings," she said, gesturing for Gwen to sit down. "There's no middle ground about them. They're either hypocritical or heartbreaking."

Gwen laughed. "Which category do you fit Waterford into?"

"Waterford into the first. You into the second." Her gaze met Gwen's. "Are you quite sure you won't come with me?" she asked. "I know that I can get you at least as much as they've offered you here for your trial period as editor."

Gwen shook her head.

Nadine leaned across the desk. "I'll admit I'm being selfish. Seven years is a long time, Gwen. We get along well, and we work together well. I'd like to take you with me. But I wouldn't ask you if I thought you were staying because you had a burning desire for all this." She waved a dainty hand around her. "I wouldn't push you, because I can understand that type of desire—I've been driven by it all my life. But I've never recognized its signs in you."

Gwen's gaze swept the cubicle. "I'd be a liar if I didn't admit I was flattered when the job was offered to me. I may not have wanted it a month ago, but I want it now."

"Well, that's it then." Nadine rose, put on her coat, picked up her pocketbook. "I'm going now. I don't want to stay and embarrass everyone by my presence any longer than I have to. Especially Cam Eckhart. You'd think he was old Doc Waterford's bastard son, the way he carries on about loyalty to the company. Don't ever get caught in that line, Gwen. I've been around long enough and worked in enough places to know that employers are loyal only to themselves. Their employees should go and do likewise."

Gwen held up her hand. "Spare me the lecture," she said. "I'm staying only out of loyalty to myself."

Both women laughed, and Nadine took Gwen's hand. Her smile faded, and once more her eyes were searching Gwen's. "It should work the same way outside the office too," she said quietly.

It was the first time in the seven years they'd worked together that the women had come so close to intimacy. They shared an awkward closeness for a moment. And then the moment was gone.

Still smiling, Gwen withdrew her hand. "Let's have lunch together someday soon, Nadine."

"Good idea," Nadine said. Then she laughed. "Whose expense account shall we use?"

"Wouldn't it be great if we could have it charged to Cam Eckhart?"

Nadine laughed again. "I'll call you soon. Good-by. Good luck."

"Good luck."

Alone, Gwen walked around the cubicle, now opening a file drawer, now leafing through a book in one of the bookcases. The sounds of the outer office floated in—typewriters clacking, phones ringing, secretaries laughing, Bill Saxon booming out in exaltation over a particularly sexy coverline.

She sank into the chair at the desk, trying it for size. It was too high for her. She stood up, twirled it around a few times to lower it, then tried it again. That was better—a perfect fit. It felt right and good, as though she belonged in it. Smiling to herself, she ran her hand over the edge of the desk, then swiveled around to gaze out the window. In the distance, the New Jersey shore was shrouded in smog, but she could still make out the Hudson and the huge orange stacks of a steamer that was pulling out. Then it came over her again, the same slow, sinking feeling she had experienced in the midst of the excitement of Jason Bart's asking her to be editor—the feeling that life was closing in on her. It had dogged her at unexpected moments ever since. Determined to shake it off, she jumped from the chair and turned to examine the contents of a bookcase.

A sudden gaping silence announced the arrival of five o'clock better than a chiming clock might have done. Gwen started across the room. Before she reached the door, Cameron Eckhart pushed it open and poked his ingratiating head in.

"Say, I've been looking for you. How about a drink to celebrate?"

He came in and closed the door. If Plato was right and heaven is indeed the sphere of ideal forms, Cameron Eckhart was patterned as near as a mortal can be to the one labeled "editor, sophisticated men's magazine." Lean and tall, he always managed to look as though he had just stepped off one of his fashion pages. His ruddy complexion was topped by fashionably long sandy hair, and his upper lip and square chin bore one of the few mustaches and beards in America that did not look seedy, pretentious or ridiculous. His mind was patterned after the ideal too. For forty-five years, he had managed to convince himself that he was living in a man's world where women, no matter how intelligent or what their position, were placed solely for man's pleasure.

Gwen shook her head. "Thanks, Cam. But I've already drunk enough today to float a battleship."

"Then surely one more won't hurt."

Because he sounded so sure of himself, she was ready to stand by her refusal. She realized, however, that Cam wouldn't be put off easily. If she refused now, it would only mean having to drink with him some other time. She might as well get it over with. She shrugged. "All right, Cam."

Bill Saxon popped his head in before she got to the door. "How about a celebration?"

Instantly, Gwen brightened. "That's just what Cam was suggesting."

Bill perched on the edge of the desk and took out a cigarette. "Swell. I'll join the party and see to it that you're not seduced."

Cam smiled, but his heart didn't seem to be in it.

Back at her own desk, Gwen pulled out a mirror and ran a comb through her hair. A gray strand caught her eye. She made a motion to pull it out, then checked herself. Why bother? After all, she was thirty-one; she'd have to expect gray hairs now. Unlike Terri Ainsworth, the self-styled office sexpot who had long ago left her twenties behind, Gwen had never attempted to delude herself into believing that she had discovered the fountain of youth.

She slipped the mirror back into her drawer and went out to join the men. She found them waiting at the bank of elevators in the main corridor, Cam in the middle of a long dissertation on reader mail. Bill was lounging against the wall, his eyes sparkling behind his dark-rimmed glasses. Obviously, he'd been at one of his favorite pastimes—baiting Cam.

"Have you fellows stopped bickering long enough to ring for the elevator?"

Bill snapped his fingers and pressed the button with a flourish. "Brilliant suggestion. No wonder they made you an editor. Where to? Nick's?"

"Where else?" she asked.

Ten years ago, when Gwen and Bill and his wife, Shari, had just started at Waterford, they'd been introduced to the dingy little bar and grill just off Seventh Avenue. The drinks there were bad and the food was worse, but years before, ancestral editors, for reasons unknown, but most likely masochistic, had established Nick's as an after-hours Waterford headquarters. Headquarters it had remained, being passed down from one generation of editors to the next and accepted by all as a family weakness that has proved to be carried by a dominant gene. Nick retired nine years ago and passed the business on to his son-in-law, Beauregard, who had once taken a six-week extension course in restaurant administration at Cornell University. The keys to the place still cold in his hand, Beauregard washed the street windows, substituted the word *restaurant* for *grille* on the sign, and stopped watering the drinks. Horrified Waterfordians shook their heads in dismay and wondered what would happen next. They didn't have long to wait. Six months later, the springs in the booths were repaired, and a massive man named Sam, who could make almost palatable spaghetti, relieved the dishwasher of his cooking duties. But the worst was yet to come: A year later, Beauregard sent his wife to Cornell for the extension course. Within a week of her return, white linen cloths draped every table, it was discovered that Sam was a direct descendent of Lucullus's chef, the restaurant's name was changed to Apollo's Grotto, and a real, honest-to-God, imitation olive tree sprang up from the center of the floor overnight. Waterfordians grumbled. They might have to put up with the other renovations, but the restaurant had always been "Nick's" to them, and, olive tree or no olive tree, "Nick's" it would remain.

Beauregard, wearing his perpetual smile and shiny tuxedo, greeted them at the door. The years since he'd been maître d' had thickened his waist and thinned his hair, so that now he had to remind himself constantly to hold his stomach in and to tilt his head back and slightly to the right so that his bald spot would not be immediately obvious to the person he was facing. This, coupled with his quick, jerky movements, and his tendency to repeat everything, gave his customers the impression that they were being greeted by a life-size marionette.

"Good evening, good evening," he said, greeting them all by name. "It's been a long time since I've seen you. And you especially, Mr. Eckhart. A long time."

He began leading the way to a table at the back. They exchanged greetings with some Waterford people they passed on the way, waved to Terri Ainsworth, who had cornered Neil Mennen at the bar.

"Watch out for the—" Gwen heard a warning voice call out. Then she heard laughter. Turning, she saw Cam, red from beard to hairline, a branch of the plastic olive tree caught in his jacket.

"Why don't you prune this damn thing?" he grated, extricating himself.

For once, Beauregard's smile faded. He went bobbing

back to Cam. "I'm so sorry," he said, alternately brushing Cam off and bending the branch upward. "So sorry. Some prankster must have bent this down. I hope no damage was done."

"Only to his ego," Bill said. "He can't sue you for that."

"Ah, yes, yes," Beauregard said. He clasped his hands and smiled once more, though the smile was a little weak. Then he led them to their table without further incident.

While they waited for their drinks, Bill whipped a ballpoint pen from his pocket and held it to his mouth as if it were a microphone. "Now that you're officially the editor of *True Affairs,* tell us, Miss Hadley, what are your plans for the magazine?" He extended the pen toward her.

Playing along, Gwen addressed the pen with mock seriousness: "To make it the best damn confession magazine on the market."

"Kidding aside," Bill said, replacing the pen in his pocket, "what are your plans? Have you decided on any changes?"

"My head has been buzzing with ideas ever since Jason said the job was mine." Leaning forward, she began outlining some of her plans, her eyes sparkling and her cheeks flushed with excitement.

Bill listened attentively, greeting her ideas with enthusiasm. Cam nodded politely, his mind obviously elsewhere.

Their drinks served, Bill raised his Scotch and soda and nodded at Gwen, his eyes warm with affection. "To you. Long may your blue pencil wave."

They drank.

Cam studied his martini. "Well," he said, "this is the first toast I've drunk today that I've meant."

Gwen laughed. "Jealous of Nadine, Cam?" she teased.

"Of course not," he bristled. "I wouldn't want to change places with her. After all, there's such a thing as having principles."

"And the fat raise Nadine will get from *Intimate* is a hell of a good principal, if you ask me," Bill said.

Cam's nostrils flared. "I wouldn't expect you to understand such a thing as loyalty to the company, Bill," he said, "but I'm sure Gwen does."

"My God, Cam! You're in the wrong business. You should

be president of a fertilizer company." Bill leaned across the table, laughing. "You can't really believe this loyalty-to-the-company shit! How loyal do you think the company would be to us if anything came up? Just let either of us miss his guarantee a few months in a row, and we'd be out on our asses so fast we wouldn't know what hit us. Do you think that the Brothers Three would give a damn that I have a wife and three kids to support or that you have a wife and seven mistresses?"

Shrugging, Cam sipped his drink. "In an age known for its lack of moral backbone, you fit in well."

Bill's eyes still sparkled behind his glasses. "The long line of secretaries who have been recipients of feels behind filing cabinets would no doubt be happy to testify to your efforts at conformity too."

Gwen was enjoying the argument, but she knew that Cam had had a great deal to drink that day, and she was afraid to let it go too far. "If you two keep it up," she warned them, "I'll pick up my marbles and go home."

Bill spread his hands, palms upward, in a gesture of obedience. "No more fisticuffs," he promised.

Cam picked up his drink.

For a moment there was silence at the table.

"Now see what you've done?" Bill complained. "There's nothing we can talk about if you won't let us fight."

Almost as though he had received a signal, Beauregard popped over. "Another round?"

"Why not?" Bill said.

Cam hesitated a second, looking at his watch. "I'll have to skip this one. I just have time to make my train." He pushed his chair back. "Good luck, Gwen. Thanks for the drink, Bill. I'll see you both Monday."

It was hard for Bill and Gwen to keep from laughing as they watched Cam make his way to the exit. Bill shook his head. "There goes a smooth operator. If he doesn't get the girl, he won't pay for the drink. You're lucky I'm here. Otherwise, you might have been stuck with the check."

"A price I would have willingly paid for getting rid of him." Gwen shuddered slightly. "He's one of the most obnoxious men I know."

Bill's eyebrows shot up. "I'm not madly in love with him myself, but I can't say I find him totally obnoxious."

"No, a man wouldn't. It's his attitude toward women I'm talking about. He thinks we're playthings who couldn't possibly have anything better on our minds than pleasing him. A lot of men think along those lines, but when you find a man as intelligent and as well educated as Cam guilty of it, it's doubly insulting."

"There seem to be a significant number of women around who don't think it's insulting."

"Oh, I don't deny that. He's very attractive, and to many women that's adequate compensation for being treated like something just slightly higher on the evolutionary scale than a pet dog."

"But that's not enough for you."

She shook her head emphatically. "You're damn right it's not enough for me."

Bill raised his fresh Scotch and soda. "I'll drink to that," he said.

Terri Ainsworth got up from the bar and walked over to their table. She smiled at Bill, tilting her head at a coquettish angle. Taking a deep breath, she forced her small breasts to strain halfheartedly against the confines of her tight sweater. "Are you coming, Bill?" she asked throatily. "We don't have much time to make our train."

"Fair maiden," Bill said, placing the back of his hand against his brow dramatically, "you must tell the engineer to carry on without me tonight. Business awaits me in the city."

Terri imitated the laugh she had heard Elizabeth Taylor use some twenty years ago. It emerged sounding halfway between a giggle and a croak. "I'll miss you," she said. "Well, have a nice weekend. Good night, Gwen."

They watched her undulating departure. "There," Bill said, an amused smile playing on his lips, "goes the *femme fatale* of the 5:49. Have you ever watched that gal in action?"

"Constantly. I didn't know she was ever out of it."

"True, true. You know, I might be flattered by her flirting if it wasn't so indiscriminate. A pox on the day she moved to a town on my line of the Long Island Rail Road! She sits with the same group of guys every morning and night. You have to see it to believe the way she carries on. She seems to think of herself as a combination of Elizabeth Taylor and Raquel Welch. The guys play right along with her, and she never seems to realize that they're laughing at her all the time." He shook his head. "I'm catching another train tonight. After all I had to drink today, I couldn't trust my stomach if I had to be part of the audience."

"You could always sit in another car."

Bill laughed. "And miss the show? I'm drawn to it like a magnet when she's on the train. I'm like the patient in the dentist's waiting room who keeps looking at the pictures of incurable gum disease in the journals on the tables. Terri fascinates me in the same sick way. She seems to be the incarnation of the spinster Robert Burns wished cursed with eternal desire and damned with endless disappointment."

"Hey!" Gwen chided. "Go easy on us old maids, huh?"

Bill leaned across the table, the laughter suddenly gone from his eyes. "Listen, there's no comparison between you and a dame like Terri. She's an old maid, but you're a woman who just doesn't happen to be married. There's a hell of a big difference."

Gwen burst out laughing. "You should have been born my big brother, Bill. Your lectures are wonderful."

His seriousness vanished as quickly as it had appeared. "Brother!" he boomed. "That's a hell of a compliment if I ever heard one! Now if you wanted me as a lover, I'd be willing to accommodate you, but you'll have to adopt someone else if you want a brother."

"Oh, shut up before you find yourself wearing a whiskey sour over your ear." The threat was far from menacing.

Bill glanced at his watch. "I'll be wearing dinner over my head if I miss that next train. I told Shari I'd be out celebrating with you, but I promised not to be too late."

Gwen slipped into her trench coat while Bill paid for the drinks. They walked outside. The foggy evening seemed fresh compared to the overheated smokiness of Nick's. The rush hour was over but the dinner hour had not yet begun, and the street was nearly deserted. Side by side, they strolled in silence, past the brightly lighted shop windows. Gwen's hands were deep in her pockets, her purse thumping softly and rhythmically against her thigh; Bill held a rolled-up copy of a rival magazine in his right hand, occasionally tapping it against his left.

Gwen had used the word *brother* in connection with Bill before, and it was true that he and Shari were like brother and sister to her, and she like a sister to them. They had all come to Waterford at about the same time ten years before, but from different backgrounds—Gwen from a public city college, Shari from a private out-of-town one, Bill from a marking-time job with which he'd supported himself while achieving his bachelor's and then his master's degree at night. Though their temperaments and backgrounds had differed, their journalistic dream had been the same. It wasn't the dream that drew them together, however, for the dream was long since outgrown, but their friendship was not. Beneath Bill's bombast, Shari's vivacity, and Gwen's quietness there was a certain sensitivity that they shared.

When Bill and Shari fell in love, their relationship with Gwen hadn't really changed. She had then become their collective friend instead of the friend of each separately. When, soon after their marriage, Shari had left Waterford to pursue her new dream of motherhood, the friendship had remained unaltered. Gwen may have seen her friends less often, but when she did, the old sensitivity, the old understanding, were still there.

To Gwen, Bill and Shari were linked together in her mind as a unit. They were a couple in the true sense of the word, each giving something so fine and vital to the other that it was sometimes difficult to think of them individually. Of the two, perhaps she treasured Bill's friendship more. For it is a rare gift when a man allows a woman to share his thoughts on an equal footing with no strings attached. This worked both ways, of course, and she was aware that Bill valued her openness with him equally.

It was that very communicativeness that prompted him to ask his question now, in his usual brusque way: "What's been eating you lately?"

She stared up at a street lamp, watching it break the fog into tiny particles of light. "If I ever find out, you'll be the second to know."

"Who'll be the first?"

"Me."

"You can't solve it till you face it."

"Assuming there is a solution."

He shot a quizzical look her way, but evidently sensing her reluctance to talk, dropped the subject.

They walked on in silence. When they reached the subway, Bill jiggled some coins in his pocket. "Care to join me? I'll be a sport and treat."

She shook her head. "Thanks. I think I'll walk a bit."

"Shari's been after me to ask when you're coming out to see us. How about tomorrow?"

"Not tomorrow. Next Saturday maybe."

"No maybe about it. Do you want to get me in trouble? Shari said not to let you be indefinite."

"All right. Next Saturday. Definitely."

"Fine. I'll see you Monday. Good night."

"Good night. Love to Shari and the kids. Thanks for the drinks and the lecture. I needed them both."

"Did they help?"

"Do they ever?"

He extended one lip in the manner of Maurice Chevalier and attempted a Gallic shrug.

Turning her collar up, Gwen continued along the street. The fog was denser now; it clung to her coat and condensed into tiny, sparkling droplets on her hair. She had the feeling she could write her name in it if she tried. Wasn't there something in the Bible about names being writ on water? Well, perhaps hers was destined to be writ on fog.

What a whiner I'm turning into! she thought. Hunching her shoulders against the dampness of the evening and the sudden darkness of her thoughts, she made her way to the subway and home to her apartment on Eastern Parkway in Brooklyn.

Her father was dozing over a well-thumbed copy of the *National Enquirer* when she came in. He was a massive man, well over six feet tall, with feet and hands the size of hams. Often in their childhood, Gwen and her older sister had felt the brute power of those hands against their cheeks in blows that left their ears ringing for days. His face was that of a

Love After Hours 15

pugilist, dominated by beetling black brows and a nose whose every bump had been won on the battlefield of barroom floors. Barnabas Hadley was a septuagenarian, and he bore his age as a medal of merit. Indeed, it was probably the only admirable accomplishment of his life. "I'm seventy-two," he was fond of telling everyone he met. He'd curl his massive hand into a fist, bending his arm at the elbow. "Just feel that muscle. Made of iron. I'll be seventy-three come next July eighteen, and never been sick a day in my life." What he always avoided mentioning was that, aside from some sporadic goldbricking as a porter in the Fulton Fish Market, he had never done an honest day's work in his life—a factor that had greatly contributed to his longevity and robust health.

He woke as Gwen walked in. His eyes, glassy from sleep, gave him the appearance of an angry bullfrog as they peered from beneath his dark brows. "Where's the beer?"

She slipped out of her wet coat. "Still on the shelf in the store, where it belongs."

"The hell you say!" He curled the fingers of one hand as though they were encompassing the body of a massive bottle. "This is where it belongs. Right here in my hand."

"Dad, please. I'm in no mood to argue—or to put up with one of your beer drunks."

Her mother came bustling out of the kitchen. Agnes Hadley was as small as her husband was large. She had the type of face which, in youth, is considered adorable. As with so many faces in that category, when Agnes's youth had fled, her small, sharply tilted nose and almost nonexistent chin had become pathetically out of place amid the network of wrinkles that led to a shock of white hair.

Agnes had spent her girlhood and youth caring for an ailing father. Barnabas Hadley had come into her life when she was thirty, just a few weeks before her father died. To the shock of her relatives, she married him less than a month later, before her father was cold in the grave. Impressed by Barney's big body and big talk, she had married him thinking he would be a steady man who would protect her from the outside world and shield her from making decisions as her father had always done. Impressed by her house and affected speech, Barney had married her thinking she was an heiress who would put him on easy street. They were both poor judges. It wasn't long before Agnes discovered that the only thing steady about her husband was his hand as he lifted a drink or lowered a blow. Barney, in turn, discovered that, her father having lived on a pension that stopped with his death, Agnes's inheritance amounted to sixty-seven dollars and forty-four cents, not to mention a fourteen-carat gold-filled stick pin; the house, he learned, had belonged to Agnes's stepmother and had been her father's for his lifetime only, after which it reverted to his second wife's son. Arguments ensued in which each accused the other of misrepresentation. Variations on that theme had been a daily ritual for forty years. Agnes never left her husband because the thought of being on her own petrified her. Barney never left his wife because he clung to the hope that one day, out of sheer desperation, she'd go out and get a job. Eventually, they became parents and pinned their hopes on their daughters. Barney demanded that the girls grow up as soon as possible so that they could go out and find work. Agnes was more subtle. She smothered the girls with love, constantly reminding them of the excruciating agony she had endured bringing them into the world and of the continuous sacrifices she had made to bring them up; every day brought several reminiscences of the devoted daughter she herself had been. When her propagandizing bore no fruit with Nora, her older daughter, who ran off and married at eighteen, Agnes refused to accept defeat and redoubled her efforts with Gwen.

Now Agnes emerged from the kitchen, wiping her hands on her apron. She always wore an apron, tying it around her waist the moment she arose in the morning and never removing it until she was preparing for bed; it gave her the appearance of never having a moment's rest. "Where have you been?" she asked her daughter in a tone that was halfway between an accusation and a whine.

"I told you this morning I might be late."

Agnes ignored the reminder. "You should have called, dear," she chided gently. "I was getting worried."

"A hell of a lot *she* cares!" Barney growled. "She's too

much of a skinflint to buy her father a bottle of beer. Do you think she'd spend a dime on a phone call to you?"

Agnes whirled on her husband, her tongue becoming as sharp as her eyes. "You shut up!" she grated. "If you want your filthy beer so much, go out and work for it."

Growling, Barney brandished a fist at his wife, but only sank deeper into the cushions of the sofa.

Agnes turned back to her daughter, her face immediately resuming its look of injured innocence, her voice returning to its tone of martyrdom. "It's all right, dear. But try to remember to tell me next time. Dad and I ate. You know how he hates to be kept waiting for meals."

"Don't worry about it, Mom. I'll fix something for myself later."

"Nonsense. I'll warm your dinner up now."

"No, please. I don't want anything."

"Of course you do. It will just take a minute."

"Mom, I won't eat it."

Gwen's tone made her mother stop short before going into the kitchen. Agnes wasn't used to being crossed. She turned around, smiling brightly. "Of course you will. I'll have everything ready before you know it."

Gwen began to tremble. "For the love of God, Mom! I don't want to eat!" Though the words rose progressively higher, their volume had been measured with great effort and never increased. "I'm thirty-one years old. If I'm not a competent judge of my appetite by now, I should be in an institution for the mentally retarded."

Great tears welled in Agnes's eyes. Her lower lip began to quiver. She balled the hem of her apron in her hand. "I didn't mean any harm." Her voice was thin and quaking. "Is it so wrong for a mother to want to make sure her child receives proper nutrition and takes care of herself?"

Gwen sighed. She should have known better than to lose control. In a second, she was across the room, consoling her mother. She kept all trace of tension from her voice now. "I'm sorry, Mom. You know I didn't mean it that way. It's just that I'm tired. Let me rest a while. Then you can cook up a storm for me if you want."

Wiping her eyes, Agnes smiled her forgiveness. A delayed victory was a victory nevertheless.

Gwen went into her room. The voices of her mother and father suddenly lost in an argument thirty or forty years old followed her. She shut her door on them and lay down on her bed, staring up at her ceiling. Closing her eyes, she tried to rekindle the excitement she had felt earlier in the day—at the luncheon, at Nick's—but the sounds of her parents' quarrel kept intruding. Add to them the sounds that surrounded her at the office—typewriters clacking, phones ringing—and she'd have the sounds of her life. She rolled over and pounded her pillow in frustration. *Is this all there is?* she thought. *Is this all there will ever be?*

Chapter Two

*Bi*ll Saxon came storming into Gwen's office, a memo clenched in his hand. "How do you like that son of a bitch?" he said.

It was mid-August now—three months since she'd become editor, more than three weeks since Jason Bart had told her she could forget about the trial period. He liked what she was doing with the magazine, and advertisers who had been informed of her innovations with child-care and household features were responding by increasing their space. If newsstand sales went up—as he was sure they would—she'd soon receive a substantial salary increase.

Gwen looked up from the Kodachromes that were strewn over her desk. All morning, she had been sorting them out, choosing from them the four-color section that would grace her December issue. A suggestion of a smile played at the corners of her mouth. "*Which* son of a bitch?" she asked.

Narrowing his eyes, Bill bobbed his head in his best Charlie Chan fashion. "Number-one son," he intoned. Then, waving the memo in the direction of the offices at the opposite end of the floor, "Cam. Who else?" He extended the paper to her. "Weren't you honored with one of these today?"

She glanced at it. "Oh—the memo about the paint job. What about it?"

"Green! A cool, sea green!" The words sounded like a curse. He read from the middle of the memo: " 'I have taken the liberty to inform Jason Bart that a cool, sea green would be best suited to our floor.' Who the hell gave him the liberty? Bart told me that you and Cam and I should get together and decide the color. Cam never said a word to me about it. What about you?"

Gwen shrugged. "No, but what's the sense of fighting with him about it? He'll only make a stink or give us one of his long speeches. I don't have the time or patience for either. Green wouldn't have been my first choice, but—so what? As long as Cam keeps his nose out of my magazine and his hands off me, I'm happy. I'd let him paint purple-and-orange stripes on the wall for that kind of peace of mind."

"Woman, where's your fighting spirit? Very well, I, Sir William, will fight your battles for you." At the door of her office, he turned back, his eyes laughing. "You're right, of course. It really isn't worth fighting about," he admitted. "But I'll be damned before I'll let him get away with it!"

In another second, she heard him striding through the outer office bellowing, "Eckhart!"

Laughing, she picked up her phone and dialed the company's photography studio. Holding one of the Kodachromes up to the light, she waited for Boyd Larson, the studio director, to pick up the other end of the line. "Boyd," she begged, "please, from now on when I ask for an older woman in a picture, don't get me a model who's doddering on the brink of the old folks' home. My shooting script specifically said 'sexy older woman'—not 'senile.' "

Good-natured Boyd fell back on his usual excuses of being understaffed and overworked, and his usual promise to try to follow her shooting script more carefully next time.

"But that still leaves me stuck with this old biddy."

"Maybe you can work around her—crop her out entirely," Boyd suggested cheerfully.

"Oh, sure! She's only the protagonist!" Gwen sighed. "All right. I'll see what my art man can do with her. But next time, stick to the script—*please!*"

"Gotcha."

As she hung up, she heard Cam Eckhart's voice from the other end of the outer office. She couldn't comprehend the words above the clatter of typewriters, but the tone was one of righteous indignation.

It wasn't long before Cam came striding into her office. He gave her his most charming smile, but it didn't mask the anger lurking in his eyes. "How's my best girl?" he beamed.

Gwen's sigh of impatience was almost imperceptible. "I don't know. Didn't you ask her before you left the house?"

The cheerless smile flashed again, and he strolled to the window as if he had nothing in particular on his mind.

Gwen glanced over a critique attached to a manuscript on top of the huge pile on her desk and wrote her own reject on the bottom.

"Pale green," he sighed in a stage whisper, "the color of the sea."

"The color of bile too." Gwen reached for another manuscript.

Cam's right hand smoothed his beard into a point, and he chewed the corner of his mustache as he always did when he grew impatient. "Be serious for a moment. Close your eyes and envision these dull, gray walls a cool, pale green. What does it make you think of?"

Playing along for a second, Gwen leaned back and closed her eyes. Then she straightened abruptly and screwed her face up. "Paint smell," she said matter-of-factly.

There was no masking of the anger in Cam's eyes now. "That's the trouble with you and Saxon. You make a joke out of everything. Did you ever stop to think that the color of an office affects the attitude of the workers? A cool, sea green would be pleasant, relaxing."

"It might put them to sleep. If you want something conducive to work, why not try a hot, burnt orange with busy red polka dots all over it?"

His fingers tugged at the side of his mustache. "Why can't you take me seriously?"

She laughed. "I'll do that someday—when you extend the same courtesy to me." Quickly she glanced through the next critique and placed another R and her initials at the bottom. "Look, Cam, it's almost lunchtime, and I've got a date with—"

There was a brisk knock. The door of her office opened, and a beautifully coiffured blond head poked in. "Hi! Are you ready?"

"Hi! I was just about to mention your name," Gwen said. "Come on in, Andrea. I didn't realize it was twelve already. I'll be only a minute."

The door opened wide, and Andrea Langford, the statuesque beauty editor for the Waterford Women's Group, stepped in. Tall and willowy, Andrea dressed impeccably, and, by applying makeup with an artist's hand, had long ago learned how to turn her attractiveness into a cold but stunning beauty. She walked with the grace of a model, always leaving her beholders a little surprised not to see the folds of a filmy chiffon gown billowing out behind her.

Cam stiffened, then started toward the door. "Think about what I've said," he told Gwen.

Smiling, Gwen scanned her crowded desk top. "If there's one thing I don't need, it's more to think about. You and Bill fight it out between you. As long as the walls aren't black, I really don't care what color they are. I rarely look at them anyway."

Cam's mouth opened. Then, glancing at Andrea, he seemed to think the better of what he was about to say. With a curt nod in Andrea's direction, he continued toward the door.

Andrea returned the barest of nods—the type a democratic lady-in-waiting might bestow upon the queen's bootblack—and then obviously thought no more about him.

His back stiff, Cam left the room. Years ago, when he had tried to initiate an affair with her, Andrea had told him publicly to go to hell. Ever since then, he'd made no secret of the fact that he thought her a bitch and couldn't stand her condescending attitude.

The door slammed.

"Well!" Andrea raised a neatly curved eyebrow. "I hope that's as final as the door-slamming in *The Doll's House*."

"I should have such luck!" Gwen said, taking out her mirror and her lipstick. "How's Marge?"

Mention of her daughter was the one thing in life that brought warmth to Andrea's eyes. Cruelly jilted by a social-climbing law student when she was in college, Andrea had resolved never to relive such a degrading experience. Not the type to wallow in self-pity, she had dried her sparse tears and set about grooming herself to become a self-sufficient woman who needed neither love nor help from any man. Within a very short time after entering the editorial field, she had pushed herself to the top, becoming a highly respected—and highly paid—beauty editor. By the age of twenty-four, she was able to count herself a success: She had money—a great deal of it inherited from a maiden aunt—position, security, a luxurious apartment, and beautiful clothes. There was nothing more she wanted from life.

Then, at twenty-five, she decided that there *was* something more. Most of her friends were married by that time. She pitied them in their split-level prisons, where they had to suppress their individuality and could achieve success only through their husband's advancement. Only one aspect of their tedious lives did she envy—the maternal. The more she pondered the situation, the more positive she became that her life would be complete if she had a child to love. Of course, she would never fall into the same trap as her friends had simply to fulfill her maternal longings, but she could see no reason why her indifference to men should preclude her becoming a mother.

With the air of a buyer going to market, she selected the candidate likeliest to have the best set of genes. Harley—or was it Harvey?—she no longer was sure of his name, and probably would not recognize him if she saw him on the street—was tall, handsome, intelligent, and, to all outward appearances, healthy. She seduced him, continuing their affair for the six and a half weeks it took for her to be certain of pregnancy. Then she dropped him, virtually never thinking of him again. To those who, in those dark days before women's liberation protected innovators like her, raised eyebrows about her condition, she gave a story about a whirlwind courtship and elopement that led to a disastrous awakening and a quickie divorce; to most, and that included Marjorie herself, she made no secret of the fact that, wanting a child, she had simply gone and had one.

Seventeen years had passed since Marjorie's birth, and not once in all that time had Andrea felt the need of a male figure in her home. Marjorie, of course, had had questions about her lack of a daddy when she was little, but Andrea had always answered them frankly. She believed that girls should learn as soon as possible that men were dullards who tried to bolster their weak egos by marrying women and suppressing their egos, and that an intelligent woman needed a man only to assist her in the act of procreation. A bright, perceptive child, Marjorie soon recognized the validity of her mother's reasoning, for she very early stopped questioning it. Andrea saw to it that Marjorie attended the best private schools and that she had everything a girl could want. As was to be expected, when she reached her teens, Marjorie began to date. Andrea had no objection to this. A male escort was a necessary entrée to many social functions, and she herself often had to condescend to being escorted. Her observance of her daughter's comings and goings, however, assured her that, like her mother, Marjorie was a level-headed girl who kept a fellow in his place.

"Marjorie?" Andrea repeated, the name emerging from her lips like a verbal caress. "She's fine. She's been accepted at Vassar, you know. She'll be starting there in the fall."

"Already?" Gwen stood up, shaking her head in surprise. "It seems only yesterday I ran into the two of you in Lord and Taylor's. She was only a little girl."

The smile on Andrea's lips was wistful and loving. "She's almost eighteen now. She's turned into a beautiful young woman."

"Well, look whom she has to take after!"

As the two women started toward the elevators, Cam Eckhart's voice reverberated from the direction of Bill's office. "Now see here, Saxon! You're being a mule about this!"

Andrea's lips curled. "They're at it again."

Gwen shook her head and laughed. "No," she said, pressing the elevator button. "They're *still* at it."

The argument about the color of the walls continued over the next two weeks like a running gag in a mediocre comedy. As the deadline for the paint job edged closer, Cam intensified his campaign, bringing the fourteenth-floor color scheme into every conversation he had with Gwen and Bill. One Thursday in late August, the morning crush in the elevator edged Bill and Cam into close proximity. To Cam, a man who would have much preferred a pert secretary's cute little rear pressed against his side, the mischievous smile of his archenemy was more a red flag than a greeting. Cam's nostrils flared, and his mustache twitched.

"You're behaving like a schoolboy about the painting," he grated. "Green's the obvious choice."

The elevator stopped at fourteen. Emerging, Cam managed to brush his hand against the generous bosom of a file clerk. The ride hadn't been a total loss.

"Beige seems obvious to me.". Bill's voice was calm and genial. "I like warm, earthy colors."

"Earthy colors be damned! I warn you, Saxon, Bart's going to hear about this!" Cam stormed down the corridor toward his office.

Having wormed her way out from the rear of the elevator, Gwen stood beside Bill, watching Cam's exit. "Are you two still locking horns over the paint job?"

Bill swung open the door that led to their offices. "It's not just the paint job that's bugging him. He's been burning since he found out Paul Lockhart is going to write a monthly column for me. Here I am, the lowly editor of *Virile*, and I had the gall to go out and ask Paul Lockhart, one of the country's biggest best-selling authors, to free-lance a monthly column for my magazine—and Lockhart actually agreed. That's a big feather in my cap and a mighty bitter pill for Cam to swallow. He's furious that he didn't come up with the idea. So now he's pushing his weight around about the paint job, trying to show who's *really* top shit around here."

"Why don't you take pity on the guy and let him have his way?"

"That's his problem—he gets it too often. Let him struggle for a change."

Shaking her head in amused hopelessness, Gwen started to turn away.

"Say, if you get a minute around four or four-thirty, pop into my office and meet Lockhart," Bill called after her. "He's dropping in to discuss the column."

"Thanks for the invitation, but I've got shooting scripts scheduled. I think it's great that you could get a celebrity like Lockhart to write a column for you, but I can't say I mind passing up the privilege of meeting him. I don't have much of a stomach for his books."

Bill shrugged. "How about giving Terri a thrill and sending her in instead? Just breathing the same air as the guy who writes such sexy spy novels should give her an orgasm."

Gwen laughed in spite of herself. "Go to hell," she said, and headed toward her office.

It was a hellish day. One of her best writers bombed out on a cover-lined article; Jason Bart sent her a memo about cutting expenses; production was breathing down her neck for late copy; and, like a recurring, cacophonic theme, Cam had been popping in and out, extolling the merits of the color green. It was after four-thirty when she finished dictating the scene and situation she wanted set up to illustrate the last story for the four-color section of her January issue.

With an air of finality, she returned the manuscript she was holding to its envelope. "That's it, Betsy. You can start typing them up now and finish them in the morning."

Betsy stood shifting her weight, glancing at the dictation pad in her hand as though it were a salver holding ignominious calling cards.

"Anything wrong?" Gwen asked.

"I was just wondering— Well, I mean, it's *practically* five o'clock, and I'm supposed to meet my boyfriend at his office so we can go shopping. If I left now, I could be there by the time he gets out."

Gwen smiled, wondering if she'd be losing a secretary soon. "Shopping for a ring?"

"Oh, no! Nothing like that. At least, not yet." Betsy shook her head, giggled, and stepped closer, giving Gwen an "I-have-him-where-I want-him" look. "We're going to get him a pair of elevated shoes. You see, he's a little shorter than I am, and when I wear high heels, I practically *tower* over him."

"What's so terrible about that? Where is it written that a woman can't be taller than the man she dates?"

"You sound just like Gary," Betsy said, shaking her head at the density her boss and her boyfriend shared. "He says he wouldn't care if I were six feet tall and wore high heels on top of that. But the man's *supposed* to be taller than the woman. That's just the way it is."

"It shouldn't be that way, and it doesn't have to be," Gwen pointed out. "But if it means so much to you not to appear taller than Gary, why not wear flats and spare him the humiliation of elevated shoes?"

"What humiliation? It's only a pair of shoes."

"It's not the shoes—it's what they represent. By insisting he buy them, you're not very subtly telling Gary that you consider a physical aspect over which he has no control a flaw. You're making it apparent that he doesn't measure up to your vision of the ideal man. That's a pretty shattering thing to do to someone you care about. What if Gary envisioned his ideal woman with a forty-inch bustline and asked you to wear a padded bra so you'd measure up to it?"

Betsy burst into laughter. It was evidently the silliest idea that had ever been presented to her.

With a sigh and a smile, Gwen gave up. "Forget it," she said. "Go ahead—take off."

Betsy's laughter still echoing in her ears, Gwen reached for a paper on her desk. Then she frowned as she started to go over Terri Ainsworth's exploitation sheet on the November issue. The sheet, which contained capsule comments on all the stories and articles in the magazine, was sent out every month to Waterford salesmen. An interoffice publicity gimmick, it was intended to fire the salesmen's enthusiasm sufficiently to induce them to convince dealers that every issue was a virtual goldmine. The dealers, in turn (it was hoped), would react not only by ordering more copies than ever before, but also by giving the issue prominent display—instead of tucking it behind all the other confession magazines (as they usually did) with only the first two and a half letters of a provocative cover line exposed. Though all editors regarded the influence of the exploitation sheet with cynicism, it was a matter of pride to give the salesmen the most catching and imaginative phrases with which to line their wastepaper baskets. Laura Faber, who had done a crackerjack job on the exploitations for Nadine, used to say that writing them was like painting a picture intended to be hung on the walls of a darkroom.

When Gwen became editor, she had moved Laura up to second in command. Realizing that, with all her new duties,

Laura could not continue to handle the exploitation, she had intended to give the job to Frances Hascomb, the new associate editor. Terri, however, had begged for a chance at it. Gwen sighed, remembering. Poor Terri! How she longed to be creative, but, one by one, Nadine had been forced to take any job that called for creativity away from her: Her editing had been a disaster, and her attempts at thinking up imaginative and exciting titles and cover lines pathetic. Terri now spent most of her time proofreading and writing critiques, neither of which she did very well. There was nothing that any of the editors she worked for could do about it. Terri had started out with Waterford when she was fresh out of high school, way back when old Doc Waterford was still running the company with an iron hand. Since then, many magazines had come and gone, but a place had always been found for Terri, who, throughout all the years of great turnover, had managed to chalk up one of the company's longest employment records. Had she been a better worker, her position would have been more precarious, for more would have been expected of her. Her muddling mediocrity, however, had secured her a lifetime of second-rate security.

Aware of Terri's disappointment at being passed over for the managing editorship in favor of Laura, who was much younger and had no seniority, Gwen had found it impossible to turn aside her pleas for a chance to write the exploitation. Now, she studied the cliché-riddled paper that might easily have been a heavy-handed parody of promotion writing. Shaking her head, she realized that she would have been wiser and kinder to have remained firm, thus saving Terri the hurt of having yet another job taken away. "Save personal feelings for personal relationships, and personal relationships for after five," Nadine Osgood had always said. Perhaps that was why Nadine was so good at her job, and how she had gone so far.

Gwen tapped her pencil against her desk a moment, then dialed Laura's extension. "Come into my office, please."

A few seconds later, a pale, pretty girl of about twenty-four was standing across from her. Laura's prettiness might have been only average had it not been for her large dark eyes; they signaled intelligence tempered by human understanding—a rare combination in one so young—and so set her apart from other merely pretty girls. She had a habit when working of unconsciously running her fingers through her short-cropped bangs, and they stood out around her forehead now like the slightly askew tiara of a tipsy princess.

Gwen extended the exploitation sheet toward her, the blue-pencil marks she had been making on it disappearing toward the middle of the page, where she had finally given up hope of revision. "I know you're swamped, but do you think you can do this over from scratch tomorrow?"

Laura smiled when she saw what it was. "I feel like one of our narrators who finds that the past isn't buried after all."

"It's only for this issue," Gwen assured her. "Next month, we'll break Frances in on it."

"Does Terri know?" The smile had left her voice and it was softer now.

"Tomorrow is soon enough to—"

Almost as though talk of her had conjured her up, Terri's head popped through the door. "Sorry to interrupt, but this is important."

Both women turned toward her, Laura quietly slipping the exploitation sheet behind her back, out of sight.

Despite her rather pasty complexion, Terri was glowing like a bride. Obviously, someone had asked her for a date. Terri always acted like a bride around any man who showed even a glimmering of interest in her, spending so much time extolling her own cooking and other homebody virtues that she quickly scared the poor fellow away. It had been years since she'd had any repeaters. To Terri, a man's asking for a date was virtually tantamount to his asking for her hand. As she was fond of telling anyone who took her out, a marriage license cost less than dinner for two at a decent restaurant.

"I just got a call from this guy I ride with on the train," she said. "His wife's in the hospital, and he asked me to meet him for a drink. Okay if I leave now?"

"Sure."

She whirled away before the word was fully out of Gwen's mouth. A few seconds later, she was back, hair combed, lipstick freshened.

"Do either of you have any perfume?" she asked breathlessly. "Wouldn't you know that today of all days I'd leave mine at home?"

Gwen rummaged in a drawer and came up with an almost empty bottle of April Violets.

Terri sniffed the delicate fragrance and grimaced. "It's not really *me*," she sighed, "but it will have to do." And she proceeded to splash most of the contents on her arms and neck.

A mirror unavailable, she primped in front of the glass-topped partition. "You know," she giggled, "I once asked him to guess my age, and he said twenty-seven." She applied a little saliva to the loose adhesive of a false eyelash. "Of course, he wasn't *so* far from wrong."

Laura looked down, and the shake of Gwen's head was barely perceptible. It was obvious to everyone except Terri herself and, perhaps, her mother that Terri Ainsworth was pushing forty, and pushing it from the wrong side.

Extending a leg, Terri smoothed an imaginary wrinkle from her black pantyhose. Proud of her shapely legs, she always wore short skirts and dark stockings to show them off. She wouldn't be caught dead in a pantsuit. She took a deep breath to extend her chest and attempted to tighten her belt a notch. The gestures were futile and a little pathetic: From the hips up, Terri might have been a boy.

"What's wrong with his wife?" Gwen asked.

"Who knows? Some kind of pains. Harry says she's in the hospital for observation." She bit her lip and gazed into space a moment, then went on pensively, "I hope it's nothing serious. Harry probably wouldn't want to divorce her then. It would look bad, and he has an important position to keep up." She shrugged. "On the other hand, if it *is* serious, how long could she last? A month, six weeks? Then the way would be clear for us. . . ." Terri was always one to look at the bright side.

For a second, Gwen's shocked glance locked with Laura's. Almost anyone else's eyes would have been mocking, but Laura's were filled with pity. Was it for Terri? Gwen wondered. Or for Harry's wife? Probably for both.

Terri hiked her skirt up a little and put her sunglasses on.

"Well, I'm off," she said, with a pat to her bleached-blond French knot. "I'll tell you all about it tomorrow."

"Do." Gwen's voice was so dry, the word nearly broke on the air.

Shaking her head slowly, Laura followed Terri out of the office.

Gwen read through a few critiques, then tossed her pencil down. It was five o'clock, and she did not want to prolong a hellish day. She combed her hair, dabbed on what remained of her eau de cologne, and turned off her light.

The lonely staccato of a solitary typewriter greeted her as she closed her office door. It was Laura, pounding out a new exploitation sheet.

"Hey!" Gwen chastised her affectionately. "That can wait until tomorrow. You have a husband to cook dinner for."

"That's okay. David's working late tonight, so I might as well, too. We'll meet and go home together." With her lipstick worn off by concentration and her bangs sticking out above her forehead, Laura looked almost like a child, and it seemed incredible that she was one of the best young editors Waterford had seen in years.

"I don't know what I'd do without you." Gwen's tone was as warm as her smile. "You've really got a fine career ahead of you."

"Thanks." Laura swung back to her typing, and Gwen attributed the quick shift of her eyes to modesty.

"Say hello to David."

Laura looked up briefly and nodded, her eyes glowing a little as they always did at the mention of her husband.

Looks as though everyone is meeting someone tonight but me, Gwen thought, heading toward the doorway to the hall.

As she was passing Bill's office, his door opened, and Bill and another man emerged. If she hadn't known that Bill had been meeting with Paul Lockhart that afternoon, Gwen would have assumed that the tall man at his side was a visiting don from Oxford. His comfortable tweeds, short-clipped hair that, singularly, was gray on top and dark at the temples, and his intelligent gray eyes seemed to bespeak the scholar rather than the writer of popular sexploitation spy novels. Even his slightly crooked nose might have been the souvenir of a tumultuous rugby match in his undergraduate days.

"Hey, I'm glad you didn't leave yet!" Bill said. "I'd like you to meet Paul Lockhart. Paul, this is Gwen Hadley, the editor of *True Affairs*."

Paul removed his pipe from his mouth, and it was difficult not to be surprised when his "pleased to meet you" emerged without an English accent. The hand he extended was a writer's hand, fine-boned, sensitive, yet strong. Gwen shook it, rather puzzled that his eyes didn't reflect the mocking amusement she generally met with when men heard her position. It was particularly strange in a man who seemed to reduce women to mere vessels of pleasure in his books. She wondered if that was why she seemed to recoil from him suddenly, withdrawing her hand quickly. Was it because she didn't like the male chauvinism he was reputed to express in his books? She couldn't accept that. After all, she was crazy about Bill, and he edited a magazine devoted to such bilge. No, it was more than that. But what, she wondered, searching his face for a clue. Perhaps it was his self-assurance—and his eyes, eyes that gave the impression that they could penetrate to depths no human being had a right to invade in another's soul.

She glanced away. "I'm happy to meet you too," she lied.

They stepped into the corridor, Gwen half hoping some coworker would be waiting for an elevator so that she would have an excuse to disengage herself from the two men. There was no one. It was five past five, and the only signs of life on the floor were the three of them and the lonely sound of Laura's typewriter, conjuring visions of a ghostly editor damned to meet an ever-pressing deadline that, like the sword of Damocles, hung suspended eternally above her head.

"We're off to Nick's," Bill said as the elevator doors closed behind them. "Come join us for a drink."

Even with the huge elevator all to themselves, she felt somehow cornered, confined. "No, thanks." She glanced from Bill to Paul, then quickly away. "You two have business to discuss."

Love After Hours

"The business discussion is over. This is purely for pleasure. Please join us." Paul's voice was polite, gentle. But his eyes were measuring her, challenging her. They seemed to be noting her apprehension, and to be waiting to see how she would wiggle out of his gentlemanly offer.

Well, she wouldn't. She had nothing to hide from him. No secrets. No depths. Who did he think he was, anyway? She drew herself up, and for the first time, met his gaze with a challenge of her own. "All right then. Thank you."

Cam Eckhart was ahead of them on the street, drifting leisurely through the sea of workers that rushed from the open floodgates of the surrounding buildings. His arm encircled the waist of Neil Mennen's voluptuous new secretary. They paused before a travel agent's window, where a waterskier, poised forever upon blue waters, said in a caption that she had paid only twenty-five dollars down to fly to Hawaii. Cam's fingers moved gently up and down the girl's back, fingering her bra fasteners through the thin material of her blouse.

"Brown!" Bill shouted as the threesome passed.

Cam's back stiffened, but he pretended not to hear.

Bill laughed, and Gwen shook her head, smiling.

"A private joke?" Paul asked.

"An office joke," Gwen said. "One that, I'm afraid, would lose all humor in the explanation."

Shrugging, Paul held the door to Nick's open for her.

"Ah, Miss Hadley, Mr. Saxon." Beauregard rubbed his pudgy hands together, and bobbed his head slightly to the right. "This way, please. This way." They followed his bouncing figure to a table in the rear.

"The usual for you two?" he asked when they were seated. And when they nodded, "Ah, the usual. The usual. And for your friend?"

"Scotch on the rocks," their friend said.

"Ah, very good. Very good." He bounced away.

"Is he praising my choice or his Scotch?" Paul asked.

Bill mulled it over. "Perhaps only his memory."

They exchanged pleasantries until the drinks arrived.

Bill raised his glass. "To our reading public."

"Right," Gwen said, "and *vive la différence*."

Paul swirled the Scotch around his ice. "Do you really think there's a difference?"

Bill's laugh boomed out. "Well, in the first place, old man, hers are women and mine are men. I'd say that's a difference."

"Only physical. They're both buying dreams."

"Oh, come on!" Gwen said. "That's true of Bill's readers, but not of mine. Mine are serious, dedicated wives and mothers. They're interested in life situations, family problems, and that's what they get. Bill's stories are from another world."

"In a way, yours are too." Paul said. "Both your magazines present an exaggerated view of life. It's obvious that Bill's magazine, and others like it, represent the fantasies of a young man's libido gone wild. Men read them for escape, well aware that it's far from what life is like. But women read your magazine because they think it *is* what life is like. And it's a totally distorted picture."

"Obviously, you've never read a confession magazine." Gwen was bristling. "If you were at all familiar with our market, you'd know that our stories *are* true."

"I am familiar with your market. When I first started out writing, I submitted a few episodes from my own life to confession magazines, but they were rejected. The editors said they were too downbeat and sordid."

"Do I detect a note of sour grapes?" Bill teased.

Paul laughed. "Not likely! I got a hell of a lot of rejection slips in those days—many of them from magazines I'm selling to right now—and, I have to admit, most of them deservedly so."

"What makes you think our market's rejections weren't just as well deserved?" Gwen asked.

"I never meant to imply that they weren't. I do think, though, that they prove my point that your stories present a distorted view of life."

"How can truth be a distortion?" Gwen persisted.

"Not in itself," Paul said, "but it can be presented in distorted ways. By rejecting stories that show the sordid, depressing side of things, you're presenting a distorted view of life."

Love After Hours

Gwen put her glass down. "If our readers want to know about depravity, all they have to do is read a newspaper. They come to us for answers—answers to real, down-to-earth problems—marriage problems, family problems, sex problems. By reading the stories of women who have solved those problems, they're able to find answers to their own."

Paul shook his head. "I think your stories may create more problems than they solve."

"Not so!" Gwen's voice was sharp. "Our stories give our readers examples to pattern their lives on. They give them hope and renew their faith."

"That's just it!" The argument was beginning to grow heated. "We don't need hope and faith to live in this world—we need courage." He gestured toward the door. "How many men and women out there are as mature, perceptive, and understanding as the people whose stories you choose to print? Your stories probably inspire more envy than emulation."

"You're wrong, and every letter-to-the-editor I receive proves it." Gwen picked up her drink. "You sell human nature far too short."

"And you give it too much credit."

"The question is," Bill interposed, "which is the lesser evil?"

"I doubt that I sell people short," Paul said. "I think I see them for what they are, and life for what it is. We're talking about editorial viewpoints now, anyway, not personal ones. What it boils down to is that Gwen's magazine places too much emphasis on people's good qualities, and yours places too much on their bad. Both distortions are harmful."

Bill regarded him over the rim of his glass. "How so?"

Paul lighted his pipe, took a deep draw, then pointed the stem at Bill. "Though it's one of the least offensive of its type on the market, your magazine draws human beings as walking, talking, living, breathing genitals, reducing human relationships *ad absurdum*. If its warped view of women sells them short, its cockeyed view of men sells them short too, because men are occasionally concerned with things other than coitus." Now the pipe stem moved toward Gwen. "Your magazine, on the other hand, by choosing to show people only at their best, sews the seeds of discontent."

"You may be right in a few isolated cases," Gwen admitted. "There are always malcontents who prefer to envy others rather than to learn from them. They don't number themselves among our faithful readers, though. There are millions of women who read confession magazines month after month, year after year, and their ranks are growing. If they didn't find both entertainment and help in our pages, they wouldn't keep coming back for more. Obviously, we're doing a hell of a lot more right than wrong."

"Hear, hear!" Bill said.

Gwen leaned back, tired of being on the defensive. "And what about your novels?" she asked Paul. "How do you rationalize *your* distortions—with your characters always involved in fantastic adventures and constantly jumping in and out of bed? Surely, you can't pretend you're depicting life as it is."

"Not as it is, but as it's becoming, with human relationships becoming more and more depersonalized, and human beings realizing less and less of their potential by seeking to stifle their true emotions and better cravings in quest of superficial thrills."

Gwen had read only halfway through the first two chapters of one of Paul's books, and, having lost patience with what she had considered to be his superficiality and insensitivity, she had dismissed it never to try another. "You must admit it's a moral your public has failed to draw," she said.

"That they use my books as a vicarious means to some of those thrills tends to prove my point rather than negate it."

Beauregard bobbed over with the second round Bill had ordered, and Paul and Gwen continued the discussion, neither budging from his view. At last, Bill drained his glass, saying, "I feel as though I've been watching a tennis match."

"What's the score?" Paul laughed.

"I don't have the final figure, but I can say for sure that it doesn't include love."

"Ah, but it was still a friendly match—I hope." Paul smiled, his eyes on Gwen. The smile was friendly. There was nothing condescending in his look or his tone as there might have been in another man's. Indeed, throughout the entire discussion, he had listened to her and argued with her as an equal. Yet she bristled with resentment and was possessed by an unexplainable need to be on her guard.

She knew the smile she returned to him was not as genuine as his, and that made her angry too. Flustered, she looked at her watch. "I have to run."

Paul and Bill rose to leave with her.

"I'm taking a cab to the Village," Paul said when they were in the street. "May I drop you both someplace?"

"No, thanks." Gwen's refusal came out sharper than she had intended.

"I'll take you up on that," Bill said. "You can drop me at Penn Station."

Gwen wondered if he were trying to make up for her rudeness.

Paul hailed a cab. As it pulled away, Gwen turned toward the subway, an odd sense of relief—and loss—washing over her.

On Gwen's desk the next morning was a memo reminding her to advise her staff members to remove all articles from the tops of desks and file cabinets as the floor was to be painted over the weekend. Gwen penciled her initials and those of the rest of the staff in the margin. Then, crossing her own off, she handed the paper to Betsy, asking her to pass it around before it was filed.

Among her mail was an engraved invitation with the Waterford insignia—a waterfall splashing over a golden W, superimposed on what would have to be the soggy pages of an open book—requesting the honor of her presence at the annual executive dinner-dance. It was to be held, as usual, in the grand ballroom of the Pinnacle Hotel, on a Saturday evening in mid-September, only a few weeks away. Actually, the company would have preferred to hold the event on a Friday or a Sunday evening when ballroom rentals were slightly lower, but it did not want to risk employees leaving early on Friday to change clothes or coming in late on the morning-after Monday.

The event itself was a glorified pep rally, intended to spark editors on to higher guarantees, and sales executives on to greater sales. To achieve this end, speeches were made, and name writers published by Waterford were paraded—if their editors could induce them to come. Gwen shuddered a little as she slipped the invitation back into its envelope. She looked upon those dinners as planned tension or endurance tests. She'd have to get out her old black cocktail dress and send it to the cleaner's. How many years had she worn it? Oh, well, it was good enough.

Betsy buzzed her. "Mr. Saxon on two."

Gwen picked up her telephone. "Hi, Bill."

"Yea team, gung-ho, and all that."

"I see you got yours too."

"Now that you're no longer a lowly managing editor, Shari and I can pick you up, and we can go to the Waterford suite for cocktails together."

She'd forgotten about the Waterford cocktail party that preceded the dinner. Hitherto, she'd been excluded because, though the dinner-dance itself included managing editors and some lesser employees, the cocktail party was limited to top executives and editors.

"I'm not so sure about that," she said. "Nothing was said on my invitation."

"Impossible! Check the envelope. There should be another card."

There was—a smaller one tucked down in the corner: *Mr. and Mrs. Archer Waterford, Mr. and Mrs. Bruce Waterford, Mr. and Mrs. Charles Waterford cordially invite you for cocktails. 7:30. Suite 1700.* Once again, she marveled at the first Mrs. Waterford's lack of imagination—A,B,C.

"Here it is. I passed over it first time around."

"Purely Freudian. You didn't want to prolong the agony. Say, I'm sorry you and Lockhart didn't hit it off too well yesterday."

She gave a start at the mention of his name. "Just one of those things." She hoped her voice sounded casual.

"I put him down for an invitation to this shindig. He probably won't come, but I thought he should have the dubious honor of being asked. You never can tell with a guy like that. If he does show, Cam will split a gut."

"That should make your night. Now go peddle your magazines. I have work to do."

She replaced the receiver and gazed out the window. Maybe she *would* buy a new dress for the dinner. After all, she was the editor now. She should dress the part. . . .

She went over the exploitation sheet Laura had placed on her desk last evening. It was like a breath of fresh air after Terri's bumbling effort. After making a few minor changes, she called Betsy in. "You can type this up and Xerox it. Send Terri in, too, please." Might as well get it over with.

There was a knock. Then Terri bounced in, obviously under the impression that Gwen wanted to gossip about her big date the night before.

"We had *two* drinks, and he said we'd have to do it again sometime." Her eyes sparkled. Two drinks and the possibility of another date were, to Terri, tantamount to a deposit on an engagement ring. She grew pensive a moment. "Do you know anything about sixteen-year-old boys?"

"Not much outside of the fact that next year they'll be seventeen."

Terri pursed her lips and pressed a well-manicured finger against them. "That's the only thing that has me worried. He has a sixteen-year-old son, and I don't know *anything* about raising boys. If his wife's all right and there's a divorce, she'll take him. But if not—I'll be stuck. Oh, well! He's sixteen now. Before I know it, he'll be away at college and out of my hair."

Gwen swallowed back the nausea that rose in the back of her throat. "Did Harry say anything about marriage?" she couldn't resist asking.

Terri's look said it was obvious that Gwen had had little experience with men. "Of course not—with everything about his wife up in the air! But don't worry—I'm in there working on him. Mama always says most men need a little push."

With a bulldozer? Gwen wondered. She picked up a pencil and tapped it gently on the desk. "About the exploitation sheet you did yesterday. You came up with some interesting turns of phrase, but it isn't quite what they want upstairs. Laura did it over, and Frances will be doing it from now on."

Gwen tensed, but the pouts and grumbles she had expected did not come. Instead, Terri stood there, bestowing upon her a rather superior, pitying look that seemed to say she couldn't be concerned with mundane things like that anymore. After all, she'd be Mrs. Harry Somebody before you knew it.

"All right. I'm really swamped with other work anyway. If Frances needs any pointers, though, you can have her ask me." She gave herself the satisfaction of slamming the door.

Sighing, Gwen picked up her phone and dialed Frances Hascomb's extension. "Will you come in, please?" she asked.

A moment later a tall young woman in her mid-twenties walked in. Frances Hascomb was an ardent worker in the women's rights movement, and everything about her—from the efficient swish of her long brown hair that she wore severely parted in the middle to the undulation of her unfettered breasts beneath her body suit—seemed to give evidence of her own personal liberation. Because she wore no makeup on her finely chiseled features and covered her warm brown eyes with a pair of uglifying steel-rimmed circular glasses, one had to look at her face closely to recognize that she was a very attractive woman; that she was voluptuous was immediately obvious. She crossed the room and seated herself opposite Gwen, tossing her long hair back off her shoulders with a quick movement of her head.

Gwen picked up a folder she had pulled out of a filing cabinet earlier and handed it to Frances. "These are the exploitation sheets for the past year. I'd like you to look them over to get the hang of what's wanted. You'll be handling them from now on. If you have any questions, Laura will be glad to answer them for you."

Frances riffled through the contents of the folder. "When's the next one due?"

"Not till the fifteenth of next month. Laura took care of the current one."

"Bless her."

Smiling, Gwen nodded in agreement. "In more ways than one."

Frances rose and tapped the folder. "Don't worry. I'll do my homework."

"I'm sure you will. You've been doing a fine job on the blurbs for the table of contents, and I know you'll come through just as well on this."

At the door, Frances paused. "I'd like to take the three days' vacation I have coming to me at the end of next week. We're having a mass meeting in Washington to plan strategy for our fall campaign aimed at liberalizing abortion laws throughout the country. It's important that I be there."

Gwen glanced at the calendar on her desk. "If you have the copy in shape by then, I have no objection."

"No problem," she said, opening the door. "I'll be ready for the fifty-percent deadline by Monday afternoon."

"Then the end of the week is yours."

Almost immediately after the door closed behind Frances, the phone rang.

Betsy buzzed the intercom. "Paul Lockhart's on one!" she squealed.

Gwen's heart gave a little lurch. "He must want Bill Saxon. The operator probably made a mistake."

"No. He asked for you! Wow! I didn't know you knew—"

Gwen cut her off, her hand going cold as she reached for the phone, pushing down the lighted button marked *extension one*. "Hello."

"Hi. I called to apologize for yesterday. Well, not really to apologize. I meant what I said, but I was talking about confessions in general, not your magazine in particular."

"Does it make any difference?"

"To me it does. I don't want you to think it was a personal attack."

"Rather love-me-love-my-dog in reverse?"

He laughed. "That's one way of putting it."

"Don't worry. If I took it personally every time someone knocked my magazine, or confessions in general, I'd have drowned in a pool of tears long ago."

"I wasn't 'knocking' confessions. I think they're a fine thing of their sort."

"You're full of contradictions. Sometimes I'm not sure what side you're on."

"It's not a matter of choosing sides. It's a matter of seeing things as they are. I can appreciate the high quality of your stories; I can also appreciate the high morality they hope to inspire; but at the same time, I can see them for what they are—one-way tickets to discontent."

As she listened, Gwen could visualize the way he'd looked the day before. She shook her head, trying to erase the image.

"How about pursuing this over lunch? That's what I really called about."

Mentally, she backed away. "Sorry," she said, "but I'm tied up."

"Monday then?"

She glanced at her calendar, relieved to see that she had the name of a feature writer penciled in for noon. "I'm in conference with one of my feature writers on Monday," she said.

"Well, that takes care of that for a while. I'm leaving for the Coast on Tuesday and won't be back for a few weeks. Maybe then . . ."

"Yes, maybe then." She could afford to sound as though she would look forward to it. After all, in two weeks, he most likely would have forgotten her. Wishing him a pleasant trip, she hung up.

No sooner was the phone out of her hand than Betsy bustled in with some letters for her to sign. She had obviously been watching the light on her extension for the first sign that the conversation was over. Her eyes sparkled with curiosity—it wasn't every day that the country's most popular writer of sexy books called her boss—but Gwen had no intention of satisfying it. She signed the papers and returned them without a word, and Betsy reluctantly went back to her desk.

Gwen picked up a manuscript that had been edited, and started giving it a final check before it went off to the printer. She planned to dismiss Paul Lockhart from her mind as quickly as she hoped he would dismiss her from his. Still, throughout the hectic day, snatches of her conversation with Paul the evening before and on the phone that morning intruded on her thoughts like naughty children who *would* be heard. And hovering in the back of her mind was the memory of the way he had looked at her.

Love After Hours

At five o'clock, she turned down Cam's invitation to celebrate Bill's eight-hour silence in the color war the two had been waging, a silence Cam interpreted as a surrender. Instead, she strolled over to the nearest library. When she emerged, she had three of Paul Lockhart's novels under her arm. She spent the weekend in her room reading them, her door and her mind closed to the background music of her mother's whines and her father's rages. By Monday morning, having discovered to her surprise that Paul's books were all he had said they were intended to be, she felt a strong respect for his work and a new appreciation of his purpose and artistry as a writer. That respect and appreciation, however, in no way diminished the nameless apprehension that the memory of his eyes still shot through her.

It was almost ten when she arrived downtown that Monday morning. For the better part of an hour, she and hundreds of co-passengers had stood, bodies pressed together, hot breaths mingling, like grotesque sweethearts trapped on a nightmarish ride through a bizarre tunnel of love.

Cam Eckhart came up behind her. "So you were stuck on that train too? I don't understand why the conductor never uses that loudspeaker of his to tell people what's wrong and when the train will get moving again."

"Those speakers have so much static, no one would be able to understand them even if they did offer an explanation," Gwen laughed. "Besides, what's the fun of stranding people two hundred feet beneath the surface of the earth if you're going to give them hope that they'll get out alive? I have a pet theory that the conductors and engineers are agents of the devil, and one day they're going to take us all careening into hell."

They crossed the street and began walking toward the Waterford Building. Cam slipped his arm around her waist, bending his head so close to her that his beard tickled her ear. "Ah, if you ever go to the devil, I'm the man who'd like to come along with you."

He never stopped trying. If he were up before a woman judge, he wouldn't be able to resist making a pun about laying down the law, and he'd try to arrange an assignation for the day after his sentence was up.

Gwen stopped and looked up at him. "Cam," she said in the tone of a mother almost—but not quite—out of patience with a forgetful child, "don't you have pockets in your trousers?"

Obviously, the question startled him, but, ever the impeccably dressed editor of a top men's magazine, he lifted the hem of his jacket to show off the roomy slash pockets on either side of the hips of his double-knit magenta slacks.

"Well, for God's sake, put your hands in them! What do you think they're there for?"

Like an obedient child, he did as he was told. "You're a hard woman, Gwendolyn Hadley."

Gwen laughed. "If you know that, why do you keep feeling for soft spots?"

They entered the building in silence.

The acrid fumes of day-old paint rushed to greet them like a maiden aunt with sour breath the moment they stepped off the elevator.

Gwen recoiled a bit. "Oh, Lord! I forgot about the paint job. I hope they didn't leave a mess."

Cam, on the other hand, took a deep breath, his nostrils and chest expanding, as though he were inhaling revitalizing mountain air. "Forgot? How could you forget something like this?" Barely glancing at the corridor, which remained the same institutional ivory of all Waterford elevator corridors—perhaps in deference to the messenger boys whose graffiti showed up better on white—he grasped her elbow and propelled her toward the door at the other end, which led toward the two-thirds of the floor occupied by the offices of *Real*. The remaining third of the floor was divided between her offices and Bill's. Cam swung open the door, and the sound of busy typewriters crescendoed. Secretaries were pounding away while senior, associate and assistant editors, each in his own little cubicle, toiled halfheartedly at their desks in pursuit of "the real thing," for less than which, according to the magazine's masthead, the discerning reader would not settle. In accordance with the Law of Diminishing Guarantees, Cam, whose monthly magazine had the largest circulation in the Waterford chain, was given a staff of twenty to put out a product that needed approximately the same amount of work as Bill's and Gwen's, but for which they were given staffs of seven and six, respectively, in accordance with their position on the guarantee scale. The size of one's staff depended, therefore, not on the amount of work to be done, but, rather, on the prestige of one's magazine and the amount of income it brought into the company. Bill, whose guarantee had been climbing steadily lately, had already been promised another associate editor. Just two more associate editors—or one associate editor and two assistant editors—and he'd be allowed a pair of drapes too.

"Look at that!" Cam said, his eyes sweeping the walls. "As cool and calm as the sea on a summer day."

"Lovely," Gwen said, and tried to head toward her office, but his grip tightened on her arm, and they continued to walk along, surveying his domain. When they reached her office, she tried to slip away, but he propelled her past it toward Bill's.

"Really, Cam! It's beautiful, but all green walls are the same, and I've got a deadline to—"

"Christ!" Cam went rigid, the fire that crept up his cheeks turning to a blaze in his eyes.

Gwen's gaze followed his to the farthest corner of the floor, the corner that contained Bill's office. "Well," she said weakly, "perhaps not all green walls are the same after all. There's one that looks decidedly brown."

If he heard her attempt at humor, Cam refused to be diverted by it. He burst into Bill's office like a storm trooper. "Saxon!" he bellowed. "What's the meaning of this?"

Unruffled, Bill looked up from the layouts he had been going over. "I told you I like brown," he said simply.

"You like brown! *You* like brown!" Cam's voice rose higher with every word, and Gwen, who had followed him in, hoping to prevent a homocide, had the feeling that he was about to explode with rage like a cartoon character.

"Um," Bill said. "I like brown." And he returned to his layouts.

"Have you any idea how ridiculous this makes the entire floor look? What kind of impression this is going to make on visitors? They'll think we're all idiots!"

"If they're idiotic enough to be impressed by the color of office walls, let's hope we're smart enough to find them out."

Cam's arm gestured frantically toward the wall. "Green here—brown there. It looks like hell!"

"If it bothers you so much, maybe we can have the whole floor done over in brown." Bill initialed a layout and set it aside without looking up.

His serenity seemed to infuriate Cam even more than his taste, but it also served to make Cam struggle to get a rein on his temper. His voice lowered to the righteous-indignation tone of outraged authority. "I'm warning you, Saxon! This time you've gone a little too far with your practical jokes. Jason Bart's going to hear about this."

Bill okayed another layout. "Oh, he already has. It seems that when an editor's guarantee keeps rising, Waterford's willing to allow him a few idiosyncrasies—like choosing the color of his own office wall."

Cam was thunderstruck. No one had ever crossed him before with sanction from above. His eyes blazed, and Gwen regarded his dilating nostrils in awe, half-expecting fire to come spewing from them.

Bill looked up, regarding Cam levelly. The strong lenses of his glasses enlarged his eyes, giving him an almost innocent appearance. "Look upon it as your own private wailing wall, Cam. You can come here and tear your hair before it any time you like."

All the control Cam had struggled to maintain was lost in a second. "Shit!" he spat. "Shit! Shit! *Shit!*"

For the first time since they'd rushed into his office, Bill turned and studied the wall behind him. The face he turned back to Cam was deadpan, but his eyes sparkled just a little. Pursing his lips, he rubbed his chin in the manner of an art connoisseur about to pronounce on a rare work. "No," he said thoughtfully. "I'd say it's more like the color of coffee with a lot of cream in it."

"*You* can go to hell!" Cam growled, and he stormed out of the room.

"Just like Rumpelstiltskin," Gwen said as she listened to his footsteps pounding off into the distance.

Love After Hours

"That's the little fellow who tore himself asunder in rage, isn't it? We'd never be so lucky."

"Well, certainly you can't be blamed for not trying to drive him to it."

Smiling a little, Bill swiveled back in his chair. Hands folded over his stomach, he looked like a gourmet who has just had the pleasure of partaking of nectar and ambrosia with the gods.

Gwen shook her head. "Why do you keep after him all the time? He's not really worth all the effort you put into it."

Bill leaned forward, smiling mischievously. "Ah, but I'm his nemesis, and I take my role very seriously. We should all have a nemesis—it makes better people of us."

"You're incorrigible!" Gwen laughed and started out the door.

"Hey!" Bill's voice stopped her. "Speaking of nemeses—I had a call this morning from someone who may be one of yours—Paul Lockhart."

"Oh?" She tried not to sound curious.

"He received the invitation to the Waterford blast. Wanted to know if you'd be there."

"Probably to help him decide if he should come or stay far away."

His eyes were measuring her. "That's the way I figure it."

"What did you tell him?"

"That you'd be there."

She gave a dramatic shrug and sigh. "Well, there go your chances of showing him off and having Cam split another gut."

"That's *not* the way I figure it."

She made a face and hurried to her office.

Often that day, Gwen looked up from her work, a little smile playing on her lips. Then, her eyes clouding, she'd return to her manuscripts with a vengeance.

Chapter Three

Agnes Hadley dabbed her eyes with the hem of her ever-present apron as Gwen emerged from her room the night of the Waterford dinner-dance. "You look lovely, dear. Just lovely." Gingerly, she touched the emerald-green silk sheath that offered a flattering contrast to Gwen's auburn hair while it deepened the green of her eyes and hugged her well-proportioned body like loving arms. "I had a ribbon just this color when I was a girl. I used to tie it in my hair when I went to Sunday school. Sometimes Joseph Rogers would chase me and pull it off so my hair would fall loose." For a moment, her face filled with memories, her wrinkles seemed to disappear and she looked almost like that Sunday-school girl of long ago. "Oh, I was pretty then!"

Gwen put her hand on her mother's thin shoulder. "You're still pretty, Mom."

Pleased, Agnes patted her white hair. "Well, not as pretty as you are tonight. That dress looks as though it was custom-made."

When Gwen thought of the price she had paid for it, she realized it might as well have been. But she had excused her extravagance on the ground that she rarely indulged herself.

Barney roused himself from the depths of the sofa cushions. "You've got a closet full of clothes," he growled. "What the hell do you need a new dress for? Do you know how many bottles of good Irish whiskey you could have bought for the price of that thing?"

Agnes was on him in a flash. "You shut up about your whiskey! What do you know?"

He stretched out his hamlike hand, his fingers curled in the air. "I know the feel of a glass in my hand, the burn of the whiskey as it goes down my throat, the fire of it in my veins. That's all I have to know, woman. That's all anyone has to know."

"That's the devil's talk."

"You and your devil. You must be in love with him, you talk about him so goddam much."

"How dare you!" Agnes shrilled.

Gwen closed her eyes, trying to push down the old, trapped feeling that was beginning to crawl from her stomach up to her chest. "Just this once," she said through her teeth, "let me walk out the door without the sounds of an argument following me."

"It's not *my* fault," Agnes whined in a tone of injured innocence. "*He* started it!"

Barney's face reddened, his bullfrog eyes bulging. "That's a goddam lie!"

"You see!" Agnes cried triumphantly. "He's always contradicting me!"

Barney raised a halfhearted fist. "You and your goddam prissy-pants ways! If you were a man, I'd—"

"Don't you raise your hand to me, you drunken bum! How dare you—" Agnes stopped in mid-sentence as she saw Gwen pick up her purse and start toward the door. She hurried after her, her tone quickly reverting to that of a woman resigned to martyrdom. "What time will you be home, dear?"

"I don't know. Don't wait up."

"You know I can't sleep a wink until you get in. You must have some idea when it will be."

Gwen sighed. "Mom, I'm a grown woman now. At least allow me the dignity of not having to check in and out like a child."

Agnes's eyes filled with tears. "You may be a woman, but you'll always be *my* child. When I think of the hours of pain and torment I went through to bring you into this world! And this is the thanks I get—you won't even tell me what time to expect you home!"

Though she had the urge to stamp her foot like a two-year-old, Gwen kept her voice calm. "Mother, I don't *know* what time I'll be home. And if I did, I really don't think I'd tell you." The minute the words were out of her mouth, Gwen regretted them; she knew they would push Agnes to the apron-twisting stage.

"The pain I suffered to bear you! The years of my life I gave up to care for you! And this is all the appreciation you can show me!" Her hands worked over her apron hem as though they would wring thirty-one years of tears from it. "You were never like this before, Gwendolyn. I don't know what's gotten into you lately."

Gwen knew the answer Nora, her high-spirited sister, would have given: *I didn't ask to be born* or *I have my own life to live*. But in the face of Agnes's tears, Gwen had never been able to let those words pass her own lips, and, looking into the fading blue eyes of the tiny lady with the wispy white hair, she couldn't bring herself to say them now.

She brushed a stray strand of hair off Agnes's forehead and kissed her withered cheek. "I don't know, Mom," she said softly. "I guess I'm suffering from a case of delayed adolescence." She opened the door. "But I really *don't* know what time I'll be home."

The minute the door closed behind her, Agnes and Barney were at it again, their voices following her down the hall where she waited for the elevator.

"Get your feet off that table, Barnabas Hadley! You may have been brought up in a pigsty, but you're not in one now!"

"The hell I will! It's my table!"

"*Your* table! I suppose *you* earned the money to pay for it!"

"Well, you goddam well didn't."

"One of these days—"

The elevator door closed on Agnes's words, but Gwen could fill them in for herself. She'd heard them often enough.

She hurried through the lobby and out to the street to wait for Bill and Shari. A Good Humor truck was parked near the corner. Close by, some black girls were jumping double-Dutch. Gwen marveled at the expertness of the jumper, who managed to lick a Lucky Jet and never miss her footing. Little Marcy Houston, one of the turners and her upstairs neighbor, waved to her. Returning her smile, Gwen waved back.

Many years ago, Eastern Parkway had been known as the Champs-Elysées of Brooklyn, one of the most prestigious upper-middle-class addresses in New York. When Gwen had found a vacant rent-controlled apartment there for herself and her parents shortly after she had started at Waterford, she had considered herself extremely lucky. Even then, the area had begun to go downhill, but it had been a far cry from the tenement existence she was leaving behind. Over the years, however, the rampaging pestilence of neighborhood blight had begun to spread, leaving its festering sores of garbage, crime, and fear everywhere. Landlords, aware that they would never want for tenants and that it is the tenant who must make all the promises in the lease—not they— continued to let their property deteriorate. Legislators, impressed more by the money and the power of the few than by the needs of the many, made no move to right matters. The poor, the downtrodden, the misfits, with their different standards of life and cleanliness, moved in, and the middle class, ever on the run from them, moved out.

Now, the side streets were inhabited by the hard-working poor who tried desperately to maintain their dignity in the face of the odds stacked against them by society. They struggled to maintain an identity separate from their drug-addicted, mugging, thieving neighbors who victimized them as much as the rich and the middle class. The Parkway itself was integrated, populated by elderly whites, young whites, and middle-class blacks. The elderly shook their heads, lamenting a world long gone when halls were clean, every door manned by a doorman, every elevator run by an operator. Unable to afford the outlandish rents of new housing, they kept to their apartments in fear at night, and sat on the benches along The Parkway during the day. (One dared not venture into the beautiful park across the street anymore, even in daylight, they would tell each other, amid much clucking of tongues and nodding of heads, whenever a new mugging came to light.) The women gossiped, purseless, their money pinned inside their dresses; the men dozed, their pensions tucked inside their shoes. Together, they sat, vacantly watching the traffic roar by. The young white mothers, dressed in jeans and tie-dyed sweatshirts, saw their similarly clad bearded husbands off to graduate school in the morning, thankful for the rent-controlled apartment that kept their expenses down. Later, they pushed their baby carriages along The Parkway, their long hair flying in the breeze. They spoke knowingly among each other of toilet training, teething and Marcuse, of how the man who mugged old Mrs. Reilly was the victim of the society their parents had so sorely bungled, and of how, by their example, they would teach their children to live with, to love and to understand all peoples. Then, their children reaching school age, they would realize that it was important for the youngsters to live with, to love and to understand nature too, and, accepting the gift of a down payment from their own parents, they would head for a home in the suburbs. The middle-class blacks, who had finally been allowed by society to afford and to move into an apartment on The Parkway, saw the same filth and walked in the same fear as everybody else.

Gwen took her post at the curb beside a tree whose only foliage was some tattered newspaper pages trapped among its branches. At its base, a corroded plaque announced to the dogs and litterers who violated it that the tree had been planted in 1918 "in loving memory of Corporal John R. Hollender, who lay down his life for his country in Flanders at the age of 20, during the Great War." With the toe of her shoe, Gwen moved some litter aside, clearing a little space around the young corporal's ignored memorial.

She looked down the street, but saw no sign of Bill's car. Three teen-aged boys were standing at the Good Humor truck. Walking away, they tossed their ice-cream wrappers on the sidewalk. One of them waved his popsicle in her direction as they approached.

"Wanna bite?"

Another copied the gesture. "Yeah. How about we give you a piece, and you give us a piece—of ass!"

Gwen stared ahead in stony silence, and the three walked on, laughing uproariously at their scintillating wit.

A car pulled up. "Hey, lady! You looking for some action?"

Gwen laughed in relief at Bill's voice.

"What did you wait in the street for? We were going to come up for you."

"I know. That's why I came down."

Bill knew all about her parents. "One of those days, eh?" He got out of the car and held the door while she climbed in next to Shari. As the two women kissed and complimented each other, Bill headed the car downtown.

Shari was wearing a red chiffon dress, and, with her dark-brown hair swept up over her heart-shaped face, she looked like a valentine. Always vivacious, she was even more animated than usual, laughter and quips bubbling from her as though they were pressurized steam escaping from a suddenly loose valve. Occasionally, though, Gwen would catch an almost brooding look in her velvet-brown eyes, and more than once she noticed Shari's long, slender fingers toying nervously with the catch on her purse.

Thinking Shari was preoccupied because one of the children was sick, Gwen asked after their health, mentioning each by name.

They were fine, Shari assured her, and, pulling her gaze back from the impenetrable distances it seemed to be pursuing, she launched into an hilarious account of the day John, the middle child, had decided to launder the paper napkins in the washing machine. As she spoke, the cloud lifted from her face, and by the time they arrived at the Pinnacle, Gwen couldn't be sure she had seen it there at all.

In the lobby, they paused a moment while Shari adjusted Bill's tie, teasing that the editor of a men's magazine should know enough to tie it straight in the first place.

"Ah, that's where you're wrong," Bill informed her. "If a man learns anything from reading my magazine, it's the subtle trick of always leaving his formal bow tie just a little crooked so that some beautiful woman will come along and be unable to resist straightening it—and jumping into bed with him immediately afterward, of course."

"Cad!" Shari said, but the word was like a caress, and the

look that passed between them was as warm and tender as a kiss.

Basking as always in the circle of their love, Gwen felt a rush of affection for her two friends. As long as there were couples like them around, she felt that life would have meaning and there would be hope for the world.

Bill swept the two women into the elevator and pressed seventeen. When entertaining lucrative advertising clients, the Waterfords always rented the Presidential Suite, but for something as unremunerative as the cocktail party preceding the company dinner, a smallish suite on the seventeenth floor was considered opulent enough. The Waterfords didn't want their employees to get the ridiculous idea that the company was doing so well it could afford to give them all lucrative raises—even if that were the case.

A white-haired butler dressed in tails opened the door to their knock, looking every bit as though he had been flown over from England for the event. When he opened his mouth to invite them in, however, the image was ruined; he spoke with a heavy Bronx accent.

"They should pay that fellow to keep his mouth shut," Bill whispered, as they edged their way into the crowded room.

They greeted their co-workers and said hello to spouses they didn't see from one company dinner to the next, all the while wending their way over to the huge picture window in front of which the three Waterford brothers were stationed, trying to look like benevolent despots. The brothers knew Bill on sight, but Gwen had to remind them of her identity.

Archer extended a cold, limp hand. "Oh, yes. Nice job you've been doing. Nice job." His lips curled up in what was evidently supposed to be a warm, encouraging smile, but the feeling never reached his cold, impassive eyes. He turned to Bruce. "Guinevere took over from that Osgood woman," he briefed him.

Another limp hand and impassive smile came her way. "Oh, yes. Good job you've been doing. We're well rid of that other one." He turned to Charles. "You know Genevieve—took over after the Osgood woman left."

Charles extended a hand colder and limper than the others, his blank gaze focused in the vicinity of Gwen's left ear.

"Of course I know Jennifer. That's a fine job you've been doing."

It was difficult for Gwen to keep her smile from bubbling over into laughter. Obviously the Waterford brothers hadn't opened her magazine in years—if ever—leaving all editorial matters under the supervision of Jason Bart. They dealt strictly with the business angle, seeing her magazine and all the others in the chain in the black-and-white figures of guarantees and dollars and cents. To them, editors existed for the purpose of filling the blank pages between the all-important advertisements with something—anything—that would keep the readers and advertisers coming back. When a magazine fell on good times, the advertising salesmen were given bonuses; when it fell on bad times, the editor was shown the door.

Gwen withdrew her hand, resisting the impulse to wipe it on her dress. As she and Bill stood exchanging empty pleasantries with the three brothers, she wondered whether it was ancestry or attitude that made them look so much alike, and considered whether there was anything or anyone in the world that could cause an emotion to break through the passivity that was always registered on their faces.

"You must say hello to Father," Archer was saying when suddenly Gwen's unasked question was answered. All three pairs of eyes before her lit up with joy; all three faces flushed with enthusiasm. "Skipper!" the brothers cried out, and Gwen, Bill and Shari turned to see R. L. "Skipper" Harrison, the advertising director, making his approach like a conquering hero. Now the Waterford handshakes were strong and warm. Now the conversation was animated. There was even some back-slapping.

"And that's what they mean by 'money talks,'" Bill whispered to Gwen as he took Shari's hand. "Come on. Let's find Doc."

Doc Waterford was sitting off by himself in one of the bedrooms of the suite, a brandy snifter in one hand, a huge, unlit cigar in the other. His large paunch extending from his unbuttoned dinner jacket, he sat in a high-backed wing chair, looking rather like a court jester trying out the king's throne. What his head lacked in hair was more than made up for by his bushy white eyebrows and mustache. He was sitting so still that the three of them hesitated on the threshold, thinking he might be asleep.

"If you think I'm dead, why the hell don't you call a mortician? And if you think I'm alive, why the hell don't you talk?" a gravelly voice growled out at last. His paunch shaking with laughter, Doc popped his cigar into his mouth and held out a slightly trembling hand. "Bill Saxon, come over here and let me see you, boy!"

Bill approached and clasped the hand in both of his. "How are you, sir?"

"Rotten. How else can a man be when they don't let him work and limit him to one cigar and three brandies a day?" He looked up at Gwen and Shari through his beetling brows. "You ladies will have to forgive me for not standing up, but the old bones make a racket when I change position, and I can never be sure that I'll be able to get back down again."

"What you need," Bill said, "is some of Dr. Waterford's Sparkling Elixir."

"The hell I do! If I took that, I'd have been dead these fifty years, and all those sycophants in there would be out of jobs!" The big paunch shook with laughter again, the diamond studs on the old man's shirt front sparkling with every undulation.

Right after World War I, Doc Waterford had been a medicine man, hawking his homemade wares from the back of a horse-drawn wagon. He got the idea of printing articles on health on the handbills he used to advertise his products, and, eventually, he came to realize that his handbills were more popular than his cures. So he stopped selling his medicine and began selling his handbills. Thus *Doctor Waterford's Way to Health* (now known as *American Health Ways*), the first magazine in the Waterford chain, was born. A shrewd businessman as well as an astute editor, he had always been quick to sense the public's tastes and needs, and, by World War II, his chain had become one of the biggest in the country. After that, he had added paperback books, and the company's growth had continued on an upward course that so far saw no limit. It was all there, the company's past, present, and future, in the *Waterford Handbook*, the little

Love After Hours

pamphlet of rules and regulations given to all new Waterford employees.

Old age and failing health had forced Doc into semi-retirement the year Bill and Shari had married, but he had kept a sensitive finger on the pulse of the company and a fond eye on Bill, whom he regarded as one of the brightest young editors in the business.

After asking Shari politely about the children, he turned shrewd, questioning eyes on Gwen. Bill made the introduction.

"Ah, yes, Gwendolyn Hadley." The hand he extended was trembling, but his grip was warm and firm. "Nadine Osgood tried to fix us, didn't she? But we fixed her. We've got you."

"I don't think Nadine was trying to fix anyone but herself, sir," Gwen said, her gaze never wavering from the old man's eyes. "As a businessman, you should be able to appreciate that."

The bushy white brows contracted, but the flash of anger in the old man's eyes quickly turned to a sparkle as he removed his cigar from his mouth, chuckling. "You're right, by God, you know! It's just that we businessmen have been giving people the shaft for so damn long we think we own all the options on it." He gestured with his cigar toward Bill. "How about a light, young fella?" When he popped the cigar into his mouth, however, he began coughing, and Bill hesitated.

"Dammit, boy!" Doc said, the cigar clamped firmly between his teeth. "You're the editor of *Virile*, not *Health Ways*! Gimme a light!"

Bill complied, and the old man took a long drag, letting the smoke out slowly, luxuriously, savoring every bit of it. He turned and took Gwen's measure through the silvery haze. "Gwendolyn Hadley, I've been watching you. You've done some damn good things with the magazine. I like the new layouts—softer, more feminine. You're grabbing the readers in their minds with the sexy titles, and appealing to their emotions with the softer layouts. That's sharp thinking. I like those new features you've been putting in too. You keep that up, girl. You're going places with us."

"Thank you, sir. I'll try."

His eyes flashed. "You thank flatterers. You agree with people who simply state the truth."

Gwen laughed. "All right, sir. I *have* been doing a good job, and I *will* keep it up."

"That's better." He took another puff on his cigar, then looked around at the three of them. "Well, why are you all standing around here talking to an old relic like me? Go out to the party and have yourselves a couple of drinks. *Party!*" He spat out the last word as though it had a bad taste. "Dressing up in monkey suits and drinking fancy cocktails! In my day, I'd crack open a case of whiskey in the office whenever there was something to celebrate, and we'd all fall to. Now *those* were real parties!" For a moment, his eyes misted over, and he was back at one of his old Waterford blasts. Then they snapped back to the present. "Well, go on—get the hell out there—and have a couple for me!"

They said good-by, and left the old man to his one cigar, his three brandies, and his memories.

The sitting room was noisy and crowded, most of the guests having arrived. The men in their flamboyant dinner jackets, bright cummerbunds and ruffled shirts looked like peacocks on parade and competed with their beautifully gowned wives for the attention of the wandering eye. Most of the women there were wives, for Gwen was one of the few women at Waterford in a top editorial position. Men were the editors-in-chief of all the other magazines, even those in the women's market. Across the room, dressed in white chiffon and statuesquely silhouetted in a window, stood Andrea Langford, the only other female employee invited to the cocktail party. At the dinner, there would be a grand total of five more women waiting to join their ranks—all managing editors.

Bill beckoned to a waiter who was passing with a tray of champagne cocktails. He handed glasses to Shari and Gwen, then took one for himself, and raised it in the direction of the threshold they had recently passed through. "To Doc."

"Long may he puff his cigars," Gwen said.

The three touched glasses and drank.

From across the room, Peter Gregson, from advertising, called to Bill, who took Shari's hand, beckoning Gwen to follow. She shook her head, indicating that she'd join them later, and took another sip of her drink.

For a second, she closed her eyes and listened. Voices droned on all around her, like the buzzing of persistent bees, all noise and little meaning.

"I'm telling you, Bob, you're crazy not to build a pool. You ask a couple of prospects out for drinks and a swim, and then you can take it off your income tax as a business expense. . . ."

"Jesus! If you'd seen the blues the printer sent me this month! He must have a new guy working there. I called him and said, 'Listen, Phil, send your man to school on someone else's magazine. . . .' "

"We found this great little island about a hundred miles from Bermuda, had it all to ourselves. . . ."

"I figure two more lunches at The Four Seasons, and I'll have that account all tied up. . . ."

Shaking her head, she opened her eyes and looked around her. The guests not only sounded like bees, they looked like them too—sipping amber nectar from the glasses in their hands, flitting from one colorfully dressed person to another as though from flower to flower.

Her gaze wandered, pausing here and there on some of the more familiar figures. Two vice-presidents and a Waterford brother were paying court to Andrea Langford, who remained silhouetted in the large picture window like a Renaissance portrait of a bored, rather disdainful Venetian noblewoman. Cam Eckhart, looking as though he had stepped off one of his own fashion pages in his apricot dinner jacket and burnt-orange cummerbund, was turning all his charm on one of the Mrs. Waterfords, while Miriam, his thin shadow of a wife, stood beside him, nervously twisting her gloves. Jason Bart downed his fifth martini and headed toward the bar for another, his gait as straight as a Methodist minister's.

A heavy hand descended on her shoulder. "Hey, I've got a confession to make, and it's true," a voice slurred. "Wanna hear it?"

Gwen turned and smiled at Nolan West, the editor of *American Health Ways*, wondering what his readers would say if they could see him now, half-drunk, a dish of high-cholesterol hors d'oeuvres in his hand. "Bet your wife would want to hear it more."

Nolan looked like a man who had just discovered he'd misplaced his wallet. "Say! I left her around here someplace. Went to get her a drink and got a little sidetracked. You haven't seen her, have you?"

Gwen's eyes swept the room until she spotted a pudgy, lost-looking little woman. "There she is—by the door."

Nodding, Nolan took a drink from a passing tray and began weaving his way toward his wife. Gwen watched him go, noting that he had consumed half the contents of the glass before he gave it to her.

Her gaze drifted from Mrs. West to the nearby door, which was being opened to admit a late arrival. Paul Lockhart stood framed in the doorway, his eyes scanning the room. A buzzing began inside her head, mounting until it seemed to surround her, and she took a quick swallow of her drink, hoping to still the trembling coldness that seemed to be rising from deep inside her. She fought down an almost irresistible urge to flee. Never before had she felt that way in the presence of a man, and she hated herself for her weakness almost as much as she hated Paul for conjuring up the feeling in her. She tore her eyes from his face and turned her back before their glances could meet.

In a dim corner of the room, she spotted Janmarie, Neil Mennen's pretty wife, obviously trying desperately not to look as bored as she felt. Quickly, Gwen seated herself beside her and began asking her about her children. Immediately, Janmarie came to life, and within seconds Gwen was poring over the yard of family portraits she carried in her purse. The smiling faces that stared out at Gwen differed little from those of countless other children, but she exclaimed and lingered over every picture, never once lifting her eyes, because, with her whole body, she was aware of Paul's eyes on her, willing her to look up.

Moments later, a waiter walked through the room requesting everyone who would not be seated at the head table to go to the main ballroom and take their seats for dinner. Gwen pretended that she hadn't heard. It wasn't long, however, before Bill and Shari came to fetch her.

Love After Hours 61

"Come on," Shari said. "It's time for phase two."

Gwen gave the pictures back to Janmarie with compliments and rose.

"Did you see who came in before?" Bill asked.

Gwen pretended ignorance.

"Paul Lockhart. I was right. Cam nearly split a gut when he showed up. He's the only writer who accepted an invitation. Lockhart asked for you, but I couldn't spot you from where we were standing."

"Pity," Gwen said dryly. The few minutes she'd spent with Janmarie had helped her regain her composure.

"What have you got against the guy?"

Gwen shrugged, wishing she knew herself.

"Women!" Bill shook his head, took Gwen's arm and Shari's, and began steering them out of the room.

On the way out they passed Paul, who had been cornered by the editor of the paperback division devoted to reprints. As his gaze met hers, Gwen nodded and smiled, complimenting herself on a coolness that she felt was equal to Andrea Langford's. She assured herself that she wasn't ruffled, even though she could feel his eyes following her all the way out of the room.

In the ballroom, the managing editors, their spouses, and the other lesser executives and theirs were standing around, drinks they had bought for themselves at the hotel bar in their hands, waiting like so many parcels for their bosses to come and claim them.

Gwen found Laura and David Faber deep in conversation, tall, bespectacled David seeming to hang on to every word Laura was saying. Just as Gwen came up to them, David was reaching out to smooth Laura's bangs, which she'd messed, as usual, in the intensity of making a point. The gesture was like a caress, and it reminded Gwen of the magic shared by Shari and Bill.

"Have you been here long?" Gwen asked.

Laura made a little face. "Ages."

David smiled. "She means it seems that way. This kind of thing really isn't our meat."

"I know the feeling," Gwen said. "Bill Saxon says we should look upon it as planned tension, a challenge to our endurance. There's one cheering thought, though. Some firms give Christmas parties too. At least we're spared that."

They found their way to the table they were to share with Bill and Shari and *Virile*'s managing editor and his wife, and joined the others. As soon as everyone in the room was seated, the five-piece orchestra hired for the momentous occasion struck up a fanfare, and all rose as the Waterford nobility and honored guests marched to their places at the head table to a few jazzed-up bars from Handel's *Water Music*. Paul Lockhart, who, as a famous best-selling author was considered too illustrious a personage to be allowed to sit with Bill, the lowly editor who had captured some of his talent, was among them. Noting that he seemed to be having a difficult time keeping a straight face, Gwen felt a momentary warmth for him.

Between courses, the band played, and Waterfordians tested their agility on the tiny dance floor. Gwen had her turns with Bill and David, and returned to the table relieved that her token dances were over and that the couples could now relax and enjoy themselves as they should. But, between the soup and the roast beef, Cam Eckhart came over and extended an invitation that, on this comradely occasion, she really couldn't refuse.

They started out a respectable distance apart, but gradually Cam's grip tightened, his bearded cheek coming down to rest against her smooth one. "We dance well together," he said. "We should do this more often."

"How about every morning between ten and ten-fifteen in Jason Bart's office? He has plenty of floor space."

"You never take me seriously," he pouted.

"You've never given me any reason to."

He pulled her closer, rocking his upper torso from side to side so that his chest could take the measure of her breasts.

She managed to pull away a little. "Look, Cam, I agreed to dance, not to indulge in a vertical petting session."

Cam laughed and pulled her close again. "I love your sense of humor."

"And I never cease to wonder at your lack of one."

Cam saw her back to her table, where he greeted all the

Love After Hours

others—especially the ladies—cordially, and cut Bill, as he had been doing ever since the incident of the brown wall.

The meal progressed, made merry by Bill's humor and his caustic preview of the speeches that were yet to come. Just before the baked Alaska, Paul descended from the dais and asked Gwen to dance. His was one of the few plain white dinner jackets and frill-less shirts present, and he looked as natural in the outfit as he did in tweeds.

"Are these affairs always so deadly?" he asked as they moved onto the dance floor.

"They are if you're sitting on the dais. It gets worse before it gets better. The speeches are next."

He groaned.

"Don't expect sympathy from me," Gwen warned him. "I *have* to be here. You're a free-lance writer. You don't work for the company. You could easily have turned down your invitation."

"I had my reasons."

His eyes never left hers, and again she felt that strange fluttering begin somewhere deep inside her. She fought it down and laughed, keeping her voice light. "Masochism?"

He laughed too. "Perhaps!"

The pressure of his hand on her back grew firmer as he whirled her into the waltz rhythm the band had just switched to. Their long legs moved smoothly together; they could anticipate each other's every step, as if they had been dancing together all their lives.

"How about waltzing right through one of those exits and down Park Avenue, far from the sound of the speeches to come?" he asked.

"Sounds tempting," Gwen admitted, "but if I did that, the Waterfords would soon have me dancing to a different tune."

"Afterward then, when the speeches are over."

"Waltz down Park Avenue?"

"I'd settle for walking, or even riding."

It wasn't idle banter anymore, and Gwen stiffened, causing them to miss a step. "I—I came with Bill and Shari."

"You're looking for excuses. You know they wouldn't mind if you left with me."

"Perhaps," she said, trying to laugh a little, "I mind."

His eyes never wavered from hers. "You mind, but you want to come too." There was no egotism in what he said, no smugness. He was simply stating a truth he had read in her eyes. It was a truth Gwen did not want to face but found she could not deny.

He did not try to press his advantage. "Leave with me," he said gently. "I'm not a man who says please easily, but I'll say it now."

For a moment, it was as though she could see into his soul too, and she shuddered at the loneliness she saw there. "All right," she said.

The music stopped, and as its strains died away, so did their moment of closeness. She returned to her table perhaps a little more quickly than she should have, but Paul kept up with her and held her chair. Then, with a little half-smile, he went back to his own seat.

As soon as the waiters had cleared away the last of the dessert dishes, Archer Waterford appeared at the lectern and microphone that had been placed at the center of the head table, directly above a shimmering, sequined replica of the Waterford trademark. In a voice as expressionless as the face from which it emanated, he stretched the few words he promised to say about the company's progress over the last year into the longest twenty-minute speech on record. His report was positive and optimistic, though not so positive and optimistic as to encourage anyone in the room to ask for a raise. He stood in his custom-made evening clothes and shoes, the smoke from his five-dollar cigar curling lazily from the ashtray beside him, and informed his executive staff that the company was functioning on an austerity budget; they should not be fooled by the rises in sales; inflation had greatly reduced the company's real profit, and what little there was had to be plowed back in to absorb increased production costs; things would get worse before they got better, for the same recession that was always lurking around the corner when he made his annual speeches was lurking there again, waiting to pounce on them if they became even a little careless; executives must warn their staffs of the

Love After Hours 65

dangers and push them harder (at no increase in pay, of course) to keep the company operating in the black.

Nearby, his wife, wearing a Pucci original, sat grim-faced nodding agreement to his every word. Plain-spoken and truthful, she had not been too proud to try to hide her financial difficulties from the wives she had chatted with earlier at the cocktail party. Candidly, she had told them that she had been forced of late to wait until Altman's had a sale before buying gifts for her grandchildren, and frankly she had admitted having placed her cook under orders to prepare hamburger for the family dinner at least once a week. A generous woman, she had offered to supply the other wives with some of her favorite recipes for that starvation-diet food—her special favorite being one that called for asparagus tips, mushrooms, and truffles, and a French burgundy, preferably one bottled in 1949.

The laughter that greeted Archer's time-worn jokes was too hearty to be genuine, but the applause that broke out at the end of his speech rang with a sincerity born of relief. After it died down, he introduced his brother Bruce, whose speech had all the earmarks of a replay. Charles was given the honor of bestowing the Waterford Awards—tiny gold lapel-pin replicas of the trademark—upon the men responsible for bringing in the most advertising during the past year, and the paperback publishers who had been lucky enough to secure the reprint rights to best sellers. So far, no editor had ever received a pin, for rules and regulations ordained that it would go to an editor only upon retiring from the company with honor after twenty-five years; so far, any editor who had the ability to accrue the honor also had the ambition to leave long before the time requirement was fulfilled.

The awards given, Charles introduced his father, and the old man was helped to the microphone by Archer and Bruce. This time the applause was warm and genuine.

Doc's sharp eyes looked out on his employees, seeming to meet every pair projected upon him. He fanned a wrinkled hand before his face. "The air around this microphone is too damned hot for an old codger like me to stand and talk in. I don't know about you, but I've listened to enough yakking for one night. It's time we had some more music besides the tinkling of pennies in my sons' tin cups. You fellers over there, play something lively. I want to see everybody dance!" He waved, and, shrugging off his sons' support, shuffled back to his seat.

As instructed, the band struck up a lively number, and Waterfordians rose to dance the aches of boredom from their limbs. From the corner of her eye, Gwen could see that Paul was taking leave of the members of the head table, and, before the first song was over, he was standing behind her chair.

"Shall we go?" he asked.

Bill, who was just returning from the dance floor with Shari, shot Gwen a questioning look, obviously meant to indicate that he'd be willing to insist she go home with him if that was what she wanted. She answered with an almost imperceptible shake of her head. Exasperated by the conflicting emotions Paul Lockhart had the power to arouse in her, she was determined to rid herself of them by spending a few moments alone in his company. She kissed Shari, and, taking leave of the others, let Paul guide her to the nearest exit.

A warm September breeze descended upon them when they emerged from the air-conditioned hotel. It was well past midnight, and there was little traffic and few people on the street.

Paul paused to light his pipe, the flame from his match chasing the shadows from his face and reflecting off the silvery hair on top of his head. "Would you like to walk for a while?"

Gwen nodded, and they began to stroll downtown along Park Avenue.

"When I was a kid," Gwen said, looking around at the miles of towering fortresses that shelter New York's rich from some of the problems of city life, "I used to walk along this street and try to imagine how much money one would have to earn to be able to afford the thousands of dollars one has to pay in rent for an apartment here. I always wound up with a headache. It was like trying to contemplate infinity."

"That's rather how the money housed on this street runs—*ad infinitum*. Did you dream of growing up and living here?"

"My imagination couldn't stretch that far. My idea of being rich in those days was to be able to afford an apartment on the Grand Concourse, Eastern Parkway or in Washington Heights."

"That was a pretty practical imagination. At least it came up with goals you could achieve."

She smiled a little sadly, thinking of how little happiness she had found in achieving that goal of an Eastern Parkway apartment. She was finding it easier to talk to him now, walking along in the artificial twilight of the street lamps, her eyes straight ahead.

"And you?" she asked. "Did you imagine yourself living here?"

"I had neither the imagination nor the desire. Even as a kid, I was a realist. I couldn't walk along this street without being haunted by a vision of the tenements around the corner, tenements that probably housed the workers whose labors made the tenants of these houses richer and richer."

"Sounds like a fun childhood," Gwen teased.

"With pretensions that didn't extend beyond the likes of Washington Heights, I'd say yours wasn't exactly ideal either."

They walked on a while in silence, Paul puffing his pipe, his hands in his pockets, Gwen holding her purse close to her body.

Suddenly Paul stopped and knocked the ashes from his pipe. "Here comes a taxi," he said, as though they'd been looking for one all evening. "Let's take it down to the Battery for a night ferry."

Before Gwen could either agree or protest, he had flagged down the cab and was holding the door open for her. Obediently, she climbed in and settled back as Paul told the driver where they wanted to go.

As the taxi made its way downtown, they talked of the dinner they had come from, Gwen filling Paul in on the history of the affair and on who was who.

The taxi stopped at South Ferry, and Paul paid the driver through the little slot in the bullet-proof plastic shield that protected him from his less law-abiding passengers.

Gwen gestured at the thick partition. "I almost never take

cabs anymore because of that," she said. "I find it too depressing."

"It's a lot less depressing than all the shot-up cabbies we used to have," Paul said as he slammed the door.

They entered the terminal just in time to catch the next ferry. Grabbing her hand, Paul made a dash for the gangplank. Almost as soon as they were on board, an attendant fastened the chains across the entrance way, and the big boat began lumbering away from the dock like an unwieldy but graceful whale.

They had the boat almost to themselves, and they went, past a few necking couples and sleepy commuters, up the narrow stairs that led to the upper deck. Not until they were on the outer deck did Gwen realize that her hand was still in Paul's. Quickly, she withdrew it, folding her arms along the rail.

Paul slipped his hands into his pockets, jiggling some change. He breathed deeply. "As long as the Staten Island Ferry exists, one can almost forgive New York City all her sins."

In silence they looked out over the black waters of the Hudson. To the west, the Statue of Liberty held her torch aloft, though the diamond tiara that was the receding Manhattan skyline needed no further illumination. On the opposite shore, the scattered lights of Richmond winked and blinked and beckoned like so many lonely flirts.

"It's so beautiful," Gwen said.

"From here," Paul amended. He gestured toward the skyline. "From there, it's just the illumination of office windows behind which countless people plod away at jobs they hate; the shining of lights behind shuttered shops that are barred and wired against the advent of thieves; the glow of street lamps, beyond the rim of which there are probably twenty people being mugged this minute."

Gwen shook her head. "Do you always have to see only the ugliness in everything?"

"Not the ugliness—the reality." He stepped closer. "I look at life and see it as it is, not as I'd like it to be, as you do."

"As I do!" Gwen turned sharply and met his gaze. "You barely know me. How can you presume to know how I look at life?"

"Because the key is there in so many things you say and do. You look at the skyline, and you see only a post card, not the concrete and grime that it really is; if something's a reminder of the realities of living—a bullet-proof partition, for instance—you turn your back on it, and try to pretend it isn't there."

"That's not true!" Anger warmed Gwen's cheeks. "You talk as though I've lived in an ivory tower all my life. Well, I haven't. I've seen plenty of harsh realities—enough to have earned the privilege of ignoring them occasionally."

There was neither anger nor condemnation in Paul's eyes. "I never said you lived in an ivory tower—never thought it. Even in the short time we've known each other, it's obvious that nothing could be further from the truth. All the more reason why you don't want to face up to reality. All the more reason why you're running scared."

Gwen's hand tightened on the guard rail in frustration. "You're outrageously unfair. I'd expect more from a man of your intelligence than to judge me without knowing me."

"Dammit!" His voice held an answering sharpness. "Don't you see? That's the problem. I *want* to get to know you, and you're too damn scared to let me!"

Suddenly she felt a trembling rising inside her, a trembling that was close to the very fear Paul was talking about. Sensing that they were skirting on the edge of a truth she could not bear to see, she searched her mind frantically for something to say—anything that would keep them from pursuing the argument. Drawing a deep breath, she said as lightly as she could, "Why do we always wind up fighting?"

His face was uncomfortably close. "Don't you know?" he asked softly.

She wanted to tear her eyes away, but his gaze held them locked with his.

"Arguing is another of your dodges," he went on, "another escape from reality. Surely, you've known from our first meeting—just as I have—what the only other alternative for us is. You're afraid of that alternative, and you're fighting to cover your retreat." Gently, he took her by the shoulders. "Why are you so afraid of me?"

She shrank a little from his touch. "You flatter yourself. I'm not afraid of anyone." She tried to keep her voice steady, haughty.

He stood there a moment, his eyes searching her face. "I don't believe you," he said simply.

Had he said the words in anger, she might have rallied and fought back. But she had no defense against his gentleness. Her lips quivering, she tore herself from his grasp. "All right!" she cried. "Maybe I *am* afraid. But for God's sake, stop cross-examining me! I don't *know* why I'm afraid. I've never been afraid of a man before in my life." She whirled from him and looked out over the water.

"Perhaps," he said gently, "it's because you never met a man like me." There was nothing egotistical in the remark. He was simply stating, in his stark, realistic way, the truth as he saw it.

Gwen made no attempt to answer. She stood at the rail, staring out over the water, the short, shallow breaths she was taking making her chest quiver like that of a cornered animal.

"Somewhere along the line," Paul went on, "there has been a man in your life—a man who has soured you so much that you've built iron-clad defenses against us all."

A vision of Barnabas Hadley, with his bulging, angry eyes, his snarling mouth, his hamlike fists, flashed before her, and she shuddered. She used to blame her parents for her single state; Barney and Agnes had done all they could to chase away those whom they called her "gentlemen callers." Whenever a young man had walked through the door, Agnes had tearfully told him what a good daughter Gwen was— how she'd been supporting her parents ever since she went to work. Then Barney had growled that she'd damn well better support them: After all, they'd brought her into the world and raised her; she owed them that much and more. After having been exposed to such a scene, the young men had always quickly faded from her life. And she had never really minded. Now, with Paul's words still ringing in her ears,

Love After Hours

Gwen realized that perhaps her situation wasn't her parents' doing after all, but her own. If she had wanted to have a serious relationship with a man, she would have found a way, even if it had meant running off and marrying, as her sister had done the minute she got out of high school. She certainly would never have brought men home to endure a scene that she knew would deal the *coup de grâce* to any possibility of building a stronger relationship. It was a disquieting thought.

"Perhaps," Paul's voice cut into her thoughts, "I'm the only man who has come along who has stood a chance of crumbling those defenses."

Again, her father's face flashed before her, and the hell her parents visited upon each other seemed, for a second, to be pressing down upon her, smothering her. She turned to him, her eyes brimming with tears. "Then, for God's sake," she whispered, "have pity, and don't try."

He shook his head sadly. "Don't you see that the pity for both of us would lie in exactly that—not trying."

"Oh, God!" she whispered, more to herself than to him. She turned and sat upon the bench behind them, her shoulders hunched, her forehead resting in her hands.

"Do you know that I'm married?" he asked.

She shook her head, not looking up.

He sighed. "Well, I am, and will be for a long time to come." He turned and gazed at the river. "I don't know what attracted me to a woman like Verna. I suppose she represents my one attempt to escape from the harshness of reality that I'd always forced myself to face. I'd just come back from Korea. The war was over when I was there, but I still saw plenty of bloodshed. What I hated even more was the starvation and misery I'd seen at the bottom of society, and the gluttony and greed at the top."

He shook his head, remembering. "After my discharge, I took a room in the Village and began spilling my guts on paper. Verna had the room across the hall. She was determined to be the great American actress. I guess what fascinated me most was her complete dedication to that goal—to the extent of being totally oblivious to the world around her.

In those days, I suppose, I half wished I could be oblivious too. At any rate, we went out and got a little drunk one night, drove to Maryland, and got married."

He tapped his fingers against the railing, and Gwen looked up, her heart beating painfully as she waited for him to begin again.

"It wasn't too bad the first few years," he went on, his back still toward her. "We were both too busy trying to get a leg up on our careers to pay much attention to each other, or to get on each other's nerves. The trouble began when I started to make a name for myself, and she still had nothing to show for all her efforts but worn-out shoe leather. She became bitter and jealous and almost impossible to live with. I was ready to walk out on her when she told me she was pregnant, so I stayed, hoping we could work things out. We couldn't. We've lived together—but apart—from the time of Melanie's birth. Verna's never cared for Melanie, but she clings to her as an excuse for giving up the career she never had in the first place."

He turned, his eyes meeting Gwen's. "I've begged her to let me have a divorce and give me Melanie, but she refuses. She's jealous of me and can't stand me, but she seems to get a certain pleasure out of being my wife because of my position. I have a feeling she thinks being married to me will bring her the break she needs. She swears that if I leave her, she'll get a divorce and keep Melanie away from me for good. She could do it, too. She may be lousy on stage, but off it, Verna Greene's the best damn actress in the country."

The lines on his face seemed to deepen. "Melanie's only twelve—just halfway between a girl and a woman. We mean so much to each other. I couldn't abandon her to her mother's clutches. Verna would kill all that's good in her within a year—and that would kill me too."

Gwen had forgotten her fear as she listened to his sorrow, and, walking over to him, she reached out and touched his arm. "I'm sorry," she said. "I really am."

He gazed down on her a moment and smiled a little. "You know," he said, "you're not the only one who has built defenses. During my life with Verna, I've built some pretty solid ones of my own. But the first time I saw you, they all came tumbling down. You're the kind of woman most men can only dream about—intelligent, perceptive, sensitive—and beautiful, too. Don't hold yourself back from me."

For a second, her old fear flashed in her eyes, and she started to move away. "Please, Paul—" she whispered. But he put his hands on her shoulders, holding her where she was. This time she didn't shrink beneath his gentle touch.

"Gwen," he pleaded, "I'm not asking you to marry me; I can't. I'm not even asking you to be my mistress; I couldn't be so presumptuous. I'm only asking you to be my friend. God knows, I need a friend like you—a woman I can share my thoughts and feelings with. And I think that you could use a friend like me. That's all I ask for now."

Her eyes searched his. "And for tomorrow?" she asked, her heart pounding.

He smiled and drew her close, pressing her head against his chest, gently smoothing her hair. "We'll face our tomorrows when they come."

She closed her eyes over her tears. Deep inside, she felt as though a glacier were receding before the warming rays of a bright new sun.

The ferry jerked suddenly as it bumped against its mooring, thrusting them apart.

"Staten Island," Paul said, taking her hand. "Come on, friend. I'll buy you a cup of coffee while we wait for the next boat home."

Chapter Four

1

*B*y one a.m., the Waterford party was drawing to a close. For the past half-hour, Waterfordians by threes and fours had been taking their leave of the benevolent despots on the dais and working their way toward the exits, those following them always spacing their approach to the dais so that there would be no impression of a stampede for freedom. Gwen's table had long since been deserted by the friends and co-workers she had left behind; only a few crumbs, overlooked by a sleepy busboy, were left to testify to its former occupancy.

A few tables away, Andrea Langford and Skipper Harrison, the advertising director, rose. They had arrived separately, but during the evening, Andrea had agreed to let Skipper take her home. They went up to the head table to say good night to all the Waterfords save Doc, who, under much protest, had been ushered off to bed shortly after midnight. The Waterford brothers beamed at Skipper and cast longing glances after Andrea as she walked by his side toward the exit; at one time or another, each of them had tried to procure her for his mistress, but none had been able to vault her wall of ice.

Outside, as the warm September air rushed over them, the doorman hailed a cab. They climbed in, Skipper giving the driver his own address.

Andrea arched an eyebrow. "I haven't moved."

"I thought we'd stop at my place for a nightcap."

She shrugged and settled back in the seat. It was going to be a longer evening than she had anticipated.

Skipper withdrew a gold cigarette case from his pocket—a second-anniversary present from his third wife, or perhaps a third-anniversary present from his second wife—and offered its contents for Andrea's inspection. She shook her head, opening the window near her a little wider. Taking the hint, Skipper returned the case to his pocket, its contents undisturbed.

A tall, muscular man in his early fifties, Skipper wore his steel-gray hair fashionably long and sported sideburns that could be described only as modified mutton-chop. Eyes whose gray looked as though it had been penciled in peered out from a complexion made leathery and tan by many leisure hours spent on the yacht he kept moored at Oyster Bay.

With the ease of a master salesman, he kept up a running conversation all the way to his apartment house at Sixty-fifth and Park. If he was aware that Andrea's responses were cool and monosyllabic, he did not give himself away.

Ever playing the role of the ingenuous, wholesome outdoors man who indulges in business only as an afterthought —it was amazing how many prospects the pose won over— Skipper loosened his tie the moment they entered his apartment.

"Make yourself comfortable," he told Andrea, as he switched the lamps on to low.

She removed her chiffon stole and placed it on the arm of the zebra-patterned sofa.

"What'll you drink?"

"Scotch on the rocks." It was the most she had said to him since they climbed into the cab. Andrea Langford was not one to make the mechanics of seduction easy for a man. While Skipper was mixing the drinks, she inspected the sports trophies that were placed in conspicuous positions around the room. She prodded the tiger skin that lay before the artificial fireplace with the toe of a silver-shod foot. "Real?"

Standing behind the bar, Skipper nodded. "Bagged it on safari about a year ago."

Aware that he was a great outdoors man only because he found through it an avenue to being an even greater salesman, Andrea said dryly, "And bagged a big contract at the same time, no doubt."

Skipper contracted the proper facial muscles for evoking a look of injured innocence. "I go on safari for the sport, pitting my mind against the cunning of the beast in his own natural habitat."

"And your cunning against that of the advertising prospect who just happens to be along."

"Ah, you're much too cynical," he said with an indulgent smile, handing her her drink.

"Not cynical—truthful." She looked around at the plush furnishings of the room. "If you're an outdoors man, Skipper, it's because your favorite sport is making money. It's no secret to me. My beauty columns aren't written to help readers or to court their good will, but to pave the way for the people in your department to bring in millions of dollars worth of beauty-aid advertising. You can drop the pose with me. I'm in the business too."

She raised the tiger's eternally snarling head on her toe, then let it drop back to the floor. "If you left the comforts of this apartment to go on a safari, it was to bag a lot more than a tiger."

They faced each other a moment, Andrea's eyes mocking, Skipper's measuring. Finally, he gave her the just-between-us smile he reserved for only those who shared privileged information.

"As a matter of fact," he said, rolling forward slightly on the balls of his feet, "Art Alexander was there too, and he signed with us for a couple of million dollars worth of cigarette advertising."

Andrea showed no sign of being impressed by either the confidence or the sum involved. "And when you landed that?" she asked, indicating the sailfish mounted over the fireplace.

His chest expanded a little. "Landed the biggest damned deodorant contract in history." His gaze followed Andrea's to a golf trophy. "That brings in a hell of a lot of good will. You'd be surprised how many avid golfers keep their accounts with us because of that."

Andrea settled herself on the sofa, saying nothing. She was never surprised by the childish motivations behind some of the biggest wheelings and dealings of businessmen.

Skipper quickly sat down beside her. "But let's not talk about business," he said, raising his glass. "To us."

Andrea raised her glass too. "To you and to me," she corrected.

Reaching over, Skipper touched a switch on the end table, and the room was flooded with soft music. Inching closer, he began to extol the virtues of yachting. "Why don't you come out with me one weekend? There's nothing like being alone, surrounded by ocean and sky."

As if to keep the ocean breezes from disturbing her well-coiffured hair, Andrea touched it with her hand. "I'm not much of a sailor."

"But a lot of woman." He took her glass from her and placed it next to his on the cocktail table, where the gleaming wood mirrored their reflection, as well as that of a cigarette caddy and lighter in the form of a golfbag and ball.

Her perfectly painted lips curved upward in a mildly mocking smile. "And now you intend to prove to me that you're a lot of man."

"A *hell* of a lot of man."

He was so close that she could feel the warm puffs of his breath as they landed on an area just above her décolletage. The smile never leaving her lips, she turned away to retrieve her drink. With the skill of a practiced hunter closing in for the kill, Skipper blocked her retreat with the curve of his left arm, and, taking her face in his right hand, he turned it back toward his. In a moment, his warm moist mouth was vainly caressing her soft unresponsive lips: Andrea had long ago learned that lack of response wounded the male ego a great deal more than a struggle did.

At last Skipper released her. "I'd get more response if I necked with a marlin," he said in disgust.

As though nothing had happened to break off the motion she had been going through before the kiss, Andrea once more reached for her drink—this time successfully. "Then you should ask one up for a drink sometime."

Skipper had no intention of accepting such an early defeat. "I might get more response from one, but I'd much rather work on getting it from you."

He leaned closer, but this time, Andrea slipped away and

walked over to the fireplace. "I don't play games," she said calmly.

Once again, his face took on the lines of injured innocence. "Neither do I."

Andrea's eyes swept over all the trophies and sport mementos in the room. "Oh, really?"

He rose and began a stealthy approach. "Not with you."

"I should have thought women were one of your favorite sports. With three wives and a long line of mistresses, it would seem you were intent on setting some kind of world record."

His eyes shone with a sudden enlightenment, and he quickened his advance. "You're jealous!"

Her laughter was like the tinkle of wind chimes carved from icicles. "You'd love that, wouldn't you?"

"There's no need to pretend with me." His voice exuded a sincerity that, being pumped straight from his heart to his mouth, necessarily missed being channeled into his eyes. "All the others were nothing compared to you. It's as if they were meant to prepare me for this moment—and the many others that I know we're destined to share."

As he spoke, his face descended closer and closer to hers, and his lips cut off the laugh that was bubbling up to hers. Once again, she was limp and unresponsive.

At last he thrust her away, his impatience beginning to show. "What the hell is it with you? What do you want from a man?"

"Nothing at all. You're the one who is doing the wanting."

He pulled her back to him. "It's impossible to be near you and not want you. Surely, you feel the same magnetic force that is drawing us together—the entire room seems to be vibrating with it."

"The only force that is drawing us together is a pair of hairy arms that happen to be attached to your muscle-bound shoulders." She slipped from his grasp like ice eluding hot tongs.

A man who was used to having things his way, Skipper did not take lightly to being foiled. Now that it was obvious that Andrea would not succumb to his formerly irresistible

Love After Hours

charm, he no longer tried to smother his anger. His eyes flashed. "What the hell did you come up here for then?"

She raised her almost-empty glass before his face. "I seem to recall being invited for a drink."

He was incredulous. "You're no sweet young innocent. You knew there would be more to it than that."

"Did I? To me, a drink is a drink." She drained her glass and placed it on the mantel. "Now I've had mine. If you didn't get yours in the process, that's your problem. Too bad you didn't mention what you really had in mind in the cab. You would have saved yourself a jigger of good Scotch." She started across the room to retrieve her stole.

A deep flush mounted beneath Skipper's carefully cultivated sportsman's tan. "Do you know what they call you at the office?"

"I imagine I'm about to find out."

"The Ice Queen."

The words came out clipped and measured, like three carefully aimed shots in the dark. It was clear from Andrea's unmoved serenity that they had not met their mark.

"That's rather pretty," she said.

"I've got a better name for you," he grated.

She laughed. "Oh, I'm sure you have. But it's probably not as pretty."

"You're damned right it's not!" He crossed to the bar and downed another drink. "What are you anyway? A goddam lesbian?"

She shook her head, the mocking smile never leaving her lips. "You'd love that, wouldn't you? You and all the others like you. It would salve those pathetic male egos of yours. Well, I hate to disappoint you, but the idea of sexual relations with someone of my sex revolts me just as much as the idea of relations with someone of yours."

"How do you get your kicks?" he sneered. "Masturbation?"

"Chalk up another disappointment. My life is free of perversions." She slipped her stole around her shoulders. "You'll just have to swallow it, Skipper. I don't need sex; I don't need men; I don't need you."

"Then you must be frigid."

Her laughter rang out once more. "Why is it so difficult for men to accept the fact that there are women who can function perfectly well and find happiness without them?"

He tossed off another drink. "Because it's a goddam lie!"

She looked rather like an avenging archangel as she approached him. Her face never lost its serenity, but her voice dripped with the venom of controlled fury. "Don't you believe it, R. L. Harrison! The biggest liars walking this planet are men like you. You accuse women of being the weaker sex, and try to force us into a mold so you can bolster your own deep-seated feelings of inferiority by walking all over us. When we prove we're equal or better and can survive very well without you, you shout *lesbian!* or *pervert!* And all the while, you're the ones who are the worst perverts around."

She held up a hand to silence the protest she saw coming to his lips. "Yes, perverts! When a man looks upon a woman as an inferior being, someone only good for answering his correspondence in the office and picking up after him at home, when he strips her of her individuality and turns her into a sex object good only for relieving his own biological urges—*that's* perversion—the filthiest kind of perversion on the face of the earth!"

She picked up her purse and started toward the door. "A woman needs a man like she needs a rattlesnake in her bed."

"Like hell you don't need us!" Skipper sneered. He slammed his glass down on the bar. "You couldn't walk out on the streets at this time of night without being raped."

"That doesn't negate my point—it proves it."

Skipper came from behind the bar. "I'll see you home," he said, like a man volunteering for the dirtiest job in town.

"Calling me a cab will do just as well."

In front of his building, he hailed a taxi. She got in, gave the driver her address, and slammed the door on Skipper. "Thanks for the drink."

As the cab pulled away, she heard him snarl, "Damned lesbian bitch!"

She settled back for the ride, her lips curling into an amused, self-satisfied smile. She felt as she always did when she had thwarted a seduction: revitalized, strong, and proud.

Once more, she reveled in the knowledge that she was in complete control of her life and her destiny. She would never need the love or the help of any man.

She was still smiling five minutes later when the driver pulled up in front of her luxurious apartment house and the doorman rushed over to assist her. Her smile faded, however, when she discovered that only one of the three locks on her apartment door was secured. Wondering if she had finally joined the ever-growing ranks of tenants who had been burglarized, she eased her door open apprehensively.

Light, and the aroma of freshly brewed coffee—not destruction and disorder—greeted her. Still she hesitated, wondering whether it was safe to cross the threshold. Then a tall, slender beauty of eighteen emerged from the kitchen.

"Surprise!" the girl cried.

"Marge!" The warmth that only her daughter could evoke flooded Andrea's face as she took the girl in her arms. "I didn't know you were coming down this weekend!"

"Neither did I until the last minute."

Andrea held Marge away from her, smiling tenderly as she searched her face. "It's too early in the term to be sent down for poor grades, and in this day and age, there doesn't seem to be anything a student can do that would be considered bad enough to call for expulsion. So what can it be? Don't tell me you're homesick already?"

"Not exactly." Marge's eyes were as evasive as her words. She slipped from Andrea's grasp. "I made some coffee. Go sit down, and I'll get it."

Sighing contentedly, Andrea walked into the living room, slipped off her shoes and curled up on the blue velvet sofa. Whatever the reason for her surprise visit, it was good to have Marge home for a little while. She missed her more than she liked to admit. She had heard often about parents who thought the sun rose and set around their children, and she knew she had to number herself among them. Whenever Marge was away, it was as though the light had gone out of her life.

Marge came out of the kitchen, tray in hand. Though she lacked her mother's cool grace, her movements as she walked hinted at an inner warmth and vigor that were no less striking. Setting the tray on the cocktail table in front of the sofa, she busied herself with pouring the coffee and adding cream and sugar.

In a glow of love and pride, Andrea watched her child-turned-woman serving their coffee. She never tired of studying her daughter's beauty. Marge's high cheekbones and finely chiseled nose were, she knew, like her own, while the luxuriant chestnut hair that cascaded over her shoulders and the full, rich lips that seemed so prone to smiles were throwbacks to Andrea's own mother. The wide, almost purple eyes that looked rather like pansies in the morning dew were a mystery, however. Perhaps they were a contribution from Marge's father, though it seemed to Andrea that she would have remembered if Harlan—or was it Harvey?—had had eyes like that. More than likely, they could be traced to a recessive gene on her own side.

Smiling tenderly, she accepted the cup proffered to her, but not without noticing that the hand that offered it was trembling a little. "Tired, dear?"

"Not really."

Both women masked the little pause that followed by sipping from their cups.

"Have you been given some special holiday," Andrea asked at last, "or do you have to go back tomorrow?"

Marge seemed to be searching for the answer in the bottom of her cup. At last she said, in a voice that was little more than a whisper, "I'm not going back."

"You mean—not tomorrow?"

Marge took a sip of coffee, and, as if gaining strength from it, brought her eyes to meet her mother's. "I mean," she said softly, "not ever." Though her voice was not trembling, the cup and saucer in her hand began to rattle. She placed them on the table and brought her gaze back to Andrea's.

For a moment, Andrea looked puzzled. Then, the explanation for her daughter's declaration suddenly occurring to her, she leaned forward, laughing indulgently. "So it seems as bad as all that, does it? College frightens all freshmen at first—all those tough assignments being thrown at you, all those demanding teachers. Give it a chance, Marge. If anyone can make it, you can!"

"That's not it, Mother. I *can* make it, but I don't want to anymore." She drew the corner of her lower lip between her teeth.

"Don't do that, dear," Andrea said absently.

Immediately, Marge obeyed. She leaned forward, her eyes filling with excitement. "You see, Mother, I want—"

Andrea cut her off with a knowing little laugh. "Oh, I know what you want! You want all the glamor and excitement of getting a job, being independent. Though what kind of job you expect to get without a degree, I can't imagine. I suppose you think I'll come up with something."

Marge shook her head vigorously. "No, really! I—"

Andrea held up her hand. "Don't deny it," she scolded tenderly. "You know that's what's at the back of your mind. Maybe it's not such a bad idea after all." She got up and walked to the sliding glass doors that led to the terrace, gazing past them at the glittering lights of the city. "With all the people I know, I certainly should be able to come up with something. You'd soon learn how little glamor there is in the working world. At the end of six months, you'd be twice as anxious to get back to your books as you are to leave them now."

For a moment, there was no comment from Marge, who had settled back on the sofa, evidently realizing that Andrea would have to have her say before she could hope to have hers. Then she dropped her bomb: "I don't want a job. I want to get married."

Andrea whirled from the window. "Married!" she gasped. Her tone and look might have been that of a saint whose daughter had just announced she was entering a pagan brothel. She searched her daughter's eyes, longing to find the glint of mischief that would signify a joke was under way, but the sincerity met with in Marge's gaze turned her glimmer of hope into an icy fear. "You're really serious, aren't you?"

Marge nodded her head, slowly, deliberately.

"But why?"

Marge leaned forward, her eyes sparkling, her face glowing. "Because we love each other—that's the usual answer, isn't it?"

Andrea's fear gave way to anger. "The usual answer, yes! But you're not a usual girl. Surely, I raised you to know better than to fall for that kind of line!"

Marge walked over, reaching out for her mother's hands. "But it's not a line, Mother. Mark does love me, and I love him."

"And so the whole world has to stop? You have to toss away your schooling, forget about your own plans for your life? Marge, Marge! Don't you see it's all part of the same rotten pattern men have been forcing on women down through the ages?"

"You talk as though Mark were man incarnate, but he isn't. He's just Mark—good, kind, gentle Mark, who would never do anything to hurt me. You'd know that if you'd ever taken the time to get to know him when he's come here to take me out."

Andrea's eyes flashed. "I know everything about him that I need to know. He's asking you to sacrifice your education, isn't he? It may be his first demand, but it certainly won't be his last."

The eagerness in Marge's eyes began to give way to impatience. "You're being terribly unfair, Mother, convicting Mark without a trial. He hasn't asked me to give up anything. I'm the one who suggested leaving school." She ran her hand through her hair. "He signed on with an engineering crew that's going down to South America. They're leaving at the end of the week. He'd have been willing to let me stay here and finish college. It was my idea to drop out. He never asked me to give it up."

"Then, for heaven's sake, why do it? Let him go. You'll soon have him out of your system."

"I'll never have him out of my system."

"I assure you, my dear, that he'll soon have you out of his. That's the way it is with men."

"Men! *Men!* Don't you ever have a decent word for them?" Marge cried. "Don't you realize that the idea of female superiority is as vile as that of male supremacy?"

Andrea was visibly shocked. "I've never preached female superiority or supremacy!"

"My God, Mother! How blind can you be? Your whole life is an offering on the altar of female superiority."

"That's untrue! My life is my own, not an exercise in philosophy. If it signifies anything, it's certainly not female superiority, but simply the existence of a female alternative —that a woman has as much right to independence as a man, that she has a right to choose her own mode of living."

"Then I have a right to choose too!" Marge cried, her hands balling into fists. "And I choose marriage!"

"You choose suicide!"

Marge's eyes filled with tears. "Oh, Mother! Why can't you see things as they are?" She flung herself on the sofa and began to cry.

"The trouble is," Andrea said, "I *do* see things as they are. I'm afraid you're the one who's wearing rose-colored glasses." Her face softening, she went over and sat beside Marge, placing a hand on her shoulder. "You really have it bad, don't you?" she asked softly.

Marge looked up, her lips quivering into a little smile. "Oh, Mother, I love him so much!"

Andrea sighed. "Then go with him—but don't marry him."

Marge's face fell. "Don't marry him!"

Amused, Andrea raised an eyebrow. "Don't look so shocked, dear. There *is* such a thing as living with a man without benefit of clergy, you know. A good many of your generation act as though they invented the idea."

Marge pulled away from Andrea. "They can have it! It's not for Mark and me. Animals cohabitate. We consider ourselves a shade above that. We're not ashamed to swear ourselves bound by love in front of witnesses."

Smiling, Andrea shook her head. "My! You almost make that sound more revolutionary than the other way. But you must admit, the other way has its advantages. When things are over, there are no messy legal tangles and lawyer's fees."

"There's no reason why it has to end!"

"No more is there why it has to continue."

Marge jumped up. "You make me so furious! You sit there like such an expert—and what do you know? You've never been married, never even *tried* marriage."

"Need I remind you that neither have you?"

"All right, so we're even." Marge brushed her hair back from her face impatiently. "But you made your choice long ago. Why can't you have the good grace to let me make mine now, without trying to tear it down?"

"I'm not trying to tear it down, dear. If what I say makes your dreams come tumbling down, it's not my fault. If you wanted reassurance about marriage, you should have known better than to come to me. I'm the last—" Suddenly Andrea stopped, growing pale. "But why should you want reassurance, unless. . . ." She got up and walked over to where Marge stood by the window. ". . . Unless the choice isn't really yours—unless you think you *have* to get married. Marge, are you pregnant? Because if you are, you of all people should know there are a great many other choices available."

Marge's laugh was bitter. "No, I'm not pregnant. So you can spare yourself the trouble of listing all the so-called advantages of abortion, adoption, and raising a child alone. I'm marrying Mark because I *want* to marry him, and when I do become pregnant, it will be because I want to be."

"You're a fool if you marry because you want children. There are other, better ways to fulfill that desire."

"Other ways, yes. But better? Definitely not."

Andrea's eyes widened. "How can you say that when you yourself are—"

"The product of just such an alternative?" Marge cut her off. "That's exactly why I can say it with so much authority."

Andrea flinched at the words, an icy feeling of dread closing around her heart. Deep inside her, she seemed to sense that the argument was taking a dangerous turn. But even as she longed to turn it back to a safer path a need to defend herself forced her to spur it on.

"Perhaps there are some for whom our way might not work," Andrea said with all her usual calm. "But you'll have to admit that for us it has."

"Has it?"

"Oh, come now! You can't deny that you've had everything you've ever needed or wanted."

"How would you know?" Marge cried. "Did you ever ask me?"

At last, Andrea's wall of reserve came tumbling down, and her voice rose with emotion. "There was no need to ask!" she insisted. "I saw what you needed, and I gave it willingly. We've been happy enough together until this minute. So if you're thinking of pulling the usual adolescent trick of denying that I've given you love, you can forget it. You know it would be a lie. If there's one thing I've reassured you of all your life, it's that you're here because I wanted you."

Eighteen years of frustration welled up in Marge's eyes. "Yes! Because *you* wanted me! I suppose you think I should thank you for that—thank you for making me the product of your narcissism. You wanted a child who was flesh of *your* flesh only and not of another's. Well, I don't. I think the whole idea is so sick it stinks!"

"You're twisting everything around!" Andrea gasped. "There's nothing wrong with a woman having a child if she wants one. It's her right!"

"And what about the child's rights—her right to look back upon the forces that brought her into existence with respect, even awe? Her right to a father and a father's love?"

"You talk as though you were the only child to be brought up without a father. What about those whose fathers are dead, or those from broken homes?"

"I count them among the lucky ones. At least, they can look back and say: 'Once our parents loved, and we're the living proof of it.' No matter how hard their lives are after their fathers are gone, they have that much dignity left to them." She drew a ragged breath, and when she spoke again, her voice was calmer, but no less heavy with emotion. "And what have you given me to say of my beginnings? That my mother wanted to perpetuate herself, so she went out and found a stud."

In a flash, Andrea's hand shot out and slapped her daughter's cheek. The sound of it seemed to fill the room, growing louder in memory as the actual vibrations ceased. Horrified, Andrea watched as five red marks began to glow on Marge's cheek. Gasping, she pressed the back of the offending hand to her lips, reaching out toward her daughter with the other. "Oh, darling! Forgive me!" she cried.

Backing out of reach, Marge covered her cheek with her own hand. "This slap is the least you should ask forgiveness for, Mother," she said. Then she turned and left the room.

Andrea stood alone by the window, listening to the almost imperceptible rummaging sounds coming from behind Marge's closed door. She felt as though her heart and her brain were functioning in slow motion. "It's not true," she whispered over and over. "It's not true." But somewhere in a corner of her numbed brain another whisper countered: *If it's not true, why do you have no rebuttal save denial?*

Tears hesitated on the brim of her eyelids. Then slowly, like strangers wending a hesitant path through virgin territory, they began to trickle down her pale cheeks. One by one, they dropped onto her bosom and her gown, taking little traces of makeup with them. A trembling that had begun deep inside her radiated out until it reached her legs and arms. Unable to stand any longer, she handed herself from one piece of furniture to another until she reached the sofa. Then she sank down, staring at the coffee service on the cocktail table.

Was it ten minutes or ten centuries ago that she'd watched Marge serving coffee with such delight? A lifetime ago, when she was a college girl herself, she'd read Plato's description of Socrates' death, the numbing hemlock creeping slowly up his body from one limb to another. A memory of it flashed before her now, as an almost deathlike coldness began slowly creeping throughout her body too. Shivering, she reached for the coffeepot and held it to her. But the little vestiges of warmth that remained in it could not penetrate her flesh to reach the coldness in her soul.

Marge emerged, an overnight bag in her hand. "Mark's picking me up. I'll stay with his folks until the wedding."

Andrea looked up. "You're wrong, Marge."

"About marrying?"

"About everything."

Marge shook her head. "No, Mother. You're the one who's wrong. The miracle is that, after living with you for eighteen years, I've still got my head on straight enough to

Love After Hours

see things the right way. To see that I have a right to be married, and that my children have a right to be created out of love. You wanted *a* child—I want *Mark's* children, created in his image and in the image of our love. There's a world of difference."

The intercom buzzed, and Marge went to answer it.

"Mr. Mark Porter's waiting in the lobby, miss," the doorman's voice announced.

"Thank you. I'll be right down."

Marge opened the door and stood there for a moment, gazing at Andrea. "I've always been thankful for one thing," she said quietly, "that I wasn't born a boy. You did your best to warp my outlook, but I shudder to think what would have happened if you'd had a son and brought him up to believe that men are good for nothing except stud services."

Andrea shook her head slowly, her voice seeming to come from far away. "I wouldn't have said that to a son."

"No," Marge said. "You would have done worse: You would have used your whole way of life to *show* him."

The door closed behind her with a little click.

For a long time afterward, Andrea sat alone, still clutching the coffeepot, shaking her beautifully coiffured head.

Chapter Five

October was a golden month. Summer, reluctant to take her final bow, and autumn, hesitant about making her entrance, compromised, treating the city to an extended run of brisk, sun-warmed days and cool, clear nights. It was a golden time for Gwen and Paul, too—that enchanted time at the beginning of a friendship when not every tale has yet been told and when every meeting brings new revelations. Over leisurely lunches and quiet dinners, on twilight strolls and afternoon excursions, they opened their minds and hearts to each other as they had never been able to do with any other person in their lives. There was no dream too foolish, no thought too lofty to share. Previously haunted by vague fears that life was passing her by, Gwen now felt that it was unfolding all around her like the petals of a magnificent rose. Its heady fragrance buoyed her to reach new heights and to perceive new depths. At work, she was innovative and able to accomplish more than ever before; at home, she was serene and untouched by her parents' querulousness.

Friendship—that's all Paul had asked for in the beginning. And, for both of them, all through that lovely October that was enough. It was enough to see, to talk, and occasionally to touch.

Then November came with its damp, gray days and its dreary, chilling rains, forcing them to abandon their ambles through Central Park, their ferry rides and their window-shopping tours. Now all their meetings were indoors. They ate quiet lunches in intimate booths, sipped cocktails and had dinner at tiny tables, where their knees touched and their faces, reflected in the soft glow of candlelight, seemed only a kiss apart. More and more, they found that they had less and less to say to each other. Talk was no longer what they needed.

It was during lunch a few days before Thanksgiving that Paul finally made them face the facts. They were seated at a wall table at La Champagne, an exclusive French restaurant where patrons paid nobility prices for the privilege of eating amid peasant decor. To fill in one of the pauses that had been falling in their conversation so frequently, Gwen had begun to tell Paul about a celebrity series she was planning to run—short, first-person articles in which actors and actresses revealed how their faith in God helped them along the way. The series would be called, "With My Hand in His," and it was the type of article her readers would gobble up.

Suddenly she stopped speaking and shook her head. "You haven't been listening to a word I've said," she chastised gently.

The wrinkles at the corners of Paul's eyes deepened as he smiled. "I've been listening," he said, "but not to your words." He reached for her hand. "I've been listening to your eyes—and I think you've been listening to mine. We've been talking on two levels for a long time now."

Never taking her gaze from his, she curled her fingers around his hand, which felt warm and strong in hers. "So it's tomorrow," she said.

"Tomorrow?"

"The tomorrow you said we'd have to face one day."

He ran his thumb over the soft, smooth flesh of her wrist. "Yes," he said, "I guess it is. What are we going to do about it?"

"You mean—do we face it, or do we pretend it never happened?"

"You know we can't pretend for long." He smiled sadly. "We've been rotten pretenders these last few weeks."

For a moment they sat in silence, their gazes locked, their fingers entwined. Gwen heard her pulse pounding in her ears like the roll of a hundred tiny drums.

"I love you, Gwendolyn Hadley," Paul said at last. "I love you with a love more awesome than any I could conjure in my wildest dreams or most fantastic fiction. I wish with all my heart that I could proclaim it before the whole world, instead of being forced to say it in a whisper that only you can hear."

"That's loud enough for me. I'll hear its echoes for the rest of my life." Tears thickened her voice and blurred her vision. "Oh, Paul! I love you, too." It was the first time she had said those words to any man, and they left her feeling weak, yet strangely strengthened. She felt his hand trembling on hers.

"God! I wish I could kiss you!"

"Not here. Not now." She could barely hear her voice above the pounding in her ears.

"Tonight?"

She nodded, not trusting herself to speak. She used to laugh at the heroines of eighteenth-century novels who swooned with love, but now she thought she knew exactly how they must have felt.

Paul signaled the waiter who had been hovering nearby, a gentle reminder that though La Champagne never hurried its patrons, rush hour was nonetheless rush hour. Gwen watched Paul adoringly as he paid the bill.

When they rose from their table, she caught sight of Bill Saxon lunching nearby with a well-known literary agent. He answered her wave with a smile, but his eyes seemed troubled, and she could feel him watching her as she and Paul began to weave their way toward the exit.

Hand in hand, Paul and Gwen walked the few blocks back to her office. Neither was willing to speak, for fear of breaking the warm cocoon of love and anticipation that their last words had spun around them. When they reached the massive glass doors of the Waterford Building, Paul bent down and gently brushed her lips with his. It was a dispassionate sort of kiss that went unnoticed by the milling crowd of workers on their way to and from lunch. Yet for Paul and Gwen, it held a thrilling promise that left them weak.

Paul smiled, taking Gwen's hands in his. "That's a preview of things to come."

She tried to match his forced lightness. "I can't wait until the feature goes on."

"I wish you didn't have to go up," he said, more serious now.

Love After Hours

"Me too. But deadlines don't wait."

"I know. Neither do conferences. I've got one with my agent and a Broadway producer at four. I'll pick you up as soon after five as I can make it. Nick's?"

She nodded.

He held her hands a moment longer. "I love you."

Her heart pounding, she gazed into his eyes. "I love you too," she said, gently withdrawing her hands. But it was the echo of his words, not her own, that followed her up to her office.

She sat at her desk, her eyes closed, her swivel chair tilted back, remembering every word that had been exchanged, savoring all the new emotions that were churning within her, delighting in their sweetly frightening strangeness. Then she drew a long breath, pressuring them to return to her heart where they belonged and to allow her mind to take over. She reached for the phone and dialed home.

"I'll be very late tonight," she told her mother. "Don't wait up for me."

"Of course I'll wait up," Agnes whined. "You know that I can't sleep a wink until I know you're home safely."

"Well, starting tonight, you'd better try. I may be staying out late quite often."

She heard Agnes's quick intake of breath, and could visualize her biting her lip, twisting her apron. "Where are you going?"

"Just out."

"With a man?"

"Yes."

There was another pained gasp. Then: "It's that Paul fellow who came to call here a few times, isn't it?"

Not bothering to answer, Gwen sighed and held the receiver away from her ear. On the few occasions when Paul had called for her at home, Agnes and Barney had subjected him to The Treatment. Obviously rattled at the good-natured way in which he took it, and by the fact that he had not immediately dropped out of the picture the way all Gwen's former suitors had, Agnes had disparaged him at every opportunity, hoping to convince Gwen to break off the relationship.

"He's no good for you, Gwendolyn. He's just a handsome face and nothing more. If there were any substance to him, he'd have been married long ago. You're wasting your time on him, and wrecking your health running around so much."

Gwen wondered how Agnes would take it if she told her Paul *was* married. Be relieved, probably. "On the contrary, Mother, people tell me I've never looked better. Certainly, I've never felt better."

"Well, they don't know you—and you don't know yourself —the way I do. A mother can tell about these things. I can tell it's doing you more harm than good. Believe me, all I want is what's best for you." Agnes sniffed, working herself up to audible tears. "When I think of all the agony I went through to bring you into this world! And this is the thanks I get—that you won't even listen to my advice—"

Smiling to herself, Gwen closed her eyes, remembering Paul's words instead of listening to her mother.

"We'll talk about it some other time, Mom," she said at last. "Right now, I have work to do. Remember, don't wait up." She hung up before Agnes could offer another protest.

She attacked the edited manuscript awaiting her approval with a vengeance born of the joy surging within her, finishing it in record time.

Betsy came in to pick it up for the printer's pouch. She paused in the doorway a moment, the manuscript in her hand. "All right if I leave a little early tonight?"

The way Gwen felt, she would have been willing to let the whole office take off early. Today *should* be a holiday. Still, she had to give lip service to the rules. "How early?"

"Half an hour?"

"Big date?"

Betsy nodded.

"Okay. Have fun."

"Thanks."

Betsy started to swing through the door, when Gwen called her back puzzled. "Is that what you're wearing?"

Ducking her head, Betsy checked over her bright red dress and matching flats, then looked up. "Something wrong with it?"

Gwen shook her head. "No, but I thought you always wore high heels for dates."

"I used to but—" Her cheeks flamed. "Well, the night we went to get Gary's elevated shoes, I told him the joke you made about getting a padded bra . . ." Her voice trailed off.

"And he didn't think it was so funny?" Gwen filled in for her.

She nodded, subdued, then quickly perked up, holding up one foot and admiring her shoe. "So we decided to stick with each other the way nature made us."

"Good for you!" Gwen laughed. "May it be the biggest sacrifice you ever have to make for love. Now hurry and get that manuscript to Terri before she closes the pouch."

Betsy swung out of the office, and Gwen turned back to the work piled on her desk.

At five o'clock, the members of her staff began to poke their heads into her office to say good night. Terri Ainsworth was, as usual, the first. She was wearing the mink jacket she had saved for years to buy, and she paused a moment in the doorway, brushing imaginary lint from it, to make sure Gwen would notice.

When it was obvious that Terri intended to maintain her post until she passed comment on her apparel, Gwen sighed inwardly and gave in. "You look gorgeous this evening. Are you going out?"

Terri smoothed the fur lovingly, her eyes lighting with an I've-got-a-secret look. "Not really."

All dressed up with no place to go, Gwen thought sadly. She remembered the time Terri had worn the jacket to the office last year: The day before, obviously in an effort to escape from the corner Terri's overbearing flirting had maneuvered him into, a handsome bachelor from accounting had tossed out the line: "We must have a drink sometime." Terri, of course, had taken it as a definite invitation—a preliminary to the wedding march—and had shown up the next day dressed to kill ("It doesn't hurt to let them know you have money of your own," she had confided to Gwen), only to find that the fellow had taken off early for a long skiing weekend. Now Gwen looked at Terri, a year older, but, obviously, not wiser, and wondered whose words she had misinterpreted this time.

"Well, you certainly look great," she said rather lamely, and tried to turn back to the manuscript she had almost finished reading.

Terri was not ready to be dismissed. "It does a girl's morale good to get dressed up once in a while. Besides," she stepped closer, a conspiratorial look on her face, "it doesn't hurt to keep them guessing."

"Them?"

"The guys I ride with." Terri giggled. "They all jumped to the conclusion that I had a big lunch date. I played along with them."

I'll bet you did! Gwen thought.

"Let them eat their hearts out!" Terri laughed. "Especially Harry. A little jealousy might do him good."

Gwen took the bait. "Harry?"

"You know—the guy I've been seeing. The one whose wife is sick."

Gwen racked her brain a moment, then remembered back to the August evening when Terri had announced her big date—which had turned out to consist of two cocktails—with Harry. It was the same evening she had met Paul.

"I didn't realize you two were still dating."

"Well, not exactly dating." Terri took out a compact and checked the makeup that did little to hide her pasty complexion. "But we see each other every day on the train."

Each other and a few hundred other commuters, Gwen thought.

"What's wrong with his wife?"

"Harry doesn't talk about it much, but it looks like cancer." Her eyes hardened and her mouth drooped into a pout. "Of course, Harry wouldn't think of divorcing her now, and she's so selfish—she wants him with her all the time."

Gwen waved to Frances and Laura, who had stopped to say good night, but Terri did not take the hint, and continued to stand there pouting. "It's really unfair," she whined.

That she doesn't have the good grace to die? Gwen wondered, but she said, "Well, some people *are* inconsiderate."

Love After Hours   97

Terri didn't seem to notice the coldness in Gwen's eyes, or to catch the heavy sarcasm in her voice. "You're so right! I mean, everything's over for her, and yet she keeps hanging on."

Feeling a desperate need for fresh air in the room, Gwen got up and opened a window. "It's time you learned that there will always be people around who will take advantage of your good nature."

Terri sighed in agreement. "Yes, I suppose I should be used to it by now." She perked up and gave her jacket a loving pat. "I've got to run. I want to stop into a florist and pick up a corsage for myself. That will *really* give them something to think about!" Giggling, she hurried out of the room.

Gwen stood at the open window a moment, hoping the cold air would blow away the nausea she felt. Pressing her forehead against the cold glass, she willed herself to cleanse her mind of all thoughts of Terri and her morbid aspirations. This was to be her own night. She pushed the image of Terri's face from her mind and visualized Paul instead, the look in his eyes as he told her he loved her. She saw his strong jaw, high cheekbones, aristocratic nose, his hair, so dark at the temples, so silvery on top—how long had she been yearning to run her fingers through it? Soon, soon—in only a matter of hours—she would be doing all that—and so much, much more.

Her heart pounding with anticipation, she returned to her desk, slipped the unfinished manuscript back into its envelope, turned off her lamp.

Though Bill's coat was on his coat tree and his light was still burning—illuminating his brown wailing wall in all its glory—he wasn't in his office when she looked in to say good night. Buttoning her coat, she hurried into the elevator that was taking the last stragglers down to the street.

"No, no," Beauregard told her when she arrived at Nick's. Mr. Lockhart had not yet come. Bobbing and bowing, he led her to a table at the back where she could await him.

"You have a fine view of the door from here," he told her, "a fine view. You'll be able to see your friend the minute he comes in, the minute he comes in."

Gwen refrained from telling him that she did not have to

see Paul to know when he entered a room; she could feel his presence with every fiber of her being. She ordered a daiquiri, then sat back to enjoy her fine view of the door.

Right after her drink arrived, Bill Saxon did too. She saw him scan the crowd and then say a few words to Beauregard, who had bobbed over to him like a cork on a choppy sea. In answer, Beauregard gesticulated in the direction of Gwen's table, then led the way to it.

"You're a popular lady this evening, Miss Hadley, a popular lady," he said, cocking his head to one side like a bright-eyed parrot. He took Bill's order and jogged away.

Bill looked after him. "I always wondered who worked his strings. Probably his wife." He turned back to Gwen. "I thought I might find you here."

"Do I look as though I've taken to drink lately?"

"No. Just male intuition."

Gwen smiled. "I stopped by to say good night, but you weren't there."

Bill stretched his long legs out under the table. "I was up in Bart's office, having a go-around about a series I want to publish. I've got a crack writer lined up to delve into the really hot spots of every major city—from the plushest to the seamiest."

"Sounds promising. What did Jason have against it?"

"Money—what else? Didn't want to come through with the writer's price."

"Who won?"

"I did. Don't I always? I convinced him that it would be a drop in the bucket compared to the advertising it will bring in, and it's bound to grab enough new readers to boost my guarantee at least another ten thousand." He spotted Cam Eckhart at another table and straightened up long enough to call over, "Watch out, Cam! I'm gaining on you!"

Cam stiffened a little, but made no response, continuing to shower his attention on the buxom young redhead he was plying with drink.

"What would you do without Cam?" Gwen laughed.

"I'd invent someone just like him." He picked up the highball a waiter had just placed before him, tilting it first toward

Love After Hours

Gwen and then toward Cam. "To friends and enemies," he said and drank.

Gwen toyed with her daiquiri. Ordinarily she loved talking with Bill, but now she felt she was only marking time until Paul's arrival.

Bill studied her, his eyes growing serious. "Beauregard tells me you're waiting for someone. Paul?"

She nodded.

"May I offer a little brotherly advice?"

"Please don't," she said softly, trying not to let his obvious concern dampen the embers glowing inside her.

Conversation cut off temporarily by her plea, the two of them experienced the first awkward pause they had ever known. Bill drank his highball while Gwen toyed with her glass.

Finally, unable to bring himself to respect her request any longer, Bill put his drink down and leaned across the table. "You know he's married?"

She nodded.

"Then for your own sake, think before you go on with him. Don't get in too deep."

She smiled indulgently. "You should know that thinking is impossible in a situation like this. And as for getting in too deep—love is like quicksand: If you can find the bottom, it isn't love, is it?"

Sighing, Bill downed the last of his drink.

"Don't look so tragic," Gwen begged. "For God's sake, Bill! We're all adults. You're the one who introduced us. You kept teasing me about him. What did you think would happen?"

"I'm not sure. I certainly didn't mean for things to get out of control." He ran a hand through his hair, and Gwen noticed that it was getting thinner, grayer at the temples. "I suppose if I thought about it at all, I thought along the lines of friendship—at the most, light romance." He shook his head. "I saw you today at La Champagne. There was nothing light about the way you were looking at each other."

Smiling, Gwen thought back to her lunch with Paul. "It shows so much?"

"You might as well have been carrying ten-foot banners proclaiming it to the world."

"I *feel* like waving ten-foot banners. I feel better than I've ever felt in my whole life." She leaned toward him putting her hand on his arm. "Don't spoil it by going 'big brother' on me."

Bill pulled his arm back and took her hand in his, forcing a laugh. "I guess it is way the hell out of character, isn't it? Okay, I'll button my big fat lip." He stole a glance at his watch. "I'm sure you don't need me hanging around here. If I hurry, I can just make the Ainsworth special."

Despite his promise of a moment before, he stood at the table a second looking down at Gwen as though about to proffer more advice. Then, seeming to think the better of it, he gave his Gallic shrug and mock salute, saying, "Take it easy, kid."

"You bet," Gwen said quietly. "Love to Shari and the kids."

He made an okay sign with his hand and turned to leave. Gwen watched him make his way to the door, where he met Paul, who was just entering. The two men shook hands and spoke a moment. Then Paul wove his way past the olive tree to Gwen's table without the help of Beauregard, who was detained elsewhere.

"Sorry to keep you waiting," he said, sitting down and taking her hand. "Some complications came up. As long as I have to be on the Coast next week for the premiere of *To Satan with Love,* my damn agent arranged for me to be on some talk shows without checking with me first. I'm going to have to leave tomorrow."

"Tomorrow!" Gwen's heart sank. "How long will you be gone?"

"About two weeks. No longer, because I have to be back here to help with the finishing touches on the script we're making of *Raw Flesh* before it goes into rehearsal."

"Two weeks," Gwen sighed. "It will feel like two years."

Paul nodded, his hand tightening around hers. "At least we have tonight," he said. "We'll make enough memories to last us."

Love After Hours

Their gazes locked, and they had no more need for words or regrets—only sweet anticipation.

After they had a drink, they left Nick's, and hand in hand, oblivious of the chill air, walked the eight blocks to the restaurant they had chosen for dinner.

The Dickens House echoed the elegant tone and leisurely pace of the Gay Nineties—gas lights, snowy-white linen, gleaming silverware, sparkling crystal. Waiters in tuxedos and waitresses wearing frilly white aprons over modest black dresses seemed to operate by some elaborate system of ESP, materializing swiftly and silently at a patron's table whenever they were wanted, but never a moment before. Paul and Gwen settled themselves in a richly upholstered rear booth and prolonged their meal, acutely aware that anticipation heightens all delights.

It was almost eight o'clock when Paul called for the bill. Gwen's stomach tightened and her mouth went a little dry as she slipped on her coat. Outside, little clusters of people huddled together as though for protection from the cold as they hurried toward theaters and other evening entertainments.

Paul took Gwen's hand and drew it through his arm. "Cold?" he asked, pressing his palm against her trembling fingers.

"No."

They walked on in silence for a while. Unlike the silences they had shared in the past, this one was separate and awkward. Each of them was lost in private thoughts.

Unconsciously, Paul massaged her fingers. "I reserved a room at the Garrick this afternoon. I wish we could go someplace better, but anyplace better I might be recognized. If word got back to Verna, she'd take Melanie away from me for good." He stopped a moment, gently turning her to face him. "It's not such a bad hotel. You understand, darling, don't you?"

Her eyes met his, a sad, gentle smile turning up the corners of her mouth. She understood a great many things: that they had to hide their love in seamy places; that their time could never be their own; that she could never—or, at least, not for years—come first with him.

"I understand," she said softly, and they began to walk again, slowly, arm in arm, like a couple walking down an aisle. Only their aisle was not a carpeted one strewn with orange-blossom petals; it was a New York pavement littered with papers.

Unable to find a cab, they continued toward their destination on foot. About two blocks from the Garrick, Gwen stopped short, a coldness washing over her. "I just thought of something."

"What?"

She smiled ironically. "I don't take birth-control pills. I'm not protected."

"There's a drugstore on the next block. I'll pick up something there."

Gwen accompanied Paul into the store, busying herself at a display of sunglasses while he made his purchase. From the corner of her eye, she saw the clerk giving her the once-over, and she cringed beneath his smirk.

Their silence was heavier than before as they covered the last block to the hotel.

Like the middle-aged to elderly widows and bachelors it catered to, the Garrick had once seen better days, and pretended to an elegance and an income that had long since faded away. It was a dying enterprise, a last haven for the hopeless, and the shadow of death could be seen reflected everywhere, from the fading eyes of its guests to the fading paper that clung to its walls. Frayed velvet drapes hung limply at the lobby windows, and a threadbare Oriental carpet, its design obliterated by a half-century of feet, made a halfhearted attempt at covering the floor. Here and there, moth-eaten-looking potted palms reached listlessly toward the ceiling. Rickety tables strewn with battered magazines stood before sagging chairs and sofas whose indentations hinted at the possibility of ghostly occupants. The overheated air seemed laden with the lethargy of hopelessness, and it greeted Gwen and Paul when they arrived with its musty kiss of despair. For a moment, they stood on the threshold, surveying the scene.

Paul squeezed her hand. "Sit down for a minute. I'll take care of the registration."

She nodded, and walked over to one of the ancient chairs, slowly sinking into it. Her heart thudded painfully as she looked around the room, her eyes taking in every depressing detail. The joy of anticipation had vanished and a nagging ache filled the void. So this would be the beginning of the best part of her life—this shabby, dreary hotel. How many more like it would follow—and for how many years?

Suddenly she was aware of Paul's presence beside her, and longing for his strength, she reached up, putting her hand in his. But his gaze did not meet hers, and she saw that, his face immobile, his eyes were taking the same path hers had just traveled.

At last, their tour complete, his eyes returned to hers, seeming to penetrate past the love on the surface to the doubts and fears that were churning somewhere deep within her. The lines around his mouth hardened, and his right hand tightened on hers as he dangled the key he held in his left hand between them.

"So this is it," he said unsmiling. "This is how it all begins." He took another disdainful glance around the room, then flipped the key into his hand. "The hell it is!" he said. He pulled her to her feet, and grasping her hand tightly so that she had no choice but to scurry along behind him, he strode across the floor, tossed the key back on the desk, and dragged her out into the night.

"Paul!" she cried after they'd covered half a block. "For God's sake! Stop a minute. Talk to me! Tell me what's the matter!"

"Everything's the matter!" he said, jerking to a stop. "Every goddam thing!"

Her relief at leaving the hotel was washed away in a rush of fear and uncertainty. "But I don't understand!"

"You do," he insisted. "I saw it in your eyes back there. You felt it too. It was wrong—all wrong!"

"Wrong?" A lump rose in her throat, and the single word she forced over it came out in a whisper. Was he suddenly becoming moral about their situation?

"Don't look at me that way!" He ran his hand through his hair impatiently. "Surely you know me better than that. I don't mean we're wrong. I mean that stinking, rotten place and all it represents is wrong."

"But what else can we do?"

"I don't know—maybe nothing. But, God knows, *nothing* is better than turning what we have into transient sex—going from one seedy hotel to another. I love you too much to subject you to that."

They walked on a while in silence, Paul staring straight ahead, Gwen trying desperately to fight back her tears.

"Where do we go from here?" she asked finally, slipping her hand into his.

He pulled her hand up, rubbing its softness against his cheek. "I wish I knew."

"We can't go back, can we?" she whispered.

"No one can ever go back. When you reach a crossroad, you can either take it or turn aside."

Her eyes filled with tears. "Then I wish this afternoon had never happened."

He turned her to him beneath a street light, gently tracing the glistening trail of a tear with his thumb. "My little ostrich," he said softly. "Would you rob me of one of the most beautiful afternoons of my life—the few short hours I had of pretending we could live happily ever after?" He shook his head sadly. "We couldn't have gone on the way we were much longer. Sooner or later, we had to admit our love. The miracle is that we were able to hide from it so long."

"But I want you," was all she managed to whisper.

He gripped her shoulders hard, his eyes flashing. "Do you think I don't want you too? Good God! I want you so much, the pain is tearing me apart." He gestured angrily in the direction of the hotel. "But not that way. That way would be our death."

"But why would it have to be?" she cried, ignoring the fact that she had felt the same way back at the hotel. "Don't you think our love is strong enough to be untouched by its surroundings?"

"Only a strong love *can* be tainted," he insisted. "Sordid relationships don't show the dirt because they spring from it." He shook his head. "I can't do that to you—reduce this feeling we have to transient sex. We'd start out by cheapen-

Love After Hours

ing our love, and end up feeling cheap ourselves, hating each other for it. We'd be fighting all the time."

She pulled away. "But we're fighting now too! We can't go on this way either, or we'll always be at each other's throat."

"I know." He slipped his arm around her, and they began to walk again.

Gwen slumped against him, needing to feel the hardness of his chest and side against her. Never had she felt so alive—she was aware of every inch of flesh and bone; her entire being vibrated and ached with the exquisite pain that only heartbreak can bring.

"Then it's over between us—over before it even had a chance to begin."

"No!" She felt him stiffen.

"But what else is there? If we won't go forward, and we can't go back—then all we can do is stop."

"But not now—not this minute." His eyes reflected the same pain and fear that was raging through her.

"Then when?" she cried.

He took a deep breath, as though forcing himself to be objective, matter-of-fact. "When I get back from California, we'll get together, talk things over. Maybe we'll come up with something if we can talk about it when we're not tied up in knots."

She shook her head. "There's nothing else. Nothing else." Tears were pushing painfully past her eyelids and coursing down her cheeks. "Please, Paul, if it has to end, let it end now. Don't make me wait two weeks, knowing that all I have to look forward to is saying good-by. That would only increase my misery, not ease it."

His shoulders slumping, he took her face between his hands. "But surely we can see each other at least one more time."

His face blurred as she searched it through her tears. "How many times do we have to say good-by? Each time would hurt more than the last. No, if it's over, let it be over now. Once and for all. It's better that way—for both of us."

"But there are so many things to be said—"

"None of them matter after 'good-by.'" Unable to bear

the sweet agony of his touch, she pulled away, looking anxiously toward the street. "There's a cab. Call it, please."

"Let it go," he pleaded. "We'll stop in someplace, have coffee..."

"No, no! It will only prolong our agony. Only make it worse." She didn't know how much longer she could maintain any vestiges of outward control. "It's almost here—hail it!"

"Gwen, please—"

"Taxi! Taxi!" She waved her arms frantically.

With a screech of brakes, the cab coasted to the curb.

"You're running away," Paul accused her.

"Would it be any easier if I walked?" It was difficult for her trembling lips to form the words.

Sadly, he shook his head. "No. I suppose that no matter how or when we say good-by the pain will always be the same."

She looked at his face as though she were trying to memorize every line on it. "I love you," she whispered at last.

Tenderly, he caressed her hair, then moved his hand across her cheek, gently tracing the outline of her lips with his finger. "My darling Gwen." His voice broke on her name.

"Hey, lady! You want a taxi or not?" The driver's harsh, impatient voice cut through their moment of closeness like the crack of a bullwhip.

Paul reached down and opened the taxi door. "I'll see you home."

She shook her head. "That would only make it worse." Settling herself in the cab, she reached through the open window for his hand.

"I'll call you when I get back."

Tears welled up in her eyes. "For God's sake—for *my* sake!—don't do that. I couldn't stand to hear from you, knowing nothing could come of it."

For a moment they remained that way, gazes and hands locked, neither willing to say that most final of all words. Then, slowly, Gwen withdrew her hand and gave the driver her address. As the taxi pulled away, she turned in her seat, straining to watch Paul, who remained immobile on the sidewalk, staring after her. Then the driver turned a corner, and a building blocked her view. But the vision of Paul standing alone, hands in pockets, shoulders slumped, followed her all the way home.

The moment she heard Gwen's key in the lock, Agnes scurried to the door to greet her. "You're home early after all, dear," she said.

Nodding, Gwen went to the hall closet to hang up her coat. She did it slowly, methodically, every small movement she made causing her an agonizing effort.

Agnes stood close at her heels. "I knew I could count on my girl not to keep her poor mother worrying."

Gwen went rigid, her hand tight on the closet doorknob, her knuckles white. *It's only about forty steps from here to my room*, she thought. *I can make it if she'll just leave me alone.*

"Even at this time of night, though, I worry about you. So many terrible things happen in the city. Not that you care about how much I worry—"

Only thirty more steps.

"Well, at least you're home now, and my worries are over until the next time you decide to go gallivanting around. You look cold. I'll make you a nice hot cup of tea."

Twenty more steps.

"Now come into the kitchen like a good girl, and I'll—"

"Goddam it! I don't want to be a good girl, and I don't want any of your filthy tea!" Gwen ran the last few steps to her room, then slammed and locked the door.

"Now listen to me, young lady!" Agnes's voice came through the door. "Just because you've had some kind of a tiff with your so-called boyfriend is no excuse for rudeness. I'm your mother. I deserve some respect!"

Gwen grabbed her pillow off her bed and hurled it at the door. "Go away! Go away and leave me alone!"

"How can you say that to me? When I think of all I've done for you! And this is the thanks I get—my own daughter telling me to leave her alone!"

Biting her fist in frustration, Gwen sank onto her bed. The

silent sobs that had been building up inside her for the past hour, pressing painfully against her chest, rising precariously in the back of her throat, now nearly ripped her apart in their rush for freedom.

Outside her door, Agnes's voice droned on and on.

Chapter Six

―•◆•―

*U*nlike most Waterfordians, Frances Hascomb welcomed the company policy that expected everyone at his desk, alert and industrious, at nine o'clock on the Friday after Thanksgiving. It gave her the perfect excuse to leave her sister's Thanksgiving dinner early, thus evading the unpleasant possibility of being cornered into staying the weekend. As a child, she had worshiped Nancy, who was five years her senior, but now she could take Nancy and her family only in small doses. It wasn't simply that she could not abide Mike, the male-chauvinist dentist Nancy had been foolish enough to marry, but also that she could not bear to see her lovely, intelligent sister wasting herself on a life of thankless drudgery. Only the fact that Nancy would be hurt if she didn't come prompted her to accept the invitation in the first place.

At eleven-fifteen Thanksgiving morning, she reluctantly left her Greenwich Village apartment, and, shopping bag of presents and goodies in hand, made her way to Penn Station. There she boarded a Long Island Rail Road train for the suburbs. The train was crowded with families on their way to spend the day with relatives, and despite the fact that she had to stand for most of the seventy-minute trip with the shoe of a small boy planted firmly on her toes, she found herself being caught up in the holiday spirit that surrounded her. She was still feeling lighthearted when she emerged from the taxi she took from the station to her sister's home.

The door was opened by her brother-in-law, a tall, well-built man of thirty-five, whose ruggedly handsome features were framed by dark hair and graying sideburns. "Well," he said, smiling, "if it isn't Betty Friedan's self-appointed right-hand girl. Happy Thanksgiving. Come on in."

Determined not to let Mike's remark get under her skin, she smiled up at him. "How are you, Mike?"

"Fine, fine." He stepped aside so that she could enter, then insisted on helping her remove her coat, though he knew she preferred to dispense with such vestiges of chivalry.

"I see they still haven't given you a raise," he said, after hanging her coat in the closet.

Puzzled, she furrowed her brow in question.

He glanced down at the ample, slightly pendulous breasts that hung free beneath her dress, its red-knit material clinging to and boldly detailing them. "You still can't afford a bra."

"Very funny." Her tone said, *Ho hum,* and her eyes said, *Go to hell.* "Where's Nancy?"

"In the kitchen." As though she hadn't been there countless times before, he led the way to the gleaming turquoise-and-white kitchen at the rear of the house. "Look who's here," he called.

"Hi!" Nancy turned from stirring the contents of a pot and rushed over to hug Frances. With her face flushed and shining from the heat of the stove and her soft, light-brown hair clinging to her head in damp little ringlets, she looked much younger than her thirty-one years. "It's Aunt Frances," she announced to her three children, who were regarding the visitor with indifference.

She gave Frances another squeeze. "You see? You shouldn't be such a stranger. They hardly know you. Give Aunt Frances a kiss, Michael."

Shyly, his eyes fastened solemnly on Frances's face, four-year-old Michael, who looked like a miniature Nancy, advanced and placed his sticky lips against the cheek Frances bent to offer him.

"You too, Michelle," Nancy coaxed.

But two-and-a-half-year-old Michelle shook her brown ringlets and remained standing on a chair at the table.

"Let her be," Frances said, half-relieved, noting that Michelle's hands were elbow deep in a little bowl that contained half the portion of sticky biscuit dough her mother had doled out to her earlier; the remainder of the dough decorated her cherubic face, pudgy arms and hands and tiny apron.

Love After Hours

"Well, here's one who can't get away," Nancy laughed, swooping Donny, the eleven-month-old baby, up from the floor where he'd been sitting, banging a spoon on a pot.

Frances took him and nuzzled his cheek. "Oh, he's grown so! They all have!"

Donny squirmed in her arms, but she was sure he could not feel more uncomfortable than she did. She loved her niece and nephews and wished them well, but, since she was not maternal, she felt awkward and ill at ease around them. Sensing her discomfort, they responded in kind. Donny, his face reddening preparatory to emitting a wail, wiggled some more and banged her firmly on the forehead with his spoon.

"I guess he wants to go back down," she said, trying not to show her relief as she placed him back on the floor near his battered pot.

Michael, in the meantime, had been hovering near the shopping bag she had placed on the floor when she entered the room, trying not to look too interested. Curiosity finally got the better of him, however, and when Frances turned around, he was bent so far over the bag that he seemed in danger of falling into it.

"Michael!" Nancy remonstrated.

He shot up, shamefaced, clasping his hands behind his back.

"That's all right." Frances tried to ward off a scolding for the child. "It's high time I handed out the loot."

She gave Michael the game, Donny the toy kangaroo, and Michelle (when Nancy had cleaned the biscuit batter from her hands) the pull toy she had bought on her lunch hour the day before. Then she steeled herself for the thank-you-kiss routine. That over, Michelle and Michael ran from the room like prisoners granted a parole. Danny remained, banging his pot with the kangaroo instead of his spoon. For the grown-ups, she'd brought wine and Scotch.

Thanking her, Mike placed the bottle of Scotch on the kitchen counter and handed Nancy the wine. "Put that in the refrigerator, hon."

Frances was tempted to ask him why he couldn't walk over and put it in himself, but she bit back the question.

Donny, catching sight of the gleaming bottle of Scotch,

crawled to the counter, hoisted himself up, and reached for it. Racing over from the refrigerator, Nancy grabbed him away just in time to avert an accident.

"You'd better take him out of here." She held Donny out to Mike. "I'm going to be too busy to watch him for a while."

Mike took the baby and nuzzled his neck. "Come on, buster," he said tenderly. "You can watch the game with me. I'll explain the rules of football."

Gurgling, Donny patted Mike's cheek.

Nancy watched them out of the room, smiling, then busied herself cleaning up the mess Michelle had made.

"Anything I can do to help?" Frances asked.

"You can fix the relish plate while I make the salad."

Frances took the makings from the refrigerator and set to work on her project. "Anyone else coming?"

Nancy shook her head. "Just you. Mike's folks went up to Albany to spend the weekend with his sister."

Their own mother had moved to Florida the year before. Neither of them knew or cared where their father would be spending the holiday; he had deserted the family when Frances was five.

Stifling a yawn, Nancy began rinsing the salad greens.

Frances looked at her more closely, observing a heaviness beneath her eyes that she had not noticed when she came in. "You look tired."

"I am. I was up most of the night with Donny. He's teething."

"You should have tried to make up for it by sleeping late this morning."

"Are you kidding? Michael and Michelle are up at seven every day. I swear, they have built-in alarm clocks. I had to get up and make their breakfast."

"What about Mike? Couldn't he have done it?"

She laughed. "On his days off, Mike never budges out of bed until after eleven. You know Mike!"

The corners of Frances's mouth turned down in disgust. Yes, she knew Mike, all right—Mr. Typical American Husband—a man who demanded that his wife be smart enough and strong enough to run his home, bring up his children, be a nursemaid and slave to him, and at the same time not use all the intelligence she needed for those jobs to question his right to force them on her. At every meeting of Frances's women's action group at least one new member married to someone exactly like Mike would show up.

"You should insist that he help you," she said. "It's his home, and they're his children too."

Nancy sighed wearily. "We've been through this a million times before, Frances. How can I make you understand that I don't mind doing what I do? Mike's tired when he gets home from the office. He's entitled to some rest." She went over to the oven and began basting the turkey.

Frances followed her. "Come off it, Nancy! He's not out digging ditches from dawn to dusk, seven days a week. How tired can he be from drilling holes in people's teeth a few hours a day, four or five days a week?"

"He doesn't only work in his office. He puts in time at the clinic too. And he has to spend a lot of time reading and keeping up with all the new discoveries and techniques."

"So he puts in thirty or thirty-five hours a week like the rest of us. That's nothing compared with the twenty-four-hour-a-day job you're responsible for around here."

Shrugging, Nancy closed the oven door and stood up. "Yes, but his job is work; mine's a labor of love. There's a big difference."

"I'll say! In pay, and in time and energy invested. And the overload is all on your side of the scale. It's time you woke up to that."

Nancy laughed, brushing her short curls back from her forehead. "Do you really think I'm so dense that I'm not aware of the situation?"

"Then why don't you do something about it?"

"Because the price of the alternative is too great. I know Mike. He does what he feels is his share of the duties. If I started insisting he do more, we'd be arguing all the time. It's just not worth it to me to turn this place into an armed camp. I love Mike and our children too much to do that."

Frances shook her head in exasperation. "So you sacrifice yourself on the altar of his male chauvinism?"

"No. On the altar of our love. And it's not such a very

great sacrifice to make when you consider the love, peace, and happiness I get in return." Her eyes softening, she reached out and touched Frances's arm. "If you were married, you'd understand. I often wish that things had worked out for you and Bob. He was a nice guy, and he certainly would have been a perfect husband for a woman with views like yours."

Frances stiffened at the mention of Robert Matthews. She and Bob had met three years ago when they were both on the staff of a suburban newspaper in New Jersey. Crazy about each other, they'd taken an apartment together in Trenton, splitting everything down the middle, from bills to chores. The setup was perfect until Bob had begun showing his true male colors by becoming possessive, wanting her to cleave only unto him, even going so far as talking marriage and a family. That kind of bondage was not for her. She was her own woman and would consent to belong to no man, no matter how much he meant to her. She broke with Bob, moved to New York, setting up housekeeping alone in the Village, and taking a job on a trade magazine, where she'd worked until going to Waterford. There had been many men since then, but she never made the mistake of letting one of them move in. Of course, she'd never been tempted to. It was unlikely that she could ever feel for any other man what she had felt for Bob.

Abruptly, she turned away from Nancy's gaze and touch. "If there's one thing I'll never be crazy enough to do, it's chain myself to a man."

"It's better," Nancy said softly, "to chain yourself to a man than to an idea."

Rather than answer, Frances began slicing pickles with a vengeance.

A few seconds later Mike entered, holding Donny at arm's length. "He has to be changed, honey."

Nancy cast an anxious glance at the pots and pans on the stove, then took the baby. "I'll be back in a minute," she told Frances. "Keep an eye on things here, will you?"

"Sure. Mike'll help me." But the irony in her voice was lost on Mike, who had already left the room.

By the time Nancy returned with a clean-diapered and

freshly powdered Donny, Frances had managed to quell the cold tremor that always attacked her when thoughts of Bob forced their way into her mind. She mashed the potatoes while Nancy made the gravy, then set the dining-room table while Nancy fed Donny.

When she came downstairs after putting Donny in for a nap, Nancy put the finishing touches on dinner, rounded up Michael and Michelle, cleaned them up and sat them in their places at the dining-room table, insisting that Frances join them. Then she brought out the turkey, and while Mike carved it, she brought the rest of the food to the table. Having at last finished serving the children's plates and cutting up their turkey, she sat down in her own place and began serving herself.

Mike had already begun to attack the food he had piled on his plate. "Say, honey," he said through a mouthful of mashed potatoes, "didn't you forget something?"

Nancy looked around the table quizzically. "Not that I can think of."

"The cranberry sauce!" Mike reminded her, beaming like a child who has come up with the answer to a riddle. "We can't have Thanksgiving dinner without the cranberry sauce, can we?"

"That would be a disaster," Nancy said, and pushing her chair back with a sigh, went out to the kitchen.

Frances had reached her boiling point. "For God's sake!" she hissed when Nancy was out of earshot. "Couldn't you have done that?"

Now it was Mike's turn to look puzzled. "Done what?"

"Gotten up off your rear and gone out for the cranberry sauce!"

His look of surprise made it obvious that the thought had never occurred to him. Now that, with Frances's help, it had, he dismissed it quickly. "Oh, Nancy takes care of all that."

"Why?"

He shrugged. "Well, she knows where everything is, for one thing."

"And you're too damn lazy to give her a hand, for another."

Not about to lose his holiday mood, he smiled. "Hey,

that's hitting below the belt. I'm not a lazy guy. I work hard for a living."

She sighed, exasperated with his thickheadedness. "Hasn't it ever occurred to you that you leave the office behind you every day, but Nancy's never away from *her* work?"

"Look," he said, frowning, "if you're about to read me another of your women's lib lectures, you can forget it. You're always quick to tell me how I 'abuse' your sister, but did you ever stop to notice that I've given her a hell of a lot too?" He waved a hand around the room. "A nice home, a good living, security."

"And for that, she's supposed to be your doting, willing slave!"

"No," he said quietly, the anger leaving his eyes. "For that she's supposed to love me, just as I love her." He leaned forward. "You know, Frances, I love Nancy very much. There isn't anything I wouldn't do for her."

Frances burst out laughing. "Except give her a little help around the house!"

Nancy returned with the cranberry sauce, and Frances and Mike immediately stopped talking.

"You two look like Michael and Michelle when they get caught with their hands in the cookie jar," she said. "What were you doing—fighting again?"

Mike helped himself to cranberry sauce. "Not fighting," he said good-humoredly, "just having a friendly discussion about what a lousy husband I am."

Nancy threw Frances an impatient look. "I think I'm the only one qualified to judge *that*, and *I* say you're a good husband."

"Seems you're overruled by a higher court," Mike said, triumphant.

Frances shrugged. "I defer to the decision in this case, but it's far from the rule. There are too many women in similar situations who feel otherwise."

"Then that's their problem, not mine or yours," Nancy said.

"Male hypocrisy is the problem of all women," Frances insisted.

"Hypocrisy isn't limited to one sex," Mike put in. "Men are victims of female hypocrisy too."

"In certain isolated cases, yes," Frances conceded. "But not as a matter of course, the way we are."

A hearty, disparaging laugh was Mike's only answer.

"The way you're trying to laugh it off is better proof of what I'm saying than any argument against it," Frances said. "You men have always been two-faced in your dealings with us. Even most men who give lip service to our Movement still, in their private lives, regard women mainly as sex objects."

"Which is exactly how a lot of you want to be regarded."

"Like hell it is!" Her eyes snapped, and a cutting edge came into her voice. "We're individuals, and we demand that we be treated as such."

"Sure!" Mike's voice was heavy with sarcasm. "That's why you run around in skin-tight jeans and tight sweaters, with your breasts flopping all over the place—because you don't want us lowly men to notice you're girls."

Her cheeks flamed with anger. "We've a right to dress as we please! And we've given up bras because they're unnatural, designed to accentuate the breasts and call attention to them."

"Oh, yeah? Well, you just walk two gals down the street— one in the unnatural fetters of her attention-getting bra, and the other with her tits flying free, and we'll see which one the passing men will think of as a sex object."

"Mike!" Nancy admonished, with a glance toward Michael and Michelle, who were all ears and eyes. "The children!"

"What's tits, Mommy?" Michael asked.

"It's an impolite way of referring to a lady's bosom," Nancy said, with a pointed look at Mike. "Daddy was only fooling."

"Tits, tits, tits!" Michelle sang, banging her spoon against her plate. "Tits, tits, tits!"

"If you men get the wrong idea, it's your problem, not ours," Frances said above Michael's questions and Michelle's chants.

"That's a lot of sh—" Mike looked at the children and

quickly lowered his tone. "—of baloney. You can't scrawl a dirty word on a wall in letters six-feet high, and then expect people to look at it and see only the color it's painted in. If you don't want men to think of you as sex objects, you should stop dressing like them."

"And let you men have the right to dress any way you—"

"For God's sake!" Nancy slammed down her knife and fork. "Will you two cut it out? This is supposed to be a pleasant holiday meal. Obviously, neither one of you is about to change the other's position on anything. So let's talk about something neutral. I've had enough of your fighting for one day."

Obediently, they turned the conversation to other subjects, and the rest of the meal passed in an armed truce, as did the remainder of the day. Frances was vastly relieved when it was finally time to go.

"It's a shame you have to work tomorrow," Nancy said, kissing her good-by. "We could have made a weekend of it."

"That's the way it goes." Frances tried to sigh convincingly.

Mike drove her to the station, keeping up a stream of small talk, perhaps to cover her stony silence. They arrived ten minutes before train time, and he suggested she stay in the car, where it was warm, instead of standing on the open-air platform.

"A little fresh air won't hurt me," she said, reaching for the door handle.

He reached over and put his hand on hers. "We're not talking about a little fresh air," he said. "We're talking about nineteen-degree temperatures and twenty-five-mile-an-hour winds. Come on. You put up with me all day—ten minutes more won't kill you. Besides, if Nancy thought I'd let you wait out there in the cold, she'd chew me out."

Frances sank back against the car seat and gave him an incredulous look. "Nancy chew you out? That'll be the day!"

He laughed. "Do you find that so hard to believe? Then you don't know your sister. She gives me hell plenty of times. Maybe not about things *you* think she should get on my back about, but about things she thinks are important. And she's usually right."

Frances continued to look skeptical.

"You think I'm kidding?" Mike shook his head. "I'm not. You shouldn't try to judge other people's lives. No outsider can do that. Nancy and I have a good marriage—maybe not by your standards, but by ours."

"Look, Mike, if you're trying to start another argument, I may as well get out of the car now—" Frances began.

"Christ! Why do you get your back up every time I open my mouth?" He waved his hand. "All right. I know a lot of it's my fault. Plenty of times I say things I don't even believe, just to rile you. Don't think I won't have hell to pay for that when I get home too. But that wasn't what I was doing just now." She'd never seen him look so earnest. "What I was trying to tell you now is that I meant what I said earlier. I love your sister. Nancy and the kids—they're my whole life. Everything I do, I do for them. Maybe that's why I needle you so much—because it gets to me, the way you're always trying to make me come out looking like a lousy husband."

"If the shoe fits . . ." Frances said with a shrug.

"But, don't you see, it's your shoe, not Nancy's. All those things you say about women being slaves and sex objects—that doesn't go at our house. Do you really think that's how I think of my wife, how I'd want people to think of my little girl? To me, Nancy is a princess, and she always will be."

Obviously he meant every word he was saying, and if she wasn't so irritated by his outlook, Frances might almost have felt sorry for him.

"Look," she said with exaggerated patience, "don't you understand that putting a woman on a pedestal is just another sneaky way of forcing her into a role that keeps her under your thumb?"

Mike shook his head, uncomprehending. "I love Nancy. There's no one else in the world like her. She *is* a princess. You don't understand how it is when you love someone."

"And you don't understand—Oh, forget it!"

"Maybe we should forget it," Mike agreed as the bell signaling that the train would soon arrive began to ring. "I mean, I guess Nancy was right when she said we'd never be able to see things from each other's point of view. So how about calling a truce for her sake? Will you come out for Christmas? I know she'd like that."

The thought was not particularly appealing. "I don't know, Mike...."

"I promise I'll stay off your back all day—if you'll stay off mine."

When she still hesitated, he added, "I'll even put out the cranberry sauce. Come on, say you'll come. Can't you do it—for Nancy?"

The train was pulling into the station. "All right," she said, opening the car door. "For Nancy."

"It's a truce then?"

"It's a truce. But you better not be kidding about the cranberry sauce."

He made an okay sign with his right hand, and she turned and ran for the train.

Like the employees who had to drag themselves to the office after a day of overindulgence in food and drink, Friday turned out to be gray, solemn and sleepy. Even the hands of the huge clock on the fourteenth-floor wall were affected by the lethargic atmosphere, seeming to take twice as long as usual to push themselves around to five o'clock. Ten minutes before that magic moment was reached, all desks had been cleared, all typewriters had been covered, and all Waterfordians had begun the week's final countdown to freedom.

Once on the street, Frances hesitated. She had pulled what her feminist group called "desexregating-maintenance" duty that evening, and was scheduled to spend the two hours between nine and eleven in Roscoe's Beer Garden, a formerly all-male watering hole. Roscoe's, as well as several others like it in the city, had finally had its policy of sex-discrimination declared unconstitutional when women's groups protested and filed suit. Determined not to allow old sexist patterns to re-establish themselves by permitting the victory to become one in name only, her group had elected to send pairs of women to all such establishments at least four times a week.

Tonight, she and Rosalie Montague were to do their share in keeping Roscoe's desexregated.

Now she walked slowly to the corner, wondering if she should go home, or grab a quick bite and spend the remainder of the time between five and nine in a movie. She was opting for the movie when a hand closed over her elbow, and a deep voice close to her ear asked, "How about a drink to brighten a gray day?"

She didn't have to look up to discern that the voice belonged to Cam Eckhart, and she felt a faint surge of excitement in spite of her basic dislike for him. For though she abhorred his male chauvinism, she found him extremely attractive physically, and was intrigued by the idea of sleeping with him. Evidently disconcerted by her militancy, however, he had kept his distance from her, and she wondered why, after virtually ignoring her all the months she had been at Waterford, he had suddenly taken an interest in her. Then she realized that most of the sweet young things who were his usual targets were probably too tired and too dyspeptic after yesterday's feasting and festing to be tempted by an invitation from Don Juan himself.

"Sounds fine to me," she said.

"Nick's?"

"Why not my place? I have plenty in stock."

The suggestion obviously took him by surprise but pleased him. "Great. Where do you live?"

Before she could finish giving him her address, he had hailed a cab. As the driver crawled through the rush-hour traffic, they settled back and chatted. It was the first time she had talked to Cam on an intimate, one-to-one basis, and Frances tried to penetrate the store of banalities he relied upon in all his conversations with women. By the time the taxi pulled up in front of her Greenwich Village brownstone, she had begun to think it was an impossible task.

As she preceded Cam up the three narrow flights of stairs to her apartment, she was aware of his eyes on her buttocks every inch of the way. Smiling to herself, she accentuated her wiggle. Though socially she detested Don Juans and girl watchers, she had often found them quite satisfactory sexually, and she had no compunctions about going after what she wanted from them. If Cam turned out to be half as good as he claimed to be, she thought as she opened her door, she might keep him in her menagerie a while.

While she hung up his coat, Cam glanced around her small living room in which the sharp angles and curves of the starkly modern furniture were echoed in the geometric op art that decorated the walls.

"Tiny, isn't it?" she said, opening the door of a vermilion, cube-shaped end table to reveal a supply of liquor. "I think the landlord created this grand three-room suite by converting two and a half closets."

Cam sat down on the canary-colored sofa. "I like it. It's cozy—" He dropped his voice an octave and looked at her meaningfully. "—intimate."

She nodded toward the bottles on display. "What's your pleasure?" she asked. "Besides sex, that is."

He laughed with the false heartiness of a man who prefers innuendo to candor in women. "Do you have the fixings for a martini?"

"Not only do I have the fixings, I happen to make the best ones this side of West Eighth Street."

She disappeared into her tiny kitchen with a bottle of gin and a bottle of vermouth, and was soon back, stirring their contents in a tall refrigerator jar.

"One of these days, I'll have to get a martini pitcher," she said.

"I'll buy one and bring it next time," Cam told her, his eyes on the cleavage exposed by her only partially buttoned blouse as she bent to pour their drinks.

She settled next to him on the sofa and raised her glass. "Thanks, but I never accept gifts from men. I take care of myself."

He raised an eyebrow. "I know you're a very independent young lady, but isn't that carrying things a bit too far?"

"A woman's independence can never be carried too far."

They drained their glasses, and she refilled them.

"You know," Cam said, "we've been working in the same office for some months now, but we don't really know each other. Tell me something about the *real* you—" He moved a little closer. "—the soft, warm woman I can sense pulsating under that militant, independent façade."

She'd wondered what line he'd try to feed her, and now that he'd gone into action, she burst into laughter. "I'm sorry to disappoint you, but that militant independence is no façade—it's the real me."

"Oh, you'd like me to believe that, but I know better." His lids half-closed over his eyes as he slipped his arm around her. "I know that underneath it all, you're warm and sympathetic—the kind of girl who can understand a man like me."

She shook her head in amusement. "For Christ's sake, Cam, can it!" she said. "You don't have to make me feel sorry for you or use flattery to get me into bed. Why the hell do you think I invited you to come home with me?"

Bristling, Cam jerked his arm back and stroked his beard. "I can't vouch for *your* motives, but I know mine were honorable—to have a drink and some conversation with a beautiful, sympathetic woman."

"Bullshit!" Laughing, she put down her empty glass, thinking that getting Cam to face up to his lecherous self might bring her as much intellectual pleasure as going to bed with him would bring her physical gratification. "You probably haven't had an honorable motive toward a woman since puberty. You came up here because you wanted a good lay, and I invited you because I want the same thing. Why waste time on an unnecessary con job?"

He drained his glass, then turned to her, his eyes puzzled. "I don't understand you. If you question my sincerity so strongly, why did you ask me up here in the first place?"

"I thought I made that crystal clear." The words came out with an exasperated sigh. "Look. You men have no compunctions about going to bed with a dumb broad you hardly know and don't particularly like as long as she's stacked. Well, I claim the same prerogative. I'll admit, I think you're a shithead when it comes to women, but I find you physically attractive—as you obviously find me, or you wouldn't be here—so I'm not averse to a little screwing. After all, men down through the ages have proved that you don't have to be intellectually companionable for that."

His face flushed. "Do you realize that you're being highly insulting?"

She shrugged. "Don't be ridiculous. I'm simply putting into words an attitude that until recently was considered the privilege of the male, and staking a claim to it. The only difference is that you *think* it while I *say* it."

Biting his mustache, he rose as though preparing to take his leave. "I must say—"

Shaking her long brown hair back off her face, Frances rose also. "Your problem, Cam, is that you say too much about far too little." Slowly, she began unbuttoning her blouse the remainder of the way, giving view to her voluptuous, unfettered breasts. Cam's eyes widened, and she smiled to herself as she heard his sharp intake of breath. "Now shut up," she said, holding her arms out to him, "and let's see some action."

He did not have to be invited again. Within seconds, they were in each other's arms; then, like the experts they were, they easily maneuvered themselves into her bedroom, stripped the bed of its bedspread and themselves of their clothes. Moaning and panting, they fell onto the bed, kissing and touching each other everywhere at once. Then, almost as abruptly as it had begun, the act was completed, and, drawing a long, quivering breath, Cam rolled over on his back.

"You really are something!" he sighed. Then he lay there, eyes closed, trying to catch his breath.

Frances, her body only partly aroused and not even fractionally gratified, stared at him incredulously. So this was the Waterford Casanova! Not since her days as a virginal novice had she been so totally disappointed in a sexual encounter. Propping herself up on her elbow, she looked down on Cam, her frustration quickly turning to anger. "You're really something too!" she said.

Not catching the irony in her voice, he smiled up at her. "We'll have to make a habit of it."

"The hell we will!" She got out of bed, picked up his clothes, and threw them at him. "Do you think I'm a masochist?"

It was his turn to look incredulous. "What the hell are you talking about?"

"I'm talking about the fiasco that just took place on my bed. It was too little too soon—strictly a one-man show. I'm not about to allow a repeat performance."

He sat up, his face reddening with indignation. "Just what are you insinuating?"

"I'm not insinuating, buster, I'm telling you. There's no room in my life for a slam-bam-thank-you-ma'am lover. I *like* sex, and I have as much right to enjoy it as you do. There's no higher insult a man can deliver than to behave as though his sex partner is no more than a mechanical receptacle for the by-product of his lust."

She went to her closet and ripped a blue karate robe off a hanger. By the time she had wrapped it around her, Cam was in his trousers.

His eyes flashed with anger and indignation. "You're way off base. I'm a lot older than you are, and I've had many more women than you've had men—and not one of them has complained about my style."

Her laugh was bitter and derisive. "Women! I've seen the kind of women you go after—sweet young things who've had few men to compare you to and are probably too shy to tell you you're a lousy lover."

Cam's chest puffed with self-righteousness. "That, my girl, is sour grapes. They haven't complained because there's nothing to complain about."

She whirled on him. "How do you know? Did you ever ask them? When was the last time you turned to a woman in bed and said, 'Was it good for you?' or 'What can I do to please you?'"

He slipped on his shirt and began buttoning it. "I don't have to do that. I happen to know—"

"You know from nothing when it comes to women!" It was no longer just Cam she was raging against, but male chauvinism itself. "You know only your own selfish needs and warped visions. 'It pleases me, *ergo*, it pleases her' is your philosophy. Well, I've got news for you, buddy—that's a lot of shit. It takes a hell of a lot more than a few passionate kisses and feels and a couple of bangs to please any woman."

He dismissed her statement with a shrug. "That's women's lib talk."

"It wouldn't be women's lib talk if it weren't a solid fact of life. Don't take my word for it. Ask any of the clinging-vine types you usually go for. Ask your wife."

"My wife wouldn't agree," he said triumphantly. "She doesn't go in for sex."

"There's no such thing as a wife who can't be turned on by sex—there are only husbands who are too stupid or too inconsiderate to find the proper switches." She tossed her hair off her shoulders with a contemptuous shake of her head. "If your wife doesn't go in for sex with you, you can be damn certain she goes in for it with someone else."

"Not my wife!" he insisted, his eyes flashing, his nostrils flaring. "She'd never do such a thing!"

"Why? Because you're such a paragon of virtue, she wouldn't want to hurt you?" Her laughter was like a sword cutting through the air. "If she hasn't found a lover yet, she will. It's only a matter of time."

He put on his tie, ducked down so that he could see himself in her vanity mirror, and carefully combed his hair and smoothed his beard. "You don't know Miriam." He shrugged off the possibility.

She walked over to her night table, slipped on her eyeglasses, and rummaged around in a drawer for a pack of cigarettes. "You're the one who doesn't know her." She lit her cigarette, sat down on the bed and stretched out her long, shapely legs.

He continued to smooth his beard. "Even if she would consider such a thing, I doubt she'd find any takers. After all, she's forty-three, not exactly in the prime of life."

"Come off it, Cam! You're more than forty-three, and I'm sure you don't consider yourself past your prime." She tried to keep the anger his pretentiousness provoked from getting out of control.

"It's different with a man."

"Like hell it is! Your wife has the same needs and desires you had at her age, maybe more. She'll find someone to satisfy them."

"Who?" he asked in the tone of a man who is calling a bluff.

"Oh, I know!" she said, calmly exhaling a puff of smoke. "You think all men are like you—slightly repressed child-molesters who are interested mainly in screwing girls young enough to be their daughters. But there's the other side of the coin, you know—young men who are looking for mother figures to screw. And there are even a few oddballs who go for women of their own age. And if the man your wife latches onto knows how to please her, believe me, she'll know how to please him—and to keep him. She'll have him around long after the kids you chase after will be regarding you as over the hill. You only have a few more years left of being attractive to the post-diaper set, you know, and you certainly don't have what it takes to keep any older woman interested for long."

He turned from the mirror, his face gray. "You're sick."

She stretched and wiggled her toes luxuriously. "No, just truthful: You're a lecher and a lousy lover. When everything starts coming apart for you, remember where you heard it first."

A muscle in his jaw began to jump, and his hands shook with rage. "You're a goddam lying bitch!"

She laughed.

"Go ahead—laugh!" His face was almost purple now. "But I'll laugh last after I talk to Jason Bart on Monday. We don't need your kind at Waterford. You'll be out on that round little ass of yours so fast you won't know what hit you."

She sat up straighter, cold fury glinting in her eyes, knifing through her every word. "Try it," she challenged him, "and right after I throw a women's rights picket line around our office building and in front of your home, I'll just take that round little ass of mine straight to the Human Rights Commission. In my hot little hand, I'll have a complete report on everything that has transpired here, and a dossier on all your other office seductions. Then we'll see who laughs last."

His face paling, he tugged his beard in fury. "You bitch! You goddam lying, conniving bitch!"

"You're repeating yourself." She heaved a bored sigh. "I have an appointment for later this evening, so if you don't mind. . . . It's a small apartment. I'm sure you can find your way out."

"You're goddam right I can!" He grabbed his jacket and stormed out of the room.

"Your coat's in the hall closet," she called after him.

"Go to hell!" he growled back as she heard the closet door swinging open, then shut.

"The same to you, pussycat." Her tone was all sweetness and light.

The bed shook under her as the outer door slammed.

Her lips curling in a smile of secret pleasure, Frances finished smoking her cigarette. Then she showered, dressed in a low-cut ivory body shirt and navy-blue knit slacks, and fixed her dinner. At a quarter to nine, she left her apartment and took a taxi to Roscoe's Beer Garden.

As she suspected would be the case, Rosalie was not there. A lesbian who was as fickle in her relationships as most men were in theirs, Rosalie was always chasing after some new love, and neglecting all important organization matters while in pursuit. Frances had noticed Rosalie and one of the group's newer members making eyes at each other during the last meeting a few days ago, and she surmised that they were off together someplace now, completely oblivious of the time and of more important obligations. Frances gave Rosalie another ten minutes in which to remember that the rights of all women come before the love of one, then decided to carry out their assignment on her own.

She hesitated a moment before pushing open the heavy, paneled door. When she and Bob Matthews were living together, he had confessed to her once that he often spent time in Roscoe's when their New Jersey newspaper sent him to New York to cover a story. That had occasioned their first real battle; Bob had maintained, despite his staunch support of women's rights, that each sex was entitled to have places off-bounds to the other, where its members could relax, let down their hair and their guard. The argument had ended in a stalemate. At that time, she had thought they could never have a more violent argument, but looking back now, it seemed a mere exchange of pleasantries compared to the fights they had at the end over Bob's demands that they get married.

With a sigh, she shrugged off her memories and pressed against the door. The musty odor of beer, cigarette smoke, and sawdust that rushed at her nostrils was quickly followed by razzings and catcalls from the all-male clientele.

"What's the matter, baby—Schrafft's burn down?"

"Why don't you go home and send out for a bottle, like other red-blooded women?"

"She's probably not here for a drink at all—just wants to use the *men's* room."

Frances stared down the hecklers with icy contempt.

"Hey, cut it out, you guys!" the bartender called out finally. "This place is open to all the public now, remember?"

Frances walked over to the bar, perched on a stool, and slipped off her coat, evoking some whistles.

The bartender, a burly man of about fifty who looked as though he'd be more at home in a wrestling ring than behind a counter, came over. "There's a couple of tables not taken yet," he said, nodding toward the back of the room.

Frances had no intention of allowing herself to be stashed away out of sight. There was no sense in desexregation unless it was visible. "No, thanks. I'm perfectly comfortable here."

Before he had a chance to extol the merits of a back table further, she ordered a Seven and Seven. While she was waiting, she glanced around the room. Though she'd had picket duty outside the bar several times before the law was changed, she'd never been inside. The decor was not too different from that of several of the other men's bars she'd been in: sturdy, no-nonsense tables and chairs; unpolished, sawdust-covered floors; dark, wood-paneled walls, covered with autographed photos of male athletes and movie stars who played rugged he-man roles.

After putting her glass down, the bartender remained standing in front of her, eyeing her suspiciously. "You're not a hooker, are you? Because I don't want no—"

"Oh, for Christ's sake!" she cut him off, putting her money down on the bartop. "I'm just an ordinary woman exercising her right to quench her thirst here, making sure no one forgets that that right exists."

"Jeez! One of them women's libbers!" Obviously he'd have been more pleased at the prospect of being arrested for allowing soliciting on the premises. "When are you dames going to get off my back? There were two of you here throwing your weight around a couple of nights ago, and two a few nights before that. When are you going to get it through your heads that I'm not going to try to keep you out, and stop coming? You're going to ruin the business."

Frances glanced around the crowded room. "You don't seem to be doing so badly."

"Yeah, but for how long? Look, you've made your point, won your rights. Now why don't you be sensible, and forget the whole thing?"

"Because forgetting the whole thing wouldn't be sensible." She took a sip of her drink. "You're going to have to get used to having us around. By the way, how come you don't have any pictures of women athletes on the walls?"

"Jesus Christ! Haven't I done enough, letting you in? Are you broads going to bug me about that too?"

"Could be."

"I'll try to dig up a picture of Babe Ruth in bloomers for you, girlie."

He walked away, shaking his head and tugging at one of his rather scraggly sideburns.

Smiling, she reached into her purse for a cigarette. Before she could strike a match, a rather unsteady hand to her right extended a lighter.

"Thanks," she said, striking her match anyway, "but I light my own."

The lighter was snapped shut and withdrawn. "Independent, huh?"

Her chivalrous knight took her nod as an invitation to move to the bar stool next to her. He was about fifty-five, paunchy, and more than a little drunk. He leaned as close to her as he could and still maintain his balance on the stool.

"But we both know there's one thing you can't do without a man."

This time she didn't bother to nod.

Love After Hours   131

"You know, you're a mighty attractive girl." The whiskey on his breath was stronger than her own drink. "I could go for you."

"Then by all means do—go away, that is."

She could smell his laugh before she heard it. "A sense of humor, eh? That's the way I like 'em—with spirit!"

She continued to stare straight ahead.

"How about we go up to my place, have some fun?"

"I'm having all the fun I care to have right here."

"Aw, come on! Don't play hard to get. Everybody knows girls like you hand it out all the time."

For the first time, she turned to look at him, her cold eyes boring into his bleary ones. "I hand it out when I please and to whom I please. I do not please to hand it out to you."

His mouth went slack, then curled into a sneer. "Independent, huh?"

"I believe that's where you came in. Why don't you use it for an exit line too?"

"Now don't get high-hat with me, girlie—"

"I think the lady just told you to get lost."

The words came from close behind her, and all that prevented Frances from snapping that she could handle her own problems was the voice that spoke them. Her hands went cold, and her heart rose up in her throat blocking the passage of her usual cutting retort. Swinging around on her stool, she found herself looking up into the warm brown eyes of Bob Matthews.

"Hello, Frances."

Bob was the only person she knew who could make her name sound beautiful.

"Hello, Bob."

After studying their locked gaze, the drunk shrugged his shoulders philosophically. "Sorry, fella. I didn't know the lady was with you." Picking up his drink, he moved further down the bar, and Bob slipped onto the stool he had vacated.

Frances took a long drag on her cigarette, hoping to calm her nerves, which had begun to quiver like furniture during an earth tremor. The only phrase her brain could select from the chaos in her mind was, "Fancy meeting you here."

Bob's smile still tilted more to the left than to the right and crinkled the lines around his eyes, exactly as she remembered it.

"It's really not so extraordinary when you think about it," he said. "In fact, I had a feeling I might run into you."

Her heart raced at the thought that he had deliberately set out to search for her, but quickly slowed to a painful thud as he explained that he had been on the staff of one of the city's intellectual weeklies for some time now, and was currently engaged in doing a follow-up story on the integration of the sexes in formerly all-male bars and restaurants.

"Knowing your feelings on the subject, I rather thought I'd see you at one place or another."

She took a sip of her drink, wishing she didn't feel so disappointed at his use of the word *thought* instead of *hoped*.

"Well," she said with a forced smile. "It looks as though you were right."

"Are you here on your own, or as the representative of a group?"

"Are you asking that as a friend or as a reporter?"

"Both. And the answer?"

"Both."

Their laughter broke down the awkwardness that the two years since their last meeting had placed between them. By the time the laughter dwindled to smiles, it seemed to Frances that the two years had been erased—that they were back where they were when life had been a dancing bubble of love, long before Bob had burst it with his possessiveness and she had been forced to flee. She looked at him, her eyes warm with memories.

"You haven't changed," she said at last.

He shrugged in his old self-deprecating way. "A little thinner on top and thicker in the middle, maybe. But you certainly haven't. Tell me what you've been doing."

They ordered fresh drinks, and when she insisted on paying for her own, he knew better than to argue. As they sipped, they filled each other in on the last two years. Personal history covered, they moved on to more general topics, their old rapport so quickly reasserting itself that they soon were able to anticipate each other in thought as well as in words. Though they never mentioned their life together, their laughter was a gentle reminder of its best of times, and all the tender memories it held for them were hinted at in the warmth of their tone.

Not for two years had Frances felt so totally alive and yet so thoroughly at peace. Being apart, she realized now, had only served to show her how much they had together. Surely, it had shown Bob too, and made him regret the possessiveness that had driven them apart. Now they could start over again, avoiding the pitfalls of the past. Her heart pounded at the prospect.

Bob glanced down at his watch, and a flood of warmth rushed over her as she studied the rugged lines of his profile. God! How she loved him!

"Let's go home," she said, her voice husky with emotion. Whose home didn't matter, as long as they were there together.

He looked up, his eyes troubled. "Home? We broke up our home two years ago—remember?"

"Let's not talk about it here." She reached for her coat, and while she slipped it on, he went over to a coat tree for his own.

Outside, the frigid air froze their breath and tossed it back into their faces, making talk impossible. Hunching over against the wind, they hugged their coats around them and hurried to Bob's car. It was the same green Volkswagen he'd driven when they were together.

"Still gets me there and back," he said, unlocking the door.

Slipping inside the car was like stepping into a time machine that eradicated the present. Nothing was changed—from the broken clock on the dashboard with its hands forever pointing to half-past two to the pile of junk on the back seat.

Bob saw her looking at the clock. "Still doesn't work," he said, "but even at that, it tells the truth twice a day."

"That's a better record than a lot of people I know," Frances said, and gave him her address.

Bob had little to say on the drive to her apartment, but she felt no awkwardness in their silence. She welcomed the chance to lean her head back against the seat, close her eyes and breathe in the past that hung heavy in the air around them. When Bob finally brought the car to a stop, she was almost surprised to open her eyes and see that they were in front of her Greenwich Village brownstone, and not their old apartment house in Trenton.

For the second time that evening, she went up the stairs with a man behind her. But this time, her heart was pounding so hard in anticipation that her ears burned and throbbed from the echo of its beats.

She opened her door and flicked on the light.

"Nice place," Bob said, as they shrugged out of their coats. "You always had a way with decorating. My place looks like me—all thrown together."

She poured some brandy to warm them up. "Where do you live?"

"Up near Columbia, but I've been looking around for something else. That neighborhood's become so tough that burglars get mugged on their way home from pulling jobs."

"Well, you won't have to look any more," she said, making a little gesture with her glass that seemed to encompass her entire apartment. "This place isn't huge, but it's big enough for two."

Instead of answering, he took a long swallow of his drink, then walked over to the window. "And where do you propose we start?" His back was to her, but the strain he felt was audible in his voice and visible in the tense line of his shoulders. "Where we began—or where we left off?"

A tiny seed of fear took root inside her at the hesitation she sensed in him. "Where we began, of course," she said softly, walking over to him. "Where we left off, there was too much hurt."

He turned and looked down at her, and the memory of that hurt was so vivid in his eyes that for a second she seemed to hear the echoes of their screaming battles all around her.

Gently, she touched his arm. "We've been apart two years too long, Bob. Surely, you felt that as strongly as I did when we met again tonight."

His eyes searched hers, as though he were trying to penetrate to the depths of her soul. "You can never go back," he said, his arm trembling beneath her touch.

"Then we'll go forward."

She pressed closer, and he pulled her to him with a cry that seemed almost more despair than joy, his lips engulfing hers until her whole mind and body seemed sucked into the whirlpool of his kiss. His lips moved from her mouth to her cheek to her neck to her breast, one hand clutching her hair, the other moving up and down her back.

"My God!" he cried. "How could I have thought I'd gotten over you?"

Kiss for kiss, touch for touch, she responded until the whole room seemed to be vibrating with their need. The bedroom too far or forgotten, they slipped down to the rug and gave way to their desire, like a parched couple diving into a stream. Then, their thirst quenched, they languished in the aftermath of love.

Finally, Bob disengaged an arm from beneath Frances's back and stretched it stiffly in front of him. "Floors aren't exactly my specialty," he said with a wry smile.

"Nor mine," she said, sitting up and rubbing a hand against her stiff neck.

Laughing, they slipped back into their clothes, then sat down on the sofa, picking up their forgotten drinks.

"To the second time around," she said, "without the mistakes of the first."

Bob touched his glass to hers and they drank, then kissed.

"When will you move in?" she asked, nestling her head on his shoulder.

He rubbed his cheek against her hair. "As soon as I can get things straightened out, and we can get a license. A couple of weeks, I guess."

She stiffened. "A license?"

"Um." He kissed the top of her head. "You want to get married, don't you? You just said we wouldn't make the mistakes we made before."

"But that's exactly the mistake that drove us apart before," she said, trying desperately to keep calm. "You were trying to own me."

Hurt, he pulled away and looked down at her. "I never tried to own you. All I asked from you was the same commitment I was ready to give to you."

She stood up, trying to laugh the whole thing off. "Come on now, Bob. You sound absolutely medieval. Surely you've outgrown those childish ideas in the past two years."

"If anything, I've matured enough for them to become even more entrenched." He walked over and turned her around to him. "I need you. I'm not ashamed to admit it. I want you to belong to me in the same way I want to belong to you. Is that too much to ask?"

"It's not only too much to ask, it's wrong to ask." She pulled away, her heart pounding painfully. Why did he have to be this way when they were so close to happiness? "I love you. I'll live with you. But I won't belong exclusively to you or any man. I have to be free."

His face reddened. "Free to do what—to be consumed by fear?"

"Fear?" she demanded. "Fear of what?"

"Of love!"

"Of love! That's a lie! I lived with you for a year, didn't I? And God knows how many lovers I've had before and after. For somebody who's afraid of love, I seem to have had a hell of a lot of it!"

"You've had a hell of a lot of sex. You had only one year of love, and you ran like the devil the minute you realized I wanted more than kid stuff. For you, there was always safety in numbers. One day you'll discover that there's such a thing as being a slave to freedom."

Her eyes filled with tears of frustration. "We just found each other again. Why do you have to ruin it all with this silly fighting? What difference does it make whether I hang onto my freedom while we live together? The main thing is that we'd be together!"

He ran his hand over his eyes. "Once that was enough for me," he said wearily, "but it could never be enough again. It's a rotten world out there. Everyone needs one person out of all the others in the world whom he can be sure of if he's to survive. If there's one thing these two years of going from bed to bed and broad to broad have taught me, it's that sex isn't enough. Strings are important."

"Not to me they aren't!"

"Obviously." He walked over to a chair and picked up his coat.

Her heart seemed to skid to a stop. "Where are you going?"

He shrugged. "Back out of your life."

"You're running away!" she accused.

He shook his head. "*You're* running away, not me. I'm running *toward*." He put on his coat and began to button it. "There's a girl I know who believes in commitments. She hasn't been afraid to admit she needs me. Up till tonight, I thought I needed her too. Then I saw you again, and I couldn't resist trying to recapture the past—not the past as it was, but as I wanted it to have been." He looked up, his face drawn and tired. "You can't recapture something that never existed in the first place."

"So now you're going back to her?" It was hard for her to get the words out.

He nodded.

"But you don't love her the way you love me."

"Not yet. But then, she doesn't love me the way you do, either. There's a lot of hope in that."

Her insides seemed to shrivel, leaving an awful emptiness behind them. "You'll regret it," she warned. "You'll come to hate being tied down, and so will she."

"It's only the ties we're afraid to make that strangle us," he said quietly.

She forced a smile and a shrug, managing to keep her voice light. "That's what *you* think!"

He looked long and deeply into her eyes, taking his last leave. "It's what, deep down, we both know."

She closed the door behind him, then stood pressed against it, listening to his footsteps recede down the stairs. Deep inside her was an urgent need to call him back, but she clamped her teeth against it. Calling him back would mean humbling herself, giving in to *his* terms, becoming his wife and doting slave. No man was worth that kind of sacrifice.

The faint sound of the street door closing drifted up to her. He was gone for good. She was safe from temptation.

She moved away from the door. "Thank God," she said aloud, "that I didn't fall into that trap!"

Somehow, the words hung heavily in the empty apartment, not bringing all the comfort and relief they should have.

Chapter Seven

*N*ews of Doc's death spread through the Waterford offices like spilled ink radiating slowly, relentlessly, over a desk blotter. Long before the official memo was circulated announcing the demise of the founder of the company and the closing of the office on the day of his funeral, all Waterfordians were aware that the irascible old man had downed his last brandy and smoked his last cigar. Looking properly somber, clerks, secretaries and minor editors and administrators contemplated the luxury of an unforeseen holiday. Assuming a solemnity that befitted the occasion, top-echelon administrators contemplated the luxury of having a free hand at last. Here and there, on all levels, there were actually a few employees who felt a genuine sadness at the old man's passing. Gwen and Bill were numbered among those few. As editors of their magazines, they were expected to attend the funeral services; as individuals, they wanted to.

The service was to be held at ten a.m. on the first Wednesday of December, and Gwen and Bill arranged to meet a half-hour early a block from the chapel. It was a raw, bitter day. Murky gray clouds, heavy with the threat of snow or sleet, hung low over the city, blocking all view of the sun. As soon as Gwen emerged from the subway, an icy wind pounced on her, biting her cheeks, tossing back the skirt of her coat, threatening to rip away her green tam-o'-shanter. Pulling the cap more securely over her ears, she took a few deep breaths, then hunched her shoulders in preparation for a three-block battle with the wind. It was a ruthless, capricious adversary, lying in ominous wait for a few seconds, then suddenly attacking from the side or from behind. The icy forages it made against her front-line defenses of bent head and hunched shoulders brought tears to her eyes and took her breath away. Pushing on, Gwen tried to overcome the onslaught by playing a game she'd made up in her childhood for days such as this one: *If I can just get past this next doorway, the wind will die down,* she told herself. Then: *If I can make it to the corner, the going will be easier. . . . If I can manage to cross the street. . . .* And so on.

She had been resorting to versions of that game more and more over the past weeks: In the office, when she submerged herself in her work; at home, when she willed herself to block out her parents' quarrels. Over and over, she'd tell herself that if she could just get through that day, everything would be all right; tomorrow would be better—tomorrow, it wouldn't hurt so much when she thought of Paul.

But tomorrow never came. Instead of waning, her pain increased. Every morning, the feeling of dread that washed over her after a fitful, restless sleep was just a little colder. Every day, her leaden heart was that much heavier, that much more difficult to carry around. There was a constant pain in her throat caused by all the lumps she had to swallow back, and her eyelids felt taut and strained from their endless vigil against tears. Even worse than the ragged pain was the dull, aching hopelessness that always followed in its wake.

It was that numbness that enveloped her now as she pushed her way through the wind to her destination. She found Bill huddled in a doorway in a futile effort to escape the cold.

"Have you been waiting long?"

"It only seems that way. Besides, I've been told that blue is a good color for me." He stepped out of his shelter and took her arm. "I'd suggest coffee, but it's getting late."

She nodded, and they struggled with the wind the rest of the way in silence.

At the chapel, they entered the family room first to pay their condolences to the brothers Waterford. Standing together, dressed in almost identical black suits, the three brothers looked like an aging vaudeville group halfheartedly awaiting a cue to go into their act. As she approached them, Gwen half-expected them to extend their right hands and nod their heads in unison, perhaps even break into a soft-shoe. There was no sign of tears, grief, or even moderate sadness on their impassive faces. But then, there was no reason for such emotions. After all, Doc had not taken the Waterford power, money, and prestige with him.

With his guarantee climbing as it had been, Bill was immediately recognized by the brothers, but he had to remind them of Gwen's identity. Then, with sincerity, Gwen and Bill told the brothers how sorry they were.

"Thank you," Archer said, extending a limp hand.

"Yes, we'll all miss him," Bruce mumbled vaguely, his mind obviously elsewhere.

"Good of you to come," Charles said, his gaze managing to elude them.

After a few words with the Waterford wives, Gwen and Bill entered the chapel and viewed the remains.

"Poor Doc," Gwen said, gazing down on the now-relaxed brow, the eyes that would never again open and shoot sparks, the mouth that would never again growl or laugh lustily.

"No," Bill said, "not poor Doc. Not really. He had a long life and a full one. He was a man who knew how to live every minute to its fullest. It's poor us—to have been robbed of his example." He touched Gwen's arm and led her to a pew.

On their way, they exchanged subdued greetings with other Waterfordians, who had automatically arranged themselves from the front pews back in order of descending rank. Cam Eckhart, whose status as editor of Waterford's prestige men's magazine should have placed him in the fourth pew, behind the editors of the more lucrative and prestigious paperback-book divisions in the third pew, but in front of Gwen, Bill, Neil Mennen and Nolan West in the fifth, had managed to insinuate himself in the second pew between Jason Bart and a vice-president. Having assumed the grave countenance befitting the occasion, he carried on an animated business conversation with the vice-president, managing to tear himself away from it only long enough to nod to Gwen and to cut Bill.

At the rear of the chapel, ignored by the others, sat the few true Waterfordian mourners—a little handful of elderly, long-since-retired men who were all that remained of Doc's original employees. There, age and death having leveled all ranks between them, two of Doc's first editors sat in easy comradery with his first mail clerk and his first janitor.

As they slipped into their pew, Bill nodded toward Cam. "He's always at it, isn't he? The paperback boys look ready to jump through their skins."

Gwen sighed and sat back. "Of all places for office politics to rear its ugly head! It's a desecration."

"You'll find that ugly head anyplace you have office people. The desecration is having office people here at all. Even the two of us, as fond of Doc as we were, don't belong here. Only family and friends, or that sad little group back there—people who had strong emotional ties with him—belong near him at a time like this. They're the ones who come for the dead—to take one last look, to say a final good-by. The rest come only for the living—out of duty, or worse, to see and be seen. Doc would have known that. If he could, I'm sure he would tell us all to get the hell out."

"You're right, of course," Gwen whispered. "But then, funerals have always been more for the living than for the dead."

They cut off their conversation to nod to a few other co-workers who were making their way to their pews. Andrea Langford, looking as though she had stepped from one of her beauty pages, was among them. Andrea's beauty and grace seemed the same as ever on the surface, yet over the past few months, Gwen had been aware of a significant, though almost imperceptible, change in her: Her model's bearing now seemed to be the result of conscious will rather than an innate grace, and more than once Gwen thought she had seen doubts and questions fleetingly poke their heads above the thin ice of a glance that had once held only frozen certainty. The most noticeable and puzzling change, however, had been Andrea's evasion of all questions about Marge, the former light of her life. Now, nodding woodenly to the others in the pew, Andrea took a seat at the far end.

At last, the chapel filled, the service began. Genuinely fond of Doc, Gwen had meant to listen to the prayers and the eulogy, but the minister's monotone could not penetrate her emotionally comatose state. The heavy fragrance of the many wreaths filled her lungs, and entered her bloodstream like a fast-acting depressant. The soft, deep tones of the organ music pumped in through hidden speakers seemed to seek her out and swirl slowly around her, as though enveloping her in a leaden shroud. Dully, her eyes sought out the now closed casket that held all that remained of a once vibrant, throbbing life. She tried to rouse herself, to tear her gaze away—to look at the minister, at Bill, at Cam, at anyone—but she could not. It was as though she could see Doc's steely eyes staring out at her once more, and her own eyes remained riveted to them.

We're both dead, Gwen thought.

But I'm the lucky one, Doc seemed to mock from his casket. *They're burying me.*

Suddenly, the light pressure of Bill's hand on her arm made her realize that the service was over. She rose with the rest of the congregants as the mourners and the casket left the chapel.

"Are you all right?" Bill whispered.

She nodded.

But he kept his hand on her elbow as though to steady her as they made their way to the exit.

Outside, the cold, polluted city air was a welcome change from the heavily scented, oppressive atmosphere of the chapel. Not heading for the cemetery, Waterfordians clustered on the sidewalk in little groups, chatting. One of the groups drew them in, but Gwen managed to extricate herself, and she stood to one side, listlessly watching her co-workers.

There is no time in life when people feel more alive than immediately after attending a funeral—especially if they have no strong emotional ties to the deceased. The fact that they are able to gaze upon death, participate in the ceremonies that surround it, and then walk away under their own power, sends an awareness of self and being surging through every pore of their bodies—an awareness that for many borders on a sense of indestructibility, and for the rest results in at least a momentary affirmation of life that takes much of the sting from the unpleasant confrontation they have just had with its inevitable end.

Gwen observed this renewal of life in her co-workers as

they stood talking, their faces animated, their eyes sparkling, their gestures sharp and vigorous. Once, she might have felt such a resurgence too, but not anymore. Scanning the group, her eyes came to rest on Andrea Langford, standing tall and beautiful as she listened to Jason Bart expostulating. Andrea's gaze was vague and her gestures automatic, however, and Gwen wondered for a moment if Andrea numbered herself among the living dead too.

Gradually, the groups began to disperse, people walking off together or alone. Andrea walked toward the corner, and Jason Bart started across the street, obviously headed for the bar that was located midblock.

"That's not such a bad idea," Bill said, coming over to Gwen and nodding toward Jason's retreating back. "Want a drink?"

She shook her head.

"Coffee then?"

"No, thanks."

Harry Anders, Waterford's top circulation man, came over and clapped a hand on Bill's shoulder. "Say, Bill, I've been wanting to have a talk with you. How about a drink?"

"Go ahead," Gwen said, as Bill started to shake his head.

"You too, of course," Harry said halfheartedly, suddenly aware of Gwen's presence.

"Thanks, but I have to get home."

Skipper Harrison, who was standing a little way off, called to Harry.

"Be with you in a minute, Bill," Harry said, and went over to Skipper.

"The hell with him," Bill said. "Let him talk business on business hours. Let me take you for a drink. You look like you could use one."

"I don't want one. Really."

"Then I'll walk you to the subway."

"I'd really rather you didn't. I feel like being alone."

He pushed his glasses up on his nose, his eyes taking her measure. "Sometimes that's the worst thing to be."

"Bill!" Harry called over.

Forcing a smile, Gwen averted her eyes from Bill's searching gaze. "Go ahead," she said. "That's the future calling to Waterford's brightest rising star."

"You're sure you're okay?"

"I'm fine. Go on now. Give my love to Shari and the kids when you get home." Mustering her energy, she managed a brisk walk halfway to the corner. Then, sure he wasn't watching her any longer, she slowed down.

Across the street, she paused for a moment to watch the cars in the funeral cortege, which had finally lined up, begin their procession to the cemetery.

"So long, Doc," she whispered, as the gleaming hearse passed by.

Some people, she mused, had to wait until they died to be chauffeured in a Cadillac. Not Doc. He had ridden in the best cars, lived in the best houses, known the best people. He had taken life in both hands and forced it into his own mold. He had lived every moment that he breathed.

And what will people think about me when my hearse passes? Gwen wondered. *That I've been dead since I was thirty-one, and alive for only a few weeks before that?*

The wind had died down, but the cold still nipped around her like an angry little dog who had delusions of being a ferocious bear. Too numb to notice it, Gwen started off toward the subway again, walking so slowly she might have been a funeral procession of one. It seemed to her that the rest of her life stretched before her like the grim, gray street she was treading. Like the street, which had no purpose except to go from one river to another across Manhattan, her life too had no purpose but to go from birth to death, in the meantime providing a thoroughfare along which the Waterford brothers could tread, adding to their millions, and her parents could scurry, indulging their weaknesses. It didn't seem fair. But then, life wasn't fair, was it? She smiled sadly to herself. If Paul had been there, he would have reminded her of that quickly enough.

Oh, Paul! she thought. *Why did it have to end before it even began? Why did we bring ourselves to the gates of heaven only to slam them in our own faces?*

But, of course, he'd been right: There was no other way.

Staying in hotels would have debased their love, and they would have ended by despising each other. At least by breaking off as they did, they had left their love unharmed. But not their hearts.

She paused for a moment at the top of the subway stairs. Then slowly, reluctantly, she began to descend them, as though they were a ladder that led to a bottomless pit of despair, the lonely, joyless hell in which she must spend the rest of her days.

"Down," her feet seemed to say as they hit against the metal grating of the steps. "Down, down, down."

Tightening her hand on the railing, she willed herself to continue the descent. *Go down*, she told herself. *Down, because Paul was right. Down, because there is no other way.*

Abruptly, she stopped, as a memory that had been blurred until now suddenly came into focus with a painful vividness. She saw Paul's face as it had been in their last moment together, the lines seeming to deepen, the eyes so full of love and pain. And she heard his words, loud and sharp and clear.

He had not said: *There is no other way.* Those were her words—and her interpretation of his. What he had said was: *Not this way.*

Another way, then?

Of course, another way! One Paul, who knew her so well, perceived that she would have to recognize herself if there were to be any hope of it succeeding. Before she could walk with him, she'd have to throw away her crutches and learn to walk alone.

A warm rush of musty air came up from the subway as a train pulled into the station. A few people brushed past her on their way to the upper regions of the earth. Still Gwen stood on the stairway as though transfixed. Inside her immobile body, however, there was a bustle of activity. Her mind was working like a frenzied teletype, and the messages it was conveying activated her pulses to joyous speeds. She felt like a prisoner on death row who has suddenly been handed a reprieve. She longed to run up and down the stairs in a burst of exuberance, but settled for a sharp tug of her hat into place over her ears and a quick dart back to the street.

Once back on the sidewalk, she took a deep breath of frigid air, then headed toward a drugstore-luncheonette she had passed on her way.

From the drugstore, she called her mother, and told her not to expect her for lunch.

"But I made a nice pot of soup!" Agnes protested. "I'll keep some warm for you."

"Don't bother," Gwen insisted, a new note of determination in her voice. "I may not be home for dinner either."

"But—"

"I'll see you later, Mother. Much later. Good-by."

She bought a copy of *The Times*, and ordered a cup of coffee. Then, ignoring the headlines, she opened the newspaper to the classified-advertisement section and began to study the columns listed under the heading: "Apartments Unfur.—Manhattan."

Three ads looked promising. The first apartment had been rented by the time she arrived on the scene. The second, a luxury apartment with rooms as small as closets and closets so small they seemed not to exist, she turned down, realizing that the only luxury it had to offer was its astronomical rent. The third apartment, three sunny, high-ceilinged rooms in a renovated brownstone in the East Sixties, she fell in love with and rented on the spot.

The remainder of the afternoon she spent in the delightful task of going from store to store, choosing essential furniture. That accomplished, she exchanged a dollar for a handful of dimes, found a phone booth, and settled down to the not-so-pleasant task of informing her sister, Nora, of her plans.

Two years older than Gwen, Nora had been a rebellious child, refusing to cringe before Barney's growls and Agnes's whines. As soon as she had been graduated from high school, she had eloped with Earl Richards of the football team and settled in New Jersey, where Earl got a job driving a truck. Earl was now a dispatcher, and they lived comfortably in their own home with their two boisterous boys. Nora's contact with her parents was limited to rare phone calls and rarer duty visits. She frequently invited Gwen out for weekends, however, to baby-sit with her boys, while she and Earl took off for a few days of fun and relaxation at luxury hotels. Because she was so fond of her nephews, Gwen never let Nora know that she was aware Nora was taking advantage of her. She was also aware that Nora was taking advantage of her by allowing her to take care of their parents unaided all these years. Up to this moment it had never really mattered; perhaps she'd even unconsciously welcomed the barrier her responsibility had built around her. But now she had outgrown that need, and she was determined to leap the barrier, clearing it by a considerable margin.

Nora listened silently as Gwen told her of her decision to live on her own, and as she suggested that the two of them chip in to supplement their parents' meager social security checks, which would never come close to paying their expenses. Then, as though she had a list taped to the wall by the telephone for just such emergencies, Nora began to enumerate all the overwhelming expenses she and Earl had: mortgage payments, taxes, car payments, food, clothing, gas and electricity, summer camp for the boys, Danny's braces, Robbie's tuba lessons . . . .

Gwen, however, was prepared too. "You poor kid!" she sympathized. "I hadn't realized things were so bad. Look, when I get home tonight, I'll explain it all to Mom and Dad. I'm sure they won't mind giving up the apartment and moving into that lovely spare room you have. I'll have them packed and ready by the weekend. If Earl can't drive in to pick them up, I'll rent a car and drive them out to you myself. Don't worry about a thing."

"Well, let's not be hasty."

Gwen could almost see the wheels in Nora's mind spinning around.

"I mean, the folks are so old, a change like that might not be good for them. I—I'll talk to Earl. Maybe we can cut down somewhere so we can scrape up enough to help them keep their own place."

"You're sure now?" Gwen was all sweetness and solicitousness. "Because I'm not going to let you make any unnecessary sacrifices. The minute it appears that it's too much of a struggle for you to keep up your end, I'll have them packed and out to you. It will be no bother at all."

"Oh, no!" Nora said nervously. "Earl's really a good manager. I'm sure he'll be able to come up with something!"

"All right then. But remember, I can always have them there in a jiffy."

As Gwen hung up, a feeling of power and freedom unlike any she had ever known surged through her. She rushed from the phone booth, almost drunk on this never-before-tasted elixir. Rather than sobering her, the cold wind whipped her to greater heights, and in a burst of exuberance and prodigality, she hailed a cab, which she took to her doctor's office to keep the appointment she had phoned for earlier in the afternoon. By the end of the day, she would be on the Pill.

Chapter Eight

It was not the fact that her current employers might have frowned upon her going that kept Nadine Osgood from attending Doc Waterford's funeral; she would never tolerate company-dictated policy on personal matters, and now that she was no longer in the employ of the Waterford sons, the admiration she felt for Doc could be labeled only as purely personal. It was, instead, the fact that she had an appointment scheduled with Horton Norwich, the president of Norwich-McAllister, at the very moment that Doc's funeral service was scheduled to begin. Old Doc, she realized as she set out for Horton's office, would have been the first to recognize that, between the hours of nine and five, business came first.

Horton Norwich was a tall, thin man in his mid-sixties whose hair was too dark and thick to be genuine, and whose eyes were too sharp to let any advantage pass. McAllister having died some five or six years before, Horton ruled the N-M empire of paperback books and pulps and slick magazines alone from the penthouse located atop the N-M Building. Nadine was ushered into his presence by a male secretary whose burly build hinted at possible sideline duties as a bodyguard.

Horton's bright blue eyes met Nadine's the instant she crossed the threshold. "Come in, Nadine. Sit down."

Furnished with elegantly austere modern furniture in tones of gold, apricot, and brown, the room resembled a sitting room rather than an office, an appearance that was accentuated by the absence of a desk and the presence of an elaborate, well-stocked bar. Dressed as fashionably as the room was furnished, in a pale blue knit suit, royal blue shirt with

Love After Hours 151

white pinstripes, and a wide tie, patterned with blue, pink and green flowers, Horton sat in a high-backed gold chair, looking more like the court fop than the absolute monarch of a publishing empire. It was with a monarch's gracious yet condescending gesture that he indicated the chair at his right on the other side of the low glass-topped table.

Swiftly and gracefully, Nadine crossed the thick-carpeted floor and took the seat. "Thank you, Horton."

Nadine had risen as high and as fast as she had in the business world partly because she allowed no man to place her on a lower footing than himself. The moment a man addressed her by her first name, she made it immediately clear that the privilege was to be a mutual one or it was not to be taken at all.

Horton's eyes flickered at the sound of his Christian name, but he passed no comment, plunging, instead, into the subject of their meeting. "I don't know whether you are aware of it, but many of the magazines in our chain are not doing as well as the one you're editing."

An amused smile played about Nadine's lips. "Horton, if I weren't perceptive enough to be aware of the troubles of the other magazines—as well as to be aware of the fact that I am the reason why my own magazine isn't floundering—you wouldn't have asked me here."

He raised an eyebrow, his own lips curling in amusement. "Ralph Christie told me you didn't believe in beating about the bush."

Christie was the vice-president who had been delegated to lure Nadine away from Waterford by offering her the editorship of *Intimate Experiences* and hinting strongly that a greater opportunity was in store.

"It saves a great deal of time and leaves no room for misunderstandings."

"It's an attitude I admire." He leaned forward. "All right then. We'll cut the polite fencing. We both know the periodicals are slipping. Bob Richards, our editorial director, hasn't had a new idea since he decided to add a TV section to *Air Waves* twenty-five years ago. We need fresh blood in that post." He sat back, nonchalantly toying with the huge knot in his fashionable tie. "Of course, we don't know who else might be available in the field, but we want you to know that you're under consideration."

It was the greatest opportunity of her career, but not a single eyelash flicked over Nadine's eyes. "I've known that since I came to N-M. I think you're bush-beating again."

"Not at all. It's an important decision, and we want to wait until we are sure we have the right person."

"If you wait much longer, you may have fewer magazines to place under that person's authority."

Laughing, he rose and walked over to the bar. "You do cut through to the bone, don't you?"

"If I couldn't, you wouldn't be interested in me for the position."

Though his expression didn't change, it was obvious in his eyes that she'd gone up several notches in his estimation. "True." He raised a crystal decanter. "Drink?"

"That depends."

"On what?"

"Whether there's something to drink to. Are you going to make me a definite offer of the job?"

Smiling, he spread his hands. "All right. I'm making a definite offer."

Her heart quickened, but her face remained immobile. "On what terms?"

He seemed taken aback, as though he expected her to be so grateful that she would accept any terms the company offered. He blew out his cheeks and made deprecating little circles in the air with his right hand. "Of course, you'll be new at the job, and not having the experience of a man like Bob, you can't expect to command the salary he's making when you take over."

Laughing, she shook her head. "Oh, come now, Horton! There aren't that many editorial directors floating around the country. Every one of them was new at the job when he started. And do you really expect me to believe that I can't command the same salary as the man who's put you into the hole you expect me to pull you out of? If you want me, you'll pay me every cent you're paying Bob Richards, and at the end of a year, when you've seen what I can do for you, you'll pay me a great deal more."

He was obviously shocked. "Most women would be ecstatic with this position at any pay."

The amused smile never left her lips, nor did her eyes waver from his. "Oh, really? Then perhaps that's why you were discerning enough to offer it to *me*."

For a moment, their eyes held. Then Horton laughed. "Christ! Christie was right when he singled you out as the one we need. The job's yours—on your terms."

She walked over and shook the hand he held out to her. "Now," she said, "I'll take that drink."

For the rest of the day she felt much taller than her four-foot-eleven. She had made it—all the way to the top. She longed to call her husband, Mitchell, and share the news, but she could not risk using the office phone for the announcement. Over their drinks, Horton had made it clear that the promotion could not take effect until the end of January when many other changes were to be instituted, and that it be kept strictly confidential until then.

As she left the office that evening, her mind went back over the events of the day. She had done very well for herself, she thought with pride. It had taken her less than twenty years to reach the top of her profession—surely, for a woman, that constituted a record. She smiled inwardly, trying to imagine how the news would be taken at Waterford. The Waterford brothers and Jason Bart would probably be furious because she knew so much about the competition. Well, it was their own fault. She had gone to them asking for more to do, and they had turned her down, implying that, as a woman, she could expect no more than the editorship she already had, and that she should be grateful for that much. Just as they could not understand that a woman might want to rise higher, they could also not admit that she might deserve to.

Doc, on the other hand, would have understood. In the old days, when he'd still had a firm hand in the Waterford business, he had recognized her abilities. If he could have known what had taken place in Horton's office, he would have been pleased for her, she was sure. It was a pity she had had to miss his funeral; she would have liked to say good-by. Pulling her coat tighter against the frigid wind, she squinted up at the first stars in the purple twilight, as if half expecting to see the irascible old fellow's soul flit by.

Not wanting to spoil her euphoric mood, she decided to take a taxi home rather than become part of the snarling, jostling crowd on the subway or the bus. She had the driver drop her a few blocks from her midtown apartment house, so that she could pick up a bottle of champagne and some flowers for the table.

"Good evening, ma'am. A frigid night," Mike, the doorman, greeted her as he swung open the entranceway door when she finally arrived home.

"Yes, bitter. It's good to be inside." She had hardly noticed the weather, but it was the only subject Mike ever discussed with the tenants. She hurried through the marble-and-mirror-walled lobby to the mail alcove, where she extracted some bills and a few Christmas cards from her box.

Upstairs in her apartment, the delicious aroma of *coq au vin* greeted her. Sally, her housekeeper, always prepared dinner before leaving for the day. Nadine put the wine in the refrigerator and arranged the flowers in a crystal bowl.

It was not quite a quarter to six when she finished setting the table. Since Mitchell had told her that morning that he would be home a little late, she decided to use the extra time to bathe and change into something more festive. After luxuriating in a steamy bubble bath, she put on a low-cut lavender hostess gown that accentuated her fair skin and dark hair. She brushed her medium-length hair until it gleamed. Then, on impulse, she went out to the dining alcove and removed one of the yellow roses from the centerpiece she had arranged earlier. Back at her mirror, she combed her hair away from her face on the left side and fastened it with the rose and a bobby pin.

Before leaving the bedroom, she took a long look at herself in the full-length mirror on her closet door. The lovely, sensual woman who stared back at her was very different from the starkly tailored, efficient career woman who had

Love After Hours

entered the apartment a short time before. Nadine attributed her success in life to her ability and determination to keep her career and her private life separate.

Her eyes sparkling with warmth and anticipation, she ran her hands over the silky material of her gown, straightening its folds, giving it a tug at the waistline so that its décolletage would slip a little lower. Maybe that would do the trick, she thought. Mitchell seemed to need a little inspiration lately.

Sighing, she went out to the kitchen to warm the chicken and put the dressing on the salad, still thinking about their waning sex life. It puzzled her. Of course, after nearly sixteen years of marriage, she didn't expect a honeymoon pace of six times a week and twice on Sunday, but she and Mitchell had always been a passionate couple, and his sudden drop in ardor was disturbing. For months now, they never made love unless she initiated it, and it wasn't the same as it had been before. As enterprising as she was in the business world, she never felt truly comfortable with being aggressive in bed, and she could tell that Mitchell's responses were, for the most part, mechanical. It couldn't be age; at thirty-nine and forty-seven, they were in the prime of life. Certainly, the older she became, the more she enjoyed sex, and she couldn't believe that it could be different for a man. It was probably a simple matter of overwork. For the past six months, Mitchell's firm had been making more and more demands on his time; he'd been expected to stay late to file reports, and even to see clients after hours and on weekends. Well, now that she had a promotion coming up, maybe he'd consider making a change too. No job was worth sacrificing so much time and the pleasures that time might bring.

A half hour later, realizing that Mitchell was going to be later than either of them had anticipated, she turned off the heat under the chicken and returned the salad to the refrigerator. After putting some Mozart on the stereo, she curled up with a book in one of the high-backed winged chairs that Mitchell used to say dwarfed her diminutive size so much that she looked like a doll. It had been a long time since he'd said things like that.

Several unheard records and unread chapters later, she

heard Mitchell's key in the lock. It was almost eleven o'clock. She stood up, her body stiff, and hurried to the door.
"Hi."
"Hi."

Mitchell kissed her, but his heart didn't seem to be in it. Tall, with the build of an athlete and the face of a movie idol, he usually looked much younger than his age, despite his graying, sandy-colored hair. But tonight he looked tired and drawn. He hung his coat in the hall closet and turned away, his shoulders slumping as though they held an invisible but heavy pack.

Nadine's heart lurched as she watched him. She loved him so much! She couldn't bear to see how he was killing himself with work. Maybe before she took over her new job, they could arrange to get away for a while. Cannes would be nice. Or, perhaps, Italy. Even if it were only for a few days. . . .

"You must be starving," she said.

He shrugged. "No. I grabbed a bite downtown." They passed the dining alcove, and he noticed the table. "You shouldn't have waited dinner. I thought I told you ages ago that if I'm delayed past seven, you should eat."

She shrugged as though it didn't matter, but a wave of disappointment washed over her. "I kept thinking you'd be home any minute." Impulsively, she took his hand and led him to the table. "Whatever you had, I'm sure it wasn't much. It's too late for Sally's *coq au vin*, but how about some cheese and crackers and champagne?"

"Champagne?"

"Mmm." She smiled mysteriously. "We have a celebration coming up."

His own smile was a little weak, but he sat down. "I've never been known to say no to a celebration."

Out in the kitchen, Nadine put the chicken in the refrigerator and arranged a tray with crackers, cheese and the bottle of champagne. By the time she returned to the table, her disappointment had disappeared. Late or early, what difference did it make? Mitchell was home now. That was all that mattered. Being together was all that ever mattered.

Glowing, she handed him the bottle with a flourish. "Will you do the honors?"

"My pleasure."

He had removed his jacket and rolled up his sleeves. As though hypnotized, she watched the muscles in his arms quiver as he manipulated the cork. How she longed for him to pull her into those arms the way he used to, with all the roughness of passion and the tenderness of love, and press her head tight against his massive chest, where she'd rub her cheek in the short, crisp curls of hair and listen to his pounding heart. Tonight it would happen. She could feel it. They'd drink their champagne, laugh and talk his tiredness and tension away. When they went to bed—

With a loud pop the cork flew across the room. Quickly, Nadine grabbed a glass and held it out to catch the frothy liquid cascading down the bottle.

"Did you get any on you?" she asked, laughing.

Mitchell laughed too, as he brushed at a couple of damp spots on his trouser leg. "Who can complain about a shower of champagne?" He filled his own glass. "Now, what are we drinking to?"

Nadine's smile and gaze softened. "To what we always drink to—to us and our dreams that are always coming true."

Giving a little nod, he raised his glass, but his eyes didn't seem to be seeing the same memories hers were.

"Do you remember," she asked, holding her glass out, "when we used to drink with arms linked, the French way?"

He smiled but made no move to complete the gesture, saying, "That was a long time ago. We were kids then."

Slowly, Nadine brought her arm back and lowered her glass to the table. "Not such kids. I was twenty-two and you were thirty when we met."

He gazed into his glass, as if expecting to find the image of those long-ago days. "All of which places our youth even further behind us." He took a long swallow.

"We're far from old, Mitchell."

He quickly withdrew the hand she was covering with her own to reach for a cracker and some cheese.

"Aside from the usual toast," he said, as though the past had never been mentioned, "what's the special occasion that prompted this?" He nodded toward the champagne.

With a teasing smile, she paused just long enough to heighten suspense, then said, "You're looking at Norwich-McAllister's new editorial director in charge of periodicals."

It took a moment for the news to penetrate. Then Mitchell beamed, emitting what might have been a sigh of pleasure or relief.

"Congratulations, Naddie! That's marvelous! Really marvelous! I always knew you'd get to the top." He refilled their glasses and raised his. "To the new editorial director."

Glowing with pleasure, Nadine drank, thanking heaven, as she had so often throughout their marriage, that she had a man like Mitchell—a man who supported her ambitions and believed in her abilities just as she believed in his, a man too mature to feel threatened by her having an identity and life of her own, a man who loved her too much to see her as a rival in the business world. True, their fields were different—he was in securities—but he never resented the fact that her rise had been slightly faster than his, and it would never occur to him to be jealous of the fact that she would soon be earning a great deal more money than he was. Each was ambitious enough and capable enough to want and to gain his own success—and sensitive enough and wise enough to recognize that success was meaningless unless they had each other.

Her eyes sparkled. "Oh, Mitchell! We'll be able to do so much more now. We'll buy that weekend house on the bay, and the kind of boat you've always wanted. We'll get to Europe more, and—"

"Hey, slow down!" His tone was gentle, but his laughter seemed a little forced. Once again he extracted his hand from beneath the one she had impetuously closed over it and reached for some cheese and crackers. "I'm hungrier than I thought," he explained, yet he seemed to be chewing and swallowing with difficulty. "Now tell me more about the job. When does it begin? What will you be doing?"

So, while he kept her glass filled, she told him about the meeting with Horton, the changes that would be taking place at the company, the responsibilities she would be expected to take on. Every time she tried to bring the conversation back to what her promotion would mean to the two of them, he seemed to have another question about the job itself.

Finally, stretching a little, Mitchell stood up. "It's really great," he said. "I can't tell you how happy I am for you—and how proud. But it's getting late. I think it's time we turned in. I don't know about you, but I'm exhausted."

The disappointment she felt at his abrupt termination of their celebration quickly turned to a flush of anticipation when he insisted on clearing up by himself, telling her to get ready for bed. Evidently, he wasn't too tired to want her as much as she wanted him.

Hurrying into the bedroom, she took mental stock of her large collection of lingerie and decided on a full-length black gown whose sheerness belied the innocence of its cut. Quickly, she slipped into it and a matching peignoir, then turned down the bed. She checked her hair and lipstick in the mirror, trailed drops of Crêpe de Chine along her arms, throat, thighs, between her breasts, behind her ears and knees.

She listened for Mitchell's footsteps, but heard only the sounds of his rattling around in the kitchen. How long could it take a man to put a few dishes in the dishwasher and return crackers and cheese to the cupboard and refrigerator? For the first time since she was a bride, she felt awkward and ill at ease. If she got into bed, the seductive sheerness of her gown would be wasted under the covers. But she couldn't just stand there in the middle of the room. Sitting down on the occasional chair with a book would look artificial too. Finally, she opted for brushing her hair at the vanity.

Her arm was aching by the time Mitchell walked in.

"Still up?" he asked, barely glancing her way. He hung his jacket in his closet and removed his tie, yawning. "God! I'm exhausted."

Her heart sinking a little, she put the brush down. Why did he keep telling her how tired he was!

He began unbuttoning his shirt. She watched him, as fascinated as a virgin. When, she wondered, would the designers of men's so-called sexy clothes like tank shirts and body suits learn that nothing turns women on more than a dress shirt with sleeves rolled up and collar open?

Once again he yawned. "It's been a long day."

"But a good one." She walked over and put her arms around him, pressing her cheek and breasts hard against his chest. "Oh, Mitchell! Life has been so good to us. And now it's going to be even better."

He brought his arms up from his sides and placed them loosely around her.

Startled by the halfheartedness of the gesture, she pulled away, studying his face. "You *are* tired, aren't you?" she asked with concern, noting the lines of strain traced on his face, the weariness in his eyes.

Nodding, he took advantage of her own loosened grip to move away.

"You've been working too hard, darling. You need a rest," she insisted, slipping around so that she could be in front of him again. "Let's arrange to take a week or two off before I start this new job at the end of January. We'll go to the Riviera, the Caribbean—wherever you say."

He shook his head abruptly. "No. It can't be done."

"Then we'll do it on weekends. We can jet down to Puerto Rico or the Bahamas or—"

"No." His jaw set, he took his robe and pajamas from his closet.

"But, darling! You're overworked—so tired all the time. Surely, you could arrange to take some time—"

His face had blanched, and his hands gripped his night clothes so tightly that his knuckles showed white and shiny beneath the flesh. "No," he cut her off. "It can't be done. Let it go at that, will you?"

But she couldn't let it go. Not when she saw the difficulty he was having keeping himself under control. *What have they been putting him through at that office?* she wondered.

Her heart aching for him, she reached out and put her hand on his arm. "Darling, don't you see what all this strain has been doing to you—to us? You need a rest. You have to get away."

He jerked away from her touch as though he had been burned. His hands trembling with rage, he flung his robe and pajamas on the bed.

"Yes, I need to get away!" he cried. "But from you, goddammit! From you!"

For a moment she stood transfixed, her ears ringing as though his words were enormous cymbals that had crashed above her head. Aware that her thought processes had been slowed by the lateness of the hour and the champagne, she couldn't be sure that she had heard him right—or, if she had, she couldn't be sure what his words meant. Shaking her head did not clear it of confusion.

"From me?" she said weakly.

His eyes flashed, his hands clenched. "Yes, yes! From you! It's over. It's been over for a long time now. I want a divorce."

The words cracked against her like shots from a rifle, and she reeled back against the dresser, grabbing on to it for support.

"Divorce?" She repeated the word hollowly, like a foreigner parroting meaningless sounds.

Seeing her reaction, his face paled. "Oh, hell!" He ran his hand through his hair. "Look, I didn't mean to throw it at you like that. It's just that I've been under a strain for months now. When you started on me about a vacation, something snapped."

Her face had gone ashen, and her entire body was trembling.

"Here," he said, taking her arm and leading her over to the occasional chair. "You'd better sit down."

She obeyed like a zombie, her eyes riveted to his face. It wasn't further orders she was awaiting, though, but further explanation.

For a moment he stood there, his brow furrowed, his chest heaving, trying to sort out his thoughts. Finally, he sighed and sank down on the edge of the bed, spreading his hands.

"There's no easy way to say it. I'm in love with someone else. I want to marry her."

At his first mention of divorce, her heart seemed to stop in mid-beat, all the blood in her body rushing back to that panic-stricken source of life, leaving her frozen and numb. Now, slowly, agonizingly, it began working again, every beat sending a pain knifing through her chest.

"Just like that," she said dully.

His eyes were sad but unflinching. "Just like that."

"To ask an old and very tired question—how long has this been going on?"

"Six, maybe eight months."

Pressing her hand between her breasts did nothing to relieve the pain. "My God! And all that time you let me believe nothing was wrong. How could you make me part of such a lie?"

"It wasn't a deliberate lie. At first, I didn't say anything because I was fighting what was happening to me, hoping I'd get over it. Then. . . ." He spread his hands, his voice trailing off.

"Then?" she prompted coldly.

He rose from the bed and began pacing the room, his hands in his pockets. "Well, Christ! It isn't the easiest announcement in the world to make. I kept putting it off. Finally, I decided I'd tell you after the first of the year. It just slipped out tonight. I hadn't meant for that to happen. I wanted to wait. I didn't want to ruin your Christmas."

"How very chivalrous of you! You didn't want to ruin my Christmas. The rest of my life isn't nearly so important as that one day, evidently. It's all right to ruin that."

"For God's sake!" He turned to her, his eyes pleading for understanding. "I didn't want this to happen. It just did. Try to understand!"

She jumped from the chair, her heart pounding, her voice shaking with anger and hurt. "You take eighteen years of my life and fling them back in my face, and tell me, 'Try to understand'? What do you want me to do?" She grasped the skirt of her nightgown and held it out, making a brief curtsy. "Bow and say, 'La, sir! You've been so very kind. Thank you ever so much'? And make a graceful exit? Not on your life!"

"I'm not asking the impossible. All I'm asking is that you try to view the situation calmly and sensibly."

"I find it difficult to be calm when my life is falling around me in a shambles, and I can make no sense out of the wreckage."

Her wave of indignation receded, leaving exposed the hollow hole of hurt it had been hiding. Pressing her trembling hands to her pounding temples, she turned her back so he would not see her tears. "How did it happen? Why did it happen? What did I do wrong?"

"It wasn't anything you did or didn't do," he insisted. "It was just something that happened—that's all. Something that none of us had any control over."

She didn't respond, but her back and neck stiffened, and her throat ached with the effort of controlling the sobs rising within her.

Mitchell moistened his dry lips. "Seeing each other every day as we did, I was in love with her for quite a while before I even realized it had happened. And then it was too late."

"Seeing each other every day?" Nadine turned back to him. "Is she someone you work with? Don't tell me she's your secretary!"

"No, no. She works in the tobacco shop in my building, the place where I buy my cigarettes."

Her eyes widened in surprise. "A shopgirl?"

"Christ! Don't talk like some snobbish character in a drawing-room melodrama. There's nothing degrading about her work."

"I'm sure there isn't anything degrading—about her work. I was surprised, that's all. Please don't let me keep you from the rest of your fascinating story."

He shrugged. "There's not much to tell. Elaine and I used to talk a bit when I dropped in for my cigarettes. It was refreshing to talk to her—she was so shy and sweet and good."

Nadine closed her stinging eyes and tried to swallow back the aching lump of nausea rising in her throat.

"I ran into her one evening when I was leaving the office. She said she was going home early, that she wasn't feeling well. She looked terrible too—not physically ill but upset. I offered to buy her a drink. Over that drink, she told me about herself." He brought his eyes back to Nadine and the present. "Oh, Naddie! She's really had a rotten life! She—"

Nadine's hand shot up like a traffic cop's. "Spare me the details. I'm sure I've read them a million times over in my magazine."

His face reddened. "You don't have to be so damned contemptuous. Her life has been hell!"

"And now she's making a hell of mine!" Her voice rose to meet the timbre of his own. "What am I supposed to do—embrace her and offer her my heartfelt sympathy?"

"All right, all right! Forget it!" Jamming his hands into his pockets, he turned his back.

For a moment she studied that massive back, trying not to remember how warm and solid it felt when she snuggled close to it in the night. Her vision blurred.

"I suppose she's very young and very beautiful," she said softly.

Shaking his head, he turned back to her. "Neither. Oh, she's younger than you, if that's what you're driving at, but she's far from being a kid. And as for beauty—" He shrugged. "What she has of it comes from inside. Between the two of you, you're the prettier, more intelligent one."

She gave a little shrug. "For all the good it's done me."

"It's done you a lot of good in many ways."

"Not in the only way that counts; it didn't hold you."

His eyes softening, he took her hands in his. "Naddie, Naddie! When you get down to it, what difference does it make? You're the most intelligent, self-sufficient woman I know. I've always admired you for that, and I always will. But the truth is that because you're that way, you don't need me. And because she isn't that way, Elaine does."

Pride told her to withdraw her hands, but they felt so good in his. "Do you really believe that I don't need you? That your love doesn't sustain me? That I don't treasure it above and beyond all else in my life?"

He dropped her hands. "But she needs me more."

Unconsciously, she wiped her palms against her nightgown, as though trying to eradicate his touch and his rejection of her. "That's not sufficient reason for a divorce."

"I love her," he said. "That's sufficient reason. I want to marry her and raise a family."

Her head snapped back as though he'd slapped her. "Raise a family? But you never wanted children!"

"I want them now."

"Now—when you're old enough to be a grandfather? Why

didn't you say something to me years ago? We could have worked something out. I wouldn't have minded having one or two, if I had known you wanted them."

"But I didn't want children then. I want them now."

"All right—even now I'm not so old that I can't...." But her voice trailed off at the look in his eyes. It wasn't her children he wanted. He wanted Elaine's. She turned away.

He read her thoughts. "Naddie, don't look like that. You'll find someone else."

She whirled on him. "How can you say that without blushing? You, who admit you're marrying a girl younger than I am? You, who know damn well that all the marriageable men your age and older are chasing after girls just out of diapers? You met me when I was twenty-two, married me when I was twenty-four, and now that you've used up all the good years men consider a woman to have, you're throwing me back into the sea. Don't try to kid either me or yourself that there are rescue parties waiting around for fortyish wives whose husbands have tired of them. It's strictly a case of sink or swim."

"You're exaggerating," he insisted. "You're an attractive, intelligent woman. There are plenty of men who would be interested in you."

"Like you were—for a while? Thanks, but I'm not interested in short-run relationships."

"Nearly sixteen years of marriage isn't exactly a short run."

"It is, when you started out expecting a lifetime."

"Believe me, I never meant this to happen." His voice was edged with impatience.

"If that's supposed to be comforting, it isn't."

"Naddie, please! They were good years. We shouldn't let them end in bitterness."

His face had softened, and she could tell he was remembering the good times. She looked long and hard at his face, as though trying to memorize for all time the deep blue of his eyes, the sensuous curve of his lips, the little lines that time had etched around his eyes, the gray it had trailed through his hair.

"They didn't have to end at all," she said at last. "The

choice was yours, not mine." She turned away. "I think you'd better go."

"But we have to talk. There are things to be settled."

She held herself rigid, fighting the temptation to turn back to face him. Her lips trembled as she spoke, but she kept her voice in perfect control. "There's nothing left to say that our lawyers can't say for us."

"Naddie—"

"Good-by, Mitchell."

He hesitated. "Will you be all right?"

"It's a little late to worry about that, don't you think?"

The room was so quiet for a moment that she could almost hear the rumble of his thoughts. Then she heard him walk to the bedroom closet for his jacket, and then to the hall closet for his coat.

The soft sound of the outer door closing penetrated her breast like a shot. She stiffened, then collapsed on the bed, her body convulsed in sobs.

When she awoke in the morning, she found her head pillowed on his pajamas.

At work, it took all her will to suppress her inner turmoil. She could not afford to let the merest vestige of pain escape and intrude upon her business-world image. That image was all she had left now, and she had to depend upon it to see her through the rest of her life. The only concessions she made to her personal problems during office hours were a call to her lawyer for an appointment for the following week, and a decision to leave a half hour early.

She took a cab to Mitchell's office building. She had to see Elaine for herself.

An aroma of tobacco almost overpowered her as she opened the shop door. It was evidently the calm period before the five-o'clock rush, and the store was almost empty of customers. A woman was browsing among the pipe racks, and in a corner, a young man was inspecting a hookah. The only salespersons visible were a man of about sixty, probably the proprietor, and a dumpy woman whose back was turned as she stocked some shelves. Obviously, it was Elaine's day off. Sighing in disappointment, Nadine turned to go, wondering if she'd have the courage to come again.

"May I help you?"

The proprietor's voice startled her, and her thoughts scattered in all directions like frightened birds. She drew a long, calming breath.

"I'm not sure. I want to buy something for an uncle. A friend of mine told me you have a very helpful saleswoman here—Elaine? Is she gone for the day?"

"Not at all. Elaine!" he called, and moved away.

As the dumpy woman at the rear of the store turned and approached, Nadine grabbed onto the counter for support. She had fully believed Mitchell had been lying when he'd said his mistress was neither young nor beautiful, but now she saw that he'd been serious. *Drab* was the only word that could adequately describe the chubby, thirtyish woman walking toward her. Her medium-brown hair hung straight to her shoulders where it merged with a plain, shapeless brown dress. Her scrubbed, unmade-up, round-cheeked face was wholesome, but far from pretty. She seemed out of place behind the counter, looking as though she had just been called in from hanging out the wash in the backyard or taking home-baked cookies from the oven in the kitchen. Her eyes were her only truly attractive feature. They were large, brown, and sad—the kind of eyes men loved to have beaming up at them filled with trust and worshipful adoration.

"May I help you?" Her voice was soft and shy, as though she doubted that she could be of any real help.

"Yes. I'd like to buy some pipe tobacco." The cool, detached expression on Nadine's face and her calm voice belied the icy tremor that had taken hold of her heart.

"Any special brand?"

"Oh, I don't know." She searched around in her mind for something that would keep up the conversation. "Do you have the blend Bertrand Russell smoked? The friend I'm buying it for is a great admirer of his."

Elaine rolled up her chocolate-colored eyes. "Bertrand Russell?" She paused a moment, mulling over the name, then shook her head. "No, I don't think he shops here."

"Well, actually, he's dead. It's just that he was a famous pipe smoker, and I thought you might know his brand."

Elaine smiled and looked almost pretty. "People get famous for all sorts of crazy things these days, don't they? Wait a minute. I'll ask Mr. Sawyer if he knows."

"No, don't bother." Nadine was embarrassed for Elaine and more than a little ashamed of herself for baiting her. "Just give me something you recommend."

"Does he like aromatic or mild?"

Nadine shrugged. "Mild."

"Would you like a pound tin?"

"Fine." She was beginning to feel closed in, and was ready to take anything to get away.

Elaine turned her back and stretched her chubby arms up to reach one of the tins on the shelf behind her. "Many of our customers like this," she said, extending a bright yellow can with a picture of a sailboat on it. "It's from Holland."

"I'll take it."

"Will there be anything else?"

"No, thank you." She glanced over her shoulder. She wanted to get out of here. What if Mitchell should come in?

"Would you like me to gift-wrap it?"

"No, no. I'll do it myself."

With painful slowness, it seemed to Nadine, Elaine placed the tin in a bag, took her money and handed her her change.

"Thank you. Have a nice evening." She smiled the same sweet, shy smile that must have gone straight to Mitchell's heart. It went straight to Nadine's heart too—and through it like a stiletto.

Clenching her teeth against the venom rising inside her, Nadine ducked her head and hurried out the door. She jumped into a cab that was caught in traffic and gave the driver her home address. Settling back in her seat, she looked at the package in her hands. What was she going to do with a pound of tobacco? She shook her head. That was the least of her problems. What was she going to do with the rest of her life?

She closed her eyes over her tears, but she could not close out the vision of plump, plain, eager-to-please, but rather dull Elaine. How could a man like Mitchell fall for a woman like that—and how could a woman like that hold him? If Elaine were young and beautiful, or not so young but sexy, or strikingly intelligent, she could understand. But Elaine had nothing—nothing! No, Nadine corrected herself, Elaine had Mitchell, so she had everything. It was she herself who had nothing, who was nothing now.

"Lady, I said this is it," the cab driver called back a second time.

Startled, Nadine looked around. "Sorry. I must have been dreaming."

"Hope they were good dreams. My wife's a big dreamer too. Half the time she don't know where she's at. Specially if she's watching TV. Then you got to call and call if you want to say something to her. . . ."

His voice trailed on as Nadine rummaged in her purse for the fare. By the time she had slipped it through the slot in his bulletproof partition, Mike, the doorman, was peering at her through the window, waiting for her to unlock the door so that he could open it.

"Evening, ma'am. Bitter cold tonight."

"Yes, it is."

He hurried ahead of her in order to reach the door to the building first. He swung it open. "That's some wind out there. Brings tears to your eyes, don't it?"

Trying to smile, she blinked vigorously, but her eyes remained too bright. "Yes, wind does that to me." She shifted her purse and package and started past him, then turned back. "Do you smoke a pipe, Mike?"

The shift away from the weather to a different topic of conversation startled him, and he reddened a little, flustered. "Well, gee! I used to—I mean, years ago. I mean, I haven't smoked one for years."

She thrust her package into his hands. "In case you decide to try it again," she said, and hurried away.

"Thank you, ma'am," Mike called after her. He opened the bag and gave its contents the same hopeless, helpless glance he gave to the hideous ties his mother-in-law sent him every Christmas. "Thank you very much."

Walking into her apartment was like entering a vacuum. The silence and the emptiness rushed at her throat like ravenous beasts who'd been lying in wait too long for their prey. Flashing on the lights did not make them disappear, but only pushed them back to their lairs in the corners, where they crouched, watching her every move with hungry eyes.

Her legs weakened when, hanging her coat in the hall closet, she discovered that Mitchell's hats, coats and heavy jackets were gone. She forced herself to walk into their bedroom and open his closet. It was empty.

A blinding knot of pain began working itself from her chest through her throat to the back of her eyes. Her hand clutched the doorknob, the whites of her knuckles glowing through her flesh, as she looked around the room. She didn't have to open his drawers to know that they were empty too. Her glance fell upon the bed in which they had slept and loved for nearly sixteen years. In all that time, though they'd moved to better apartments and bought better furniture, the bed had remained the same; it had been part of their marriage—a beautiful part—and though they weren't a sentimental couple they'd never once considered exchanging it for another. Now Mitchell had left it.

A patch of white stared back at her from the top of her pillow like a glaring hole cut into the rose-colored taffeta spread. It was an envelope with her name written across it in Mitchell's firm masculine scrawl. The letter it contained was brief and to the point: He'd taken his clothes. There were a few pieces of furniture he'd like—he listed them—which he was sure she would agree he was entitled to. He'd send some men for them tomorrow. Would she please tell Sally to let them in. He also supplied her with the name and phone number of the lawyer he had consulted, because he was sure she would rather consult the lawyer who had been handling their affairs as a couple for so long.

She stood staring at the paper until it began to tremble in her hands. Then she balled it up and let it drop to the floor.

So it was over. Really over. Until that moment, though she had not dared to admit it to herself, she had half hoped that he wasn't really serious about the divorce. But you don't collect all your clothes, send for your furniture, and consult a lawyer when you're not really serious. True, she had contacted a lawyer too. But she'd made her appointment for the next week, unconsciously praying that she'd be able to cancel it.

It's over, she told herself, pacing the room. *Over, over.* Tears streamed down her cheeks.

"Over." She tried the word out loud.

She wrung her hands, wincing with a sudden pain as her diamond wedding band—the only jewelry she wore except for a watch—cut into her flesh. Extending her left hand, she studied the ring, her tears making its diamonds shimmer and shoot forth little rainbow rays of light. She'd been married wearing a plain gold band, but on their fifth anniversary, when things were going well for both of them, Mitchell had insisted on giving her the diamond ring. "Diamonds last forever," he'd told her as he'd slipped it on her finger, "like our love."

He'd been half right: Her love would last forever, but his...

With a violent tug, she pulled the ring from her finger and hurled it across the room.

"Liar!" she cried.

And then, as they had been threatening to do since she walked through the door, her legs caved in beneath her.

Chapter Nine

On the whole, Barney and Agnes took the news of Gwen's decision to move well. As Gwen had expected, Barney reacted with cursing and grumbling, and Agnes with whining and tears. As she had not expected, they did not indulge in histrionics to more than the usual degree. Perhaps that was because curses and whines multiply and thrive only in the fertile ground provided by the reaction of their recipient, and, having found her emotional independence at last, Gwen no longer needed to respond.

After making her announcement, she sat back and patiently waited for the attack to end, Barney's threats and Agnes's tears having no more effect on her than a barrage of spitballs fired at the Empire State Building. It was not that she did not care. It was that having cared too much and too long, she no longer *could* care. When Barney's roaring lowered to a growl and Agnes's whining wound down to a whimper, she quietly but firmly outlined her plans for herself and for them. Agnes's attempt at another feeble protest evoked only an indulgent smile and the calm announcement that the matter was closed: She was moving; Barney and Agnes would be provided for; there was nothing more to say.

Agnes, of course, *did* have more to say, and in the two weeks preceding Gwen's departure, she said it often and emphatically. Gently but persistently, Gwen ignored her. Old habits die hard, however, and even as Gwen was about to pass through the door for the last time as a resident of their apartment, Agnes was still trying to whine her into submission.

"I don't know what's got into you," she said. "Everything

was going so well. I thought you were back to your old self again. And then—boom!—you had to go and take an apartment. As if I can't take care of you anymore!" She wiped her eyes.

"I never questioned your ability to take care of me, Mother. I've simply decided that it's time I took care of myself. I've been a grown woman now for more years than I like to remember. It's time I was on my own."

"But everything was going so well again!" Agnes protested, ignoring Gwen's explanation.

"So well for whom?" Gwen asked. She shook her head, recalling the sorrow and pain of the days Agnes was referring to. "Mother, the time you're talking about was the most miserable period of my life."

Agnes sniffed, twisting the corner of her apron. "Misery! You'll never know what misery is until you've gone through the pain and agony of having a child, only to have her desert you when you're old and weak."

"Then, thankfully, Mother, you'll never know what it is to be miserable either. Because, though I'm leaving you, I'm not deserting you." Gwen's voice was gentle but firm. "Now won't you say good-by and wish me happiness?"

For a moment, Agnes's face softened and her eyes filled with love. Hugging her daughter, she whispered, "You know I want you to be happy." Then she pulled away, spoiling the moment by adding in a whine, "Even if it is at my expense."

"For God's sake, let her go and be damned!" Barney bellowed from the living room. "I can't hear the goddam TV with all that carrying on."

"This is where I came in," Gwen sighed. She kissed Agnes, picked up her suitcase, and walked out.

"Shut up, you old sot!" Gwen heard Agnes shrill as soon as the door closed behind her. "It's all your fault that she left. If it wasn't for your bumming around and drinking—"

"The hell it's my fault! You're the one who made her leave. You, with your sniveling and whining and carrying on. You shut your goddam trap, or I'll leave you too!"

"Ha! That will be the day! Where would you set up house —in the gutter?"

Downstairs, Gwen hailed a taxi. The driver, a long-haired youth wearing a denim jacket and a battered Anzac hat, had his radio tuned full blast to a rock station.

I wanna be me, an androgynous voice wailed over the metallic thwanging of an electric guitar. *I'm gonna be freeeee. Yeah, baby! I'm gonna be freeeee!*

"The music bother ya, lady?" the driver called out.

Ordinarily, it would have driven her to distraction, but now she laughed, stretching her legs out and tapping her fingers against her suitcase. "No," she called back. "Leave it on. They're playing my song."

Shrugging, the driver pulled out into traffic.

Though it had been difficult, Gwen had managed to wangle a week of her vacation in mid-December, and she spent that time getting her apartment into shape. She had arranged to have the walls painted, the floors sanded and buffed, and her furniture delivered before she moved in. Now she cleaned up after the workmen, vacuuming away the fine layer of pulverized floor that was coating the moldings, scraping away the Pollock-like drippings with which the painters had decorated the windows and bathroom tiles at no extra cost. She hung curtains; she shopped for odds and ends. By the time she left for work the following Monday, the apartment looked ready for life—and, she reminded herself as she locked the door behind her, love.

She ran into Bill on the elevator at work, and they paused for a moment in front of his office, chatting about the problems of setting up house, the high cost and low caliber of services, the defiant indifference of deliverymen to delivery dates. In between, they nodded to co-workers who were passing by on their way to their own desks and cubicles.

Instead of continuing on, Terri Ainsworth walked over to them. Ducking her head, she looked up at Bill coyly through her false eyelashes. "We missed you this morning," she said huskily. "Did you take an earlier train?"

Bill shook his head. "The doctor told me to give up smoking, so I've decided to resist temptation and sit in a no-smoking car from now on."

The false eyelashes batted. "We'll miss you."

"As long as you're there, I'm sure no one will notice the difference."

Terri gave him a sexy smile and then continued on to her office.

His polite smile faded quickly as he watched Terri's retreat. Then he took Gwen's arm and pulled her into his office. "I've got to talk to you," he said, tossing his coat on a chair and fumbling for a cigarette.

"So much for doctor's orders," Gwen observed, watching the orange flame of his match leap as he lit the cigarette.

He aimed the match at his ashtray. "That was the first explanation that popped into my head. I couldn't tell her the real reason."

"Which is?"

"Last Friday, after Terri got off the train, I told all those creeps she flirts with to go to hell."

He took a long drag on his cigarette, and Gwen slid out of her coat while she waited for his explanation.

"They're starting to play rough, and I don't like it."

Gwen raised her eyebrows. "Good Lord, Bill, don't tell me you're turning into a prude! Terri thrives on innuendos, and I've never known you to blush at them."

"You don't understand the half of it." He waved her words away impatiently. "Look—Terri's a poor sex-starved idiot. We both know that, and so do those bastards she flirts with on the train. Up to now, no harm's been done. It's been a kind of symbiotic relationship between her and them. A sick one, maybe, but harmless. They feed her vanity, laughing up their sleeves all the while, and she eats it up. Both sides get their kicks, and no one's really hurt. I've watched it for ages, intrigued by all the variations on a theme Terri and those guys can come up with."

Gwen followed him with her eyes as he walked around his desk and stabbed his cigarette out in the ashtray.

"And now?" she prompted him.

Bill pushed his glasses back up on his nose. "Lately, she's been concentrating on this shithead Harry Curtis—it seems he bought her a drink once. Friday, after she left the train, Harry boasted that all he has to do is take her out to lunch one time, and he can have her in bed by the end of the week. They started placing bets on it. I told them where they could shove their money."

He circled the desk and faced her. "You've got to talk to her, Gwen. She's a bubble-brain, and she's been asking for this for years, but she's human. She doesn't deserve to be hurt for a gag. No one does, no matter how great a fool."

Though Gwen had lived long enough to be well aware of the depths to which human beings will stoop to hurt each other, she had never hardened sufficiently to accept that fact of life, and every fresh cruelty filled her with as much loathing as the one before it.

"The bastards!" she said. "The stupid, egotistical bastards! Well, they're in for a surprise. Terri would never fall for such a scheme. She values her virginity as the golden key that will unlock the gates of matrimony for her. She'd never give it away without a marriage certificate in her pocket and a wedding band on her finger."

"Not even if she thought the affair was leading to marriage?"

"Especially not then. She's read too many of our stories to fall for that old line."

Bill shook his head. "Don't be too sure. People are full of surprises. And if you stop to think about it, you'd probably find that their 'unexpected' acts are very much in character after all. I think Terri's desperate enough and vain enough to fall for any line this son of a bitch throws at her."

"You may be right, but I don't see what I can do about it, Bill."

"Talk to her."

"Do you really think she would listen to me?"

"Probably not, but try anyway. Maybe something you say will penetrate before it's too late."

Gwen sighed. "Okay. I'll try to see her before the day is over."

"Thanks." He shook his head. "That poor dumb broad. I know I laugh at her a lot, but I really feel sorry for her."

"So do I."

With a little wave, she headed for her office. On the way, she glanced into the cubicle Terri shared with Frances Hascomb, but Terri wasn't at her desk. Telling herself she'd get to her later, she entered her office. There were other important things to be done.

Before going over any of the work piled on her desk, she buzzed Betsy on the intercom. "Do you have any stationery with the Waterford head on it rather than our own?"

"No, but I can get some."

"Fine. Just a sheet or two and one envelope will do. Bring it in as soon as you can."

Gwen was still going through the pile of correspondence on her desk when the intercom buzzed.

"I have that paper," Betsy told her. "Do you want me to take a letter?"

"No. Bring it in. I'll take care of it myself."

Betsy lingered at Gwen's desk, but Gwen thanked her and dismissed her, pretending not to notice the curiosity sticking out all over her like a porcupine's quills.

As soon as the door closed behind Betsy, Gwen slipped the paper into her typewriter, typed the date and Paul's name and home address. She stared out the window a moment, watching a freighter with orange stacks slowly making its way along the Hudson. Her thoughts collected, she turned back to the typewriter.

Dear Mr. Lockhart, she wrote. *I hope you will be pleased to hear that the publication difficulties we discussed at our last conference have now been solved. Alternate Plan B should prove agreeable to all parties. Your agent has the details, but if you have any questions, please feel free to contact me at my office. Yours truly, G. R. Hadley*

After addressing the envelope, she set the letter aside. Later, when Betsy was away from her desk, she would slip it among the outgoing mail. Now it was time she got down to work.

She was poring over the April dummy when Betsy buzzed her, announcing that Terri would like to see her.

"Send her in," Gwen sighed, wondering how she would steer the conversation around to the subject Bill had brought up. Terri helped her out by leaping into it herself.

"Okay if I take a long lunch today?"

"Shopping?" Gwen asked.

Terry glowed. "A date. A very important date."

He doesn't waste time, Gwen thought.

"Harry?" she asked.

Giggling like a teenager, Terri approached her conspiratorially. "He called a few minutes ago and said he wants to take me to lunch at Sardi's. Nobody takes a girl to Sardi's unless he's serious."

She sat on the corner of Gwen's desk, draping herself so that her shapely legs were in the line of view from the door. Terri believed in being prepared for all male comers.

Gwen's stomach began to sink. She'd rather pretend to listen to advice any day than presume to give it. Still, she had promised Bill.

"But can he really get serious with you?" she asked. "I mean, after all, he has a wife."

"A wife!" Terri dismissed the moribund Mrs. Curtis with a wave and a sniff. "She's nothing to him. He wouldn't even be with her except for the fact that she's dying and he's too nice a guy to walk out now. But he's got to think of himself too, and make some plans for the future."

Gwen fidgeted with some papers on her desk. "That's as it may be, but you have to look out for yourself too—and after all, he *is* a married man. It's possible he's just looking for some fun on the side."

Terri attempted a throaty laugh. "Not with me, he isn't. He knows where I stand." She primped her hair. "He's serious about me, all right. I mean, a girl can tell."

"Men can tell too sometimes—kiss and tell."

Terri's brow furrowed. "What are you getting at?"

Gwen shrugged. "Just that you should be careful and not let him take advantage of you."

"You know what I think?" Terri said, sliding off the desk and looking down on Gwen in righteous indignation. "I think you'd like to see me let this chance slip through my fingers. I think you're jealous."

Gwen couldn't help laughing. "Oh, come on, Terri! I'm concerned, but certainly not jealous."

"Well, that's the way it looks from here," Terri said, her eyes narrowing. "After all, you don't have a boyfriend, and here I am, practically engaged."

"Believe me," Gwen told her, smiling sadly, "I wish you well. I just don't want to see you hurt. Men do hurt women sometimes, you know."

Terri's face softened. "Sorry if I misjudged you, but you don't have to worry about me. This is one girl who can take care of herself." She gave a broad wink. "I know how to play my cards right."

"I'm sure you do," Gwen sighed.

"So it's okay about lunch?"

Gwen nodded and turned a page of the dummy, hoping Terri would take the hint.

Terri started out, then came back. "Do you have a needle and thread?" she asked.

Gwen opened a drawer and took out a small sewing kit.

"Thanks. I think I'll go up to the ladies' room and take my skirt up an inch. Let him eat his heart out!" Giggling, she hurried on her way.

Shaking her head, Gwen dialed Bill's extension.

"I tried," she said, when she got through to him.

"And failed?"

"Yes. She's on her way to lunch with him."

"Shit!"

The revulsion Gwen had been struggling with while she'd been talking with Terri washed over her again. "Don't waste your expletives. Terri's dancing on a dying woman's grave. Maybe she and that creep deserve each other."

"God, the world is full of crumbs, isn't it? Well, at least we tried."

They rang off.

A short time after Gwen turned back to her work, she heard Terri's quick steps nearing her door. A wolf whistle from the vicinity of the *Real* offices was quickly answered by Terri's high-pitched giggle. A second later, Terri knocked and entered, holding out the sewing kit.

"Well, I'm off!" she said. "Wish me luck."

What kind? Gwen wondered, and she shook her head as the door slammed behind the *femme fatale* of the 5:49.

Eager to make a dent in the work that had piled up while she was away, Gwen had a sandwich sent up from the lobby luncheonette and remained at her desk all day. By five, she felt that the situation was coming under control. Slipping into her portfolio a few manuscripts that, according to Laura's critiques, had possibilities for publication, she prepared to leave. She had almost finished brushing her hair when her door opened and Cam walked in.

"Ah, Venus at her toilette," he said.

"And Don Juan at his gallantries."

Smiling, Cam stroked his beard. "I hear you've taken an apartment."

"Word travels fast." She slipped her mirror into a desk drawer and stood up.

"How is it going? Are you settled now?"

"Just about."

He snatched her coat from her hands and held it for her. "In that case," he murmured, so close that his beard prickled her neck, "how about asking me up for a drink?"

She ducked away, laughing. "For heaven's sake, Cam! When are you going to give up?"

"All I suggested was a drink." Cam was all injured innocence.

For a moment, Gwen almost felt sorry enough for him to agree to a drink at Nick's. Ever since Frances Hascomb had been spreading the word that he was a lousy lover, she'd begun to view his womanizing as more pathetic than offensive. But Cam quickly put an end to her generous impulse when, mistaking her hesitation for acceptance, he slipped his arm around her and began propelling her toward the door.

"That's my girl." His voice dripped with the self-confidence of the conquering male. "Just a little celebratory drink."

"A screwdriver, no doubt," she said, slipping from his grasp.

Cam made a good show of looking shocked.

All pitying impulses extinguished now, Gwen laughed, her eyes sparkling with mischief. "Oh, come on, Cam! Don't look so shocked. We both know what you have in mind—and we both know you'll never get it. Why you knock yourself out trying is beyond me." Shaking her head and smiling, she walked back to him and put a hand on his shoulder. "You know, beneath that suave sex fiend is probably a nice guy. If you would just drop the Don Juan bit, perhaps we could be friends."

"I don't know what you're talking about," Cam sniffed. "Of course we're friends. That's all I was proposing—a friendly drink. I have only your interests at heart. After all, a woman all alone in a new place—you must be lonely."

"Oh, but I'm not alone," Gwen said with wide-eyed sweetness. "Didn't I mention that I've bought a huge German shepherd for company—one that's trained to attack on command?"

Cam's mouth was still slightly open as she picked up her portfolio and started out the door. "Do me a favor and switch off the light when you leave—friend," she laughed.

It was an endless night for Gwen—a night of doubts and longings. For hours, she lay awake in her new double bed, staring at the ceiling and the patterns of light cast by passing cars. How would Paul feel when he opened her letter? Would his heart pound as hers had when she'd written it? Had life been the same hell for him that it had been for her during the past agonizing weeks of separation? Had he walked the same dreary, deserted road, the hollow echo of his footsteps haunting him? Had he felt the same raw, gaping wound in the space where his heart had once swelled with love? Or had his wound, perhaps, begun to heal? Heal so much that he had learned to live without the memory of what they had shared haunting him? Would he be unwilling to begin again?

She wrestled with the sheets and blankets. The large bed still seemed strange to her, its unoccupied half tantalizingly mysterious and frighteningly cold. Gingerly, she reached out and stroked the other pillow. No, he couldn't have stopped caring. They'd been too close, shared too much. Their separation had been like an amputation—a loss that could never be completely forgotten. One might accept it and learn to live with it, but always, there would be the awful realization that there was something missing.

The pillowcase was cold as she touched it, and its coolness seemed to radiate, spreading its chill slowly and terrifyingly through every part of her body. Quickly, she withdrew her hand. What if she had waited too long to see how things must be between them? What if it had taken her too much time to grow up? There's a perfect time for everything in life. In her stupidity, had she let that time pass? Was it too late now?

With a cry, she sprang from the bed and closed her drapes, standing there for a moment clutching the drawstring as though it were a lifeline. Then slowly she released the cord and went back to bed. The lights from the street no longer penetrated her room, but she could not close out the chilling fears that had crept into her mind. It was not until shortly before dawn that she fell into a restless, troubled sleep.

She awoke to find that daylight had not chased the shadows—it had merely shrunk them. They followed her all the way to her office.

It was almost impossible for Gwen to concentrate on her work that morning. She was dictating shooting scripts to Betsy, but she kept glancing at her watch. Paul should have his mail by ten o'clock. By ten-thirty, surely.

At 10:45 her phone rang. Gwen froze as Betsy reached for it.

"Miss Hadley's office."

It was Boyd Larson, the studio director. Was Gwen aware that today was the deadline for June four-color shooting scripts?

Gwen swiveled around in her chair as she took the receiver, hoping Betsy would not notice that her hand was shaking. "Have I ever been late, Boyd?" It took a great deal of effort to keep her voice from cracking with disappointment. "I'm dictating them now. Betsy will have them down to you this afternoon. Don't tell me I've spoiled you by getting them there early in the past?"

Boyd cracked a good-natured joke about being overanxious to take some sexy pictures and rang off.

Sighing as though the call had been only a minor annoyance instead of a monumental disappointment, Gwen went back to setting the scene for the picture that would illustrate her lead story.

It seemed to Gwen that her phone rang incessantly all day. There were interoffice headaches to deal with and problems at the printing plant. And between calls, the phone seemed to radiate an ominous silence.

Love After Hours   183

By day's end, it was obvious that Paul was not going to call. Gwen offered any number of excuses to herself: The letter had been delayed; Paul had not been home to receive it; Paul, for some perfectly logical reason, had not been able to phone her. All of them seemed inadequate, and none counteracted the sinking certainty within her that he had not called because he no longer wanted to call.

At five o'clock she stuffed some manuscripts into her portfolio, in the hope that work might help her get through the long evening looming ahead. She slipped on her coat and stood at her window buttoning it, watching the rush-hour traffic in the street below. Workers poured from their buildings and into the subway entrances, like so many grains of sand hurtling through life's hourglass. In the morning the glass would be reversed, and they'd spew up from the subways and into the buildings. She was a grain of sand too. But unlike some of those down there who had found another grain to cling to on the trip, she was destined to travel alone.

When her phone rang, she looked at it listlessly. It would be her mother, she knew. No one else would call at after five and expect to find her in. Agnes would whine and cry and demand to know why she had not yet come home to visit. Betsy had gone for the night, and Gwen toyed with the idea of not answering. She did not feel strong enough for one of Agnes's scenes. Picking up her portfolio, she started for her door. Then she heard footsteps rushing toward Betsy's desk.

The ringing stopped, and Laura Faber's voice came over the partition: "Miss Hadley's office. Yes, I think she's still in. Hold on a moment, please."

She had no choice but to answer Laura's buzz. How would Laura take it when she asked her to tell her mother that she had left for the day? Probably without batting an eye.

"Yes, Laura?"

"Paul Lockhart on one."

All day she had waited to hear that announcement. Yet when it came, she was unprepared. The blood drained from her head as it rushed to give aid to her rapidly pounding heart. Weak with relief and trembling with anticipation, she sank into her chair. She took a deep, steadying breath before she pressed the button that would channel his voice to her ear. Still, her voice came out in little more than a whisper. "Paul!"

"Thank God you're still there! I was afraid you might have left for the day."

The sound of his voice brought memories of all their moments of closeness.

"I was about to. I was afraid you weren't going to call."

"You know me better than that."

She could hear the disappointment in his voice, and then she realized how unfounded her fears had been, how she had slighted him and all they meant to each other.

"It wasn't you I doubted," she tried to reassure him, "only my luck."

"I've been in Boston for the past few days. I arrived home only minutes ago. I was afraid I was dreaming when I saw your letter. I've been having an awful lot of wishful dreams about you—only to wake up and remember you're gone."

"I know what you mean. I couldn't stand it either. I've taken an apartment."

There was a pause as Paul absorbed the information, recognizing its implications and ramifications. She wondered if his heart was pounding as hard as hers was.

Finally he asked, "Are you sure this is what you want?"

She closed her eyes for a second as thoughts of the hiding, the lies, the sneaking that would be involved converged on her. Then she opened her eyes again.

"It's not what I want," she said simply. "It's what I'm willing to settle for."

He wanted to pick her up and take her to dinner, but she insisted that they dine at her apartment.

"We have so much time to make up for. Let's not waste any of it in public."

After she hung up, she sat staring at the phone, reliving their conversation, recalling, more than Paul's words, his loving tone. Then she opened her portfolio and put its contents back on her desk. She'd have to hurry. She hadn't set a time, and she had nothing to make for dinner. She'd stop and buy a steak; it would cook quickly. Or, perhaps, chops. It didn't really make a difference. Neither she nor Paul would notice what they were eating.

It had begun to snow just before Gwen left the office. By the time she arrived in her neighborhood with her purchases, a thin blanket of white had covered the sidewalks and the naked branches of the trees. Between patches of darkness, streetlights illuminated the lazy descent of the silvery flakes as they glided earthward, and Gwen held her face up for their feathery kisses. She had always delighted in snow, and she took its coming now as an omen of good fortune. As she had since childhood, she stepped gingerly along on the soft white carpet, choosing to make her own tracks rather than to follow in the footsteps of others.

Nearing her building, she saw a man huddled in the doorway. She didn't have to see his face to know his identity.

"Paul!" she cried, her heart racing as she ran toward him.

Her bootless feet skidded on the new-fallen snow and flew out from under her before she reached her stoop.

Paul rushed down and helped her up, brushing her off, hugging her. "Are you all right?"

"Yes, yes!" she laughed. "Or, rather, I will be, if you hold me just a second more."

He pressed his cold cheek against hers. She thought she would faint from the thrill of his nearness, the joy of being with him once more. Shakily, they drew apart and gazed at each other. He ran his hands up and down her arms. "No broken bones?"

She shook her head. "Not even a scratch."

Gently, he ran his finger along her cheek. "You look as though you're wearing a powdered wig, and you have snow flakes on your lashes."

She reached up, but he caught her hand. "No. Leave them. They'll melt all too soon."

He picked up her package and took her hand. Slowly they walked up the steps of her building, relishing every step. At the entrance, he stooped to pick up a package. "Champagne," he said.

Inside her apartment she hung their coats in the bathroom

to dry, changed her shoes, and joined him in the living room. She had toweled her hair, and it clung to her face in a soft, damp cap of coppery ringlets.

Paul's eyes glowed. "You look like a little girl after her bath," he said, taking her in his arms.

She relaxed against him, feeling she had come home at last. A little later, though, she pulled away, feeling exhilarated yet awkward, like an actress who has been awarded a coveted role and then suddenly discovers she is not quite sure how to play it.

She picked up the bottle of champagne he had placed on a table and handed it to him. "It feels as though the snow chilled it while you were waiting for me. I'll get some glasses."

He followed her into the kitchen, taking the dish towel she extended and wrapping it around the bottle.

She took two glasses from a shelf. "I hope you don't mind water tumblers. I don't have wineglasses yet."

Smiling, he filled the glasses, handing one to her. "It's not what you drink from, but whom you drink with."

Back in the living room, they settled on the couch, and Paul touched his glass to hers. "To us."

"To us."

She leaned her head against the back of the couch. "I don't need this to feel tipsy. I've been floating since you called me."

"I know the feeling. I'm still not quite sure I'm really here and you're really you."

"I'm me all right. I'm the only person I know whose heart can beat this hard without fainting. So it must be me."

She looked long and deep into his eyes. "That last night we were together, you knew then this was the answer for us, didn't you?" she asked, making a little sweep with her glass that seemed to take in her apartment.

"No. I knew it could be the answer, but only if it came from you."

"And you'd never have suggested it yourself?"

"It had to come from you. Unless it was your idea, unless you decided to do it for yourself as well as for me, it would never have worked. You see that, don't you?"

"I had to grow up first, I guess. Loneliness provides very fertile ground for growing up."

He took her hand. "You were already grown up. What you had to do was declare your independence."

Sighing, she lifted his hand and rubbed her cheek against it. "I won't argue about semantics. Whatever it was, I've done it. I'm my own woman now—and yours. I'm free."

Gently, he took her face in his hands. "Not free," he said softly. "Freedom and love are mutually exclusive terms. Love doesn't free us—it binds us. That's the beauty of it."

"I know that," she whispered, as his lips came closer. "That's why I'm here."

It started out as a gentle, tender kiss, but soon they were lost in a swirl of mounting passion, as the floodgates of their love, locked for so long, were at last released. Harder, harder, Paul's lips bore down on hers. His arms tightened around her with all the longing of the lonely nights they'd spent apart.

Gwen clung to him and moaned his name as he kissed her cheek, her neck, the hollow of her throat. "Oh, Paul! Paul!" she whispered, returning kiss for kiss. It was joy to feel the hardness of his body as he eased her down on the sofa. Then the tingle of joy turned to a chill of apprehension as his hand moved to her breast. Suddenly she felt unsure of herself, even a little frightened. Awkwardly, she drew away from him.

"I—I guess I should start our dinner," she said. "You must be starving."

She wanted to look away, but his eyes refused to let her gaze wander.

"No, I'm not," he said softly. "Are you?"

"No. Not really." A trembling—half excitement, half anxiety—was spreading through her.

He took her hand, his smile, the gentle tone of his voice, telling her he understood. "Would you like a little time alone?"

He knew her so well. That was why, she realized, she had been so afraid of him when they met, why she loved him so much now. Nodding, she pressed his hand in silent thanks and went into her bedroom.

She started to take a nightgown from her drawer, then changed her mind and went to her closet for her robe. Tossing it over her arm, she went down the hall to the bathroom.

She undressed slowly, hoping to calm herself, but her hands continued to tremble and her heart to pound. When she had removed all her clothes, she slipped into her robe. Its pale green color emphasized the green of her eyes and the red highlights in her hair, while the soft fabric clung to the curves of her body. The belt, its only fastening, accentuated her small waist.

She glanced in the mirror to check her hair and face. She had no need for makeup. Love made her eyes glow, and the blood from her pounding heart took ample care of the color in her cheeks. Taking a deep breath, she opened the door and, barefoot, crossed the hall to her bedroom.

Paul had removed the bedspread and pulled the drapes, but she was relieved to see that he had not undressed himself. Instead, with only his tie and jacket removed, he awaited her in the chair near the window.

"Hello again," he said.

"Hi."

Slowly, she walked over and placed her hands in his outstretched ones.

For a few moments they remained that way, not moving, not speaking, not thinking—only feeling the warmth and beauty of the love that surrounded them, gazing at each other as though they wanted to preserve forever this precious moment in time.

Then, gently, Paul pulled her down onto his lap, took her face between his hands. "God! How I love you!" he said, his voice trembling with emotion. "How I want you!"

Her whole body was yearning toward him, but she tensed at his words and pulled away.

"What is it?"

"There's something you should know."

"The only thing I have to know is that you love me. The past didn't exist before we met. You don't owe me any confessions."

Shaking her head, she rose and walked over to the window,

where she toyed with the drape cord. "How I wish it were a confession—a lurid confession of a sordid past."

"If it's not a confession, what is it?" His voice was puzzled, concerned.

She gave a little shrug. "Call it a revelation, but even that's too big a tag for such a pathetic fact of life."

Trying to smile, she turned to face him, but the little laugh she managed tripped over the tears in her throat. "I'm a virgin, Paul," she said. "A thirty-one-year-old virgin. Isn't that a laugh?"

"I'm not laughing," he said gently.

She tossed her head, as though trying to shake away the tears that were threatening to invade her eyes. "Well, you should be. Or perhaps you should be crying."

"Why?"

"Because a thirty-one-year-old virgin is no prize."

"According to whom?"

"According to everyone."

"The hell with everyone. Do you think I give a damn for the gutter morality that's rampant today?" Shaking his head, he crossed over to where she was standing. "When I come to you, it's to give of myself as well as to take. That's what love is all about."

He took her hands. "If your being a virgin has any significance for me at all, it's that it shows me that you feel the same way I do—that you have too much self-respect to take intimacy lightly. The fact that you waited thirty-one years before you found someone you are willing to share yourself with is no shame for you—and a great compliment to me."

Her eyes filled. "I'm not so much ashamed of my virginity as I'm embarrassed at my inexperience. Just as you want to give pleasure to me, I want to give it to you—but I'm not sure I'll know how."

He smiled. "Being in love is experience enough," he said tenderly.

This time when he kissed her, her fears were gone.

"Do you know," she whispered, "I've never seen a man naked?"

"You're not afraid anymore?"

She shook her head.

"Then it's time you did."

Fascinated, she watched him step back from her and remove his clothes. He was beautiful. She longed to run her fingers through the hair on his chest, to press her body close to his, but she waited.

Slowly, he walked toward her again. When he was very close, he paused. Her eyes never left his as she unfastened her robe and let it drop to the floor.

She heard his sharp intake of breath before he whispered, "How beautiful you are!"

He held out his hand, and she placed her own in it, letting him lead her to the bed. There, she lay down, and he sat beside her, gazing at her, stroking her, whispering to her of his love.

Her eyes were half-closed, her lips parted slightly with desire. She ran her hands over his chest, his back.

"Hold me!" she begged. "Hold me close!"

Tenderly, he took her in his arms and stretched out beside her. Gently, gently, gently, his lips and hands passed over her flesh. Slowly, he increased their pressure to meet the mounting urgency of her own kisses and caresses. Her pulses pounded as the blood surged through her body like a raging fire. The white heat of passion mounted in her until she thought she would explode from its pounding, surging pressure. Then suddenly it found release in a shock of pain and a burst of pleasure.

One in mind and one in spirit for so long, they had become one in body at last.

Chapter Ten

It was difficult for Terri Ainsworth to keep from bursting into song as she replaced the telephone receiver. Harry had called! It had taken him only three days to get around to making the date he had hinted at when they had lunch together at Sardi's. Poor Harry! Underneath his suave exterior, he was just a shy boy after all. But then she had known all along that he was putty in her hands.

Her heart beat a little faster. This was it. At last, after all the years of longing, of waiting, of having to smile mysteriously at weddings when people asked "when are we going to see *you* walk down the aisle?" her turn was coming. After twenty years of biding her time at Waterford, working for editors who didn't appreciate her abilities or who were perhaps afraid of them and so kept her tied to proofreading and production where they wouldn't have to worry that she'd outshine them, Mr. Right had finally come along.

She smiled to herself as she glanced at the galleys piled on her desk waiting to be proofread. What did it matter that she was always being passed over for promotion? Let Laura Faber be managing editor. Let Frances Hascomb do all the editing. It didn't matter to her anymore. Soon she could tell them all to go to hell. Soon she'd be Mrs. Harry Curtis.

Mrs. Harry Curtis. Mrs. Harry Curtis. She hummed the name to herself, rolling it over her tongue. Repetition brought a feeling of power and exaltation.

With pitying contempt, she looked over at Frances, who shared her office. It was really a shame the way that girl let herself go, wearing no makeup, letting her hair hang as limp as spaghetti and straight as a stick, wearing those stupid steel-rimmed eyeglasses, letting her breasts sag and flop around.

She'd never get a husband looking like that. Oh, Frances was a big one for sleeping around, but how else could such a girl keep a fella interested for even a little while? All her talk about how rotten Cam Eckhart was in bed, and the way she bad-mouthed marriage—well, all that was obviously sour grapes.

Disdain tugged at the corners of Terri's pink-frosted mouth. She longed to make Frances green with envy by telling her the news of her date. But of course she couldn't. Harry had made it clear on Monday that they'd be spending the night together. It wasn't the type of thing she cared to confide in anyone, though there was certainly nothing immoral about it. After all, if Harry's wife had stopped hanging on so selfishly and had gone ahead and died, she and Harry would have been married already. In the meantime, she had to do everything she could to keep his interest from wandering.

Not that there was much chance of that. No man could look at legs the way Harry looked at hers and lose interest. She stretched her legs out under her desk, the better to be aware of every inch of them. Hadn't Harry told her she had the best legs he'd ever seen? No, she had him in the palm of her hand all right. But she intended to see to it that he stayed there. After all, vice-presidents of corporations didn't come into a girl's life every day. She had to protect her own interests. And going to bed with Harry now would bind him to her. Absolutely.

Still, she wished he had given her some advance notice. She would have brought in a nightgown—something sexy—and a change of clothes. Now she'd have to wear the same outfit to work again tomorrow. But she shouldn't complain. It was probably the outfit that had got to Harry on the train that morning. Lovingly, she smoothed the red dress over her thighs. She'd have to remember to tell Harry that she'd made it herself. Men were impressed by women who could economize. But the girls in the office would be bound to notice when she wore the same dress two days in a row. She'd have to come up with some story about staying overnight in the city with a friend.

Good God! She'd have to come up with a story for Mama

too. Not that Mama didn't know all about Harry and give the match her blessing. But she was so set in her ways, always insisting that a girl should never, *never* sleep with a man before marriage unless she wanted to lose his respect. Mama wouldn't understand that this would make Harry hers —really hers!—for good.

She picked up the phone and dialed home. "Hello, Mama? Listen. You remember Sandy Pembroke, the girl I worked with when I first came here? The one who moved to California?" She raised her voice so Frances would be sure to hear. "Well, she just called a little while ago. . . . Yes, that's the one. She's in town on a visit, and she asked me to have dinner with her and stay over at her hotel so that we'll have plenty of time to catch up on what we've both been doing. . . . All right. . . . I'll see you tomorrow, then. Bye."

She hung up and did her afternoon's work at record speed. At four-thirty, she went up to the ladies' room, washed her face, and spent the next twenty minutes applying fresh makeup. Then she went back to her office and cleared her desk.

She met Gwen on her way out, and casually mentioned her story about Sandy as they rode down in the elevator. Gwen's thoughts appeared to be miles away, and Terri wondered, as they parted on the street, what Gwen had to look so happy about. Poor thing! Surely, she'd never get a man. Not the way she so readily admitted her age and refused to show her figure off in tight sweaters and revealing blouses. Certainly, she'd never be lucky enough to get a man like Harry.

They were to meet at five-thirty in front of the restaurant where they planned to dine. Terri was fifteen minutes early; Harry was forty-five minutes late. She spent the fifteen minutes visiting the "Electronics of the Future" exhibit in the Time-Life Building, which also housed the restaurant. She saw herself on the Videophone (looking quite young and attractive, if she did say so herself), walked through the kitchen of tomorrow (maybe she and Harry would have something like it in their home someday), pushed buttons that set sundry gadgets into motion, and fed a couple of computers silly questions.

At exactly five-thirty, not wanting to keep Harry waiting, she went back outside. Harry was nowhere in sight. She huddled in a recess in the building, trying to escape the frigid gusts of wind. The street glittered with the Christmas decorations that had been heralding peace on earth since well before Thanksgiving, and office workers, shoulders hunched against the cold, hurried along past her on their way home or to meet friends for preholiday drinks.

Terri stamped her feet and clapped her hands together. It wasn't the waiting that bothered her—she was sure all the men passing were giving her admiring glances, and a girl enjoyed *that*—it was the cold. She would have gone inside the restaurant for a drink, but nice girls didn't drink alone, even when they *were* waiting for someone.

At ten to six, she was so cold that she crossed the street and went into a luncheonette for some coffee. But fearing Harry might leave if she were not waiting when he arrived, she took only a few sips and rushed back to her vigil.

There was liquor on Harry's breath and he was in high spirits when he finally appeared.

"Hope you haven't been waiting too long," he said casually. "On my way over, I ran into a customer I owe a drink to. Gotta be nice to a guy who brings in a quarter of a million dollars worth of business every year. When he suggested dinner, though, I turned him down flat." He gave Terri a knowing look. "Told him I had a special dish of my own waiting."

Terri giggled her forgiveness, and they went into the restaurant where she drank a couple of predinner martinis to ward off frostbite. Though he had not been a victim of the cold himself, Harry kept up with her. Harry kept up with everybody when it came to drinking, and it showed in his middle-aged paunch, his double chin, his heavy-lidded, fading blue eyes, his sallow complexion. Terri thought he had a worldly look. Others, not intent on matrimony, thought him merely dissipated.

Dinner, when they finally got to it, was a jolly affair. Terri laughed at all of Harry's innuendoes and *double-entendres*, blushingly submitting a few of her own. But she remembered to show her serious side too. After all, Harry was an important man of the world. He needed more than just a party girl for his wife. He needed a girl who, in addition to being attractive, clever, and vivacious, could cook, entertain and be a credit to him.

She was quick to observe that her own *arroz con pollo* was every bit as delicious as the dish being served to them, and—what was more—she could whip it up in large quantities when entertaining a crowd.

"That right?" Harry asked through a mouthful of food.

Terri blushed as though he'd offered a great compliment. "I have a secret ingredient," she confided, leaning conspiratorially close.

With his forkful of *pollo*, Harry indicated her tiny bosom, which was grazing her plate. "That it?"

"Oh, Harry! You naughty boy!" Terri chided him through a fit of giggles.

She recovered herself, and went on to reveal her housekeeping skills and her prowess as a seamstress.

Harry was greatly impressed. "Really?" he'd say now and then, while refilling his wineglass, and sometimes, "How about that!"

When she had finally run through her résumé, he beamed at her as though she were too good to be true. "You're one talented kid!" he said.

She fluttered her lashes and dropped her voice an octave. "I have talents you haven't discovered yet."

He looked her up and down through his heavy-lidded eyes. "Not for long, baby."

She dropped her gaze in delighted embarrassment. "Oh, you!" She toyed with her napkin. "What I meant was that I used to act."

It was true. At the age of twelve, she had had the second lead in a Sunday-school play. A fellow congregant who liked her voice had hired her to do a few pre-Easter commercials for his shoe store on the local radio station.

Harry took a swig of wine. "No kidding?"

"I was with a top-notch amateur group for a while. My acting caught the eye of the right people, and I was given a job in radio. Then I got interested in editing, and then—well, here I am." She sighed. "I thought I made the right decision at the time. But sometimes I can't help wondering what would have happened if I had stuck with acting."

"You'd be in Hollywood now, instead of here, and I'd be the loneliest guy in town."

Smiling, she put her hand over his. He really had it bad, didn't he?

"Don't even think about it," she said. "After all, I *am* here."

Harry ran his free hand up her arm. "And what I want to do is get you someplace else. Let's have our coffee and get the hell out of here."

She smiled demurely as he signaled the waiter.

A half hour later, having consumed their coffee and cordials, they left. Harry hailed a cab and gave the driver the address of a hotel in the West Thirties that Terri had never heard of. It turned out to be a sleazy-looking place—a far cry from the Summit or the Americana, where she had hoped he would book their room—but she realized that Harry had probably avoided the more glamorous places in deference to her reputation. She'd see to it that he made up for it on their honeymoon.

Inside, Harry signed the register *Mr. and Mrs. John Smithers*. An original touch, Terri thought, that *ers*.

A sleepy-eyed clerk handed them a key, and they entered a creaky elevator operated by an evil-looking adolescent engrossed in a picture spread on a dog-eared copy of *Playboy*. Harry had to repeat their floor number three times before the boy, his eyes still on the magazine, set the car into motion. As they left the car, he popped his huge wad of chewing gum.

The minute they entered their room and hung up their coats Harry reached for her, but Terri pressed her hands against his chest and pushed him back a little. They were going to get married, true, but in the meantime a girl had to watch out for herself.

"Harry, do you have anything?"

"You want a drink?"

"No, no." She shook her head in embarrassment and looked toward the bed. "I mean, do you have anything to take care of things?"

Love After Hours

He looked blank.

"You *know*," she said, coloring. "Anything for birth control."

First realization, then annoyance showed in his eyes. "Hell! I thought you were taking care of that end."

Smiling demurely, she ducked her head and looked up at him through her false lashes. "How can I? You know I'm a virgin."

"Shit! I forgot about that. Okay. There's a drugstore downstairs. I'll go get something. You get ready in the meantime."

When the door closed behind him, Terri stood there wondering what to do. Harry had said to get ready, but how could she do that? She didn't have a robe or a nightgown with her, and she couldn't just take off all her clothes and sit around naked, could she? The very thought sent delightful little shocks of horror through her.

She looked around the room, wishing it were nicer. Somehow, it didn't seem appropriate after all these years to be giving up her prized virginity in a musty-smelling room with a peeling ceiling, faded green walls, scratched furniture, and a threadbare carpet. There should be perfume, soft music, satin quilts, a furry carpet, a crystal chandelier.... Never mind, she didn't need all those trappings. She had Harry, and he had her. Tonight was just to put the seal on their secret engagement.

What was it that he'd said Monday at lunch? *I can't go on seeing you like this and not having you.* And when she'd answered that he could have her forever if he'd only say the word, he'd said: *Then let's start forever with one night in town this week.*

So this was the beginning of forever. The true beginning of their marriage, though they wouldn't be able to take their actual vows until that selfish wife of his got around to dying.

Sighing, Terri removed the bedspread, noting that it was haphazardly mended in several places. What difference did it make? When they were married, she'd see to it that they had an expensive bedspread, a gorgeous Mediterranean bedroom set. She'd make it clear to Harry that he must buy her all new furniture. She wouldn't live with any of his first wife's leftovers. Harry could certainly afford it. He must be making at least fifty thousand a year.

She turned one of the pillows over so that the mending wouldn't show. Discovering a huge rip on the other side, she turned it back again.

"I thought you'd be ready," Harry said when he returned.

"I didn't have anything to put on."

"Put on? Hell! You're here to take it off." Laughing uproariously, he extracted a packet of prophylactics from the small bag he held in his hand. "Jesus Christ! I haven't worn one of these goddam things since my honeymoon."

"This is a honeymoon too, Harry," Terri said shyly as she approached him. "Our honeymoon."

"You said it, baby."

He pulled her close and planted his loose, wet lips over hers. Grinding his mouth down until her teeth cut into her lips, he crushed her close with one arm while he moved his other hand up over her breasts, then down under her skirt and up over her buttocks, where it encountered her two-way stretch. He snapped it against her thigh and pulled away.

"What the hell is that?"

She giggled. "My girdle, silly."

"Well, get out of it, will you? It feels like some goddam armor. And while you're at it, get out of the rest of that stuff." He winked and slapped her fanny. "It cramps my style."

For a moment she hesitated. She had thought he'd carry her over to the bed and lie her down gently, planting tender kisses all over her as he delicately removed her clothing without her even being aware of it.

"Well, go on!" he said, pinching her bottom.

He opened his belt, and when his hand went to his zipper, she realized that he intended to undress in front of her. With a little gasp of shock, she scurried into the bathroom, his laughter following her.

Once she had removed all her clothes, she stood for a moment, barefoot on the cracked tile floor, wondering what to do. Everything was so different from the way she'd imagined it would be. But then, it was probably just that Harry

Love After Hours 199

loved her so much, wanted her so much. A man was bound to be a little overeager when he finally found himself face to face with a girl he'd been longing for for so long. Still, she couldn't go out to him like *this*, could she?

"Are you coming out, or do I have to come in after you?" Harry called.

She whirled around and picked up her slip from her pile of clothes. "I'll be right there."

Quickly, she pulled the slip over her head. A hasty glance in the streaked mirror showed that her eyelashes were still secure and her makeup was intact. Her lipstick was a bit smeared, but not having brought her purse in with her, there wasn't much she could do about it.

"Hey!"

"I'm coming!"

She took a deep breath, opened the bathroom door, and gasped. Harry was lying on the covers, not a stitch on him. She had thought he'd at least leave on his undershorts. At least for a while.

"Come here, baby."

Slowly, she approached the bed, her eyes riveted on Harry as though hypnotized by his nakedness.

"Take a good look, baby." He laughed and patted his paunch. "Never seen a man in the flesh before, eh?"

She smiled coyly. "I've been saving myself for *you*, Harry."

"Smart girl. You'll find me well worth the wait." He gestured impatiently toward her slip. "What the hell have you got that thing on for? Come on, take it off. Give a guy a look at the goods."

"Oh, Harry!" Her tone told him that he said the nicest things. Reaching down, she pulled the slip over her head and and tossed it on the floor.

Harry propped himself up on one elbow and looked her over from head to foot. "Nice legs," he said. "Not much to the rest of you, is there?"

She giggled self-consciously. "Good things come in small packages, you know."

"Yeah. Let's hope so." He shifted over and the bed squeaked. "Come on. Get in."

She hesitated. "Harry..."

"Yeah?"

"I'm a virgin, you know."

"Sure, sure. You've told me. No sweat, baby. Now come on. Get in. We've only got the room for one night."

"What I mean," she said, still hovering over him, "is that I've always believed that a girl should save herself for her husband. And I've saved myself for you. There's never been anyone else."

"Believe me," he said, his voice growing impatient, "I don't hold it against you. Now get in!"

She obeyed.

The moment she was huddled beside him, Harry was all over her, grabbing, pinching, biting. She squeezed her eyes tight shut and gritted her teeth, refusing to complain about the hurt his probing hands brought. After all, what greater sign of his love could she have than his ardency, his eagerness?

Then came the pain. Oh, God! The pain! Mama hadn't told her it would hurt like this! Oh, God! She couldn't stand it! Not for another second!

"Harry!" she cried. "Harry! Please! It hurts! Stop! Please! *Harry!*"

But Harry didn't stop.

"Jesus Christ!" he growled when he finally rolled off her. "Will you stop that blubbering! It's not as if you're some goddam kid."

"But it hurts so much, Harry," she whimpered. "It really does. You forget, I'm a virgin."

His belly shook as his laughter filled the room. "Not anymore you're not!" he bellowed in merriment, slapping her playfully. "Old Harry took care of that for you, didn't he? Well, didn't he?"

She sniffed and nodded.

He reached for a corner of the sheet and wiped her eyes. The sheet came away black with her mascara.

"Come on now, stop crying," he ordered. "It's just the first time that it hurts so much. You'll hardly feel a thing later. You'll see."

"Later?" she asked weakly.

"Sure, later. Jeez! We've got the room for the whole night. You don't expect to just sleep here, do you? I couldn't get much sleep at any rate. Not with a babe like you in the raw beside me."

She giggled.

"That's better. Now give me a kiss."

She complied.

Harry was wrong. It hurt just as much the next time, and the time after that, but she bit down on her fist to keep from crying so that he wouldn't know. She didn't want to hurt his feelings, or—worse—give him the idea she couldn't satisfy him sexually. When he finally left her alone, she fell into an exhausted sleep.

The sunlight pouring in through a torn portion of the shade awoke her the next morning. Harry lay beside her, snoring softly, exhaling the sour stench of last night's whiskey. His hair was tousled over his eyes, and the dark whiskers that had sprouted on his face overnight emphasized the sallowness of his complexion.

As gingerly as she could, Terry extricated her arm from under one of his. Then she lay stiffly beside him, afraid that any more movement might awaken him—and reawaken his passion as well. Though she had always known she was desirable, not until last night did she realize just *how* desirable. At the moment she was sufficiently convinced of her seductiveness not to need Harry to prove it to her anew.

Moving in his sleep, Harry threw an arm across her bare midriff. He was wearing his watch, and she strained her eyes to see the time: 7:45. If she waited until a little after eight to wake him, it would give them just enough time to dress and get to their offices—without any time to spare for other things.

Slowly she stretched out her legs. Never before had she felt so aware of the lower part of her body. Never before had she felt so sore—not even when her pursuit of a husband had taken her to a dude ranch and her first horseback ride. Soreness was evidently the price she had to pay for her desirability, and when she realized that it would all serve to lead Harry straight to the altar, it didn't seem too steep a price after all.

Still, after they were married, she'd see to it that Harry cut down on sex. Once a week should be plenty for him. At least until she got pregnant. After she had a couple of kids—two was all she wanted—she'd get him to cut it out altogether.

8:15. Thank God! She'd shower and dress, then wake Harry. Slowly, she rolled toward the edge of the bed, but it wasn't slowly enough.

Harry woke up and drew her back toward him. "Where you off to? God!" he said, squinting at her. "You're a sight for sore eyes in the morning, aren't you? But I suppose I don't look much better." He began nuzzling her breast.

"Please, Harry. It's late."

He glanced at his watch. "We have plenty of time."

She tried to pull away as his hands began foraging. "Not if we both want to take showers and—"

"Tell you what," he said, pulling her close. "We'll shower together. That leaves us the time it would take for one shower for a quickie."

She bit her lip as, suddenly, he seemed to be all over her again.

"There, you see?" he said finally. "There's plenty of time left for that shower. Come on."

She tried not to limp as they walked to the bathroom. As she passed the mirror, she caught a glimpse of herself: Her hair was on end, her makeup was streaked, and one of her false eyelashes was missing. It was lucky Harry was too much in love with her to notice.

The shower was such fun! Harry had obviously had enough sex for a while, so all he was able to do was play. They carried on like a couple of kids. It made up for all the soreness.

Terri was still giggling and glowing when they left the hotel.

"Look," Harry said, running a hand over his growth of beard, "I'd like to take you to breakfast, but I've got to get to a barber and get rid of this before I go to the office." He reached into his pocket and took out a five-dollar bill. "You take this and have breakfast someplace nice."

"Oh, Harry!" She smiled demurely. "I can get my own breakfast."

He pressed the money into her hand. "I want breakfast to be on me."

"If you say so, Harry." She knew better than to argue. A man liked to think his wife would defer to him.

They parted, Harry heading toward a barber shop and Terri toward her office. She was so engrossed in planning their wedding that she forgot to stop for breakfast after all.

Chapter Eleven

Living in dread of a company shake-up themselves, workers tend to delight in such catastrophes when they occur to a competitor. More than taking joy in the troubles of the opposition, they attempt to buttress their own shaky security with the knowledge that the hand of Fate is momentarily striking its blow elsewhere. So throughout January, it was with relish and relief that Waterfordians gossiped about industry rumors that heads were about to roll at Norwich-McAllister. With omniscient nods, they reminded each other that for years N-M's book division had been behind the times, and for ages its magazines—with the exception of Nadine Osgood's *Intimate Experiences* (that woman had a golden touch!) and one or two others—had been slipping. It was obvious to everyone that it was no longer a question of whether the ax would fall, but when it would fall, and upon whom.

The answer was supplied by the *New York Times* business section one day late in January. Gwen had not purchased a newspaper that morning. Having managed to cut short a business trip, Paul had been able to stay the night, and they had prolonged for as long as possible the luxury of awakening in each other's arms. Later, in her rush to the office, Gwen had had no time to spare for a stop at the newsstand.

She had no sooner settled herself at her desk than Bill popped in waving his copy of *The Times*. "Have you seen this?"

She shook her head.

"Then read all about it. It's all right here: 'Norwich-McAllister Appoints New Executives.'"

"What's all there?"

Love After Hours

"N-M finally lowered the boom, and guess who got herself a juicy promotion?"

"Nadine?"

"None other."

She took the paper and scanned the two-column article on the editorial and administrative changes announced the previous day by Norwich-McAllister, publishers of paperback books and periodicals. Prominent among the names mentioned was that of Nadine L. Osgood, who had been promoted to editorial director of periodicals.

"How about that!" Her eyes sparkling with pleasure, Gwen returned the paper.

"I came up in the elevator with Jason Bart this morning. He looked like death warmed over. If you listen carefully, you can hear him grinding his teeth all the way down here. He's obviously afraid she knows too much about the competition—which is us."

"Good. Let him sweat it out a while. You know, it's his fault more than anyone else's that Waterford lost Nadine. She has a brilliant editorial mind, and it was no secret to me that she had begun to feel that she was stagnating here. She wanted the editorship of our Minerva Books when it fell open. But Jason said no dice. Probably because she's a woman."

"Ha!" Bill's eyes twinkled mischievously. "So she went to N-M. Hell hath no fury, et cetera, eh?"

Gwen shrugged. "Something like that."

Bill pointed to the article. "Did you know that this was in the package for her when she left?"

Gwen shook her head. "She never mentioned anything about it to me. She may have known, though. I wouldn't be surprised. She might even have insisted on it as a condition for taking over *IE*. Nadine is a gal who looks out for herself."

"That's the way it should be. God knows, no one else would look out for her in this shitty business. I'm glad she made it to the top." He gestured toward Gwen with the rolled-up newspaper. "How about you following in her footsteps? Seems to me, Jason Bart has been warming that seat upstairs far too long."

Gwen laughed. "Not me, thank you. I have neither Nadine's business head nor her ambition. I'm happy right where I am." She gave him a level look. "But I know one guy around here who might run the place a damn sight better than Jason does."

Bill shrugged. "If you mean Cam, forget it. He's holding out to take over for God."

Laughing, Gwen tossed a blue pencil at him. "Get out of here, will you? We both have work to do."

Later that morning, Gwen phoned Nadine to congratulate her.

"The whole place is buzzing with the news of your well-deserved good fortune," she told her, "and I understand that Jason is having strong second thoughts about having let you leave."

Nadine's cool laugh tinkled over the wire. "That's good to hear. For a long time, I've been under the impression that Jason never thought at all."

Before saying good-by, Nadine suggested that they get together soon.

"Fine," Gwen told her. "I'm free for lunch every day next week except Tuesday."

Nadine hesitated. "Lunch would be difficult for a while. Right now, I'm booked up with an editor a day. Why don't we meet after work and have dinner?"

Gwen's eyebrows shot up. Nadine had always been a nine-to-five woman, considering all the time after working hours to belong to her husband. Not in all the years that Gwen had known her had Nadine strayed from that routine, not even to the extent of stopping in at Nick's for a quick drink with a co-worker. Perhaps she'd found she had to change her thinking in her new job.

"Dinner would be fine," Gwen said at last, "but in that case, Thursday would be best for me." Any other night, Paul might be able to get away and come to her, but she knew he had a dinner engagement Thursday evening.

"Great," Nadine said. "How about five-thirty at The Chatterton? It's about midway between us."

They agreed, and then Nadine rang off just as it occurred to Gwen to ask if her husband would be joining them.

Her question was answered in the negative when she arrived in front of The Chatterton on Thursday and saw Nadine approaching from the opposite direction, alone. After greeting each other with affectionate hugs, they hurried inside out of the cold.

"You look marvelous," Nadine said when they'd settled at their table and ordered a drink. She cocked her head to one side, her shrewd eyes studying Gwen. "I can't put my finger on it, but somehow you've changed. Your hair's the same, and you haven't gained or lost weight. . . . No, whatever it is, it isn't physical. It's a change from the inside."

Gwen knew what it was. It was Paul. His love had brought her a glow of fulfillment.

Then Nadine's eyes, from which nothing could remain hidden for long, filled with recognition. "You're in love, aren't you? Only a man could change a woman so much."

Gwen smiled. "So you can still read everyone's secrets."

Nadine looked away. "Not everyone's." Her voice held a mixture of sadness and bitterness that took Gwen aback, yet seemed to forbid her to pursue the subject.

Their drinks were placed before them, and when the waiter left, Nadine was smiling again. "Tell me about him."

Gwen's thoughts were filled with loving phrases, but all that circumstances and convention permitted her to say was, "Not yet. Perhaps someday."

Nadine nodded knowingly and lifted her drink. "To you and your 'somedays' then."

Gwen raised her own glass. "And to your todays. Congratulations on your promotion."

"Thanks." Nadine took a quick sip and glanced away.

There was a pause in the conversation; to fill it Gwen said, "Your new responsibilities don't seem to have changed you. You're looking great."

Nadine's eyes darted back to Gwen's face, and her lips curled into a half-amused, half-sardonic smile. "Am I?"

"Yes, of course. Marvelous."

This time, Gwen was the one to avert her eyes. She'd forgotten that Nadine could spot a lie a mile away. And it *was* a lie. Nadine had changed—but not for the better. It was difficult for Gwen to identify the change, for in Nadine's case, as her own, it was nothing physical. It seemed to be a subtle change in attitude rather than in appearance. Her weight and hairdo had not altered. She was dressed with the same impeccable taste as always—from the high heels she always wore to give added height to her diminutive size to the fashionable hat—Nadine was one of the few sophisticated women who had remained faithful to the hat, and she wore one extremely well.

No, superficially, she seemed to be the same Nadine Osgood who had walked out on Waterford last spring. Yet on closer examination, she seemed to be only the shell of that woman. The spark that had once animated her features had died somewhere along the way; now her mouth seemed to droop ever so slightly, and the faint lines around her eyes were etched a little deeper. And her eyes—those marvelous eyes that could cut through superficiality like laser beams—what had happened to them? The world still seemed to parade naked before them, but the sight no longer seemed to amuse them. Gone was their cool, mocking laughter. Instead, they seemed to look upon the scene with bitter disappointment.

As though to smooth over the awkwardness she'd created by questioning Gwen's statement, Nadine shrugged and laughed. "Well, if I haven't changed yet, wait. By the end of two weeks, I should have at least ten gray hairs for every magazine under me."

Gwen laughed too. "But a call to your local beauty parlor can easily fix that. You've really done yourself proud with this promotion. We're all delighted for you. Bill, especially, told me to give you his best wishes."

"Thanks. I had a delightful note of congratulations from him the other day. He's still the same old Bill. I hope Waterford appreciates him."

"They seem to—though, of course, they're grudging about it. Do you know that if his circulation keeps rising at the rate it has been, it should be equal to Cam's before the end of the year?"

"Cam must be livid!"

"Well, it's hard to tell what color he is under that beard, but I will say this: He's been a hell of a lot quieter lately."

Love After Hours

"That should be a welcome change."

The waiter materialized, and they ordered their meal. Throughout its consumption they talked shop, Gwen bringing Nadine up to date on Waterford gossip, and Nadine filling Gwen in on office politics at N-M. On and off there were lapses in the conversation, moments when Nadine's mind would seem to wander, and she'd gaze off into space or toy with her food; moments when Gwen would study her closely, trying to identify the source of the subtle, elusive change in her friend. Always, Nadine would bring herself quickly back into the conversation, and then Gwen, too, would continue as though there had been no hiatus, while her eyes continued to search for the key.

When coffee was served, she found it. After foraging in her purse for a moment, Nadine placed a cigarette between her lips, then lifted her slightly trembling hands to light it. Gwen frowned as she observed the familiar ritual closely. There was something different about Nadine's hands. Nadine's long nails were as well manicured as always. Surely, hands can't get fatter or thinner, bigger or smaller. Nadine's hands were small, slightly dimpled at the knuckles, hands such as those eighteenth-century artists had preserved on canvas when they had painted the beauties of the day in all the glory of their powdered wigs and décolletages, their bejewelled fingers lightly caressing a pampered pet. Bejewelled! *That* was the difference! The wide, diamond-studded wedding band was missing.

Nadine's eyes followed the line of Gwen's gaze. Placing her matchbook on the table, she stretched out the fingers of her left hand.

"It's gone," she said. "And so is the man who gave it to me."

Gwen raised her shocked eyes to meet Nadine's. "You and Mitchell have separated?"

Nadine exhaled a little puff of smoke. "That's a polite way of putting it. A more accurate way would be to say he walked out on me." She rubbed the index finger of her right hand over her naked ring finger. " 'Diamonds last forever,' he told me when he gave me my wedding band. That's how long he said his love would last. Forever turned out to be not quite sixteen years."

Gwen shook her head in disbelief. "I always had yours down as one of the few perfect marriages around."

"So did I. So much for the insights of 'perceptive' women."

"But you seemed so right for each other!" Gwen protested, still unable to accept the news.

"You can credit yourself with being half right." Nadine's laugh was bitter. "It's really ironic. Here I am, the great confessions editor, and I've run the gamut of basic situations—love, marriage, the other woman, divorce. How's that for a personal research project?"

Her smile faded, and she stabbed her cigarette out in the ashtray. There was no irony or bitterness in her eyes when she raised them to meet Gwen's—only naked heartbreak. "I'm so sick of pretending to be casual about it," she said in a voice ragged with agony. "I hurt, Gwen. I hurt like hell!"

Impulsively, Gwen reached out and touched her hand. "I'm so sorry, Nadine. I wish there was something I could say."

Nadine shook her head. "There's nothing you can say. But maybe you could listen. I'm so sick of playing the cool career woman whom nothing can ruffle. If I don't talk to someone soon, I'll go out of my mind." She put her hand on Gwen's. "You're about the only person in the world I can let my hair down with. Will you come back to my place for a while?"

Gwen checked an impulse to look at her watch, for love makes the best of women selfish. Her first thought had been: *What if Paul's dinner is over early and he can come to me after all?* But she quickly pushed the thought aside. Paul would be the first to understand that the needs of an outsider must sometimes come first.

"Of course, I'll come," she said, and she signaled the waiter for their bill.

While they were slipping into their coats, Nadine glanced around the room. Her gaze came to rest on two graying women at a nearby table. They were talking animatedly between sips of champagne.

"How sad," she said, "to have to drink champagne with

another woman. Whenever Mitchell and I went to a restaurant, I used to pity the middle-aged ladies I'd see there eating together. I always thought that the only more piteous sight was to see a woman eating alone." She shrugged cynically. "Pride goeth before a fall, indeed. Now I'm one of that sorry crew."

Gwen knew only too well how she felt. "I can't offer you a very hearty welcome aboard," she said drily.

Nadine looked back at her with eyes filled with concern as she realized how her words might have hurt her friend. "I'm sorry," she said. "I didn't mean—"

"I know," Gwen cut her off gently. "Come on. Let's go."

They took a taxi to Nadine's luxury apartment house in the east Fifties. Once the apartment door closed behind them, Nadine's shoulders sagged a bit, and the change Gwen had noted in her face earlier seemed to intensify. It was as though, now that the world was safely closed out, she could remove her mask of cool sophistication and show her true disillusionment.

"Would you like coffee or something stronger?" Nadine asked after she had hung up their coats.

"Whatever you prefer."

"Something stronger then. I've been preferring something stronger quite often lately."

While Nadine busied herself with their drinks, Gwen settled herself in an easy chair and looked around the room. It had been furnished with taste and loving care after the fashion of the Georgian period. A cherrywood cocktail table stood before a long sofa which was upholstered in a brocade with a delicate pattern that combined warm tones of blues, greens, and rust. The rust was picked up in the drapes gracing the picture window, and the blue was echoed in two high-backed wing chairs flanking the artificial fireplace, above which was hung a fine Gainsborough reproduction. Two Wedgwood lamps stood upon the end tables on either side of the sofa, and the chinoiserie craze that had swept England under George IV was reflected in the Oriental rug and the delicate screen that partially hid the bar.

Yet despite its elegance, there was something vaguely unbalanced about the room. The furniture seemed huddled together here and there, while other areas were bare. It was as though a beautiful woman opened her mouth—only to reveal a gap-toothed smile. As she studied the room more carefully, Gwen realized that the effect did not result from an ungraceful arrangement of furniture, but rather because other pieces that had evidently balanced the room had been removed. Barely perceptible indentations in the rug revealed that a chair and perhaps a small table had stood in one conspicuously bare area near the window. A few scratches on the floor near a blank section of wall hinted that a bookcase—perhaps the mate to the one on the opposite side of the room—may have occupied the space. Here and there, faded patches of wall space announced the removal of pictures of varying sizes.

Handing Gwen her highball, Nadine glanced around the room too. "It looks peculiar, doesn't it?" she said, seating herself across from Gwen. "Rather like a smile someone has smashed with a fist. In a way, I guess that's what happened. Mitchell took some of his favorites with him. I don't know why I don't rearrange the furniture. At first, I guess it was because I was an optimist, hoping against hope that Mitchell would come back. Now I guess it's masochism more than anything else. Every time I walk into the room, the empty spaces gape at me like blank-faced children who keep asking, *why?*"

"There are some questions that have no answers," Gwen reminded her gently.

"But there *has* to be an answer! How can a woman spend eighteen years loving a man—nearly sixteen of them living with him—and have it all add up to nothing? It's a nightmare! Eighteen years that led to *nothing.*" She downed her drink too fast.

"But to you those years meant something," Gwen said, trying to comfort her.

"That's not enough!" Nadine leaned forward, her sharp eyes studying Gwen's. "You say you're in love, so you must know I'm right. Love is meaningless unless it's meaningful to the object. Oh God, Gwen!" She jumped up and walked to the window. "Eighteen years! *Eighteen* years!"

"But surely most of those years were meaningful to Mitchell too."

"Then they weren't meaningful enough!" she cried, whirling around to face Gwen. "And that adds up to the same damn thing!" She closed her eyes and clenched her jaw in an effort to bring herself under control. "I'm sorry," she went on finally. "I shouldn't make you take the brunt of my anger like the messengers who brought the news of lost battles in Shakespeare. You're just an innocent bystander. It's myself I've lost patience with, not you." She blinked back the tears that filled her eyes. "Can I get you another drink?"

"I'm still working on this one."

"Then I'll keep you company."

She poured herself a double.

"It's funny," she said, holding her glass toward the light and studying it as though she expected to find the answers she sought somewhere in its depths. "For years, I've rejected as phony stories in which the writer makes herself sound blameless and martyred. I was sure that when a man left a woman, she must have done something to provoke it, and that unless she recognized and accepted her share of the responsibility for the situation, her story was meaningless. Now here I am, smack in the middle of that same situation, but when I do the soul-searching I expect to find in a good story, I draw a blank."

She walked over and once more sank down on the chair opposite Gwen. Its high back accentuated her petiteness, making her look like a vulnerable child.

Gwen shook her head, her heart aching for Nadine. Remembering the way Paul had argued against confession stories on their first meeting, she said, "You know we choose only the stories with positive outlooks. You're only hurting yourself if you expect situations in your own life to conform to their patterns."

Nadine dismissed that possibility with a wave of her glass. "Of course I know better. No, I'm not trying to fit my life into a good confession plot. If I were, I'd be expecting a happy ending, and I don't. All I'm looking for is a key, a thread—a logical explanation that will help me understand."

"Didn't Mitchell offer any explanation at all?"

"Only the usual one—that he'd found someone else." She drained her glass. "What he didn't tell me was *why* he'd found someone else."

"Maybe he doesn't know why. Those things just happen sometimes."

"Not without a reason." She was back at the bar, rummaging among the bottles. Suddenly she stopped and leaned toward Gwen. "I've seen her, you know. And she's the biggest question mark of all." She went back to her search, and having found what she was looking for, proceeded to pour herself a generous amount of it. "If she were some young, sexy kid or some beautiful, intelligent woman, I might be able to understand her hold over him. But she's neither. Oh, she's younger than I am, but she certainly can't be placed in a bracket with the girls men turn to when they're trying to recapture their long-lost youth. She's thirty, if she's a day. And drab. My God, is she drab!"

Nadine began pacing the room, drink in hand, and Gwen watched her apprehensively, wondering if she should tell her she was drinking too much, hoping the liquor wouldn't lead her to say things she'd regret having revealed.

"She's a salesgirl in a tobacco shop. If that doesn't sound like something straight out of Maugham!" She laughed mirthlessly. "She's about as plain as they come—plain face, little makeup, straight brown hair, pudgy figure. The dress she was wearing had about as much style as a flour sack. I didn't let on who I was, and I struck up a conversation with her. Her personality and intelligence match her appearance —nothing! Absolutely *nothing!* She's a pathetic, helpless creature I'd pity if I didn't have such good reason to hate her. My God, Gwen! What can he see in her?"

Gwen shook her head. "I'm sure I don't know." But she had a sinking feeling in the pit of her stomach, because she was afraid that she could guess. Perhaps it was precisely the other woman's pathetic helplessness that had appealed to Mitchell after so many years with the independent, self-sufficient Nadine.

"Mitchell has such a lively, intelligent mind. What can he possibly talk to a woman like that about? Babies and recipes and the high price of bread?" She downed the rest of her drink and slammed her empty glass on the bar. "I know that makes me sound like a snot-nosed bitch. But I'm not. Not really. God knows, I've never held myself superior to any woman—only different."

She took a ragged breath. "It was that difference that attracted Mitchell. He said he loved me because I never used my femininity either as a crutch or as a weapon. Our marriage was a perfect, equal partnership all the way down the line. We weren't only lovers, we were best friends. All we needed in life was each other. From the very beginning we had decided together that the two of us was all we needed. We didn't want children, and we never regretted deciding against them. Now," her voice rose and cracked, "now he's left me to—to 'raise a family,' as he puts it, with *her*."

It was agony for Gwen to see Nadine, usually so composed, standing before her, her hands trembling, her eyes filled with tears. "Don't," she begged, as much to spare herself as to spare Nadine. "You're only hurting yourself."

"No, no." She pressed her hands to her temples. "I've got to say these things out loud. Maybe then they'll stop screaming inside my head." She shook her head as though to clear it, but her eyes still looked dazed—from too much drink or too much pain. "We never wanted children," she said softly, as though talking to herself. "It wasn't just my idea. It was his too. It was one of the things we saw eye to eye about, like so many other things. That's why we had such a good marriage." A bitter laugh escaped her. "*Good* marriage! That's a laugh, isn't it?" Her gaze came back to Gwen; her eyes were wistful, beseeching. "I didn't change, Gwen. Why did he?"

Gwen shook her head sadly. "Half the time we don't even understand our own motivations," she said. "How can we hope to guess at another's? Perhaps he thought life was slipping by too fast, and he hoped to recapture some of his youth by having a family."

Frowning, Nadine shook her head emphatically. "That can't be the answer. Mitchell is too intelligent for that kind of self-deception."

"No one's too intelligent for self-deception," Gwen protested gently.

"But it's not the answer here!" Nadine insisted. "No, it must be that woman. Somehow, *she* changed him." She sank down on the sofa. "Why did it have to be Mitchell? Of all the men who come into that tobacco store, why did she have to sink her claws into my husband?" She buried her face in her hands and burst into tears.

Her heart aching, Gwen went over and placed a hand on Nadine's shoulder.

Nadine raised her tear-streaked face and searched Gwen's eyes. "What kind of bitch will knowingly take up with a married man, knowingly break up a marriage?"

Wincing, Gwen withdrew her hand. Nadine's words stung like the lash of a whip. "We don't choose the one we fall in love with," she said softly.

"Yes, but we can choose whether to pursue that love."

"It's not always as simple as that."

Eyes flashing, Nadine jumped up. "Are you defending her?"

"No," Gwen said sadly, "I'm defending myself."

"Yourself?" Nadine echoed, sinking slowly back onto the couch.

Gwen nodded. "In simple confession jargon, I'm a married man's mistress. But there the resemblance ends. The marriage was dead long before I came on the scene, and my being on the scene will in no way end it."

"I suppose I should have guessed—when you said you couldn't talk about it."

There was an awkward pause during which Nadine stared blankly into space and Gwen stood before her silently, lost in her own conflicting thoughts.

Finally Gwen said, "I guess I'd better be going."

"No, don't." Nadine put a restraining hand on Gwen's arm. "At least, not because of what has just been said. I may be steeped in my own misery, but I hope that I haven't let it cloud my vision so much that I've lost all perspective. I know you too well to believe that you'd deliberately choose a hurtful course. You're right: Not all cases are the same, and no case is simple. I'll no more judge you than you've judged me tonight."

Gwen placed her hand over Nadine's. "Thank you."

Nadine forced a little laugh. "Thank *you*—for listening to my whole tedious tale." She stood and headed toward the kitchen. "I'll make some coffee."

"No, please!" It was getting late, and Paul might be waiting. "I really must go now."

"Oh." Nadine looked genuinely disappointed.

"But I hope you'll make some for yourself."

The old, amused smile came to Nadine's lips, and for a second, she seemed like her former self. "Don't worry. I don't make a habit of all this guzzling. As a matter of fact, since my world fell apart, I've vowed never to drink alone. I'm strictly a career girl now. I can't afford to start bad habits that might cost me my job. A company will look the other way when a man is too dependent on alcohol—as Jason Bart's long career proves—but it would never extend such indulgence to a woman."

She opened the hall closet and took out Gwen's coat. "Another gap-toothed smile," she said, looking at the numerous empty hangers. "Mitchell took everything with him but my memories. I wish to hell he'd taken them too."

"They'll hurt less as time goes by," Gwen tried to comfort her. "Someday, you'll find someone else and be happy again."

Nadine shook her head. "No. In life there are no happy endings," she said. "If we're lucky, we may get a happy beginning. Mine lasted eighteen years. Now the ending has set in."

"There can always be a new beginning."

"Not for me. I've never tried to fool anyone, much less myself, about the type of woman I am—competitive, ambitious, independent. There aren't many men around who feel secure enough emotionally to love that kind of woman. And the older I get, the less willing even those few will be to try."

She handed Gwen her purse. "No, all I have left is my career—a career I was able to build because I always had enough sense to keep it second in my life. Now I'm stuck with second-best."

"There are many women who would envy you your position," Gwen reminded her.

"There are many women who are fools."

At the door, Gwen turned and took Nadine's hand in hers. "Take care of yourself, Nadine," she said.

Nadine's lips twisted upward, and her eyes lit with the old irony. "Don't worry, I plan to. I'm well aware that I'm the only one around to do that." She gave Gwen's hand a squeeze. "Thanks for coming. Good night."

Downstairs, the doorman offered to hail a cab for Gwen, but she decided to walk a bit, hoping the frigid air would alleviate the depression that had descended upon her as soon as she left Nadine. When she didn't feel any better after walking a few blocks, she hailed a cab after all.

All through the ride home, Nadine's heartbroken question: *What kind of bitch would knowingly take up with a married man?* kept echoing in her mind. And every time, her heart sinking just a little more, she answered it: *My kind.*

There are no happy endings, Nadine had said, *only happy beginnings.* And the words returned to Gwen like a prophecy of doom. She and Paul were having their beginning—but where would they end?

Her depression was so heavy by the time the taxi pulled up in front of her house that not even the sight of Paul huddled in the vestibule could lighten it.

She hurried to him. "Have you been waiting long?"

"Only about ten minutes."

She unlocked the vestibule door. "I wish you'd take the set of keys I had made for you."

"Let's not go through that again," he said, as he followed her up the stairs. "You know how I feel about it."

"I think you're being hopelessly Victorian."

"On the contrary. A Victorian would have taken the keys. To him, they would have symbolized his rights over the woman who dwelled behind the door."

"And you think you have no rights over me?" she asked, as she closed her apartment door behind them.

"Only as many as you have over me. And since I can't grant you the privilege of coming and going as you choose in my apartment, I won't accept the key to yours."

Sighing, she slipped her keys into her purse.

"Did you have a nice evening?" he asked, helping her off with her coat.

She shrugged. "It was all right. Coffee?"

"Fine." He followed her into the kitchen and leaned against the doorjamb, watching her go through the preparations. She did everything silently, methodically, as though immersed in an elaborate procedure that demanded total concentration.

"What's wrong?" he asked finally.

"Nothing."

"There's something bothering you."

"No, really."

She took two cups down from a cabinet, but he took them from her hands, placed them on the table, and closed the cabinet doors before she could reach for saucers. Gently but firmly, he turned her toward him.

"You've hardly looked at me since you've come home. Why?"

Their gazes held for a moment. Then her lower lip began to tremble, and her eyes filled with tears.

"Oh, Paul!" she whispered. "I've had the most awful evening." She pulled away from him and leaned against the sink. "I saw the woman whom I admire and respect above all others reduced to a hollow shell because her husband has left her for someone else. And all the time I was with her, I was torn between feeling sorry for her and hating myself—because I'm one of those 'other women,' too."

He took her shoulders and turned her toward him. "When will you learn to stop using labels? You're not just an 'other woman,' you're you. Your case is entirely different from your friend's."

"But the facts are the same!" she protested.

"That's an impossibility." His eyes bore down into hers, anger mounting in them. "No two situations are the same. Every fact in any situation is colored by its own unalterable circumstances. When will you stop torturing yourself and accept that?" His hands tightened on her arms. "By your interpretation, if you're just another 'other woman,' then I'm just another lecherous, philandering husband, looking for some sex on the side. Is that how you see me? Is that how you see us? Well, is it?" He dropped his hands and turned away.

"No, you know it's not!" Her tears were flowing openly now, and she rubbed her arms where he'd held her. But it wasn't her arms that hurt, it was her heart.

He turned to her. "Then why are you trying to make us feel guilty?"

"I'm not!" she cried, afraid of his anger, afraid of her thoughts. She shook her head, wishing that she could straighten out the conflicting emotions that were raging inside her. "It's just that suddenly I'm afraid—not of what we are, but of what's to become of us. Nadine said it all tonight when she said there can be no happy endings. Somehow, I can't get it out of my mind."

"If you insist on measuring us by someone else's rule, then you're bound to sell us short. Of course there are no happy endings, but that doesn't mean that we should cut the rose down before it has a chance to bloom."

His voice softened, and gently, tenderly, he took her face in his hands. "Gwen, I love you," he said. "I love you now. I loved you yesterday. I'll love you tomorrow. We're not schoolchildren. I can't promise to love you throughout eternity. I'm not even sure eternity exists. But I can tell you that what I feel is real and lasting and will be a part of me until I die."

"Others have felt the same way and have been wrong," she whispered.

With one finger he traced the trail of tears down her cheek. "Only because somewhere along the line they've mistaken other things for love. Many things can predecease us— sex, romance, illusions, desire. But not love. That goes on as long as life itself. And it's love above all else that I feel for you."

She relaxed against his chest. "I don't know what gets into me sometimes," she whispered. "It's just that I love you so much and our love is so beautiful that I sometimes become afraid something terrible will happen."

"I can't offer you any guarantees about life. We have no control over where the next thunderbolt or drunken driver may strike. But I'm sure in my heart that when fate finally deals me the death blow, I'll go down loving you. Is that enough for you?"

Love After Hours

She pulled back and looked up at him. "You know it is. And I feel the same way." She drew a shuddering breath. "But let's not talk of death. It frightens me more than anything else."

"Let's not talk at all," he said.

His kiss routed all fear of death and desertion from her heart. When they finally broke apart, they slipped their arms around each other and went into the bedroom.

Later, as she lay in the curve of Paul's arm, deliciously warm and drowsy in the afterglow of love, Gwen wondered how she could have allowed such doubts and fears to prey upon her. There could be nothing wrong about a love that was so right. Lightly, she ran her fingers through the short curly hair on his chest. Like the hair on his head, it was graying in the center, while the rest was still dark.

"Forever and always," she whispered.

"Forever and always," he echoed, his hand gently stroking her breast.

For a while, they lay in silence, luxuriating in their nearness of body and soul. Then time, the enemy of all clandestine lovers, began to insinuate itself. A far-off church bell began to toll, and with each succeeding chime, the languor of love was broken just a little more, and the pressures and demands of the outside world which mounting passion had held at bay now rushed past his sleepy sentinels.

Sighing, Paul withdrew his arm from beneath Gwen's head. "I have to be going."

She nodded and sighed, too, raising up on one elbow, her breasts lightly brushing his chest as she gave him a gentle kiss. Then she reached over and switched on her lamp so that he could see to dress. She never pleaded with him to stay longer, for she knew he gave her every moment he could manage.

Reluctantly, Paul pushed himself from the bed and went to the chair that held their clothes. He removed his own clothes from the pile, holding up his tie and her brassiere, which had somehow become entangled.

He smiled. "There are times when a picture like this evokes a stronger sense of intimacy than the image of a kiss."

Gwen knew exactly what he meant: The supreme moments of intimacy, she had discovered, come not when a couple is in the throes of passion; for then—as magnificent as that moment is—they are completely outside themselves, lost in a throbbing crescendo of desire and abandonment that momentarily obliterates all rational thought and all sense of identity. It is only in the quiet, gentle moments, when they are as aware of their thoughts as of their emotions, that a couple can savor every aspect of their oneness and delight in all its subtleties. They had shared such a moment when they lay wordlessly in each other's arms, each acutely aware of the other's warmth and of every curve and angle of each of their bodies, until the church bells made them part. They shared it still as Gwen, her lips still moist from his kisses, lay propped against her pillow, the blankets barely covering her breasts, watching him dress.

"If I ever had a daughter and she asked me about love," she said, "I'd tell her that it can be measured best in the quiet, tender moments."

"Maybe someday you can tell that to my Melanie," Paul said. "Maybe sooner than we've ever dared to hope."

Gwen sat up. "What do you mean?"

He slipped on his shoes. "I mean, Verna's finally ready to talk divorce on my terms."

"You've told her about us?"

"God, no! That's all I'd need to do to ruin our chances. No, it's not compassion that led to her change of heart—it's ambition."

"I don't understand. Why haven't you said anything to me before?"

"I didn't say anything before tonight because I didn't want to raise any false hopes. It wasn't until dinner this evening that I got things rolling in the right direction. Then, when you came home, before I could tell you my news, we got involved in your problems."

She nodded. "You had dinner with your lawyer?"

"No. I had dinner with Sam Walters and Larry Hanks, the producer and director of *Raw Flesh*."

"I wish I knew what you were talking about."

He sat down on the edge of the bed and took her hands in his. "It's simple once you know the facts. *Raw Flesh* has been in rehearsal for weeks and is scheduled to open at the end of March. Sam and Larry had signed Marcia Endicott for the female lead, but she was in an auto accident the other day and wound up with a broken hip that will lay her up for six months."

Gwen nodded impatiently. It seemed to be taking him forever to get down to cases about the divorce. "I read about it in the papers, but I don't see what that has to do with—"

"Verna read it, too, and when she did, that mind of hers started clicking away. She decided that this could be her chance for stardom, and she insisted that I try and get her the role. When I refused, she made it clear that she was open for negotiation—the role in exchange for a divorce, including complete custody of Melanie."

"But you've said yourself that she's not a good actress. How can you convince those men to take her?"

"I already have—tonight." He squeezed her hand. "I'm afraid I used a little blackmail of my own. Sam has been dying to get the stage rights to my latest book, which will probably make an even better play. I told him I'll give him the rights only if he gives Verna the role."

"And he agreed?"

"He agreed."

Her heartbeats were tripping over themselves in joy as she threw her arms around him. "Oh, darling! I can hardly believe it!" Finally she pulled away. "Not that I care, as long as I wind up with you, but if Verna is such a bad actress, won't she ruin the play?"

"She's far from good, but she isn't absolutely rotten. Larry is one of the best directors around. With him working on her constantly, she should be passable, and I'm sure he'll try to keep her as much in the background as possible. With luck, the play might make it."

"When is she going to start divorce proceedings?"

"That's where the hitch comes in."

"The hitch?" Her hopes, at the pinnacle of expectation a second before, began a slow plunge into the depths of despair.

"She wants to milk our marriage of all the publicity and good will it might bring her in the part. She refuses to start proceedings until after the play opens."

"And if the play isn't a success?"

He smiled a little and brushed her hair back from her face. "I can be cold and calculating too. I had her sign a statement promising to start proceedings within two weeks of the opening, no matter what the critics' reaction may be."

"It's legal?"

"Very. My agent and my secretary witnessed it."

Gwen's heart began thudding painfully with a mixture of hope and fear. She bit her lip, unable to speak.

"What's wrong? I thought you'd be pleased."

"I am," she whispered. "But I'm scared too. Scared that it's too good to be true—that something will go wrong."

"Nothing can go wrong," he assured her, kissing her lightly, "as long as we continue to be careful so that she doesn't find out about us and have an excuse to throw a monkey wrench into the works. But there's little chance of that. She'll be up to her neck in rehearsals from now till the end of March. After that, we'll stop seeing each other for a while, so there'll be no chance of discovery." He pulled her close. "Oh, darling! We'll have more from life than we ever dreamed possible. Nothing can go wrong."

Forcing back her fears, she tightened her arms around him, losing herself in his kiss. Then she slipped on her robe and walked him to the door.

"When can you come again?" she asked.

He shook his head. "Not for a couple of days. Tomorrow I have to go out of town and Saturday is Melanie's birthday. I've promised her that we'd spend the entire day together."

"Verna too?" she asked, trying to fight down a pang of jealousy.

"That will be the day!" There was irony in his voice, bitterness in his eyes. "Verna boycotts all family celebrations in which she isn't the center of attention. That's why I can't possibly cut Saturday short."

A wave of compassion for the child quickly submerged Gwen's jealous thoughts of the mother. "I wouldn't want you to." She touched his hand. "I hope she has a happy birthday. I only wish that I could tell her so myself."

He covered her hand with his, his eyes thanking her for her understanding. Suddenly his grip tightened, and his face lit up. "Why don't you?" he asked.

"Why don't I what?"

"Wish her happy birthday yourself?"

She shook her head uncertainly. "But that's impossible!"

"No, it isn't." He squeezed her hand, his face animated by the idea that had just occurred to him. "Meet us Saturday and share the day with us."

She looked at him as though he'd taken leave of his senses. "You can't be serious!"

"But I am. Really." He paced the hall, planning. "I've been longing to have you meet Melanie. I know she'll love you."

"But, darling!" She tried to bring him back down to earth. "You just finished telling me a little while ago how careful we have to be. Surely, introducing me to your daughter wouldn't be very discreet."

"Melanie would never tell Verna about it," he insisted.

"But it would be wrong to ask the child to lie."

He dismissed her objection with a wave of his hand. "We wouldn't have to. Melanie would never mention it to Verna. She learned a long time ago that she can't tell her mother about any of the good times she has—unless she's prepared to pay dearly."

"But what if we're seen together?"

"How could it be interpreted as anything but innocent when I have my child along?"

She hesitated, and sensing her temptation, he moved in to take advantage of it.

"Please come. It will probably be the only chance you'll have to meet Melanie until after the divorce. Verna lets us have very little time alone together, and rather than have her make life more miserable for the child than she already does, I don't push the issue."

She considered for a moment, then shook her head, still undecided. "But it's her birthday, and she expects to be spending the day alone with you. Don't you think she'd resent the intrusion of a stranger? In her place, I think I would."

He thought a moment, then shook his head. "I think she'd welcome having someone else along—it would make it seem more like a party."

"All right," Gwen said at last. "But only on the condition that if I see she's unhappy with me there, I can plead a forgotten engagement and leave. I wouldn't want to spoil her celebration."

He took her face between his hands. "I'll accept that condition," he said, "but the fact that you're the type of person who could make it is a guarantee that you won't have to fall back on it."

"If I don't, let's come back here for dinner."

"All right." He kissed her. "Wear something warm. Melanie wants to start out in Central Park. We'll meet you at the Delacorte clock at ten."

For a long time after he left, Gwen lay awake in bed, still tingling from the warmth of his lips, still feeling the strong but gentle roughness of his day's growth of beard as he rubbed his cheek against hers. The events of the evening seemed to swirl around her until the whirlpool of the confused emotions they had evoked caught her up at last and dragged her down into the depths of sleep.

By 9:30 Saturday morning, Gwen had cleaned her apartment, baked a cake, set a festive table, bathed, and dressed in a rust-colored tweed slack suit that looked as warm and as comfortable as it felt. She slipped into her coat, pulled her tam-o'-shanter onto her head, and hurried out of her apartment.

It was a cold day, but little rays of sunlight struggled through the sky like golden threads trying to tie the clouds back and prevent them from releasing their burden of snow. Though the huge clock above the archway was striking ten as she arrived at the appointed place in Central Park, Gwen saw no sign of Paul and his daughter. She sat on a bench on the promenade.

Too early and too cold for most New Yorkers, the park

Love After Hours

was relatively deserted. Gwen hugged her purse to her and glanced around. Before long, she sighted two figures approaching from the Fifty-ninth Street entrance. Suddenly she felt apprehensive: Would Melanie like her or resent her? Turning up her collar against an inner chill, she rose from the bench and began walking toward them.

Paul smiled and waved as he caught sight of her, then turned to say something to Melanie, who turned an impassive face in Gwen's direction and quickened her pace to keep up with her father.

Trying to sound very casual, Paul made the introductions, stretching the truth a little by saying that Gwen was one of the editors who published his work. All the while, the tall, thin girl at his side was regarding Gwen with a child's frank curiosity. Were it not for the sadness that seemed to linger in their depths, the gray eyes that looked up into Gwen's from behind a pair of dark-rimmed, circular glasses might have been Paul's. Fringed by long, light lashes, the wideness of her eyes was accentuated by her high cheekbones, narrow chin, and thin face. The paleness of her skin was heightened by her gray parka and a cherry-red stocking cap from beneath which her straight, ash-blond hair cascaded past her shoulders.

Gwen held out her hand. "It's nice to meet you Melanie. Your father's told me a lot about you. Happy birthday." Though she meant them sincerely, the words sounded awkward and hollow to her ears and seemed to hang frozen in the air between them.

Then the frosty pause melted as Melanie's pale lips curved into a shy smile, and she placed a red-mittened hand in Gwen's. "Thank you. I'm glad to meet you, too."

If a rabbit could speak, Gwen thought, it would sound like that—soft and gentle and a little scared. She pressed the hand in hers, feeling a rush of warmth for the lovely child before her.

"Does everyone tell you you have your father's eyes?" she asked softly.

Shyly, Melanie glanced away and withdrew her hand. "Some people say that."

There was a pause, but Paul quickly intervened before it

could become awkward, suggesting they stroll through the zoo. They watched the seals at their antics and looked in on all the other animals except the big cats.

"I hate them," Melanie confided, hurrying Gwen and Paul past their cages with a shudder.

Hesitating, Gwen glanced back at the panther, whose sleek jet coat glistened as he prowled the confines of his man-made prison in moody majesty. "They're quite beautiful, though," she protested mildly.

"That's the worst thing about them—that they can be so beautiful and yet so sneaky and vicious at the same time." Melanie's face had paled, and there was genuine fear in her eyes. "That's why I can't stand to be near them."

Paul gave the tassel on her stocking cap a gentle tug. "It's their nature, Mellie. You can't blame them for something they can't help."

Melanie turned to Gwen. "Daddy tells me that every time we come here. I can't seem to make him understand that I don't blame them for their nature, I—I just don't like them because of it."

"I do understand," Paul assured her. "I just want to make sure that you keep seeing it that way too."

Melanie sighed and shrugged, shaking her head over the obscurities of parental logic, but Paul's eyes met Gwen's, and Gwen realized that he suspected Melanie's feelings ran far deeper than simple distaste for feline instinct.

"Well," Gwen said, trying to head the conversation to pleasanter paths, "what's your favorite animal then?"

"The deer. Come on, let's take another look at them." Brightening, she darted ahead toward their cages.

"Aren't they sweet?" she asked when Paul and Gwen caught up with her. "They're beautiful and gentle and would never harm a fly."

"Like you," Paul said, slipping his arm around Melanie's shoulders and giving her a little hug.

"Oh, Daddy!" she protested, her cheeks coloring, but she snuggled closer to him.

Smiling, Gwen looked at Melanie, realizing that Paul's comparison was not a casual one. One had only to look into those wide gray eyes to see that the child was like a deer—

sweet and gentle, unable and unwilling to hurt others, and because of this, often cruelly hurt by them.

"What's your favorite animal?" Melanie broke in on Gwen's thoughts.

"The giraffe," Gwen said. "I guess I like them for the same reasons you love the deer. But there's more too. When I was growing up, I felt as though I were all arms and legs and neck. I always admired the giraffe for being able to take those same awkward qualities and merge them into a beautiful, graceful whole. I think it gave me hope and taught me that it's not what we have that counts, but what we do with it."

Melanie nodded. "I like them too. What's your favorite, Daddy?"

"The hippopotamus," he said with mock seriousness, "because he teaches us the same lesson Gwen's giraffe does."

They all laughed.

"Well," Paul said, "where to now? The Children's Zoo?"

"Oh, Daddy! I'm thirteen now—too old for that kind of thing."

"You mean I'm going to have to wait until I have grandchildren to have an excuse to go in there again?"

Melanie giggled. "Maybe."

"I know what I'm not too old to do," Gwen said. "Take a ride on the merry-go-round."

Melanie looked wistful. Obviously, she loved the merry-go-round, but felt that at thirteen she should be too sophisticated for it.

"Please come on it with me," Gwen said. "I don't often have a chance to ride it, and it's no fun alone."

"Well, in that case . . ." Melanie's eyes sparkled with delight at being rescued from her dilemma. "How do we get there, Daddy?"

Paul glanced around to get his bearings. "We have to cut across the park. We'll take that flight of stairs near the bears' cages."

"Come on! I'll race you to the stairs!" The young sophisticate disappeared, and Melanie became a little girl again, racing ahead of them, the tail of her cherry-red stocking cap flying out behind her.

"We give up!" Paul called, laughing.

But she continued to run until she had reached the top of the stairs, where she sat down, elbows on knees, chin in hands, awaiting them.

"You're such slowpokes!" she teased.

Gwen looked at her sitting there, red-cheeked and panting, her eyes sparkling behind her glasses, and thought how very beautiful Melanie was. Instinctively, she started to reach for Paul's hand, to share the warmth she felt for his child with him. Then, remembering that as far as Melanie knew, she and Paul were only casual friends, she continued the gesture until she had brought her hand up to the top of her head where she straightened her hat. Her glance met Paul's, though, and she read in his eyes the same love and yearning for closeness that she knew he saw in hers. He pushed his hands deeper in his pockets as though to keep them from having their way and reaching out to her, and they quickened their steps.

At the top of the stairs, Paul reached down and tapped Melanie playfully on the top of her head. "What took you so long?" he asked.

Laughing, she jumped up and darted ahead again.

Paul watched her go. "You can't imagine what joy it is to see her like this. She doesn't laugh very often." He turned to Gwen, his eyes filled with love. "But soon we'll change all that for her, won't we?"

Gwen nodded, her gaze going back to Melanie, who was standing still now, her hands in the pockets of her parka, watching a squirrel digging up a nut.

"Soon," Gwen echoed, but she felt as though the word referred to something an eternity away.

They caught up with Melanie and walked three abreast the rest of the way. It wasn't long before the wind carried the strains of the calliope to them, and they quickened their steps as though under the spell of a magic piper. As they arrived, the carousel was slowing down, its fanciful horses making sleepy, slow-motion leaps as though halfheartedly trying to escape a charm cast by fairies intent on keeping them in the land of make-believe.

Love After Hours

Paul hurried to the ticket booth and came back flourishing tickets for double rides. The merry-go-round had stopped by then, and they hurried on. Gwen and Melanie mounted two gently snorting horses that were side by side, while Paul, having always wanted to ride the lion chariot, realized his dream a few rows behind them.

The gong sounded, making Gwen's heart quicken. The tinny music that inevitably evoked poignant memories of real or imagined golden days swelled, and the horses moved up and down, taking their younger riders on exciting imaginary adventures, and their older ones on the impossible pursuit of their childhood's lost illusions.

Gwen's eyes were misty at the ride's end, but she was surprised to see that Melanie's were too. They dismounted and waited for Paul, who was helping a young mother attach safety belts around her twins.

"Merry-go-rounds always make me want to cry," she confided to Melanie. "They make me miss my childhood, which is rather silly, because it really wasn't an extremely happy one."

There was a world of sad understanding in Melanie's eyes. "It isn't silly," she said softly. "I know what you mean. They don't really make you miss your childhood—they make you miss the way you wish your childhood might have been."

A shiver shot through Gwen. How sad it was to be so young and yet so wise. "Yes," she said. "That's it exactly."

For a moment, they stood there looking at each other. There was no need for more words. Each could see into the other's heart, and each was moved by what she saw there. From that moment they were friends, and the rest of the day passed in a happy haze of relaxed warmth and closeness.

They lunched on hamburgers and hot dogs at the park cafeteria, then took a bus to the Museum of Natural History, where they spent the rest of the afternoon wandering among the natural wonders of the earth. But the most magnificent wonder Gwen experienced was that she could share laughter and intimacy with the child as well as the father, that the three of them could so easily merge into a warm and comfortable unit.

As they were leaving the museum, she extended an invitation to dinner, and Melanie seemed genuinely pleased. The girl's eyes lit up when, upon arriving at Gwen's apartment, she discovered the festive table Gwen had set up in the living room with her homemade cake as the centerpiece.

Gwen smiled a little self-consciously. "To change the title of an old song—I hoped you'd be coming, so I baked a cake."

"Look at it, Daddy!" Melanie exclaimed. "Isn't it beautiful?" She turned to Gwen. "No one's ever baked a cake for me before." She stopped short and cast a worried glance at Paul, obviously afraid she'd hurt him. "Daddy's always bought me the most beautiful, delicious cakes a girl could want, though."

Paul laughed and tousled her hair. "You're not going to hurt my feelings if you admit it's not the same, Mellie. I'm as pleased with Gwen's cake as you are."

Gwen settled them in the living room, Paul with a highball, Melanie with a Coke, then went into her bedroom to get the present she had spent her entire lunch hour shopping for the day before—a cuddly stuffed panda.

Melanie squealed with delight when she opened the box. "It's adorable!" she cried, throwing her arms around Gwen and giving her an impulsive squeeze. She ran back to the box and lifted the panda out of the tissue paper. "I'm going to keep it on top of my bed all the time! It's—" Suddenly, her eyes clouded and the blood drained from her cheeks. A coldness seemed to creep into the room, and Gwen knew the child was thinking of her mother. Melanie bit her lip, her eyes full of apology. "I—I'll have to say that Daddy gave it to me."

"That's all right," Gwen told her. "Just enjoy the gift."

Paul told an amusing story while they finished their drinks, and their laughter quickly banished Verna's presence from the room.

When Gwen went to the kitchen to prepare dinner, Melanie followed, asking if she could help.

"There's not much to do," Gwen said, "but you can keep me company if you like."

"How about me?" Paul called after them.

"No boys allowed!" Melanie teased. She sat on the stepladder stool near the sink, watching Gwen as she put up water for spaghetti and prepared steaks for the broiler. They chatted freely about Melanie's school, her likes and dislikes, the books she'd read. Then they began reviewing the events of the day.

"I think," Melanie said, "that this is the happiest birthday I've ever had."

"I'm glad that I've been part of it," Gwen told her sincerely. "It's one of the nicest days I've ever had, too."

Melanie sighed. "I wish it never had to end."

Gwen took vegetables for salad from the refrigerator and began rinsing them. "You'll have your memory of it, though."

Melanie nodded, her eyes troubled. "Sometimes it's hard to keep your memories straight when someone's always trying to get at them and tear them apart."

Gwen realized this was a reference to Verna, and her heart ached at the unhappiness she saw in Melanie's eyes. But to offer sympathy at that point would have been an admission that she was more familiar with the situation than a casual acquaintance of Paul's should be.

Keeping her face impassive, she asked, "What do you mean?"

Obviously afraid she'd said too much, Melanie shrugged and attempted to laugh the remark away. "Oh, nothing. It was a stupid thing to say. I'm always saying stupid things."

Gwen's eyes never left hers. "Funny. I haven't heard you say one stupid thing all day."

Embarrassed, Melanie glanced away, then picked up one of the carrot sticks Gwen had cut and began to nibble on it.

"My mother used to tell me that eating raw carrots would keep my hair red," Gwen said lightly, trying to ease over the awkwardness and change the subject. "So for years, I refused to eat them."

Melanie's eyes widened with amused curiosity. "Why?"

Gwen laughed. "I thought that by keeping carrot dye out of my system I could change the color of my hair. I wanted it to be blond—like yours."

"Like mine?" Incredulous, Melanie glanced down at the ash-blond tresses shimmering past her shoulders, then back at Gwen. "But yours is such a pretty color. Mine's just ordinary mouse."

Gwen smiled. "Do you realize that women spend small fortunes at beauty parlors just to have their hair changed to that same mousey color? Only, they call it ash blond. You have beautiful hair, Melanie. You're a beautiful girl."

Melanie shook her head sadly. "You're nice to say that, but you don't have to. I know I'm not pretty. I'm too tall and too skinny. I'm pale. My eyes are a nothing gray, my lashes are too light." She sighed. "When I was little, I used to cry about it a lot. But I'm used to it now. I don't mind it anymore."

Gwen shook her head in disbelief. "I think we're talking about two different girls. Have you looked in the mirror lately?"

"I don't have to. I've heard it often enough."

From Verna obviously, Gwen realized, feeling a white-hot rage against the mother who would try to pulverize her daughter's ego in such a way. She pretended, however, that she suspected a different source for Melanie's warped image of herself.

"You mustn't listen to your classmates' catty remarks," she insisted. "It's obvious that they're jealous of you. There's no such thing as being too tall these days, and it's fashionable to be thin. You're not pale, you're fair. Your face has the fine bones and delicate features of a model, and your eyes are an intriguing gray. Your lashes may be light, but they're long and thick, and when you're older, you'll find that a little mascara will do wonders for them." She paused a second, holding Melanie's eyes with her own. "Don't let anyone make you sell yourself short, Melanie. You're a beautiful girl—inside and out—and you're going to grow up to be a stunning woman."

A little patch of red began staining each of Melanie's cheeks, and her eyes remained fastened on Gwen's as though they longed to take hold of the lifeline she had thrown out but was afraid it might turn out to be an imaginary one. "Do you really think so?"

Love After Hours 235

Gwen nodded. "I know so. But don't take my word for it. Look—*really* look—in the mirror the next time you wash your face or comb your hair; you'll see I'm right. I wouldn't lie to you, Melanie. I'd never lie to anyone I cared about."

The flush on her cheeks deepening, Melanie bit her lip. Her gaze remained locked with Gwen's for a moment, then her silky-lashed eyelids lowered, shading the sadness and longing in her eyes. She reached for the lettuce Gwen had rinsed.

"May I break this up in the bowl for you?" Her voice was light, as though the intimacy they'd experienced a second ago hadn't happened, but her eyes when she looked up still reflected it.

"Please," Gwen said, pushing the salad bowl toward her.

For a little while they worked in silence, but there was no awkwardness about the lack of conversation. It was the warm silence of two people who are comfortable with each other and don't need to express themselves with words.

Melanie finished with the lettuce and extended the bowl toward Gwen, who added the other vegetables she'd been slicing and dicing.

"You like my father very much, don't you?" she asked with childlike candor.

The question took Gwen by surprise. For a moment her mind raced ahead, seeking the proper answer, the perfect evasion. But when her eyes met Melanie's expectant gaze, she realized that she could not bring herself to evade the question. What she had told the girl before was true: She could not lie to her.

"Yes," she said softly. "I like him very much."

"I'm glad," she said, "because I can tell he likes you too. He seemed so—so happy today. And he laughed so much. Daddy doesn't laugh very much at home."

Gwen's eyes misted as she remembered Paul using almost the same words in reference to Melanie.

"Being with him makes me happy too," she said.

Melanie's eyes searched her face. "I hope you'll always be his friend," she said quietly. "And mine too."

Gwen slipped her arm around her. "Always," she promised. "Now let's get dinner on the table before we all faint from starvation."

Like the day that had gone before it, the evening was as warm and glowing as the candlelight on the birthday table. Paul, Gwen and Melanie talked, laughed and teased through dinner as though they were already a family. All too soon it was nine o'clock, and Paul said that he and Melanie must be going.

Gwen refused Melanie's offer to help clear up, protesting that it wouldn't take her long.

Impulsively, Melanie hugged Gwen when they were at the door. "Thank you for everything."

"Thank you for letting me share your birthday."

Melanie grew pensive. "I hope I see you again."

"You will," Gwen promised.

"Good night, and thanks." Paul's eyes conveyed the kiss he could not give her.

The apartment seemed lonelier than usual after Gwen had closed the door behind them.

Chapter Twelve

In the newsstand jungle, where to hold one's own is a prodigious feat in itself, a rise in sales is tantamount to a miracle. But editorial miracles do not just happen; they are achieved by the ability, sweat and cunning of the editors involved. Jason Bart could never have risen to the top-dog position of editorial director of Waterford Publications if he had not been cognizant of that fact, and he could never have maintained his post if he did not try to belittle these same editors, thus holding budgets and egos to a minimum. Perhaps that was why, at the end of February, instead of congratulating Gwen on the rise in sales-circulation figures for the past three months, he returned to her the latest article she wanted to purchase for her sex-and-modern-morality series with the notation that he felt the series was being overdone.

The blood rushed to Gwen's cheeks as she read the memo. She had a crack writer working on the series, and she had negotiated long and hard to get her. More important, she was convinced that it was this series, above all else, that was responsible for her rise in sales. With the manuscript and memo in one hand and a copy of her circulation figures in the other, she marched up to Jason's office and demanded to be seen.

Though he granted permission for her to enter his sanctum sanctorum the moment his secretary announced her presence, Jason did not look up, but continued signing the correspondence on his desk when she entered. Quietly, Gwen walked across the plush carpeting and seated herself in the conference chair nearest the expansive and elaborate mahogany desk that dominated the office. Everything in that spacious office seemed larger than life, as though intended to awe and intimidate visitors. Heavy gold gabardine drapes, that opened and closed at the flick of a drawstring, hung from the windows and blended perfectly with the thick-piled carpeting. Except for six feet of space allotted to an elaborate bar, bookcases lined the walls, and two exquisitely wrought, low glass-topped tables held the current issues of all the magazines in the Waterford chain.

At last Jason leaned back in his regal, high-backed chair of leather and mahogany—the kind of chair that Cam Eckhart would cheerfully have shaved his beard for. Still saying nothing, Jason leveled his gaze at Gwen. His pale brown eyes, the color of excellent Scotch, had their customary, slightly glazed look. As usual, he had probably drunk his lunch. Jason Bart's drinking was a legend among Waterfordians. The amount of liquor he was able to consume without slurring a word, missing a step, or losing an iota of mental acuteness demanded both the respect and awe of all. Now as Gwen watched him tilt back in his chair, the overhead light glinting off his iron-gray hair and showing his rugged though dissipated features to their best advantage, she wondered fleetingly which rumor about his drinking was true: the one that claimed his beautiful young wife had committed suicide twenty years ago in despair because he drank so much; or the other that claimed he began drinking twenty years ago in despair because his beautiful young wife had committed suicide. Whatever the reason, though, Jason's drinking and the scandal surrounding his wife's death remained great subjects of Waterford gossip.

"What's on your mind?" Jason finally asked.

Gwen was aware that he had deliberately kept her waiting to make her uncomfortable and nervous, but she was neither. She extended the memo she was holding in her hand. "I'd like to know what prompted this."

He pulled himself up. "I'm not in the habit of having to explain my memos. I think it's self-explanatory."

She shook her head. "Jason, you can't be serious." She tapped the manuscript in her lap. "This is a damned good article. Surely the market for sex is never satiated. Every magazine we publish carries at least one article an issue on the subject, not to mention all the books we publish that are dedicated to it."

"Different markets have different needs. I think yours has had it from the angle these articles cover."

She placed her circulation figures on his desk. "My last three issues had circulation rises. Those were the issues that carried the first three articles on sex and the new morality. I can't believe that that's a coincidence."

"Why not?" Jason asked. "No one can say definitely why the rise took place. It may be indicative only of a slight economic upswing that will affect all our other magazines as well."

"Did it affect all of them during the last three months?" Gwen demanded.

Jason pursed his lips. "That's beside the point."

"On the contrary," Gwen insisted, "I think it *is* the point. The sex articles in those three issues pulled in new readers who are obviously willing to stick with us if we keep giving them more of the same. If we don't, we're going to lose them—and perhaps some of our old readers too."

Jason tapped his well-manicured fingernails on the desk. "You're basing everything you say on pure speculation, and you're not taking into consideration the fact that the word has come down from upstairs that we're to cut budgets."

Gwen leaned forward, her eyes sparking. "The budget be damned! You're the one who decides where the cuts will be made. If you must save money, take away a couple of Cam's precious cartoons or one of his file clerks. Don't rob me of the very thing I need to survive in that newsstand jungle out there!"

Jason tilted back in his chair, his eyes taking her measure. "I'm not sure there is sufficient proof that those articles *are* what you need."

She stood up. "You're editorial director here, Jason, because your judgment of editors is considered sound. Ten months ago, you considered *my* editorial judgment sound enough to name me the editor of one of the biggest confession magazines in the country." She nodded toward the manuscript in her hand. "Is your rejection of this article a reflection on my judgment—or yours?"

For a second he rocked a little in his chair, his face expressionless. Gwen remained standing, refusing to be stared down. When he finally righted his chair, his eyes held a mixture of amusement and respect.

"All right," he said. "I'll put it through."

"Good," Gwen said, placing the manuscript in his hand. She refused to say *thank you*, because she did not want to imply that the purchase was a favor. "I hope I won't have to fight with you about future articles in the series."

"We'll see how future sales go."

It wasn't until she was in the corridor waiting for the elevator that Gwen realized she had won too easily. Obviously, Jason had purposely created the situation to test her; it was part of the cat-and-mouse game male directors felt compelled to play with female executives. She might have resented it more if she had not recalled the respect she'd seen in Jason's eyes. She had not only passed the test, she had been graduated. Without his saying a word about it, she was sure that from now on she'd have the carte blanche enjoyed by all the male editors though, of course, she'd be expected to work and fight harder than they did to maintain it.

She had been back at her desk for only a few minutes when Terri came in with some final proofs on the main section of the May issue for her okay. While she was going over them, she was aware of Terri hovering nearby, shifting her weight from one foot to the other, brushing invisible lint from her skirt, patting her hairdo, giving every impression of a child trying to catch an adult's attention.

Oh, hell! Gwen thought when she looked up at Terri's eager face. *She's in one of her just-between-us-girls moods.* Hoping to escape what was sure to be a confidence, she handed back the proofs with only a nod and turned to the manuscript she had been working on before Terri's interruption.

Still Terri remained.

Gwen sighed. Terri obviously intended to stand there until she was asked what was on her mind. Gwen hoped it wasn't another dream. Having never read Freud, Terri delighted in revealing to others the "crazy" dreams she had, never realizing that they abounded in phallic symbols and symbolic representations of coitus. Then she would giggle at the "meaninglessness" of it all while her more well-read audience cringed in embarrassment for her.

"Is there something on your mind?" Gwen asked finally.

"Well, not on my mind exactly, but I had some good news today that I knew you'd want to share."

"Really?" Gwen toyed with her pencil and tried to look politely interested.

"Yes!" Terri was positively glowing. "Harry's wife died yesterday."

The pencil dropped from Gwen's hand, and for a moment she was afraid she wouldn't be able to fight down the cold lump of nausea that catapulted from her stomach to the back of her throat. When she finally managed to get the lump under control, she asked, as evenly as she could, "What made you think I'd be glad to hear such news?"

For a moment, Terri looked puzzled. Then realization dawned on her face. "Oh, you're worried about losing me!" She waved such a tragic possibility away with a flick of her hand. "I'll be here for a good while yet. After all, we won't be able to marry for close to a year."

As she studied Terri's eager face, Gwen's feeling of revulsion increased. In the bright fluorescent light, her makeup did little to hide the puttylike hue of her complexion or to disguise the little pouches of flesh that had begun to form under her eyes. She reminded Gwen of a bright-eyed ghoul.

"Why wait?" Gwen asked drily, thinking that vultures usually swooped down the moment their victims expelled their last breath.

Terri sighed. "Believe me, it's not that we *want* to. It's just that Harry has his position to keep up, and if we married too soon, there might be talk. People can be so unfeeling."

"Yes, can't they?"

There was no indication that Terri caught the sarcasm in Gwen's voice. "And then there's Harry's son," she rushed on. "It will probably take a little while for him to adjust. I guess we'll have to take that into consideration."

"It might be a good idea."

"Of course, it shouldn't take him long. These teenagers bounce right back. And I'll do everything I can to help him."

"With a stepmother like you, how could he miss?"

Terri tried unsuccessfully to look modest at what she evidently took to be a well-deserved compliment.

Goddammit! Get out of here before I vomit! Gwen thought, clenching her teeth.

But Terri showed no sign of leaving. Instead, she clutched the proofs a little closer and leaned across the desk confidentially. "Do you think I should go to the funeral?"

"Has Harry asked you?" Gwen asked, not trying to keep the edge off her voice.

"Well, of course, he's been so busy since she took a turn for the worse that he hasn't had a chance to call. A mutual friend told me about her passing on."

Passing on to what? Gwen wondered. Something better than what Harry had offered her, she hoped.

"Anyway, do you think I should go?" Terri prodded.

Obviously, she longed to go, to insinuate herself between the dead woman and her husband, weakening even more the pathetic, feeble, final demand a corpse had on a faithless man's attention. Gwen felt a great temptation to insist that it was none of her business, thus leaving Terri open to do as she wanted—and to fall flat on her face in front of the real mourners. But she pitied them, as Terri did not, and she tried to spare them.

"I don't think it would be a good idea," she said finally.

"Oh?" Terri's face fell.

"They might doubt your sincerity," Gwen explained, when Terri continued standing there, looking blank.

"But that would be ridiculous!"

"People under emotional strain might not be able to be as perceptive as you are."

Terri sighed, her petulant mouth turning down at the corners. She started out of the office, her stride not as jaunty as before. At the door, though, she brightened. "I know what I'll do—I'll send flowers."

Before Gwen had a chance to counsel against it, Terri was out the door. Shaking her head, Gwen returned to the manuscript. *Poor Harry's wife!* she thought. *She's probably well out of it.* She might have felt sorry for Harry too—if he did not so richly deserve Terri.

By the time she had finished going over the manuscript and had signed her correspondence for the day, it was close to five o'clock. She dialed the managing editor's extension and asked Laura Faber to come in, for she had not had an opportunity to tell her about her encounter with Jason Bart.

Laura sat across the desk from her, her eyes alive with interest, and now and then she nodded her head as Gwen related to her the arguments she'd used with Jason in behalf of the sex articles.

"I'm glad you got him to see reason," Laura said when Gwen had finished. "Those articles are probably the biggest single factor contributing to our sales rise."

"Along with our celebrity-bylined religious articles. They've helped too," Gwen reminded her.

Laura laughed. "Sex and God—in that order—the two main considerations in American homes. What I don't understand is how Jason Bart could have missed that point."

"I'm sure he didn't. It occurred to me afterward that he was testing me to see if I'd stand up for something I believed in the same way a man would."

"The bastard! Did you tell him you saw through his scheme?"

Gwen shook her head. "He'd only deny that it was one. A woman in business has to learn to take these male games in her stride. I won this round, and from the way it looked when I left his office, it will be quite a while before he initiates another—if ever. I think I have him off our backs."

"Well, that's good news."

The clacking of the typewriters in the outer office ceased, signaling five o'clock. Laura rose to go.

"One thing more," Gwen said. "Now that I've got him where I want him, I intend to press for a raise for you. I'm not going to take the story he gave me at the beginning of the year, about budgets being frozen, for an answer any more."

Laura frowned. "I appreciate it, Gwen," she said slowly, "but I really don't think you should make an issue out of it."

"Of course, I should," Gwen insisted. "You're a damn good editor. You deserve a raise."

Laura stood there hesitantly, as though she were trying to decide whether it was advisable to make a revelation. Evidently deciding in favor of it, she sat down again.

"Look, I wasn't going to say anything for a while yet," she said, "but I guess I better tell you now—before you start making things uncomfortable for yourself over me. I'm not going to be here too much longer."

A coldness washed over Gwen at the thought of losing Laura. She'd miss her creativity, imagination, and plain, down-to-earth industriousness; they were qualities that were hard to come by in workers these days. Then her anger flared as she realized that the raises Jason Bart had turned down for her staff at the beginning of the year might well have been responsible for Laura's decision to leave. She was a fool not to have fought harder for that raise.

"I take it you have another job lined up?" she asked, trying to sound nonchalant.

Laura laughed, her face lighting up. "I guess you could put it that way. I'm pregnant."

Though it didn't change the basic situation, Gwen felt relieved to know that she wasn't losing Laura to a competitor.

She smiled. "Congratulations. I would never have guessed. How far along are you?"

"I'm at the end of my third month," Laura said, glowing. "I had intended to wait until I'd rounded out my fourth before saying anything. It makes a woman seem pregnant so long when she starts talking about it right away."

Gwen laughed. "I know what you mean. When my sister was pregnant with her first son, she must have told me practically ten minutes after conception. By the time she gave birth, I had the feeling she'd been carrying that baby three years."

"That's why I'd rather you didn't say anything to anyone else for a while."

"Don't worry. It's your baby and your pregnancy. Any announcements concerning it are strictly up to you." She sighed. "I'll be sorry to see you go, Laura. Are you sure that's what you want to do? Have you considered the possibility of a leave of absence? I could probably manage to arrange one for up to a year."

Laura shook her head. "I don't think I could manage it, though—raising a baby and working."

"Many women do."

"They're made of sterner stuff than I am."

"I'd say you had a lot more to offer than most of the working mothers I've seen."

"Oh, it's not that I think I couldn't measure up physically to the two jobs. It's just that I know I'm not psychologically suited for both together. There's an awful lot of talk these days about the right of a mother to a career, but very little about the right of the child to its mother's attention. Maybe I'm conceited, but I can't believe that any nurse or housekeeper could give my child the same kind of loving care I could."

Gwen smiled affectionately. "I'm sure you're right. But isn't Frances always saying that it isn't the quantity of time a mother spends with her child, but the quality?"

"I'm sure that would work for her and for a lot of women, but it wouldn't for me. I know I'd feel torn between two worlds—and I probably wouldn't be able to give my best to either." She shook her head. "My mother was widowed when I was six, and she *had* to go to work. Until I was old enough to stay by myself, baby-sitters cared for me after school. There's nothing lonelier for a child than coming home to an empty house—or to one occupied by a stranger. I have a feeling that no matter what the quality of love we give a child after five o'clock, it's the loneliness that he experiences in the hours before it that he remembers most vividly when he's grown. I want my baby too much to give him a burden of memories like that when it isn't necessary."

She stood up, smiling a little sadly. "I know Frances and many others sneer at the idea, but I still think that raising a child to be a happy, decent, well-rounded human being in this crazy world of ours is a full-time job that's at least as important as being the managing editor of a magazine."

Gwen's eyes misted. "You're wrong," she said softly. "It's a hell of a lot more important. If I were in your shoes, I'd do the same thing."

Laura smiled warmly. "Thanks. I'm glad to find someone who agrees with me. There are times when I feel like an atavism."

"If you are, you're a good one. How does David feel about it, by the way?"

At the mention of her husband, Laura's eyes glowed as they always did. "He's as thrilled about the baby as I am. As far as the decision to work or to stay home—well, he said it was entirely up to me and that he'd back me in whatever I wanted."

"He's a gem," Gwen said, "and you're another. That's going to be one lucky baby."

"Speaking of David, I'd better be off. I was supposed to meet him downstairs at five. He must be turning blue."

Just before she reached the door, there was a knock and it opened. It was David.

"Hi," he said to Gwen. "I was just about to ask you if you'd seen my wife, but I see her myself." He planted a quick kiss on Laura's cheek. "I'll wait in your office if you're busy."

"I was just leaving," Laura said. "We got to talking, and I'm afraid I forgot the time. Are you frozen?"

"My glasses fogged up a bit and I got a minor case of frostbite, that's all," David teased.

Gwen came around her desk and extended a hand toward him. "Laura tells me you're about to become parents. Congratulations."

Beaming, David took her hand. "Aren't we clever?"

Gwen laughed. "I tried to talk Laura into being a working mother, but she wouldn't hear of it."

"You didn't try very hard," Laura reminded her.

"That's because my heart wasn't in it. Good night. Have a nice evening."

"Good night."

David slipped his arm around Laura's shoulders, and Gwen could hear them laughing softly as they headed for Laura's office.

As she cleared her desk, Gwen's thoughts returned to the conversations she'd had that afternoon. In the span of a few hours, the whole life cycle had passed before her in her office—from the death of Harry's wife to the new life growing within Laura's womb. That was life. We were born; we died. And there was so little time left for what happened in between. She sighed. Thank God for Paul. If it weren't for him, it would all be so shallow, so meaningless. Soon, if all went well, they'd be free to be together always. Then they would truly feel whole and fulfilled.

If all went well. How could such little words hold so much threat? Paul kept assuring her that nothing could go wrong. And yet there were moments when she was seized by a cold panic that seemed to paralyze her. She never knew when the feeling would suddenly envelop her, like the choking, clammy embrace of a ghoul from the nethermost regions of hell. If she were with people, she would try to ignore the cold sweat, try to control the trembling of her hands. Like a lion tamer with an unruly beast, she would appear outwardly calm while using all her inner powers of concentration to bring the feeling under control, and force it back into a corner of her mind where it could do her no harm. But like the unruly lion, the fear would crouch there watching, always watching, waiting for the moment when, too self-confident, she would look away. Then it would pounce again.

Paul said that when happiness was almost within one's grasp, it was only natural to fear that something would happen to snatch it away. But nothing would happen, he assured her; everything would work out. Yet she knew he worried too. Verna wasn't doing too well in rehearsals, and there was only another month to go before the opening of the play. But there was really no way Verna could back out of her agreement, was there? So, no matter what happened with the play, everything would work out. . . .

The voices of David and Laura, soft and intimate as they laughed over some private joke on their way to the elevator, drifted in through the deserted outer office and over Gwen's partition, interrupting her thoughts. She paused, listening. How marvelous it must be to be free to love as Laura and David were, free to reveal one's feelings in public in a look, a touch, a word, a laugh, never fearing that the wrong person might see—and tell. Shrugging into her coat, she assured herself that soon she and Paul would know that freedom too.

As she rode down in the elevator, she toyed with the idea of shopping for a new pair of shoes, but the cold, damp air that rushed to meet her when she walked out of the building quickly changed her mind. It would be better to go straight home. Paul had said he might be able to drop by for a little while around seven. It would give her a chance to bathe and change. A warm bath would be more welcome now than a pair of shoes anyway.

She squeezed into a crowded subway car, and, as always, began planning her strategy for making her way through the numberless bodies that formed a human barrier between her and the opposite doors, which would open at her stop. Einstein should have devoted himself to more pragmatic matters like the relativity of subway space, she thought, as she began elbowing her way through the unyielding mass and out the doors.

Collar turned up and hands in her coat pockets, she hurried the few blocks from the station to her apartment house, her breath forming tiny frozen clouds before the wind dispersed it.

She didn't see the figure huddled on the steps leading to the upper floors until she had unlocked the vestibule door. Heart pounding, she leaped backward as it suddenly uncurled itself and came rushing toward her. Then, emerging into the light, the shape called her name, and her apprehensive shock turned to pleased surprise.

"Shari! What are you doing here?" she cried as she hugged her friend.

"Waiting for you, of course!" Shari evaded the broader range of Gwen's question. "I tried to get your super to let me into your apartment by pretending to be your sister, but he told me he wouldn't open the door for the Queen of England herself unless you had told him to do so. He was kind enough, though, to let me into the hall before the wind turned my blood to ice."

Gwen laughed. "Good old Mr. Taverat! Thank heaven he has a kind heart as well as a suspicious nature, or you might have been turning blue out there. I almost went shopping after work. I'd have kicked myself if I had missed you." She started up the stairs. "What happened? Did you spend the day in the city and then miss your train?"

"Not exactly."

"No, of course not. They leave about every fifteen minutes at this time of day, don't they?" Gwen corrected herself. They reached her landing, and she unlocked her door, swinging it open and switching on the hall light. "Well, whatever the reason, welcome."

"Thanks." Shari's voice was subdued.

Gwen pulled off her tam-o'-shanter, and shook her hair loose. "Why didn't Bill let me know you were coming? I'd have picked up something decent for dinner. Now we'll have to make do with bacon and eggs."

"Bill didn't know I was coming." Shari bit her lip, and her velvet-brown eyes drifted from Gwen's face to a suitcase propped against the wall farther down the hall. She smiled a little tremulously. "Your Mr. Taverat was less suspicious of my suitcase than he was of me. He brought it inside."

A sudden chill of foreboding shivered through Gwen as she stared at the suitcase as though it were an omen of evil. Slowly, she brought her puzzled gaze back to Shari. For the first time since encountering her downstairs, she looked hard at her friend and saw that the cheeks so often dimpled with vivacious smiles were flat planes, and the formerly laughing eyes were deeply troubled.

Shari drew a jagged breath. "I've left Bill, Gwen."

"My God, Shari! No!"

Shari didn't answer, but stood there nodding her head like a mechanical doll.

"But why? In God's name, *why?*"

Shari pressed a trembling hand to her forehead. "That's the first time I've said it out loud." Her voice was almost a whisper. "Please. Let's go sit down. I don't think I can stand up much longer."

"Of course," Gwen said. "Here. Give me your coat and go on inside. I'll be right with you."

Her brain still whirling from the impact of Shari's announcement, she hung up their coats, then followed Shari into the living room. Shari was seated on the sofa, her slender fingers toying nervously with a button on her blouse, her eyes gazing off into space. Looking at her, Gwen felt transported back in time and space, as though she were suddenly living in another time, long ago, when she had seen Shari wearing the same sad, troubled expression. But Shari was always happy, vivacious; it must have been in a dream that she had seen her looking that way. And then she remembered. It hadn't been a dream; it had been the night of the Waterford party. Shari had seemed preoccupied then. There had been moments in which Gwen had caught her toying with the catch on her purse and gazing off into space as though searching for a memory or a dream. But these had been only fleeting moments in the midst of Shari's usual exuberance. Now it was the exuberance that had fled.

"I could use a drink," Gwen said. "How about you?"

Shari nodded.

In the kitchen, Gwen mixed two strong highballs and then returned to the living room with the bottle in tow. She placed the liquor on the table. "We may be needing more of this."

Wordlessly Shari accepted her drink.

For a moment, Gwen stood staring down into her own drink. Then she sank into a chair. "I'd propose a toast, but I can't think of a damn thing to drink to."

"How about new beginnings?" Shari said, downing a good portion of her highball.

"Not when the endings hurt so much." Gwen shook her head. "I can't believe it! I was talking to Bill the other day. He never even hinted that anything might be wrong between you two."

"I guess he didn't know." Shari tilted her glass, watching the ice cubes chase each other in their amber pool.

"But how could he *not* know that you were about to walk out on him?"

"Easy. I didn't know myself until twelve o'clock this afternoon." Nervously fingering loose ends of her hair back into its French knot, Shari gazed into space as though trying to recall the circumstances.

"You can't expect me to believe that you made a snap

decision about something as important as this!" Gwen was incredulous.

As if with great effort, Shari pulled herself back from her pursuit of other thoughts and concentrated on Gwen's question.

"I suppose it seems that way on the surface," she said at last. "But it's something I've been considering for a long time in the back of my mind. Maybe even longer than I'm aware of."

"But you and Bill, of all people!" Gwen protested. "You've always been so right for each other. Your marriage seemed so perfect."

Shari sighed. "Perfect for Bill maybe. Not for me. For a long time now, I've been slowly suffocating." She got up and began mixing herself another drink.

For a moment as she watched Shari, a vision of Bill flashed before Gwen, his eyes twinkling with kindness and laughter behind his thick eyeglasses. She sucked in her breath at the pain she felt at the thought of her two best friends parting.

"Do you mean you've stopped loving Bill?" she asked.

Shari looked at Gwen thoughtfully. When she spoke, it was as though her words were a precious commodity that had to be carefully weighed. "No. No, I love Bill. I suppose I always will." For a second, her eyes glowed with tears, but she drew a deep, shuddering breath that seemed to chase them away. "It's just that I can't live with him anymore," she went on, her voice cracking a little. "For the last nine years, I've been so busy being Bill's wife and Robby, Tommy, and Allison's mother that I've lost complete track of who *I* am. Don't you see, I have to leave so I can find out who I am before it's too late?"

"But being Bill's wife and the children's mother is part of what you are."

"Part, yes, but that's not enough anymore."

She sank down on the sofa, resting her head against its back and closing her eyes. "I'm going crazy, Gwen. I'm going absolutely out of my mind!" Straightening, she turned her eyes back to Gwen, who shivered at the unhappiness she saw in them. "I spent four years of my life in college—and for what? To spend the rest of it worried about cooking dinner, doing the wash, keeping a nine-room ranch house looking clean, wiping noses, talking baby talk, driving carpools, applying Band-Aids, attending the PTA? My God! There has to be more to life than that! And I've got to find it before I'm too old to appreciate it."

"And so—just like that—you decided to walk out?" Gwen asked sadly.

"Just like that. At noon today, I was trying to wipe up Allison's spilled milk, break up a fight between the boys, and rescue the cake I'd baked for the PTA from the dog when the phone rang and my neighbor asked me to take over her turn in the Cub Scout car-pool. I suddenly felt that I couldn't take another minute. After lunch, I brought the boys back to school, put Allison in for her nap, packed a few things, called a baby-sitter, and came to the city."

Gwen shook her head. "But what can you possibly hope to find in this godforsaken place that you couldn't find at home?"

"Myself." She held up a hand to ward off any more questions that Gwen might ask. "There's no time and no place for me to be that at home. There, I'm always so busy being all things for all people that there's nothing left over for me."

She gazed off for a moment, as though trying to visualize what she had in mind. "I want to know what it's like to be independent again," she went on finally, her eyes glowing, "to work and to take care of myself. I want to be among people who talk about important things—not recipes, the latest virus, and the newest sex manual, or dollies' tea parties and making Little League. I want to be in the midst of life, not on the fringes of it. I want to be a person again! I want my dignity back!"

Gwen's heart ached for the agonizing time she knew Shari had been through, but she was impatient with her too, half-suspecting that she was acting like one of the children she longed to escape.

"For God's sake, Shari!" she cried. "Wake up to all you have! Do you know how many 'independent' women would give their eye teeth to change places with you?"

Love After Hours

Smiling sadly, Shari shook her head. "Only because they've never been there. Believe me, it's death by slow suffocation."

"And how do you expect to find your way back to life here?"

"I hoped you'd let me stay with you for a day or two until I get my head on straight. Then I'll get a job and an apartment."

"And that will be life with a capital *L*?" Gwen shook her head sadly. "Oh, Shari! You're in for a big disappointment."

"I don't think so. Please, Gwen, don't lecture me. It won't work. There isn't any argument you can toss at me that I haven't tossed at myself—and tossed away. I have to do this to save my sanity. So don't throw stones until you've walked in my moccasins—or however that saying goes. Okay?"

"Okay." Gwen smiled a little and nodded, but she didn't give up. Instead, she tried another tactic. "What about the children?"

The calm that had been in Shari's eyes a second before now vanished. "Don't keep throwing questions at me!" She ran a slender, shaking hand over her forehead. "I haven't thought everything out. I don't know. I'd like to get a housekeeper and have them with me, but they're probably better off where they are. Maybe Bill can find someone to take care of them."

"And what about Bill?" She felt like a prosecutor relentlessly pressing her case.

Shari shook her head, her eyes filling. "He's strong. He loves me, but he doesn't really need me. He'll get by. Later, I'll talk to him. But not yet. He'd only mix me up. I left him a note saying that I was going to stay at a hotel." She got up and began pacing the room. "He mustn't know where I am—not till I have myself settled. Then I'll be strong enough to face him." She stopped in front of Gwen's chair, her eyes pleading for help. "I'll talk to Bill, but it must be in my own time. Please, Gwen, help me. If he asks you, don't tell him where I am."

For a moment, her loyalties torn, Gwen hesitated.

"Please!" Shari begged. "Promise you'll help me!"

Gwen's heart went out to her. Reaching up, she took her hand. "All right," she whispered.

They were still looking at each other in a silent pledge when the doorbell rang.

Paul! Gwen disengaged her hand and hurried to the door. She greeted Paul with a quick kiss, then took his hand. "I have unexpected company," she whispered, leading him into the living room.

Having met the night of the Waterford party, Shari and Paul had no need for introductions. They greeted each other, and Paul sat down, accepting the drink Gwen offered. Conversation about trivialities flowed easily, but as soon as it was politely acceptable, Paul rose to leave.

"It was good seeing you again," he told Shari. "Give my regards to Bill."

"Thanks. I will." Shari smiled at Paul, but her eyes flashed a panicky message to Gwen, who received it with a nod.

When they were alone at the door, Gwen went into Paul's arms. Lovingly, she rubbed her cheek against the rough tweed of his overcoat.

"Shari will probably be here for a few days," she whispered at last. "Sorry."

He held her a little away from him so that she would have to look up into his eyes. "Don't be," he said tenderly. "You have a right to a life of your own, remember?"

She smiled and tried to keep her voice light, but her eyes misted. "I wish to hell I didn't."

"Soon," he whispered. "Soon." And he pulled her back, his lips crushing down on hers in a kiss that left them both dizzy.

Finally, reluctantly, Gwen pulled away. "I'd better get back to Shari. She'll wonder what's keeping me."

Paul's eyes twinkled. "I'll bet she has a vague idea." He pulled her close again, gently rubbing his cheek against hers, tenderly caressing her hair. "Take care of yourself, darling," he whispered. "I'll call."

Releasing her, he reached for the doorknob, but she placed a restraining hand on his arm. "Paul."

"Yes?"

Love After Hours

"If for any reason you should happen to speak to Bill—please don't mention that you saw Shari here."

He raised an inquisitive eyebrow.

"It's a long story. I'll tell you about it as soon as I can."

"Tell her her secret's safe with me." Once more, he brushed his lips on hers. "Good-by. I love you."

"I love you."

She leaned against the door a moment, listening to Paul's footsteps recede down the corridor and the stairs. With a sigh, she went back to Shari.

"Don't worry," she assured her. "Paul won't say a word."

"Thanks." Shari studied her a minute. "You two are in love, aren't you?"

"Bill never told you?"

Shari shook her head. "No. I wonder why?"

Gwen's heart ached with the pain of her own situation. "Perhaps he thought it wouldn't last. There are many complications."

Shari's eyes filled with sympathy. "I'm sorry," she said. "Not just sorry that you have trouble of your own, but sorry that my turning up here with mine kept you from being alone with Paul tonight."

"There'll be other nights." Suddenly her eyes misted, and when she spoke, her voice was choked with tears. "Do you have any idea what Paul and I would give for a situation like the one you're throwing aside?"

"Please!" Shari's face contorted with pain.

Gwen pulled herself together. "I'm sorry. A woman in my situation certainly has no right to criticize one in yours." She tried to force some gaiety into her voice. "Come on, let's go into the kitchen and see what we can rustle up for supper before we die of starvation."

Shari followed her, picking up the whiskey as she passed the table. "Just to make sure we don't die of thirst, either!" she said.

The two women talked long into the night, and when they finally went to bed, both fell asleep immediately, perhaps from the liquor or perhaps from emotional exhaustion—or both.

Gwen managed to rouse herself in time for work the next morning. She dressed quickly and tiptoed out to the kitchen for her usual breakfast of black coffee and toast. On the sofa—she had refused Gwen's offer of her bed—her dark hair tumbling over her shoulders, Shari slept through Gwen's preparation of breakfast, looking like an innocent madonna with nothing but visions of heaven to disturb her dreams. Gwen toyed with the idea of waking her, then changed her mind and scribbled a hasty note, which she left on the cocktail table along with the extra keys that Paul consistently refused to take.

By arriving at work a little early, she managed to avoid encountering Bill in the elevator. As soon as Betsy arrived, Gwen told her that she did not want to be disturbed with calls and visits, using the fact that she would be working on cover lines for the June issue as an excuse. In this way, she managed to get through the entire day without any contact with Bill. A check of her telephone messages later, however, showed that he hadn't tried to get in touch with her.

It was ten minutes after five, long after all signs of life had fled the office, before she felt it was safe enough to leave. It proved to be too early, though, for as she neared Bill's office, she saw that his overhead light was still burning. His door was closed, and she might easily have passed it without making her presence known. Instead, she stood there staring at the door as though by sheer willpower she could make her eyes penetrate its opaque glass and wood to discover the evidence they'd need to reassure her that Bill was indeed as strong as Shari insisted, and was taking his wife's desertion in stride. Her X-ray vision proving faulty, she convinced herself that she could look in and say a casual good night without becoming any more involved in his problems and Shari's than she already was.

Quietly, she opened the door.

Seated at his desk, his back to his brown "wailing wall," Bill was, ostensibly, going over a manuscript, but the slump of his shoulders and the way he held his head between his hands indicated that the words on the pages before him were far from the thoughts in his mind.

Love After Hours 257

Gwen bit her lip, tempted to flee before she was noticed, but at that same moment, Bill turned his head and saw her. For a moment, he regarded her as though he were not quite sure who she was. Then he gave a hazy smile and said, "Hi."

"Not 'hi'—'good-bye'!" Gwen said with a gaiety that sounded false to her own ears. "It's past the witching hour. Time to go home."

"Home? Oh." He seemed to be trying to pick up thoughts that were scattered all over the floor of his mind. He made a vague gesture toward his desk. "I still have . . . things to clear up."

"Oh. Well, then." Gwen began backing out. She couldn't stand to see him look so hurt, so bewildered, and she longed to get away. "See you."

"Gwen!"

The door had almost closed behind her. She could pretend she hadn't heard him call her name, hadn't noticed the pain in his voice. Why had she decided to look in in the first place? If only she had walked by without opening the door!

She swung the door open again.

"Yes?" Her false smile made her lips feel stiff and her cheeks ache.

"Can you spare me a minute?"

"Well, I—" With an elaborate gesture, she looked at her watch.

She was still trying to think of a way to back out when Bill ran a hand over his face and blurted: "Gwen—Shari's left me!"

She knew Shari had left him. She'd known it at least as long as he had—possibly longer. Yet the jagged edge of pain in his voice and the raw hurt in his eyes made his words hit her with the same awful impact that Shari's announcement had carried the night before.

"Oh, God, Bill! I'm sorry!" she said, and there was nothing hypocritical about the sorrow and shock mirrored in her eyes. She walked over and sank down in the chair next to his desk.

"She's gone," he said, spreading his hands helplessly. "Just like that—she's gone."

He jumped up and went over to the window, turning his back on her, but it was too late; Gwen had already seen the glint of tears in his eyes.

"How can a man who loves a woman so much drive her away without even knowing it?"

She licked her lips, but it didn't relieve the dryness in her mouth. "Maybe it has nothing to do with you."

"Then why would she leave?" He turned back to Gwen, running his trembling fingers through his hair. "Oh, God, Gwen! Do you think there's someone else?"

"No." Gwen's voice was firm, forceful. At least she could spare him that much. "Not Shari. I know her. She could never love anyone but you, Bill."

"Goddammit, she has a funny way of showing it!" Sinking down at his desk again, he drew a shuddering breath, and Gwen could see him working to control his facial muscles, to fight back his tears. "She left a note saying she'd be staying at a hotel in the city. I've called every damn one of them, and she's not registered anywhere."

"Maybe she's using a false name."

He nodded absently.

"I'm sure she'll contact you when she's ready."

"And what am I supposed to do in the meantime? What am I supposed to tell the children? What am I supposed to tell myself?"

"I don't know," Gwen whispered.

For a while, they sat in silence, Gwen squirming uncomfortably in her chair, Bill lost in his own morose thoughts.

Suddenly he slammed his hand down on the desk. "Why?" he cried. "Why would she just run off like that without an explanation?"

Gwen shook her head.

"All she said in her note was that she couldn't take it anymore. Couldn't take what? Me? The kids? The house? The neighbors?" His rage and frustration seemed to mount with each word.

"Maybe it was a combination of all that." Gwen longed to comfort Bill, yet she wasn't sure how far she should go in trying to explain actions she was supposed to have no knowledge of. "Maybe she just felt—well, trapped. It happens to

Love After Hours

many women. You know, men delight in complaining that marriage is a trap, but it's women, shut away at home with the kids, who really wear the ball and chain."

"Trapped! My God!" he cried, jumping up, his eyes blazing. "Marriage isn't a trap—life is. We're all trapped one way or another. Does she think she's unique? There isn't any one of us on this earth who has absolute freedom of choice. Does she—" He broke off in the middle of his outburst, the anger draining from his face and voice, leaving only sadness in its wake. "I'm sorry," he said, shaking his head. "I'm a heel to be yelling at you."

"It's okay. You have to let it out to someone."

"Let it out maybe. Not take it out." He pushed his glasses back up on his nose and ran his hand over his face. A nerve in his cheek jumped as he fought to control the tears that stood out in his eyes. "I love her, Gwen," he said. "I always thought our love was the only thing in this whole putrid world that had any meaning. And now she's gone. What am I going to do? How does she think I can live without her?"

So this was the strong man who didn't need his wife? Why, Gwen wondered, had Shari never guessed that his strength came through her love? Never in her life had Gwen felt more torn between two people.

Her eyes misting, she stood up and stretched out her hand to the broken man standing before her. "Oh, Bill!"

Seeing his own grief mirrored in her eyes, he stiffened and moved back. He made a visible effort to pull himself together, and a ghost of his old smile passed across his face. "Look, I didn't mean to get you involved in this."

"But I *am* involved. You and Shari are my friends."

"Yes, but you've got problems of your own—not the least of which will be explaining your lateness for the appointment I'm keeping you from." He managed to get some of the old teasing quality back into his voice, though not into his eyes.

"No, really! The appointment's nothing. I don't want to leave you like this."

"Like what? I'm fine. Go on—you're late enough already."

Though she had longed to flee from his presence before, now that she was dismissed, Gwen was reluctant to go. "You're sure you're all right?"

"You know me—I roll with the punches." He turned his back on her and looked out the window.

"Bill..."

"I'll see you tomorrow."

"Sure. Tomorrow." She walked to the door, her eyes riveted to the tense line of his shoulders, the outline of his clenched fists in his pockets.

"Bill..."

His shoulders stiffening even more, he continued to keep his back to her. "I'm smiling," he said, his cracked voice belying his words. "Will you please get the hell out while I can still manage to do so?"

Still she remained at the door, her eyes filling with sympathetic tears. Suddenly, she took her hand from the doorknob and began rummaging in her purse.

"Bill!"

His head snapped around at the sharp note of command in her voice.

"Shari's at my place." She spoke quickly, before she had time to change her mind. She tossed her keys on his desk. "She loves you, but she's one mixed-up kid. Go see if you can straighten her out. I can't."

His incredulous eyes went from Gwen to the keys that lay gleaming in the light of his desk lamp like a newly unearthed pirate's trove.

"You mean you knew all along?" It wasn't an accusation, only a hurt, bewildered man's attempt to place things in perspective.

Her cheeks burning, Gwen nodded. She felt that she was a traitor, yet she was not quite sure whom she had betrayed.

"Why didn't you say something in the beginning?"

"Don't you see that I couldn't? Shari had begged me not to tell you where she was."

Very slowly, he walked over to the desk and picked up the keys, as though afraid that too hasty a movement might frighten them away. "What made you change your mind?"

"Seeing you—and suddenly remembering that I hadn't really promised not to tell you; I'd simply promised to help her. I think this *is* helping her." She shook her head. "I feel so rotten, Bill! So torn between the two of you."

"You shouldn't. It was rotten of us to involve you." His fingers caressed the keys, and his eyes filled with gratitude. "You're a good friend, Gwen. Better than either of us deserves."

She smiled a little. "Thanks."

She opened the door, but paused on the threshold and looked back. "Oh, by the way," she said as casually as she could. "I'm on my way to visit my folks. I'll be staying overnight."

A sad half-smile flitted across Bill's face. "As I said—you're a good friend, Gwen."

"Good luck," she said, and closed the door behind her.

Chapter Thirteen

Shari extracted the key Gwen had left her from her purse, opened the door to Gwen's apartment, and slipped inside. For a moment, she stood there in the dark, feeling the strangeness of the place like an animal sniffing for danger.

It was funny, she thought, the way everyone's home seemed to have its own characteristic odor. As a child, she had never been able to think of her grandparents without her nostrils quivering in remembrance of the distinctive fragrance that pervaded their apartment—and, indeed, the home of almost everyone she'd ever met who had had his heyday in the Twenties—a rather vague mixture of camphor and incense that intimated exotic memories. Her own mother's immaculate home had the cardboard-and-tissue-paper smell of fine department stores, making the visitor think that everything in it must have just been removed from its box for the sole purpose of impressing him. And Bill's folks' place! Poor Mom Saxon never seemed able to eradicate the oniony smell of yesterday's stew, no matter how hard she worked at airing it. Gwen's apartment had its own peculiar essence—a clean, polishy fragrance of verbena that conjured thoughts of spring and of Gwen herself—wholesome, efficient, intelligent. And her own home—what was its smell? Shari wondered, as she hung her coat in the closet. But that essence, so long lived with that it could no longer be isolated, evaded her.

She walked to the living room, fumbling along the wall until her fingers reached the switch that flooded the room with light. It was a homey room, decorated in contemporary —though not severely modern—style, with comfort and aesthetics given equal reign. But other people's homes never come to life when their rightful occupants are not present, and so, though the colors were warm and the arrangement pleasing, Shari felt no sense of welcome in the room.

It was to escape that feeling of being an intruder that she had fled the apartment earlier in the day. It had been strange to awake to quiet instead of the usual morning bustle, and though she had told herself as she was eating breakfast that quiet was exactly what she needed to sort out her thoughts, the silence had soon driven her almost to distraction, and she had hastily dressed and taken flight.

Once in the street, however, she had realized that it was not only the silence she had wanted to escape, but also the doubts that had been lurking in every corner, doubts she sensed following close on her heels. She had taken a bus to the midtown area, and had spent the day walking through the streets, looking at the tall buildings, studying the people rushing in and out of them, trying to whip up the enthusiasm she knew she should be feeling for the new life she had chosen. Lunching in a restaurant that catered to business people, she had watched with admiration well-dressed, sophisticated women at the other tables who seemed surrounded by an aura of purposefulness and importance. Soon she would join their ranks again. Then when someone asked her what she did, she wouldn't have to shrivel up inside, smile apologetically, and say, "I'm a housewife," or "I'm a mother." *Mother*. That word had conjured visions of Tommy, John, and Allison, making her wonder how they were, what they were doing, whether they missed her. Realizing that if she continued to think about them, she'd become just as confused as she'd been before her final decision to leave, she had gulped down her coffee and hurried from the restaurant, hoping to leave her disquieting thoughts behind.

She'd spent most of the remainder of the afternoon window-shopping to get ideas for the wardrobe she'd have to buy. No more blue jeans or baggy slacks and T-shirts. When she had reached Fifty-ninth Street, she had turned off Fifth Avenue and entered Central Park. That had been a mistake. There had been too many mothers and children there. Too many little boys and girls who had looked too much like her own. She had rushed to the nearest bus stop and gone back to Gwen's apartment.

Now she stood in the quiet living room, the silence echoing all around her, and wondered what she should do until Gwen arrived. She sank down on a chair, then stood up. She felt so out of place. She'd have to get an apartment of her own soon. Tomorrow, she'd take a room in a hotel and stay there while she apartment-hunted. It was better to be alone in an impersonal place than in a room that was so obviously a part of someone else's life.

She picked up a magazine, then put it down again, glancing at her watch. Five o'clock. If she were home now, she'd be— No, she mustn't think that way. It wasn't home to her anymore, wouldn't be again. . . . Nervously, she twisted a loose strand of hair around her fingers. What was she going to do until Gwen got back? She'd go crazy if she just sat there. Maybe she'd take a bath and shampoo. It would relax her, and it would certainly be better than staring at the walls, fighting to keep her thoughts from wandering in the wrong direction.

Taking her robe from her suitcase, she headed for the bathroom. As she passed Gwen's bedroom, the phone on the night table caught her eye. Maybe she'd call home just to see that the children were all right. No. She couldn't do that. There would be too many questions, questions she wasn't ready to answer yet. She continued past the bedroom and the temptation of the telephone, entered the bathroom and began running the tub, helping herself to a generous amount of Gwen's bubble bath.

Much later, when she had finally roused herself enough to step out of the warm, relaxing water, she heard the outside door open and close.

"I'll be out in a minute, Gwen," she called. "I just got out of the tub."

With the water going down the drain, she could not hear Gwen's answer.

She wrapped one towel around her hair, turban fashion, and toweled herself dry with another. Then she tied her soft pink terry-cloth robe around her and, barefoot, padded out to the living room to say hello and to get a fresh change of clothes from her suitcase.

The apartment seemed uncommonly quiet, and she wondered what Gwen could be doing. Why in the world had she turned off the living-room light? Was she a nut about pinching pennies on her electric bill? She never would have thought Gwen was the type. But then, people were full of surprises, as Bill was fond of pointing out.

"I spent the day looking over the city," she called out as she flipped on the light switch.

"That's nice. I spent the day in hell."

"Bill!" The blood drained from her head, leaving her vision blurred and her brain whirling. She sank back against the wall for the support that her shaking legs could no longer provide. "My God! You scared the wits out of me!"

He didn't move from his chair by the window. "Good. Now you'll know a fraction of what I felt when I went home last night and found you gone."

As her heart stopped racing, anger began to take the place of shock. "Sitting in the dark is a childish thing to do."

"So is running away."

She let that slip by and continued her attack. "Where's Gwen?"

"At her parents' place." He held up the keys. "She gave me these."

Tears of anger and frustration crowded in her eyes at the thought of Gwen's betrayal. "Some friend! She promised me she wouldn't tell you where I was."

"No. As she tells it, she promised to help. That's what she thought she was doing."

"Help? Help whom?"

"Help both of us. You seem to forget that we're both her friends. It was a crummy thing to do, Shari, putting her in the middle."

"There shouldn't be a middle in a situation like this."

"There's always a middle." He tossed the keys on a nearby table. "Let's leave Gwen out of this. Her loyalties are her problem. We have problems of our own to discuss."

Shari pressed her lips together. She wasn't ready to talk to him. She needed more time to pull her thoughts together.

She turned toward her suitcase. "I have to get dressed. I'll be back in a minute."

"No! We'll talk now!"

"Don't be silly. I'll only take a minute." She picked out a change of underwear, a pair of slacks, a sweater.

Up to that moment, Bill had sat in the chair, a picture of calmness, his voice even, his face composed. Now something inside him seemed to snap, and he jumped up, bounded across the room to Shari, grabbed the clothes from her hands, and hurled them into a corner in a fury.

"No! I feel like I've waited an eternity for your explanation. Another minute is too long. We'll talk now!"

"For God's sake, Bill!" Shari gasped, looking at the heap of clothes against the wall. "What's got into you?"

"I could ask you the same goddam question." He grabbed her shoulders. "What's got into you? Where are your feelings? How the hell long is it going to take you to ask me how our children are?"

"I don't have to ask you," she insisted, struggling unsuccessfully to free herself from his viselike grip. "I know you'll take care of them."

His fingers tightened on her shoulders, and his face, red with rage, came closer to hers. "How can you be sure? I always trusted you to take care of them, but yesterday you turned your back on them. How can you be sure I won't do the same?"

Never before had she seen him so furious, and fear of his anger spurred her to renewed efforts to free herself from his grasp. "I won't discuss anything with you while you're trying to bully me like this!" she cried. "Let go of me! You're hurting me!"

"That's exactly what I want to do!" he said. "I want to hurt you the way you've hurt me. I want to shake the nonsense out of you and knock some sense into that idiot brain. I—"

His voice broke off as he encountered the fear in her eyes. Closing his own eyes, he shook his head as though to clear it. When he opened them again, the fury was gone and only naked hurt remained. "What I really want to do," he said softly, his voice trembling, "is hold you so tight that you'll never have a chance to leave me again."

Quick to take advantage of his change of mood, Shari slipped from his grasp, rubbing her arms where, seconds before, his fingers had bitten into them. "And we'd be right back where we started, smack in the middle of the same problems."

"What problems?" Bill asked, perplexed. "We have each other, our children, our home, a good living. *What problems?*"

"*My* problems! Don't you see that the wonderful life you think we have is driving me out of my mind? I'm sick of being stuck in a house a thousand miles from nowhere, sick of wiping noses, kissing boo-boos, driving car-pools, doing laundry. I want out!"

Bill pushed his glasses back up his nose, his eyes hurt, bewildered. "But no one forced that life on you. It's what you wanted."

Tears of frustration clouded Shari's eyes. "It's what I *thought* I wanted. I was idiot enough to think it would be sufficient. But it isn't. It's suffocating me, Bill. I've been so busy being a wife and a mother that I don't know who I am anymore."

"And you think you can find out by running away?"

"I know I can." Nervously, she caught a strand of hair that had escaped the confines of her towel turban and pushed it back into place. "Look. I know that what I've done seems sudden to you, but it wasn't for me. It was something I'd been thinking about for a long time."

"Then why didn't you talk to me about it? We might have worked something out."

"I couldn't. You wouldn't have understood."

"You might have tried."

"I'm trying right now, and you don't." Sighing, she shook her head. "No man could. You're in the mainstream of life. How could you conceive of what it's like to be stuck on an out-of-the-way island, condemned to do boring, mundane chores over and over again, with only childish intellects for company?"

"Jesus!" Bill cried, incredulous. "Do you think batting my brains out to produce a magazine that will titillate a bunch of shitheads is being in the mainstream of life? Like hell! You're the one who's in the mainstream. You're molding the minds and lives of the next generation—that's the important job."

"The hell it is! That's a typical male evasion if I ever heard one. If raising kids and running a house are so goddam important, why the hell don't you men do it?"

"Maybe because you women do it so goddam well," Bill shouted, exasperated.

"Oh, shut up! You men make me sick! You belittle everything a woman does, until she starts complaining. Then, afraid you might get stuck with some of her shitty jobs, you run scared and start shouting at the top of your lungs that hers is the most important job in the world and men shouldn't be entrusted with it. It's only another way of trying to keep us slaves, prisoners of your houses and your children."

Bill's face went livid with rage. "So now you're suddenly a slave and a prisoner! I suppose you think I'm free."

"I know you are!"

"Free to do what—jump up at six o'clock every morning so I can catch the 7:09? Free to kill myself trying to beat the competition on the newsstand, while trying to keep one step ahead of the back-stabbing competition in the office? Free to lick the asses of the big shots while placating the little ones and pretending that it doesn't disgust me that they're licking mine? If I were free, I'd be hundreds of miles from that stinking office building, sitting in a sunny room, writing a book when I wasn't out working in my garden. But I'm as much a slave of our family's financial needs as you are of its physical needs." He came ominously close. "Face it, Shari. The only freedom we get in this life comes when death releases us from all our responsibilities."

Shari backed away, but not down. "Oh, that's a lovely speech. 'Full of sound and fury and signifying nothing.' Freedom is a relative thing, and you're a hell of a lot more free than I am. I'm sick of playing the wife and mother. I want a chance to find myself, and I can do that only in your world."

"For God's sake! Don't you see you'd just be trading one

Love After Hours

set of roles for another—wife and mother for career woman and playgirl. They're equally confining, with their own sets of rules and regulations, totems and taboos."

Shari stamped her bare foot in frustration. "I don't care! I have to give it a try. I owe myself that much."

"And the children and me—do you owe us nothing?"

At the mention of their children, she recoiled as though he'd hit her. "That's dirty pool!"

"Oh, really? And your walking out on us without a word as to the why or wherefore—that's good clean cricket, I suppose!"

Her eyes filling with tears of anger and frustration, she clenched her fists at her side. "You see how you twist my words? That's why I didn't want you to know where I was for a while. I knew if you found me, you'd try to make me look like an idiot so that you could shame me into being meek and submissive and going back to being your slave."

The moment the words were out of her mouth, she regretted them as she saw Bill's fury. His eyes flashed, and a blue vein in his neck stood out against the crimson flush of his face and throat. Though he made no move to close the gap between them, Shari instinctively stepped back.

"*My* slave!" His voice was like the cry of a dangerously wounded animal. "It's one thing when you spout off about all women being enslaved by custom and biology—it's another to say *I* treat you as though you're my own personal property. When have I ever treated you as anything less than an individual—an individual whom I happen to be crazy enough to love? When have I ever asked or expected you to do anything that I haven't on occasion done myself—from cooking a meal to cleaning the house to diapering one of the kids? When?" He was inching closer now, his face becoming even redder. "Well, answer me!"

Shari continued backing away, her trembling hands readjusting the towel that held her hair, but the more his words chipped away at her argument, the more desperate she became to hold her ground.

"All right! So I'm not your personal slave!" she conceded, her voice rising to match his. "But I'm someone's or something's—call it society or custom or tradition—and I'm sick of it. I refuse to be its prisoner any longer. Obviously, you can't do anything to free me, so I'll free myself."

"So now I'm to blame! But you forget that my breadwinning role makes me as much a prisoner of society, custom and tradition as you are. How do you expect me to free you? Should I ride down on a white charger, swoop up your washing machine and dryer and set them up in my office?"

"There, you see!" she cried, pointing a finger at him in accusation. "You're doing it again. You're trying to reduce what I want to do to the ridiculous."

"Well, it's a hell of a lot more fitting than exaggerating it to the sublime. How can you believe that you'd be better off trying to make your way alone in this godforsaken jungle?"

"It's not a matter of believing, it's a matter of knowing. I'd be independent, not just someone's appendage. I'd find the happiness that comes from being independent and self-sufficient. Take a look at the career women around you, and you'll see—"

"You take a look at them!" he cut her off. "Obviously, you've been away from them too long. There's Terri Ainsworth, who can't wait to drag a guy to the altar so she can chuck her marvelous career; she must be close to menopause, but she still talks about all the children she plans to have. Then there's Angela Langford, the Ice Queen. Since her daughter ran off and married, life doesn't seem to be such a winter carnival for her anymore; her ice finally melted, but all that was left under it was hollow wood. There's Frances Hascomb, a recent addition to Waterford's happy family. She's so hung up on being a liberated woman, she's become a slave to orgasms and independence. And then there's Gwen —our Gwen. What real happiness has her independence and self-sufficiency brought her? Did she tell you that she's a married man's mistress—and that she'd probably sell her soul to the devil for a chance to live with him as we were living until yesterday?"

He came so close to using Gwen's own words that a shiver shot down Shari's spine. Instinctively, she pulled her robe a little tighter.

"Shall I name some more?"

"Don't bother," she said coldly. "You'd only choose all the

wrong ones. Besides, what other people do or want from life doesn't matter and is no ground for comparison."

"You just said it was. You're the one who dragged them into the argument, not I."

"Well, then—then I've changed my mind."

She closed her eyes a second and shook her head as though to clear it. Her heart was pounding, and she felt as though her thoughts were flying in all directions. Why did he have to come here and get her so confused, just when she was beginning to get her life straightened out? Why did he have to stand so close that she could see his gray hairs, so near that she could see his glasses slipping down his nose again and could barely resist the impulse to push them back up?

Clenching her fists, she tried to pull her thoughts together. She mustn't listen to his arguments. Her whole life was at stake. "It makes no difference what others do or have done," she insisted, her voice brittle with desperation. "What I'm doing is right for me."

"And for our children?"

"For God's sake!" she cried, pulling her robe around her with trembling hands. "Will you stop dragging them into this? I have a right to put myself first for a change. It's my life!"

"It's not your life! No one's life is his own alone. Our lives are shaped by those closest to us. They become part of us, and we can't cut them off without diminishing ourselves." He shook his head sadly. "I'm not dragging the children in. They're here. They're wherever we go, because they're part of us. Just as you and I have been part of each other."

Shari's heart began pounding, and she bit her lip. *Shut up!* she thought. *Don't come any closer. I can't stand much more!*

But he wouldn't shut up, and he did come closer. So close that she could feel the warmth of his breath, see the tears standing out in his eyes.

"From the time we met, we've been a unit—not just a *you* and a *me*, but an *us*," he pressed on. "When the children came, we expanded that unit, that *us*, to include them. Do you think for one minute that you can blow that unit apart

—change that *us* into *you, me,* and *them*—without changing us all, hurting us all?"

She pressed her trembling fingers against her temples, but they could not alleviate the pain that was pounding there, pushing against the back of her eyes.

"I'm not doing this to hurt anyone, Bill. You must believe that," she begged. "I'm doing this to help myself."

"But you *are* hurting us," Bill insisted. "You're hurting yourself too. Perhaps you're hurting yourself most of all." He put his hands on her shoulders, but now his touch was loving and gentle, without a trace of the fierce anger from before. "Come home, Shari," he said, his voice brimming with the years of tender memories they shared. "We love you and we need you, and I think you love and need us too."

"I do love you!" she cried, bursting into tears. "But I can't come home. Oh, Bill! Don't you see how unhappy I've been there?"

"And don't you see that you're acting like the guy in the old joke who wants to cut off his head to cure a headache? There are better, easier remedies." He shook his head, his eyes filled with pain. "I must have been blind or a shithead or both not to realize how unhappy you were. But now that I do know, I promise you that we'll work it out together. I know that if we just give ourselves a chance to think about the problem rationally, we'll find that there are countless options open to us. Maybe you'd like to go back to school for your master's degree. I could arrange to get home early a couple of nights a week so that you could go to classes, and I'd keep the kids out of your hair on weekends so that you could study. Or maybe you'd like to take a part-time job, or just have a day or two free for yourself during the week. I should be able to pick up some free-lance work so that we'd be able to afford a housekeeper."

He pulled her close, muffling her sobs against his shoulder. Her towel turban was opening, and gently he pulled it from her head, letting her hair tumble to her shoulders. "My poor darling," he whispered, rubbing his cheek against her damp curls. "Have you lived so long and still not learned that there's no such thing as total happiness? Everyone is discontented to some degree. You show me a person who is totally happy, and I'll show you a corpse or an idiot."

She pulled away and looked up at him through her tears. "But surely you've been happy. You always seem to be."

"Do I have to remind you that I thought *you* were happy too? I meant every word I said about my job and about wishing I could be writing and gardening instead of beating my brains out at the office."

Her heart sank at his words. For a long time, as much as she loved Bill, she had considered herself a martyr on the altar of their marriage. She had felt he was using her. Now it was suddenly uncomfortably apparent that he could hurl the same accusations her way. She had basked in the light of her martyrdom for too long to share its glow willingly with Bill. But every argument she advanced to herself to refute his words was defeated when she studied his face. The truth could be read too easily in the sadness in his eyes, in the deeply etched lines that fanned out from them, in the many silvery hairs sprinkled among the dark ones. She bit her lip, frowning. How long had it been since he had begun to turn gray, since the marks around his eyes had deepened from laugh lines into worry wrinkles? How long had it been since she had looked at him without her vision clouded by her own self-pity?

"Oh, Bill," she whispered, "why didn't you tell me you were unhappy?"

Taking a deep breath, he dropped his hands from her shoulders and slipped them deep into his pockets. "Because I knew you were making equal compromises of your own." He walked over to the window and stared down at the street. "Besides, I had made peace with the situation. Giving up a few dreams didn't seem like too great a price for having you and the kids and our little corner of peace and sanity in an insane world."

He turned around and walked back to her, taking her face in his hands. "Look at me, Shari," he said, his voice husky with emotion. "Look at me and think of all the years of love and laughter and even tears that we've shared. Think of our children, and how we've loved them and agonized over them together, sharing the miracle of watching them grow. Think of how much easier it is to grow older, not really minding that the years are catapulting by, because we're facing Time's onslaught together. Then think of what it would be like to face life all alone, and tell me that the price of our compromise would be too great."

For the first time, she thought of his sacrifices rather than her own. Her eyes brimming with tears, she studied every line on his face, and it was as though she could suddenly recall the exact moment of shared worry or heartache that had engraved it there. How many new lines, she wondered, longing to reach up and smooth them away, were her own recent actions responsible for? Suddenly, the image of life without that face by her side hovered before her like a dark tunnel that led only to an eternity of loneliness and despair.

"Tell me!" Bill urged, his eyes searching hers.

"I can't!" she whispered.

"Why not?"

"Because all I can think of with you standing so near is how much I love you and how much I've hurt you." It was difficult for her to push the words past her trembling lips. "And what a goddam fool I've been."

He stood looking down at her as though afraid she'd change her mind and take back the promise her words held.

"For God's sake!" she begged, her tears spilling over. "Kiss me! Hold me so tight that I can never run away from you again!"

When their trembling lips finally parted, she gazed up at him, gently tracing the soft lines in his cheeks that always deepened when he smiled.

"Have I ruined everything?" she asked, her eyes searching his. "Can things ever be the same for us again?"

He shook his head. "Never the same," he whispered. "Better."

He loosened her robe, and she let it slip from her shoulders to the floor. Then, gently, his lips tracing kisses over her face, her neck, and her breasts, he lowered her to the sofa. Heart pounding, she locked her arms around his neck. And, as her body flamed under his caresses and her lips pulsated under his, she yielded to her need to be one with the man she loved. She knew at last that he was right. Life would be better. Together, they would find a way for her to realize her dream of independence.

Chapter Fourteen

*T*erri Ainsworth had been one busy girl during the month that had passed since Harry's wife had finally had the good grace to die. Lunch hours and Saturdays, she spent in shops, selecting sexy lingerie for her trousseau. Evenings and Sundays, she and her mother planned and replanned the wedding and reception. And in between, she dreamed about the beautiful white lace gown with tiny seed pearls at the bodice and just a hint of a train that was currently on display in Lord and Taylor's bridal salon. Of course she knew that, technically, she was no longer qualified to wear white, not after that night with Harry, but that was only *one* night so she was still *practically* a virgin.

The worst part of all the planning, of course, was that she couldn't get the ball *really* rolling. She realized that Harry had a great deal on his mind and evidently—foolishly— thought it would be wrong for them to see each other before the first three to six months of mourning were over. Still, she wished he would get in touch. Because his schedule seemed to have changed, she no longer saw him on the train, so she couldn't drop a hint about his calling or about how discreet she would be about everything. After all, if they waited until the year of mourning was over before they even began making plans, it would be at least another half year before they could marry.

Though her mother had always maintained that a girl should never call a fella, when she still had not heard from Harry by the middle of March, Terri had begun phoning his office. As luck would have it, her timing was always off. Inevitably, his secretary would tell her he was out—and then the stupid girl would forget to give him her message, so he

Love After Hours

never called back. She couldn't call him at home, either, because his number was unlisted.

On the last day of March, she went to work determined to bypass his stupid secretary and see him. This time she would not phone; she would go straight to his office at about a quarter to five. Once they were together, she knew she'd have no trouble pinning him down about wedding plans.

In the afternoon, she asked for and received permission to leave early. She really hated having to go through that formality. After more than twenty years with a company, one should be allowed to come and go as one pleased, without having to check in and out with people who were considered "superiors."

It wasn't worth getting into a pet about, though, she thought, as she went to the ladies' room to change and apply fresh makeup. She stepped out of her skirt and slipped into a pair of burnt-orange hot pants, from which her legs, encased in black nylon pantyhose and black, form-fitting, high-heeled boots, stuck out like shapely exclamation points. After all, she reminded herself, slipping a matching burnt-orange vest over her frilly white blouse, she wouldn't be at Waterford much longer. She cleansed her face with creams and soap and water, then coated it with a makeup base guaranteed to give her a "romantic, dewy look," and worked in liquid rouge. No, she intended to quit work right after she and Harry were married. She smeared some lighter base over the dark circles under her eyes. It would give her great pleasure to hand Gwen her resignation. She smiled to herself, applying three different shades of shadow on her eyelids. Poor Gwen! She was pretty jumpy lately. Probably jealous because she realized Terri was planning her wedding, and she also knew that she didn't stand a chance for half so good a match. She licked her eyebrow pencil and painted on her brows. Of course, it was Gwen's own fault—wearing hardly any makeup, admitting to her age, having no clothes sense. No man worth his salt would be interested in a woman like that. She glued on her false eyelashes, batting her lids a few times to make sure they were secure. Well, that was Gwen's problem. Her own problems were practically over now. Sighing contentedly, she took her eyeliner and painted doe eyes on her upper lids and little vertical lines simulating long lower lashes on the puffy skin below her bottom lashes. It would be marvelous to have the right to stay home all day, doing as she pleased. With a lipstick brush, she painted a dark outline on her lips with one color of lipstick, then filled in the inside with a lighter color. Once in a while, of course, she'd come down to the office for lunch, wearing the rings and expensive furs Harry was sure to give her—just so that no one would forget that she was a married woman with a man who took care of her in style. She patted her hairdo, checking to make sure no dark roots showed, then sprayed her hair generously with Just Wonderful!

A final check in the mirror assured her that Harry would be ready to come out of his silly mourning the minute he saw her. He might even want to elope, she thought, gently brushing up the plush of her hot pants. But of course she wouldn't stand for that. Every girl was entitled to a real wedding.

At precisely 4:45 she arrived at Harry's office building. One of the city's newer skyscrapers, it looked as though it had been constructed from beer bottles and old tin cans. Duly impressed with its magnificence, Terri stood on the sidewalk for a moment, looking up toward the sixteenth floor where she knew Harry had his office. Any wife would be proud to be able to say that her husband worked in the Farnsworth Building, she thought. And a husband who was actually one of the twenty vice-presidents of Farnsworth, Incorporated—well, what could be better?

Her shallow bosom swelling with pride, she entered the building and boarded an elevator. When the doors closed, Muzak came on, and her ascent to the sixteenth floor was accompanied by one hundred invisible violins playing "Whistle While You Work."

Earlier in the day, cleverly pretending she was a secretary dispatching a messenger, she had telephoned and ascertained from a bored-sounding switchboard operator that Harry's office was in room 1603. Emerging from the elevator, she found that her timing was perfect. The sixteenth-floor receptionist was not at her desk; no doubt she was in the ladies' room combing her hair and freshening her makeup in preparation for the working girls' olympics—the forty-yard dash for the elevator at five o'clock. Terri was able to skirt past the reception desk without being stopped.

The door marked "1603, Harold L. Curtis, Marketing" opened into a rather spacious reception area, all modern sofas and paintings, ruled over by Harry's secretary, a raven-haired beauty of twenty-one or twenty-two, who, at the moment Terri entered, was applying frosted-pink lipstick to her sensuous, pouting mouth. Not until she had finished did the girl look from Terri to her watch and back again.

"May I help you?" she asked in a voice that sounded like velvet, and a tone that implied she hoped she could not.

It occurred to Terri to give the girl a severe tongue-lashing for never passing on her telephone messages to Harry, but she decided against it. She'd tell Harry instead and let him take care of it. Tomorrow, Miss Sexpot would probably find herself pounding the pavement, looking for another job.

"I'm a friend of Mr. Curtis's," she said, smiling meaningfully.

The girl looked her up and down. Then, her beautiful, pouting lips turning up ever so slightly in what was closer to a smirk than a smile, she asked, "Is he expecting you?" She reached for a button on the intercom.

"No, don't do that," Terri said, holding up a restraining hand. "I'm surprising him."

"He usually doesn't like surprises."

Terri giggled. "This one, I assure you, he'll love."

The girl looked at her watch and shrugged. "Suit yourself," she said, shaking her head and gently tossing her mane of hair back from her beautiful face. "I'm practically through here for the day anyway."

You'll be through here for a lot longer than that, my girl, Terri thought as she sauntered past her desk, *once I tell your boss about your incompetence!*

She tapped at the door marked *private*, then opened it and whirled in.

"Surprise! Surprise!" she said.

"Jesus Christ!" Harry said, dropping the hat he had been reaching for in his closet. "Where the hell did you come from?"

"From spending much too long a time away from you."

Terri pretended to pout. "You're really very naughty, Harry. I know you wanted to keep up a semblance of mourning, but you could at least have called. Do you know, I've tried to call you several times, and that stupid secretary of yours forgot to give you the messages?"

"Yes, I know." Harry picked up his hat and brushed it off.

"You *know?*" Terri batted her false eyelashes, incredulous.

"I mean," Harry said quickly, "that I know she's stupid."

"Well, you'll have to do something about her, darling. After all, we can't have her coming between us, can we?"

"Of course not." When Harry shook his head, his jowls quivered.

For a moment, there was an awkward silence. Then Harry walked over and sat down at his desk. "Well, what can I do for you?" he asked, tilting back in his chair, his pudgy hands folded over his paunch.

Perching on the edge of his desk, Terri threw him one of her sexy, sidelong looks. She wondered whether she should take off her coat and reveal her outfit now, or wait until they arrived at the cocktail lounge. Noticing the long sofa at the side of the office, she decided to wait for a more public place; she didn't want a repeat of their last night together—not until they were married. Then it would be worth the discomfort. God! Just the thought of it made her nether regions hurt.

"You might buy a girl a drink." She leaned toward him, eyes half shut, lips parted.

Apparently not noticing her invitation to a kiss, Harry rolled his chair back and checked his watch. "I think that can be arranged. I could go for one myself."

Though she stood as close as it was humanly possible to get to a man who was putting on a muffler and struggling into an overcoat, Harry did not take her in his arms. Terri understood, realizing Harry was aware that, after so long a separation, once he touched her, he might not be able to keep his passion under control. Stoically, he kept his distance in the elevator and in the street too.

Though she admired his self-control—indeed stood almost

Love After Hours

in awe of it, for she knew how difficult it was for him to withstand her charms—Terri, like all her sister *femmes fatales* through the ages, refused to take pity on him. Once they were at the rear of the dimly lit cocktail lounge, she was merciless. Standing at the tiny table they had chosen, legs apart and elbows akimbo, she began, with the slow, deliberate movements of a stripper going into her act, to unbutton her coat.

"Hang this up for me, will you, darling?" she said throatily, slipping out of it at last.

As she'd known would happen, Harry's eyes popped. "Say, that's some outfit, baby!" he said. "What are you got up for—Halloween?"

For a second, Terri was taken aback. Then she looked down and understood his meaning. "Oh, you mean the orange and the black!" She laughed, putting one of her shapely legs forward, the better for him to view it. "Honestly, Harry! You're a riot." She gave him a sidelong glance as he returned from a nearby coat tree. "What do you *really* think of it?"

"For you, baby, it's appropriate," he said, sliding his pudgy hand over her buttocks and squeezing. "Very appropriate."

Giggling, she slapped his hand away playfully. "Oh, you fresh, fresh boy!"

He pinched her rear again as she lowered herself to squeeze into the tiny U-shaped booth. "And that's the way you love me to be." Shoving in beside her, he signaled the waiter and ordered a Seven and Seven for her and a double brandy for himself.

"You're very naughty for not calling, you know," she said as they waited to be served.

Harry spread his hands. "Busy, busy. You know how it is."

"I know. I've been busy too, but—" She batted her eyelashes and moved in for the kill, remembering how men loved to be flattered. "—I've missed you."

Smirking, Harry ran his hand up her thigh. "Can't get enough of old Harry, eh?"

Coyly, she lowered her head and looked up at him. "Well, we really should start getting together. There's so much we have to talk over."

"Talk?" He threw back his head and laughed, kneading her thigh. "You can't fool me. It's not just talk you have on your mind. I gave you a taste for something else that night, didn't I?"

"Oh, Harry!" She shook her head, blushing. He was so romantic!

Their drinks came.

"Cheers," Harry said, quickly downing his and ordering another round.

Terri took a swallow of hers, disappointed that Harry hadn't toasted their coming marriage. She downed the rest of it, still waiting for him to bring up the subject. When he hadn't by the time their next round arrived, she decided to tackle it herself. Mama always said men needed a little prodding when it came to wedding plans.

"Well," she said, pressing close. "When are we going to set a date?"

"A *date?*" He leered at her. "Is that what you call it? You really do have the hots for old Harry, eh?"

"Harry, please!" she giggled. "Someone will hear!"

"Don't worry. Everyone in here is over eighteen and knows the facts of life." He downed his drink. "Look, baby, I know how you feel, but you've got to understand how it is with me. I'm an eligible bachelor now. I've got something going almost every night. I don't know when I could fit you in." He patted her leg sympathetically and winked.

That was one of the things she loved about Harry—his sense of humor. But she wished he would be serious. "Oh, Harry!" she said, smiling up at him. "You know what I *mean.*"

"Sure I know what you mean." He ran his fingers along the edge of her hot pants. "But you don't seem to understand what I'm telling you, baby. Harry can't take care of you anymore. You're going to have to find it someplace else." Shrugging, he spread his hands helplessly. "I'm in demand now. My time isn't my own."

A cold panic began to creep through her, like a deadly

glacier slowly inching its way over a continent. She studied his face, the blood draining from her own. He couldn't be serious. Not her Harry. Not after all they'd meant to each other.

"But, Harry!" she protested.

He puffed up with pride as he took in her reaction. "Look," he said, patting her hand consolingly, "I know nobody else could take care of you quite as well as I did, but that's life." The heavy lids over his eyes dropped lazily as he looked at his watch. "I'll tell you what. I have something on at seven, but—as long as you're here—if you want to come back to the office with me, I think we could work in a quickie."

The glacier began to recede in the warm relief his words brought her. He *did* still want her. The whole thing had been an act so that he could get her to bed again before they were married. Giggling, she nudged him gently with her elbow.

"Now there'll be no more of that, young man," she said with mock sternness, "until we're properly married. As if you didn't know that that was the date I was talking about all the time!"

Harry's brows shot up in surprise. "Married?" He burst out laughing. "You've got to be kidding!"

Realizing he was referring to the time element, she hastened to explain. "Oh, not right now! I know you want to wait for a decent period of mourning to pass. But weddings take time to plan. I've got to get started. There's my gown to order, the reception to arrange, the—"

"Jesus Christ!" Harry said, incredulous. "You really are serious!"

"Of course, I'm serious," Terri pouted. "You don't seem to appreciate how much time and effort go into planning a nice wedding."

"Well, take all the time you want, only plan for another guy in the role of the groom, because I'm sure as hell not going to be there." He shook his head, laughing. "Whatever gave you the crazy idea we were going to get married?"

Her hands grew cold and began to tremble as the glacier advanced again. "There *was* that night," she reminded him primly. "A man doesn't spend a night with a girl unless he's seriously interested in her."

"Seriously interested in screwing her, you mean!" His jowls shook with laughter.

There was a pain in her chest, and her eyes filled with tears. "But you said you loved me," she protested weakly.

"Did I?" He shrugged. "Well, maybe I did. But, Jesus! love is a four-letter word like all the others. It's one of the things you say when you're screwing. Like you say 'pleased to meet you' when you shake someone's hand. It doesn't mean a goddam thing."

"Well, it meant something to me." She bit her lip to keep it from trembling.

"Shit! You're no kid. You're old enough to know the score."

"But, Harry!" she cried, twisting her hands in her lap. "I gave you my virginity! You *have* to marry me now."

"Like hell I do!" His face was immobile, his eyes cold and hard. "You were anxious enough to drop your pants for me. I didn't see any strings attached to them that night. Wake up, baby, this is the twentieth century, when sex has no more meaning than shaking hands. A guy buys a girl a drink or a meal, and then he takes her home and screws her. It's the polite thing to do. It's the modern replacement of the old-fashioned good-night kiss."

"But you said—you *implied*—we were getting married." The tears were spilling out of her eyes now, smearing her cheeks with mascara.

"Bullshit! Any implying that was done took place in that fuzzy little brain of yours. I'm not responsible for that." He leaned close, and she could smell the brandy on his breath, see the red streaks in the yellowish whites of his eyes. "What the hell gave you the idea I'd marry you? Have you looked at yourself in the mirror lately? Do you really think all that glop on your face improves your looks or hides your age? And your figure—all right, you've got good legs—but, Christ!—as far as the rest of it goes, you're built like a truck. And the way you dress!" He sneered and flicked a thumb and forefinger against her hot pants. "Like a teenager, when there are women your age who are grandmothers."

"Grandmothers!" Terri gasped. His last words hurt even

more than his refusal to marry her. "I'll have you know I'm only twenty-seven!"

He burst out laughing. "Come off it! You said good-by to twenty-seven fifteen or twenty years ago. And even if you were twenty-seven, you'd be over the hill for me. I've got girls a lot younger than that chasing after me now."

Terri's temper flared. "Well, if you think it's you they're crazy about, you're wrong!" she grated. "You're no great prize yourself. It's your money they're after."

"What the hell do I care?" he asked with a lewd wink. "As long as they show their appreciation of it the right way."

"But I appreciate you for yourself," Terri said, grabbing his hand. "Doesn't that mean anything? You'd never have to wonder about the sincerity of my feelings, because you'd know I'm not interested in your money."

"Sure," he said, extricating his hand. "Money's not the main point with you. What you're sincerely interested in is nabbing yourself a husband. His financial and physical states don't matter, as long as he can stand up at the altar and say 'I do.' Well, you'll have to find another prospect."

"But how can I?" she wailed in frustration. "I've given *you* my virginity. Everyone knows that no matter how much they say they believe in free love, men want their wives to be virgins."

"What the hell is it with you and your shitty virginity?" he cried, slapping his forehead. "What do you think—that cherries are like antiques and get more valuable with age? Well, I've got news for you—the only thing that happens to an old cherry is that it gets wrinkled. There was nothing special about your pickings, baby!"

"But it was my most precious possession to give a man," she squeaked, trying to blink back her tears.

"Christ!" he bellowed, jumping up. "I paid you five bucks for it, didn't I? And it wasn't worth that. You should have paid *me!* Now will you leave me alone and get the hell out of my life? I never saw a bitch as dense as you! What the hell do I have to say to make it clear that you make me sick?"

She looked up at him, her heart pounding painfully, her tears blurring the image of her last great hope.

"Didn't that night mean anything to you at all?" Her tone was that of a little girl begging to have the existence of Santa Claus confirmed in the face of her own grave doubts.

An invisible sheet of ice seemed to fall behind his features, freezing them into a cold, hard sneer. "Sure it meant something. It meant I collected fifty bucks from our riding companions. You see, I laid you on a bet. Would you like me to split the money with you?"

Her ears rang as though he had boxed them. Slowly, she shook her head, closing her eyes over her tears. "Go away," she whispered. "Go away and leave me alone."

When she opened her eyes again, she found that he had done exactly that.

Sniffling a little, she looked around, discovering to her horror that the people at the tables nearby were looking at her. Clamping her teeth against the sobs rising in her throat, she rose and put on her coat, trying to look as though she were a queen donning her coronation robes. Then she swept out of the cocktail lounge and headed toward Penn Station.

The freezing March wind swept up inside her coat, nipping at her unprotected thighs. Relentlessly, mercilessly, it invaded the heavy coat of lacquer on her hair. Then it attacked the tears on her face as though it would freeze them in their mascaraed tracks. Pulling her coat as tightly around her as she could, Terri bent her head into the freezing onslaught and hurried on. She had to get home!

She arrived at the station just in time to board the 6:45. The rush hour now over, she had her choice of grimy seats, and still out of breath from hurrying she settled herself near one of the filthy windows. After giving a bored-looking conductor her monthly commutation ticket, she withdrew her compact from her purse. Wetting a tissue with her tongue, she attempted to remove some of the mascara stains from her face. Then, with her hands, she patted her hair into place as best she could. Mama always said a girl shouldn't comb her hair in public; it made her look cheap. And Mama was right.

Mama was right about everything! Hadn't she always said no man would buy the cow when he could get milk free? Why hadn't she listened? If she had, she and Harry would probably be together right now, planning their wedding. What was she going to do now? Every girl in the world but her seemed to be married or engaged. She'd been so sure of Harry. Oh, why hadn't she listened to Mama?

Closing her eyes, she leaned her head back. Her tears slipped through the barrier of her false eyelashes, making fresh dark tracks through her makeup.

Mama was right, the train wheels seemed to say as they raced along through the suburban towns that were themselves the off-spring of marriage and the family and could never exist without them. Periodically, the train would stop, and the conductors would bellow a garbled word. Men would rise, take their hats and attaché cases from the racks, and disembark to hurry home to their wives. So too she had been sure Harry would be coming home to her one day. *Mama was right! Mama was right!*

At her own station, Terri hurriedly disembarked, climbed into the car she had left in the parking lot in such high hopes that morning, and drove home. Once inside her house, she could hear the television going in the family room. She knew her parents must be there, but she hurried up to her own room without greeting them.

She loved her room. As a teenager, she had decorated it in frills of pink and white organdy and lace, and she had kept it that way through the years, changing nothing but the growing number of cosmetics, creams and emollients she added to the collection on her vanity. From behind the stiff organdy curtains on her window, she had watched many seasons come and go in her parents' backyard, but within her never-changing room, she could pretend that time was standing still. She could lie on her bed, staring up at the pink organdy canopy, and pretend that she was only a few years older than the teenager who had chosen it with such love and such warm optimism that she would be leaving it behind in a very short time to go to a marriage bed in a home of her own. She could sit at her lace-skirted vanity, applying her makeup in the soft light of her lamp, and pretend that it was the dictates of fashion, not the passage of time, that created the need for her many cosmetics.

Now she stood on the threshold, her back pressed against

the door, taking long, deep breaths, as though she were trying to suck up the youthful atmosphere of the room and revitalize herself with it. For once, though, the sight of the room offered no comfort. The vision of Harry's face when he'd spurned her kept getting in the way. Now the room seemed to her not a precious retreat, but a confining prison that she'd never escape.

Eyes brimming with tears, she walked over to her dresser and pulled open the bottom drawer. There, beneath the filmy lingerie she'd bought, beneath the scrapbook of brides' pictures she'd pasted together as a girl, lay the five-dollar bill Harry had given her after their night together. It had been his only gift to her, and she had treasured it, taking it out of its hiding place (Mama would never understand accepting money from a man) and lovingly fingering it every night before she went to bed.

She sank down on her vanity stool and placed the bill before her on the dressing table. Tenderly running her fingers over it, she stared at Lincoln's face with all the yearning of a lover. Then she picked the bill up and slowly, methodically, tore it to pieces, burning the little pile of rubble in her ashtray.

As the smoke dissipated in the air, there was a knock on the door, and her mother, a woman in her late sixties whose heavy body was a testimony to her own good cooking, came in.

"You're home earlier than you said you would be, Theresa."

It was more a question than a statement of fact, but Terri only nodded.

Her mother sniffed the air. "Was something burning?"

Terri shrugged. "Just a cigarette."

Picking up the ashtray, her mother shook it a little, shifting its feathery gray contents back and forth. Then she replaced it on the vanity.

"A funny kind of cigarette," she said.

Suddenly Terri jumped up from the stool and threw her arms around her mother, burying her face in her ample bosom. "Oh, Mama!" she cried. "I saw Harry tonight. He doesn't want to get married after all!"

Her mother held her close, rocking her as if she were a little child. "That's what they all say in the beginning. You mustn't pay any attention. Men are all like that. Why, I remember, your father—"

"No, Mama." Terri pulled away and peered into her mother's soft brown eyes. "Harry meant it. He said terrible things. He's even dating other girls."

Disbelief, quickly followed by disappointment, rode across the wide plane of Mrs. Ainsworth's face, leaving only hardness in their wake.

"Well!" she said at last. "It's better you found out what kind of man he is now than after the wedding. You're well rid of him. He doesn't deserve a girl like you." She patted Terri's head. "Don't waste any tears over him. He isn't worth it. There are plenty more fish in the sea."

Terri shook her head. "No one will want me now. I—I did a bad thing with Harry, Mama."

Gasping, Mrs. Ainsworth clutched at her bosom. "Terri, no! Not after all I taught you!"

Terri hung her head. "I thought I was doing the right thing."

Her mother pressed her lips together, her eyes flashing. "You smart-aleck kids make me sick! You think you know better than your parents. You have to find out the hard way that your mama is right."

Tears began slipping down Terri's cheeks again. "Mama, I'm sorry. Really I am!"

"Sorry! You think being sorry will bring him back? How many times do I have to tell you a man won't buy what he can get for free?"

Burying her face in her hands, Terri sank down on her bed, sobbing. "I know, Mama! I know! And now it's too late."

Hands on her heavy hips, Mrs. Ainsworth stood there watching her daughter sob. After a while, evidently feeling that Terri had repented sincerely and sufficiently for scorning her advice, she sat down beside her, her face softening.

"What's all this about its being too late?" she demanded.

Terri looked up. Her tears had loosened her false lashes,

and they hung slightly askew. "You always said no man would want to marry a girl who wasn't a virgin."

Mrs. Ainsworth didn't blink an eye. "But I never said a girl had to *tell* a man she wasn't a virgin."

"But you said a man could tell whether a girl was a virgin when he went to bed with her."

"So?" Mrs. Ainsworth spread her hands. "If he doesn't go to bed with her until after they're married—what can he do? And with a beautiful girl like you, a man could forgive many things."

Hope began creeping back into Terri's heart. "You really think so, Mama?"

"I know so. Virgin or no virgin—any man would be lucky to get my girl!" She stood up. "Now you wash up and come down and have some supper. You forget all about what happened with Harry. You're well rid of him. You'll meet someone else soon. You'll see."

"You really think so, Mama?"

"A beautiful virgin like you? Of course!"

They both giggled conspiratorially as her mother went out and closed the door.

As she removed her makeup and washed up, Terri wondered why she hadn't been able to see things that way for herself. Thank God for mothers like hers! They could always see things in their proper perspective.

By the time she had put on her robe and descended the stairs, she was convinced that she was the one who had broken up with Harry, and that it was the best thing she could have done. As Mama had said, better to find out about him before marriage than afterward.

She ate the meal her mother had prepared, then went back upstairs, showered, set her hair, applied her creams and emollients, and went to bed determined to get a good night's sleep. A girl needed her full eight hours if she was going to look her best.

Tomorrow, she thought, snuggling down under the covers, she'd wear her red V-neck dress and begin sitting in a different car on the train. After all, you never could tell. . . .

Chapter Fifteen

By the second week in April, Gwen's nerves were stretched as tight as the skin on a drum. Because they did not want to jeopardize his divorce, she and Paul had agreed to stop seeing each other shortly before *Raw Flesh* opened at the end of March. They had spoken on the telephone since then, but, for Gwen, the sound of Paul's voice only increased her longing for his presence.

Though the play had been politely received, it seemed destined for a short run. Verna's contribution to it had been roundly panned, and Paul confided that Verna was bitter and dragging her feet about fulfilling the agreement they had made about a divorce.

As the deadline for Verna to file suit approached, Gwen became more and more tense. She kept repeating to herself Paul's assurances that nothing could go wrong, but without Paul there to back them up, the words offered little comfort. She lost her appetite and slept poorly.

Often when she finally did fall asleep, she was awakened by an anonymous pervert who would neither respond to her pleas for identification nor hang up, but would hold the phone line open in maddening silence. The woman at the phone company was ever so solicitous, and within a few days of her reporting the calls, Gwen was issued a private number. Two days later, the calls began again. Still solicitous, the phone-company woman pointed out that there was most likely a serpent among Gwen's inner circle of friends ("you never can *tell* about people, dear"), and that if the calls kept up, Gwen might do well to consider going to the police. ("Though *they* can't really *do* anything unless he *says* something, uh, *significant*.") Did Gwen want her number changed again? No, Gwen said, she did not; if the caller could get her present number, it was likely that he could unearth her next one too. In that case, the woman said, perhaps Gwen should try blowing a whistle into the phone. It often discouraged repeat calls.

Gwen bought a whistle and blew it.

The calls continued.

Reluctant to increase Paul's own worries and tensions, Gwen did not tell him about the calls. Nor did she consider going to the police. Her suspicions about who was behind them were too strong for that. It was all she could do when the piercing rings rent through the dark silent night, like the slashing scimitar of a wild Turk, to keep from lifting the receiver and shouting into it that she knew who was there. For such an admission would have been tantamount to acknowledging her affair with Paul and putting an end to his hope for a divorce settlement that would award him custody of his child.

When she began to leave her phone off the hook at night, the calls came earlier in the evening and more frequently. She wouldn't give the caller the satisfaction of prolonging her torture by asking questions that she knew would not be answered; as soon as she heard the silence instead of a response to her "hello," she hung up. But her action was never quick enough to keep the little beads of perspiration from forming on her upper lip or prevent her hands from trembling and growing cold.

With the terrifying certainty of one guessing at her own damnation, Gwen sensed that Verna was responsible for the calls. There were times, of course, when she'd try to cheer herself with the possibility that the caller was a frustrated, neurotic reader whose story she had rejected and who was now bent on revenge. But as appealing as that idea was, its possibility became more remote as the calls dragged on. No, she was certain it was Verna—or someone employed by her. But who? The Fish, perhaps?

"The Fish" was the name with which Gwen had christened a thin, unwholesome-looking man with a low brow, receding chin, thick lips, and flat, silver-colored eyes, who had been cropping up in her life lately like a heavy-handed symbol for death in a grade-C movie. She had first become aware of him in a dream she had in March, at about the time she and Paul had decided it was no longer safe to keep seeing each other. She had dreamed that she had seen Paul waiting for her at the edge of a cliff, but when she arrived at his side, the man had turned out to be not Paul but The Fish. He had turned to her, a blank smile stretching his thick lips across his thin face, his flat, expressionless eyes looking from her to the foot of the precipice, where, following his gaze, she had seen, to her horror, Paul lying in a broken heap. Her sobs had awakened her; then, trembling, her nightgown clinging to the cold sweat that coated her body, she had jumped from her bed, fearful that more sleep might bring a return of the nightmare. Over a calming cup of tea, she had been able to see things in perspective. It had been a simple anxiety dream and nothing more, a natural outgrowth of the decision she and Paul had recently made not to see each other again until after Verna initiated divorce proceedings. She wondered, though, where her subconscious had dug up the disturbing image of the man with the fishlike face. Perhaps, she had conjectured, he was a remnant from the comic books she had read as a child.

Two days later, however, she had seen the same man in the flesh, sitting at a table near the door in the restaurant where she had lunched. She had stopped in her tracks on her way to the cashier, feeling as though someone had poured ice water down her back. Had her dream come to life? Or had she actually seen that gaping face prior to her dream? All the way back to the office, she had racked her brain, trying to remember if and when she had seen him before. It was not until she reached the Waterford Building that she remembered where and when she had seen him for the first time: It had been her last evening with Paul; they had dined in a neighborhood restaurant near her apartment, and when they had left it, they had passed the man with the fishlike face, huddled in the doorway of the store next door, no doubt waiting for someone. His face was so extraordinary that it was no wonder her subconscious mind had taken note of it. But what a coincidence, she thought, that she should see him again!

When she continued seeing him, however, she began to suspect that it was not a coincidence after all. Too often she spotted him near the Waterford Building when she left her office, or on the subway platform while she waited for her train. More than once, she caught sight of him sitting in a parked car near her apartment house. And always, even when she could not see him, she had the feeling that he was lurking somewhere behind her, his flat eyes watching, waiting. . . .

One Saturday afternoon, she spotted him as she left her parents' apartment house after a visit. Her anger at last outweighing her apprehension, she resolved to confront him.

Though it was the beginning of April, winter was still hanging doggedly on, and The Fish was seated on one of the Parkway benches facing her parents' building, his overcoat collar turned up, the ear flaps of his Russian fur cap pulled down.

Gwen crossed to the island and stood before him.

For a few seconds, he continued his struggle to hold his newspaper upright in the wind, pretending not to notice her. At last, however, he raised his eyes to hers.

"May I help you?" he asked. His voice intensified Gwen's aquatic impression of him, for it had a hollow, tinny sound, as though it were filtered through a bubble when it passed through his throat.

"Yes," Gwen snapped, her eyes flashing. "You can stop following me."

He looked over his shoulder, as though convinced that the person she was addressing must be standing behind him. Finding no one there, he turned his blank gaze back on Gwen. "Following you?" he asked, incredulous. "My dear lady, how could I be following you? I've been sitting on this bench for at least the last half hour. I have no idea where you've been, or even from what direction you approached me."

"I'm not referring to the past few minutes—I'm speaking about the last few weeks," Gwen said. "You've been following me—and doing a lousy job of it too. I spotted you from the very beginning."

He shook his head uncomprehendingly. "When you have

nearly eight million people living and working in such a small area as New York City, it's bound to happen that strangers will cross paths often. I'm flattered that you noticed me when such a coincidence happened to us. You are a very pretty lady, and I would have enjoyed noticing you too. But I'm afraid you never came to my attention before this moment."

"It has happened too many times for it to be a coincidence. You *have* been following me," Gwen insisted.

Clicking his tongue, he shook his head in mild reproach. "It's very bad manners to call someone a liar."

"It's also very bad manners to follow someone. I've seen you too often in my neighborhood to—"

"Ah!" he said, as though pleasantly surprised. "Don't tell me you live in the east Sixties too? I moved there only a few months ago. It's a great neighborhood—"

"You know perfectly well where I live," Gwen cut him off. "Just as you know where I shop, visit, and work."

His face remained expressionless. "Now that *is* a coincidence! Do you mean to say that you've seen me near your office too? My own office is in the Waterford Building. Are you located anywhere near there? Perhaps we could get together for lunch someday." His eyes traveled meaningfully from her face to her feet, then up again, pausing at her breasts. "Despite your persecution complex, you *are* a very attractive woman, and obviously you're attracted to me too." He ran his tongue over his thick lips. "I'd like to get to know you better."

Gwen ignored his lewd insinuation, her fury mounting. "If you're not following me, what are you doing sitting on a bench across from my parents' home in this frigid weather?" she demanded.

"'Every man to his own season,'" he said, shrugging. "Winter happens to be my favorite. As to your parents, I'm afraid I wouldn't know them if I saw them, and I certainly have no idea where they live. I'm in the neighborhood to visit an aunt who invited me for dinner. I arrived a little early and decided to wait here until the appointed time."

"You're lying!"

He sighed. "My, my! That's the second time you've accused me of that. You should visit your parents more often. Perhaps they'd teach you better manners."

Gwen glared at him. "I could go to the police, you know."

"Be my guest." He spread his hands in a gesture of generosity. "You'll be sure, of course, to mention that you approached me first. Or would you rather I did? I'll come along with you if you like."

"I can do it myself, thank you."

"Then, by all means, go ahead. But wouldn't you really rather give me your name and phone number?" Again, his eyes went meaningfully to her breasts. "I'm sure if we got together, I could straighten out whatever problem it is that sends you chasing after strange men with false accusations much better than the police could." His lips stretched into the same smile she had seen in her dream.

"Tell it to the judge!" she said furiously and left.

His high-pitched laughter followed her, telling her he knew she'd never go to the police. She couldn't—because it might turn out that Verna had hired him. And what would become of the divorce then?

If he had ever made an effort to conceal his movements, The Fish no longer made a pretense of doing so after that confrontation. From that day on, whenever Gwen caught sight of him, he would nod to her like an old acquaintance, his eyes never wavering from her face, his lips stretching into a lewd, suggestive smile. Quickly, Gwen would turn away, her stomach churning, her jaws tightening. *I can take it*, she would insist to herself. *It can't last much longer. It's only a matter of days now.*

Certain that the harassment was connected with Verna, she was convinced that it would stop as soon as the deadline for filing suit for divorce arrived. To Gwen it seemed obvious that Verna did not *know* about her and Paul, but only suspected, and was hoping to goad Gwen into becoming angry enough—or frightened enough—to let the truth slip. But after that isolated incident near her parents' home, Gwen kept her feelings under control.

There were still times, of course, when she tried to convince herself that Verna might not be associated with her persecutors—that The Fish and the caller might be the common, garden-variety, run-of-the-mill perverts who could be found walking almost every street in New York. But those times grew less frequent as the cold days of early April dragged on.

Finally, there were only five days left until the Monday when Verna was scheduled to file suit. Gwen went to the office that Thursday feeling better than she had in weeks; she had not had any anonymous calls the night before, and there had been no sign of The Fish on the subway or on the street. Verna, or Gwen's own private perverts—whatever the case might be—had evidently given up. She sat down at her desk and attacked her work with all the pleasure and energy born of relief.

At 11:30 her phone rang, and Betsy buzzed her to announce the caller. Without looking up from the layouts she was checking, Gwen reached over and picked up the receiver.

"Yes, Betsy?" she said absently.

"Verna Greene on extension two," Betsy announced.

The pencil dropped from Gwen's fingers. Her heart began pounding in quicktime, but the blood rushing through her body was not warm enough to counteract the cold fear that was spreading through her like the icy fingers of a slow paralysis.

"Who?" she said, asking the question more to verify that she still had control of her voice than to check the accuracy of her hearing.

"Verna Greene." Betsy enunciated the name carefully. "Do you know her?"

Gwen closed her eyes, trying to keep her voice calm and natural. "I know *of* her; she's an actress."

"An actress! Gee!" Betsy was duly impressed. "Funny, I never heard of her."

"She works mostly on the stage, I think."

"Oh. Gary and I never go to shows. They're too expensive." There was a pout in her voice. "Anyway, do you want me to put her through?"

While she was talking to Betsy, Gwen's mind had been racing ahead, debating the answer to that question. If she took the call, would Verna interpret it as an admission of guilt? But if she refused to take it, turning Verna over to

Betsy, would Verna, perhaps, give Betsy an all too vivid message? Better to take it and try to bluff her way through.

"Put her through."

Betsy pressed the extension button, releasing the hold. There was a click, and the little light went on above extension two.

"May I help you?" Gwen asked in her most crisp, businesslike voice.

"The question is, Miss Hadley, may *I* help *you*?" The voice at the other end was soft and feline.

Gwen managed a polite little laugh. "I'm afraid I don't understand."

"You *are* the editor of *True Affairs*, aren't you?"

"Yes." Closing her eyes, Gwen tried to draw a steadying breath.

"And you *do* publish a monthly feature called 'With My Hand in His,' don't you?"

"We do."

"Then it is *I* who can help you," Verna purred. "You see, I thought I'd write one of those articles for you. They're so inspiring. And I have a *very* inspiring story to tell."

"That's very kind of you, Miss Greene." Gwen wiped her perspiring hand on her skirt. "But I'm afraid that even though we run those articles in our magazine, we have very little to do with them here in this office. Arrangements for them are made through the company publicity department, which works for all Waterford magazines. The writer who's been contracted for ghosting the series lives out on the Coast, where most of the stars whose bylines we use live. You see, our readers are more familiar with movie and television stars than with the more sophisticated stage personalities like you."

"Oh, but I'm sure they'd be interested in *my* story. I'm going to be very famous soon." Her tone hinted that her words held a hidden meaning, but it was a meaning Gwen could not fathom.

"Then I'm sure they would be interested." Gwen found the effort to keep her voice impersonal almost unbearable. "But, as I said, arrangements are handled by our publicity department. If you have your agent get in touch with John Michaels, he'll make all the necessary arrangements with the writer—"

"But I intend to write it myself," Verna cut in. "That's what I wanted to talk to you about—the things I intend to say in the article. I thought we could get together for lunch today and discuss it."

Her heart was pounding so hard, Gwen was half-afraid Verna would hear it. She took a deep breath to steady her voice. "I'm sure that would be delightful, Miss Greene, but I have a very busy schedule."

"Oh, that's all right. I can always come up to your office instead." Her voice was soft, accommodating, but there was no question that her words held a threat.

Gwen's heart sank. She had to keep Verna away from the office. "Well," she said, as genially as she could, "I think I might be able to make it for lunch today, after all."

"I'm so glad!" Verna purred. "Shall we make it at one-thirty at Gino's on Forty-fourth Street? By that time, the rush will be almost over, and we'll be able to talk in peace."

"I'll be there," Gwen said, and she felt as though she were pronouncing her own doom. "By the way, I'll be wearing—"

"You don't have to describe yourself," Verna cut in. "I'll know who you are. Good-by—till one-thirty."

"Good-by."

Staring into space, Gwen held the receiver in her trembling hand for a moment after Verna had broken the connection. When she finally hung up, the receiver was wet with her perspiration. After wiping it dry with a tissue, she buzzed Betsy.

"Call Fran Carson. Tell her that something has come up, and I won't be able to keep our lunch date. Make it for one day next week, but tell her if she has any questions about the assignment she's working on, she should call me."

"Sure thing." Betsy hesitated. "Do you feel okay?"

"Certainly. Why?"

"Your voice sounds funny."

"Must be the intercom. Make that call right away, will you? I want to catch her before she leaves her house."

"Gotcha." Betsy rang off.

Gwen squeezed her eyes tight shut for a moment, then

opened them and looked at her watch. Less than two hours to go. She wished the meeting were over with—and yet she wished the time would never come. Sometimes dragging, sometimes skipping, the hands of her watch teased their way to 1:15. Gwen freshened her lipstick, slipped on her coat, and left the office.

It was cold and cloudy, and a bitter wind whipped her coat around her and tousled her hair. Hunching her shoulders against the wind, she headed for Gino's. Gwen waited in the cold for ten minutes, then she decided to check inside.

Yes, said the short, charming maître d', who looked as though he indulged in a little too much of Gino's cooking, there was a Miss Greene waiting for a Miss Hadley. This way, please. He led the way to the rear of the restaurant, where a slim, dark woman was seated alone at a table for two, gazing into the depths of a half-consumed martini.

"Your friend has arrived," he announced.

Verna looked up. Her makeup was heavy and theatrical, but expertly applied, and though Gwen was aware that in the sunlight it would add years to her face, here in the flattering, soft light of the restaurant, it made Verna look closer to thirty than to the forty Gwen knew she was. The feline quality Gwen had noticed in her voice was evident in her face also—in the eyeliner-accentuated, catlike shape of her large gray-green eyes, in her high cheekbones, narrow chin, small nose, and thin lips. The lips curved into a mirthless smile.

"Welcome, friend," she purred, repeating the maitre d's phrase. "Have a seat."

Gwen sat down, shrugging out of her coat. *She looks like a cat about to pounce,* she thought. *And I'm the mouse.* With a sudden flash of insight, she realized that Melanie must see Verna this way too—that was why the child had a morbid dislike of cats.

"I was waiting outside for about ten minutes," Gwen said at last. "I hope you haven't been here long."

Verna shrugged. "Only a little while. Hardly long enough to finish three martinis."

As the waiter approached, Verna downed the rest of her drink and ordered another. Gwen asked for a whiskey sour.

Love After Hours

While they waited for their drinks, Gwen let Verna do the talking. The topic of conversation she chose was a short, rather exaggerated account of her acting career.

"Everything was going beautifully," she was saying as the waiter delivered their drinks. "Then I had to get knocked up." Her eyes narrowed as she lifted her glass. "In those days abortions were dangerous, so I had the little bitch. I've been stuck at home with her till now. But now everything is different. She's able to look out for herself. I'm finally on my way to the top." She took a swallow of her drink, then shook her long dark hair back dramatically. "Have you seen my play?"

"I'm afraid not."

"Oh, my dear! You must get your boyfriend to take you." She smiled her slow, feline smile. "You *do* have a boyfriend, don't you?"

Gwen's stomach knotted, but she managed to smile noncommittally. "I have friends who are male."

Verna raised a well-arched brow, her lips curling in mild amusement. "More than one? My, my! Well, you'd better have *one* of them take you right away. Because soon there's going to be a stampede for tickets, and then heaven only knows when you'll get seats."

"Really?" Gwen knew from Paul that the play was about to fold, but she tried to sound as though she gave credence to Verna's wild predictions.

"Really." Verna leveled her eyes on Gwen. "You never know what might happen to spur the public's interest. By tomorrow morning, there will be a run on tickets. You wait and see."

The words had been spoken softly and with a smile, but there had been a deadly threat in Verna's eyes. A chill knifed through Gwen, as though she'd just received the kiss of death. Clasping her hands in her lap to keep them from trembling, Gwen pushed the corners of her mouth up into an answering smile. "I'm sure the producer will be pleased."

"Not half as much as I will be."

Verna finished her drink, and the waiter approached with the luncheon menu. Though she felt ill, Gwen tried to look interested as she studied the menu, finally ordering lasagna and coffee. Verna asked for ravioli and a double martini.

While they waited for their order, Verna continued to talk about herself and her role. Tensing more with every minute, Gwen listened, wondering when Verna was going to drop the bomb she so obviously intended to explode. As she watched Verna's restless eyes and slow, malicious smile, she remembered a French teacher she'd had in high school who took malicious delight in making her students squirm. Her expression when she had Josef, a recent immigrant from Hungary whose English was as poor as his French, stand before the class and struggle with page after page of sight translation was a perfect match for Verna's.

"I got the part," Verna said as their lunch was placed before them, "through Paul Lockhart, my husband. He's very devoted to me."

"How nice," Gwen said.

"Do you know my husband, Miss Hadley?"

Gwen refused to allow her gaze to waver from Verna's. "Not really. I met him once when he was a celebrity guest at a company dinner, and I've read a few of his books."

"Terrible, aren't they?" Verna's eyes darted away, and she attacked her ravioli. "I'm the one in the family with talent, but, unfortunately, he's the one who has had the luck—so far."

Methodically, Gwen chewed her lasagna, but found it difficult to ease the food past the stricture in her throat.

The smile was back on Verna's face. "Speaking of Paul reminds me of the article I'm going to write for you. After all, that's what we're here to talk about, isn't it?"

Gwen nodded and picked up her coffee cup.

"It's going to be all about how I kept him from leaving me for another woman. Your readers go for things like that, don't they?"

For a second, the room seemed to go out of focus. Then, slowly, willing her hand to be steady, Gwen replaced her cup on its saucer.

"They're very interested in that subject," she said, amazed at the calm in her voice. "But the article is supposed to be religious in tone."

"Of course! I'll make it very clear that it was God who

showed me the way. I assure you that they'll find it interesting—and educational too."

"How nice." Gwen pushed her plate away.

Verna signaled the waiter for another drink. "That will be my coffee and dessert," she told him as he placed it before her.

"Nothing else for me, thanks," Gwen said when he extended the dessert menu to her. She nodded toward her plate. "You can take that away."

"But you've hardly touched it!" Verna protested, her eyes wide with mock incredulity. "Did you lose your appetite?"

"No," Gwen lied. "I just don't want to lose my figure."

"That's something I've never had to worry about," Verna purred. "My figure has always been one of my best points. Paul's crazy about it. Can't keep his hands off me. He has another woman, you know, but she obviously can't give him enough sex. He keeps coming straight from her to me for more."

Though she knew Verna was lying, Gwen still felt every false word she said cut through her like a knife. She took a sip of coffee to steady herself. "How generous of you to let him."

"Wifely duty and all that." Her eyes darted around the room. "Besides, I'll soon have him all to myself again."

"From the way you describe him, I'm surprised that you'd want him."

Verna shrugged. "He comes in handy."

"And this plan you have for keeping him," Gwen said, sloshing the dregs of her coffee around the bottom of her cup, trying to sound casual, "you haven't mentioned what it is."

Verna smiled mysteriously. "Oh, I wouldn't want to ruin the suspense. You can read all about it in my article." She signaled the waiter for the bill.

Gwen reached for her purse, but as soon as the waiter came, Verna handed him a credit card.

Trying not to show how furious Verna's false generosity made her, Gwen extended some bills. "That's very kind of you," she said, "but I insist on paying my share."

"It's my treat," Verna said. Smiling, she put her hand on Gwen's and gently pushed it away. Her skin was cold and dry, like a snake's, her nails long and sharp. Gwen recoiled from her touch.

"That's better," Verna said. She added a tip and signed the bill. "Keep the signature," she told the waiter. "It will be worth a fortune someday."

The two women rose and put on their coats. For someone who had recently consumed at least six martinis, some of them doubles, Verna managed to keep her gait extraordinarily steady as they left the restaurant.

"Good-by," Gwen said when they were outside. "I look forward to reading your article."

Verna laughed soundlessly. "I'm sure you do. I'm looking forward to living it." She turned and walked away.

For a while, Gwen watched her retreat. Then she began trudging back to her office, concentrating only on the agonizing effort it took to place one foot in front of the other.

As Gwen passed her desk, Betsy seemed to take alarm at her paleness. "Are you all right?" she asked, jumping up as if to go to her aid.

"Yes. Yes, I'm fine." She paused at the entrance to her office. "No calls, Betsy. Unless it's Mr. Lockhart or Jason Bart."

Still looking concerned, Betsy nodded and slipped back into her chair.

As though in a trance, Gwen hung up her coat and walked over to her desk. Suddenly, all the emotions she'd fought so hard to control in Verna's presence broke loose, and, her teeth chattering, her entire body trembling, she sank down on her chair.

"What is that woman up to?" she whispered to herself. She held her head between her hands and wept.

Finally, the sounds of typing and the ringing of phones from the outer office penetrated her emotional fog. Realizing that someone might walk in on her at any moment, she made an effort to pull herself together. She opened her purse and took out her address book. It would be dangerous to call Paul at home, but she had his agent's office number. Paul had given it to her once, telling her that in an emergency his agent would be able to contact him. With trembling fingers she dialed the number, then tried to be patient as she was shifted from the switchboard operator, to the agent's secretary, to the agent.

"Mr. Phillips," she said when she got through to him at last, "I'm Gwendolyn Hadley, a friend of Paul Lockhart's. He told me once that if an emergency came up, you would probably be able to contact him for me. Well, an emergency has come up."

"I hope it isn't serious."

"If it weren't I wouldn't be calling. Can you contact him and ask him to get in touch with me?"

"He's over in Jersey today, meeting with Harry Richards to make plans about collaborating on the dramatization of his new book. He's due back late this afternoon. He's supposed to give me a ring then. Do you want me to wait until he calls, or should I try to reach him at Harry's?"

"Try to reach him there, please," Gwen begged. "It's very important."

"All right. I hope they decided to stick around the house."

"I hope so too. Thanks very much, Mr. Phillips."

She replaced the receiver on the hook and looked at her watch. 3:30. How long would it take Phillips to reach Paul —and Paul to reach her? Five minutes? Ten?

She tried to work but kept looking at the phone, willing it to ring. The few times it did, however, it couldn't have been Paul, since Betsy took the calls, and didn't put them through to her.

It was after four when Betsy finally pushed the intercom button. "Mr. Lockhart on extension one."

Not stopping to comment, Gwen switched over immediately. "Oh, Paul! Thank God!"

"Darling, what is it?" His voice was filled with concern. "We've been away from the house. Wally said he's been trying to reach me for the past half hour."

Her hands began shaking, and it was difficult for her to keep her voice under control. "It's Verna—she knows! I saw her this afternoon."

She heard his sharp intake of breath. "You *saw* her?"

Trying to regain her composure, she breathed deeply, but

the effort was futile. "She called me and insisted on a meeting. It was awful!"

"What happened? What did she say?"

"I can't go into it here." Her voice cracked with tension. "I know we agreed not to see each other, but this is an emergency. Paul, I'm so frightened. Something's going to go wrong. I know it!"

"Get hold of yourself, darling!" His voice was tender, yet commanding. "Nothing can go wrong at this stage—"

"But I have to see you! You don't know what I've been through! Please come."

"Of course, I'll come. Look—I want you to go home. You're in no condition to be at the office. I'll leave here now. With luck, I should be at your place by five."

"I'll be waiting. Drive carefully, darling."

"I will. And you be careful going home. I love you."

"I love you too."

She hung up the phone, then sat for a moment looking at the trembling hand she lifted from the receiver. She had thought talking to Paul would allay her fears, but it had only intensified them. The loving tone of his voice reminded her of all she had to lose.

She put on her coat, picked up her purse, and went out to Betsy's desk. "I'm leaving now," she said. "I don't feel very well."

Betsy gave her an I-told-you-so look. "I thought you looked a little green when you came back from lunch. Don't worry about a thing here. I'll hold down the fort."

In no state for the city subway system, she took a taxi home, glad that she had left early enough to escape heavy traffic. She rushed into her apartment like a child seeking the security of familiar surroundings, but when she closed the door behind her and switched on the lights, she found that her fears had followed her home. They remained with her, always a step behind her, as she paced the floor awaiting Paul's arrival. By the time he rang the bell, she was more tense and frightened than ever. She rushed to the door and flung it open.

It had been almost a month since they'd seen each other last, and for a moment, they stood transfixed, gazing on each other's faces as shipwrecked sailors might behold the approach of a sail. Then, suddenly, they were in each other's arms, their hearts pounding so furiously as they pressed together that it was impossible to distinguish the beat of one from the other.

"It's been so long!" she whispered when their lips finally parted.

"Too long, darling." He rubbed his cheek against hers. "But soon the waiting will be over. Whatever happened this afternoon, it can't do anything to change that."

She slipped out of his arms, her eyes filling with tears. "No. Something terrible is going to happen! I can feel it."

"You're letting your imagination blow things out of proportion," he insisted.

Her eyes flashed with fear and impatience. "It's not my imagination that I've been followed. It's not my imagination that I've been receiving anonymous phone calls. And I didn't imagine the threats behind every word Verna said to me today," she said as he led her to the sofa.

In a voice shaking with emotion, Gwen told him everything that had happened since their last meeting; finally, she gave him the details of her two conversations with Verna.

"Don't you see?" she cried when she had finished. "She has some awful, diabolical plan!"

"The bitch!"

Gwen burst into tears.

Gently, he took her face between his hands. "I wish you had told me what you've been going through long ago."

"It wouldn't have changed anything."

"No, but sharing would have eased the burden a little." Lovingly, he wiped her tears away. "You *are* making too much out of it, you know. If Verna had any concrete proof, she never would have resorted to these tactics. She gambled on scaring an admission out of you—and she lost."

"But she *does* plan to do something terrible, Paul!" Gwen insisted. "It was obvious in everything she said today."

Paul shook his head. "Don't you see that it was her final big bluff? She was playing her last hand, and she played it to the hilt. But you kept a poker face and out-bluffed her." He pulled her close. "Darling, you're worrying over nothing.

There's nothing she can do but go quietly to a lawyer on Monday."

Gwen rubbed her cheek against the rough tweed of his jacket, trying to find reassurance in his words, in his presence. But even in the comfort of his arms, she realized that her fears were not routed, only scattered and regrouping.

"Christ!" Paul stiffened suddenly and pulled away to look at his watch. "I agreed to take Verna to some goddam showbusiness cocktail party this evening. She's been after me about it all week. I was supposed to pick her up at five-thirty. It's six now."

"Do you have to go?"

"God knows I don't want to, but it was part of our agreement that she could use me for publicity purposes until she officially files for divorce. I hope it will be my last public duty for her." He stood up. "I'll call her and tell her I'll meet her there. That way we can have a few more minutes together."

While he was in the bedroom making the call, Gwen sat on the sofa, trying to cope with the fear inside her. It seemed that she could keep it at bay only when Paul was near, and soon he'd be leaving.

When Paul returned to the living room, he was frowning. "After nagging me for a week about the importance of picking her up so we could arrive together, she evidently left without me. There's no answer."

For some unknown reason, that news sent a chill coursing through Gwen. "Where's Melanie?"

"Spending the night at a friend's house. For once, Verna gave her permission without making the child eat her heart out and beg. Maybe now that she realizes she's going to lose her, she's learning some compassion." He walked over to the hall closet. "I'd better leave now if she's there already."

Gwen sat as though frozen, staring into space. "All week?" she asked in a half-dead voice. "She's been after you to take her to that party all week?"

Nodding, Paul shrugged into his coat.

Suddenly all the pieces seemed to fall into place. Jumping up, Gwen ran to Paul, her face white with fright.

Love After Hours

"Don't go!" she cried. "Whatever it is she plans to do, she's going to do it at the party! It all adds up."

Paul shook his head, puzzled. "You're imagining things, darling. Monday is only a few days away. She knows that this is the last event she can use to capitalize on my being her husband."

"All the more reason for her to make the most of it!" She clutched his hand, desperate to make him see the same horrible forewarning that had flashed before her. "She told me that tomorrow morning there would be a run on tickets for her play. Curtain's at seven-thirty. She has only a little more time to do something that will create interest in the play—or in seeing *her* in it. Don't you see? She's going to create a scene at that party or start a fight—do *something* that will cause a big scandal!"

"Verna was whistling in the dark when she gave you that story about a run on tickets," Paul insisted. "Certainly, she's low enough to think of such a scheme," he went on when he saw Gwen was about to protest, "but she's also shrewd enough to know that she could never provoke me into acting it out with her."

"How can you be sure?" Gwen demanded. "For God's sake, Paul. For *my* sake, don't go! Nothing could happen if you stayed away—and so much could happen if you went." She began to tremble, tears welling up in her eyes. "Besides," she whispered, "I need you here tonight. I'll go out of my mind after all that happened today if I have to spend the evening alone."

"That," he said tenderly, "is the strongest argument of all." Gently, he kissed her. Then, having put his coat back in the closet, he slipped his arm around her quivering shoulders and walked her back into the living room.

As they sipped their drinks and then scrounged up dinner in Gwen's tiny kitchen, they both made an effort to keep their conversation light, to banish Verna from their midst. But the shaking of Gwen's hands as she ate, the tremor that cracked through her too hearty laugh gave evidence that Verna could not be banished from her thoughts. Though Paul never alluded to it, Gwen knew her fear did not escape him, and his eyes were filled with concern.

After they cleared away the dishes, they lingered over coffee in the living room. Finally, Paul placed his hand over Gwen's as she shakily returned her cup to its saucer.

"Maybe," he said huskily, "I should go now. What you need more than anything else is a good night's sleep."

Gwen moistened her lips. "What I need more than anything else," she whispered, "is you."

Hand in hand, they walked into her bedroom, where, locked in each other's arms, they were able to create a world of their own—a world that Verna and her threats could never hope to penetrate. Then, in the sweet exhaustion of fulfillment, they drifted off to sleep.

It was Gwen who awoke first a little while later. Raising herself on one elbow, she looked down on the sleeping Paul, her gaze moving over him like a soft caress. The hands on the luminous dial of her clock read a quarter to ten, and she knew she should awaken him, but she delayed, wanting to relish his nearness as long as possible. Gingerly, she ran her fingers through the short curly hair on his chest. It seemed to her that there was much more gray among the dark hairs than when they had become lovers. The expanse of silver between his dark temples had widened too. She felt as though her love increased tenfold for every new gray hair he had gained.

In sleep, the intensity that always animated his face retreated, but his sharp, rather crooked nose, his wide jaw line, and his strong chin bore silent testimony to his inner strength. Lovingly, she traced the craggy lines of his features with a gentle finger. He did not waken, but stirring a little, he turned his head aside, leaving the line of his neck more visible than before. She bent to kiss it, but abruptly drew back, her eyes fixed on the little pulse throbbing just below his jaw. She hated that reminder that life and love hung on a thread—that the man who brought all joy and meaning to her life was encased in a flesh-and-bone machine that had to be pumped with air and lubricated with blood constantly to keep going and could stop functioning completely at any time. Recoiling from that tiny reminder of human mortality, she reached over and shook Paul, as if by awakening and animating him she could negate the transience of life and love.

"Paul. Darling. You have to leave soon."

Reaching up, he pulled her down on top of him for a lingering kiss. "Not too soon, I hope," he murmured, shifting his body gently so that she rolled over and he was looking down on her.

She reached up and took his face between her hands. "Too soon, I'm afraid. It's ten."

Neither of them would mention Verna in the sanctity of the bedroom, but uppermost in their minds was the necessity that Paul arrive home before Verna returned from the theater.

Sighing, Paul leaned down, planting a quick kiss on her lips. "All right. I'm off." He swung out of bed and began dressing.

For a while, Gwen watched in silence. Then she slipped from bed and put on her robe.

"Coffee before you go?"

He glanced at the clock. "I'd better not."

She picked up his tie, holding it for him while he slipped on his shoes. He took it from her with a kiss.

"Why do I feel so sad?" she asked.

He smiled a little, but his eyes were sad too. "Because the last mile is always the hardest."

She nodded, going to his side. Arms around each other's waists, they walked in silence to get his coat from the hall closet.

At the door, he paused and put his hands on her shoulders. "Feel better?"

She closed her eyes and managed a little smile. "A little."

"In a few more days, it will all be over," he reminded her. "The next time we meet, everything will be different."

"Thank God!"

Their kiss was light and tender.

"I love you," he whispered when their lips parted.

"And I love you."

Reaching up, she traced the outline of his mouth with her finger. He took her hand and pressed it tight against his lips. Then he turned and left.

Gwen spent the remainder of the evening in an unsuccessful attempt to read and keep her mind off the day's events. Around midnight, she went back to bed. An hour later, she was still lying there, wide-eyed, staring at the ceiling, when the phone at her bedside shrilled. Sure that it was her anonymous caller striking again, she lay there rigid, refusing to reach for the receiver.

On and on it screamed, like a spoiled baby demanding to be picked up. When she could stand it no longer, Gwen finally gave in, but she would not give the caller the satisfaction of hearing her say hello.

"Gwen, is that you? For God's sake, don't hang up!"

Her heart turned to a lump of ice. "Paul!" she cried, jumping up and switching on the lamp. "What is it? What's wrong?"

"Everything's wrong." His voice cracked with emotion. "Verna's dead."

The hair at the back of her neck prickled, and she almost dropped the receiver. "Dead?" she echoed.

He drew a ragged breath. "She killed herself tonight."

"Oh, my God, no!"

There was a pause; then, with an obvious effort, he forced himself to go on. "The hell of it is, I'm sure she didn't mean to. I think she intended that I should find her at five-thirty and rush her to the hospital in time to have her stomach pumped."

The blood drained from Gwen's head, and the room went out of focus. "And I had you come here!" she said, almost gagging on the words. "And then I made you stay."

"Don't blame yourself, darling. You couldn't have known. Neither of us could have known." But his tone said that he blamed himself. "She took God only knows how many barbiturates, and the doctor told me she had so much alcohol in her blood that she most likely would have died anyway."

"Oh, Paul! It's like a nightmare come to life."

For a moment neither said anything. Then Paul's voice, ragged with emotion, came through again. "Gwen—there's more."

"More?"

"Verna arranged to have a letter delivered to the *Daily*

Love After Hours 313

News at midnight. It named you as the cause of her suicide —said you came between us."

"Are you sure?" she gasped.

"A reporter has already started hounding me." He drew a deep breath. "Oh, darling, I'd give anything to—"

"I know, I know." She was crying now, and it was difficult to keep her voice under control.

"This was what she meant when she told you something would happen to create interest in the play. She intended to live to read the headlines and to benefit by them. She trusted me to keep her plan from backfiring." His voice broke. "It was the only time I didn't keep my word."

"And it was my fault."

"No. It was no one's fault—except maybe Verna's."

"But she—she's no longer here to take the blame."

There was another pause.

"Have you told Melanie yet?" Gwen asked at last.

"I've arranged with her friend's parents to let her sleep through the night. I'll call for her early in the morning and tell her then. I'll try to keep as much of the ugliness from her as possible, but she's a big girl. It won't be easy."

"Do you think the newspaper will print the story?"

"Would a hungry lion refuse a juicy piece of meat?"

She began to cry again. "If only—"

"Don't say it, darling. Once you begin with if onlys, there's never an end. Just try to pull yourself together and get some rest. You'll need it. The reporters are bound to start hounding you too. I'll come over tomorrow, and we'll—"

"No."

"No—what?" His voice was puzzled.

"Don't come tomorrow." It was hard for her to get the words out.

"Because of the reporters? All right. I'll call you, and we'll arrange to meet somewhere."

"No, no, no!" Her voice rose shrilly. "Don't call. Don't come. Don't meet me!" She had to force every word over the lump in her throat. "We can't see each other. Never again."

"You can't mean that!"

For a moment, she was crying so hard she could not answer. Then finally, she pushed her voice through her tears, but the effort made it emerge sounding weak and high pitched. "Everything we had is tainted now. It's over, Paul. It has to be."

"You're not thinking clearly!" he insisted, tears in his own voice. "Tomorrow you'll see things in a different light."

She shuddered. "There's only one light to see them in."

"I'll call you tomorrow," he insisted.

"No. It's over. It has to be." Her voice shook with emotion. "Oh, please, Paul! Don't make it any harder!"

"Gwen, listen to me—"

"Good-by, my darling." Sobbing, she hung up on his protests.

She collapsed on her bed, her body shuddering, shaking with tears, her mind racked with regret.

The phone began ringing again.

It was Paul. She knew it. She covered her ears with her shaking hands. If only she hadn't called him that afternoon, maybe Verna would still be alive. There would have been a scandal, but scandals blow over.

Still the phone rang.

Stop it, Paul! Stop it! she cried silently.

If only she hadn't had that crazy feeling about the cocktail party and begged Paul to stay! If only. . . . She shook her head. Paul was right. Once you began with if onlys, there was no end.

The phone rang on.

"Paul, you're only making the hurt that much worse for both of us," she whispered.

Gently, she placed a pillow over the phone. Then, tears streaming down her cheeks, she sat there staring at it, listening to the muffled rings resound in her room like muted death tolls for a lost love.

Suddenly, the ringing stopped. Tensing, she removed her hands from her ears, listening intently, as though seeking an echo. But the only sound that came back to her was the lonely, screaming silence.

Chapter Sixteen

Stories about Verna and her suicide were blasted all over the front pages of the *Daily News* the next morning, complete with photos of Verna in her heyday. *The Post* echoed it with glee in the afternoon, while *The Times* gave it a sleepy nod, with a few paragraphs on its obituary page. The more sensational stories, of course, were slanted to evoke sympathy for Verna, the aspiring actress and loving wife and mother, and antipathy toward Gwen, the *femme fatale*—editor of a confession magazine, no less—who had destroyed her happy home. Along with photos of Verna and Paul, the *News* also published one of The Fish, identifying him as T. O. Enright, the private detective to whom the heartbroken Verna had turned for help. It was Enright, the paper revealed, who had been entrusted to deliver Verna's suicide note to its night city editor, although the distraught, wronged woman had given him no idea of its contents or of her intentions.

All three newspapers were left anonymously at Gwen's door by a friendly—or perhaps unfriendly—neighbor. She read them without emotion. Her heartbreak was too great for her to feel anger at injustice. She shuddered, though, when she saw how much of her personal life had suddenly become public property.

She called in sick on Friday, and virtually barricaded herself in her apartment for the entire weekend. Except for using the phone once for what she intended to be a reassuring call to her mother—who verbally beat her thin chest and tore her gray hair, lamenting her destiny as a martyr who had gone through the agony of childbirth only to have her daughter bring shame upon the name and home she had provided—she kept her phone off the hook and refused to open her door to the reporters who incessantly banged and rang her bell.

Watching the news on television late Friday evening, she learned Verna's suicide had been a publicity gimmick that had backfired. Interviews with members of the *Raw Flesh* cast had brought to light the fact that Verna had been bragging about a media event she was about to stage that would create a stampede for tickets. She had even told her co-star that her career was the only thing that mattered to her, and that she was ready and willing to sacrifice anyone and anything to advance it. In a few hours, the media's depiction of Verna had changed from that of a heartbroken, wronged wife to an ambitious, neurotic actress. At the same time, however, Paul's relationship with Gwen continued to be milked for every last ounce of sensationalism.

Early Saturday morning, feeling unable to cope with her self-imposed solitary confinement any longer, Gwen tried to slip out for a while. The second the vestibule door closed behind her, two figures jumped up from the stoop, and Gwen staggered back, momentarily blinded by the light from a camera's flashbulb.

"How long have you and Paul Lockhart been lovers?" a metallic voice snapped at her.

Gwen rubbed her eyes, trying to restore her vision. Hazily, she made out a stocky man of about fifty with a camera poised and cocked before his eye like a well-oiled shotgun. Beside him stood a hard-faced young woman with long straight hair and round, metal-framed eyeglasses, holding a pad and pen at a menacing angle, looking like an iron-faced court officer about to read into the record the heinous charges of which her prisoner was being accused. It was obvious from the pair's rumpled clothes that they had spent the night camping on the stoop.

Another flash of light exploded in Gwen's eyes.

"Were you with him the night his wife committed suicide?" the girl barked.

Another flash of light.

"Okay, Sal," the man said. "I've got some good ones. I'll go back and print them up."

Love After Hours 317

Her heart pounding, Gwen pushed against the vestibule door, but it had locked automatically behind her.

"Great! I'll see you back at the office," the reporter said.

Again, Gwen pushed against the door, but it wouldn't yield.

"Did you know his wife was planning a phony 'publicity suicide'?" The friendliness that had been in the reporter's voice when she addressed the photographer had disappeared, and the words rapped out of her mouth like a round of bullets from a machine gun.

Frantically, Gwen groped in her purse for her keys, but her vision, still faulty from the flashbulbs' glare, was further blinded by tears.

"Have you seen Lockhart since the suicide?"

"Please!" Gwen begged.

Giving up her search, she pushed past the reporter and ran down the stairs, hurrying along the street. The girl stayed close on her heels, following Gwen like a stubborn stray, barking out insistent questions, as undaunted by Gwen's silence as she was unmoved by her tears.

Then, as her trembling hand reached for a tissue, Gwen's fingers suddenly made contact with the cold metal of her keys. Clutching them as though they were a lifeline, she turned and raced back toward her building.

The reporter changed direction as swiftly and smoothly as if she were physically attached to Gwen. "Are you glad that she's dead? Are you going to the funeral?"

On and on the reporter went, never missing a step, never mincing a word. On the stoop of Gwen's building, she placed herself between Gwen and the vestibule door and put her hand over the lock. "What are your plans for the future?"

"Get out of my way, please," Gwen said, trying to keep her mounting fury under control.

The reporter held the knob more firmly. "Are you going to marry him or move in with him?"

Gwen's face reddened, and her voice shook. "Move out of my way!"

"Oh, for Christ's sake!" Disgust and impatience flicked over the girl's hardened features as the early-morning sunlight glinted off the metal frames of her eyeglasses and the frosted glaze on her petulant mouth. "Give me a break! Be a sport and *tell* me something. Hell, there's nothing personal in this. It's just my job."

For a second, the anger drained from Gwen as she gave the girl a long, measuring look. More than infuriating, she found it sad and sickening that someone so young should be so callous and cynical.

"There's a great deal personal in it," Gwen informed the reporter finally, her eyes misting. "It happens to be my life." With one swift movement, she made a fist and brought it down sharply on the girl's hand.

Yelping in surprise and pain, the girl pulled her hand off the door. In a matter of seconds, Gwen had inserted her key in the lock, opened the door, and slammed it in the girl's face. Quick to recover, however, the reporter began rattling the knob, calling out her questions through the glass. Trying not to listen, Gwen rushed up the stairs to the sanctuary of her apartment, where she collapsed in tears.

Late that night, Paul came. Having somehow gained admittance downstairs, he rang her bell, knocked on her door, and called to her through it. Silently, Gwen sat in a chair, clutching its arms until her knuckles seemed ready to burst through her flesh. Finally, Paul gave up.

"I have to get back to Melanie," he called through the door. "But I'll come again tomorrow. Darling, we have to talk."

There was no rush of relief as she heard his footsteps echo down the hall, only another of sorrow's endless waves that washed the tension of the moment away and left her sitting deflated but far from relaxed in her chair.

"Why can't you realize that there is nothing left to say?" she whispered.

By Sunday the newspapers had other people to fry, and the reporters disappeared from Gwen's doorstep, at least for the time being. Determined to avoid the agonizing strain of Paul's next attempt to see her, Gwen tossed a few things into a suitcase, slipped out, and registered at a small hotel in a residential district.

Monday dawned chilly and damp; dark, low-slung clouds promised rain or perhaps more of the unseasonable snow

Love After Hours 319

with which New Yorkers had been visited in the past few weeks. Having left more appropriate clothing at home, Gwen had only a trench coat and a kerchief to protect her against the weather. She put them on and left the hotel much earlier than necessary, determined to be the first in the office so that she could avoid walking the gauntlet of curious, pitying or condemning eyes.

Almost as soon as she was on the street, a cold wind began driving sharp needles of a rain into her face. Trying to ward off the onslaught, she hunched her shoulders and ducked her head as she walked to the subway.

At 8:40, she entered the Waterford Building alone and rode the elevator unaccompanied to the fourteenth floor. Taking a seldom-used key from her purse, she unlocked the corridor door that gave access to the offices on the floor. The outer office greeted her with the silence of a tomb. The steel-gray desks, their typewriters covered like the heads of grieving Greek matrons, stood like so many silent monuments to all the souls that have been sacrificed on the altar of big business.

Gwen switched on the lights, and, with her footsteps echoing all around her, started across the floor. At Betsy's desk, she paused, ferreted a piece of paper from one of the drawers and wrote: *I am out to all calls except those obviously pertaining to business.* She started away, then went back and added: *Bill Saxon included.* She knew Bill would be anxious and concerned, but she didn't feel ready to talk to him yet.

In her office, she removed her coat, combed her hair, took out a manuscript, and settled down to wait for the inevitable call from Jason Bart.

A little before nine o'clock, the outer office began to stir. Doors opened and slammed, people called greetings to one another. The secretaries could be heard gossiping enthusiastically, and once or twice, though she could not make out the rest of their words, Gwen heard her name mentioned.

Betsy arrived, knocked, and slipped inside, looking like a guilt-ridden thief expecting to be discovered by the police at any moment.

"Good morning," Gwen said, her voice and attitude unchanged from her usual bearing.

"Good morning." Betsy stared at her a second, then quickly shifted her gaze to just past Gwen's left ear, as though she had discovered a smudge of dirt on Gwen's face but was too polite to call attention to it. "I, uh, got your note. Do you want me to order coffee for you?"

The condemned's last meal, Gwen thought. "Not today, thanks," she said.

Betsy toyed with the doorknob. "Do you want me to take a letter or anything?"

In spite of her depression, Gwen smiled at Betsy's awkward lack of candor. "A letter of resignation?" she asked.

A blush rushed from Betsy's neck to her forehead as her embarrassed glance met Gwen's, then fluttered quickly away. "Oh, no!" she protested. "I didn't mean—I mean—"

"It's all right," Gwen assured her soothingly. "I appreciate your conscientiousness, but I have no dictation for you right now."

Still red-faced, Betsy continued looking past Gwen's left ear. "Well, in that case . . . I have a pile of things to do. . . . I'd better get on with it. . . ."

"Yes, I guess so."

In a flash Betsy was out the door. Never in all the time Gwen had known her had she seen her so anxious to get to work.

Gwen picked up a pencil and tapped it against her desk. No, she thought, there would be no letter of resignation. She had always been a model employee, her work excellent and above reproach. If the Waterford Brothers wanted to play dirty because they disliked the scandal about her private life, she'd be damned if she'd do anything to make it easy for them.

She finished looking over some material for the printer, then dialed Terri's extension and asked her to come get it for the pouch.

Terri swooped in, looking like self-righteousness incarnate.

After saying good morning and handing her the material, Gwen attempted to turn back to her work, but Terri remained standing at her desk until Gwen looked up again.

She batted her false eyelashes. "I just want to say that I read the papers, and I don't believe what they said about you for a minute." Her look and tone said that not only did she believe every word, but she was also prepared to believe worse.

"That's very comforting." Gwen's voice was dry, almost brittle.

Terri forced a little laugh. "Of course, whatever they say, I'm sure it can't bother you. All that really matters is that your *friend's* wife is finally out of the way." Petulance pulled down the corners of her mouth, and her eyes filled with envy.

"Yes, it is all that matters, but not in the way that you think," Gwen said quietly. "Now, if you'll excuse me, I have a lot of work to catch up on."

"Certainly," Terri sniffed. Her tone was one of moral superiority, but her look as she swept out of the office said clearly that some people had all the luck.

Almost immediately after Terri left, Betsy buzzed to say that Frances had some questions about a manuscript.

Gwen sighed. "Send her in."

Frances seated herself in the chair at the other side of Gwen's desk, placing the manuscript she held in her lap.

"What's the problem?" Gwen asked.

Frances glanced down at the manuscript, then dismissed it with a wave of her hand. "Nothing with this," she confessed. "I just used it as an excuse to come in—Betsy said business only." She held up her hand as she saw Gwen frown. "But this *is* about business," she assured her hurriedly. "I came in to tell you that we're behind you one hundred percent."

"We?"

"My organization," Frances explained, leaning forward, her eyes glowing. "If those sons of bitches upstairs try anything because of what happened, we'll throw a picket line around here so fast their heads will spin. We're prepared to get you the best civil-rights lawyer around and fight them in court if necessary. We'll—"

"Please!" Gwen held up her hand, her depression deepening at the thought of adding court battles and picket lines to her troubles, "I appreciate your interest, but whatever happened down here— Well, it will be my problem, and I'll handle it in whatever way I see fit."

"But it isn't just your problem," Frances insisted. "It's the problem of all women in the business world. We're not going to let them get away with—"

"It's *my* problem first," Gwen cut in, her voice firm, "and womankind's second. Therefore, it's my prerogative to choose the way in which it will be handled—and I choose to handle it alone."

"But—"

"No buts." Gwen's voice softened, and she searched Frances's face for a sign of understanding. "Please, Frances. I have all the troubles I can bear right now. Don't ask me to take on those of half the world too."

For a second, there was a flash of sympathy in Frances's eyes. Then, their old hardness returning, she rose. "All right." She sighed like a mother reluctantly giving in to a child's outrageous whim. "But if you change your mind, you know who to come to."

Nodding, Gwen watched her leave the office. Then she picked up her blue pencil and went back to work.

At 9:40, the summons from on high finally arrived. Gwen's phone rang, and after answering it, Betsy buzzed her on the intercom. "Mr. Bart would like to see you."

"Thanks."

After a quick check in her mirror, Gwen left her office. There was a distinct lull in the activities of the outer office when she entered it, but though she felt all eyes on her, whenever she turned to meet someone's gaze, it slid away like quicksilver.

As she approached Bill's office, she noticed that his door was open. Hoping to pass by unnoticed, she quickened her pace, but Bill caught sight of her. Calling her name, he came after her, took her hand and pulled her into his cubicle.

"What the hell is it with you?" he demanded with tender sternness, closing the door behind them. "Shari and I have been going crazy trying to reach you all weekend, and this morning Betsy Boop out there tells me you won't take any calls from me."

She shook her head helplessly. "I can't talk yet, that's all—not to people I know really care."

Love After Hours

"Then for Christ's sake, just nod your head. Are you okay?"

She smiled a little in spite of herself. "I'm here, aren't I?"

"That's a bloody evasion."

"It will have to do for the time being. I can't stay here talking. Jason just sent for me."

His face became grim. "I'll go with you."

She shook her head. "It's my battle, Bill. I'll handle it alone." Her expression left no opening for argument.

He sank down on his chair. "All right. Let me know how it goes."

"I will." She opened the door.

"The minute you get back."

"Promise."

"Gwen."

Halfway out, she turned. "Yes?"

"Good luck, kid."

"Thanks."

She closed the door behind her. Then, instead of waiting for the elevator, she walked up the two flights to Jason Bart's office.

For once, Jason did not pretend to be the busy executive. His eyes followed her as she crossed the carpet to his huge mahogany desk.

"You wanted to see me," she said.

He nodded toward a conference chair.

She sat back, relaxed, completely devoid of feeling. The worst thing that could happen in her life had already happened. Any complications Jason intended to add would be purely anticlimactic. Her eyes never wavered from his. Evidently he'd already had a few drinks to start the day. It would have been flattering to think that he had taken them for courage to face this interview, but Gwen knew only too well that Jason had taken them from habit and for the normal fortification he needed to face each day. Crossing her legs, she waited.

Jason immediately came to the point. "I'm sure you've seen the papers."

"More than that, I've lived through the nightmare they report and the additional one they've created."

"Well, then," he said, leaning back, "knowing how ugly the situation is for you, you must be able to see how deplorable it is for the company."

Calmly, Gwen shook her head. "I'm afraid I don't. The 'situation,' as you call it, exists only in my personal life. It has nothing to do with the company. Therefore, the company should have no feeling about it at all."

He raised an eyebrow. "I think you're deliberately trying to evade the point."

"Then I'm sure you'll do your level best to make me see it."

"You're a perceptive woman, Gwen. I don't know why you insist that I spell it out for you, but since you do, I will." He leaned forward, his eyes hardening. "Waterford's reputation is only as good as the reputations of its employees. It cannot afford to keep on its staff someone who, even if unintentionally, has made a bad name for herself."

"And the name I made for myself over the past eleven years as a top-notch editor, the fact that I've raised the income from and the guarantee on my magazine in the past few months so that it has nosed out *Modern Movies* and become the third best seller in the company's magazine line —all that counts for nothing?"

For a second he had the grace to look a little uncomfortable, but the expression quickly fled. "Not, I'm afraid, when it's measured against your current notoriety."

Gwen began to speak, but Jason cut her off, holding up one hand and reaching for a pile of papers on his desk with the other. "These," he said, "are telegrams from advertisers demanding your removal. And these," he nodded toward another pile, "are letters from your readers demanding the same."

Gwen smiled ironically. "So, what my readers will forgive in my narrators they won't forgive in me!"

"Apparently." Having made his case, he pushed the two piles aside. "So now you see why we have to let you go."

She shook her head. "No," she said calmly. "I don't see

why at all." She nodded toward the piles of paper. "They're really not so very big. We have many more advertisers and many thousands more readers."

He spread his hands. "It's only the beginning of the week."

"Come now, Jason!" she said. "We both know human nature better than that. People who feel strongly enough to protest something in writing do it immediately or not at all. There may well be a few more letters and telegrams before the week is out—but not many."

"Whether more come in or not is not really a consideration. The Waterfords' minds are made up."

"And I've no doubt," Gwen said, gesturing toward the papers, "that their minds were made up to dismiss me before any of these arrived on the scene. They're simply happy accidents that can be put to work after the fact."

Jason sighed. "Be that as it may, they've made their decision and relayed it to me. I have no choice in the matter but to pass it on to you."

She rose, smiling bitterly. "Rather a twist on the poor-little-rich-boy theme, isn't it? The poor little editorial director who sits in his plush, gold-plated office, collecting his annual six-figure salary, and who is powerless to do anything but carry out all the decisions handed down from upstairs."

Jason leaned forward, frowning. "Now, Gwen—"

"Now Jason!" Her voice did not rise in volume, but increased in intensity. "Let's stop pussy-footing around. Being fired is no problem to me. I have worse things to contend with right now. From the minute my personal hell broke loose on Thursday, I suspected I'd be finished here. I came in today to see if you'd have the guts to give me the real reason for firing me. Now I know that you haven't."

"Obviously, you're distraught and not thinking straight." His voice was soft, his look that of a slightly bleary-eyed doctor trying to soothe a mental patient. "I gave you the reasons—the notoriety that surrounds you and the reaction of readers and advertisers."

"You gave me excuses, not reasons." Her eyes flashed. "I'm being fired because I'm a woman, and because in this male-organized world, a woman must be punished if any scandal touches her. You'd no doubt like to brand me with an *A* before you throw me out, but since that's passé, you'll settle for just throwing me out."

"I think you're taking this too personally," Jason insisted. "The Waterfords would react this way to anyone in the same situation."

"Not to a man they wouldn't, and neither would you!" Pressing her palms on his desk, she leaned toward him. "Admit it, Jason: If the same scandal had surrounded a man who had the kind of record I have, you'd have gone to bat for him the minute the Waterfords raised a triplicate eyebrow." She straightened up. "No, on second thought, you wouldn't have. But only because you wouldn't have had to—the Waterfords would never have considered firing him in the first place. They'd have snickered and winked, and the most that would have come out of the whole business would have been a memo to the man involved asking him to try to be a little more discreet about his affairs in the future."

She took a deep breath. In spite of her resolve to remain calm, her heart was pounding and the palms of her clenched hands were damp. "But a woman—oh, a woman's different, isn't she? She has Eve's curse upon her soul. She has to be made to stand naked and shamed before the world. Well, Jason, you and the Brothers Three can strip me of my job, but you can't strip me of my dignity. I'm no better and no worse than any man who ever erred."

"I assure you that you're grossly misinterpreting the facts," Jason protested.

Sighing, she shook her head wearily. "A little while ago, you told me I was a perceptive woman. I return the compliment. Don't degrade yourself by trying to stretch the hypocrisy any further. Look around you at all the men at Waterford who have weathered scandals and are here to tell the tale. I rest my case."

He blanched, and she realized that her words must have reminded him of the scandal surrounding his own wife's death. She hadn't had it in mind when she spoke and would probably not have said what she had if his situation had occurred to her. Now that the damage was done, however, she could not bring herself to feel sorry. She had been through

Love After Hours

too much lately; there was no room in her heart for pity for hypocrites. She started to walk away.

"Just a minute!" Jason called after her. "I have something more to say."

She turned back toward him, her hand on the doorknob. "At this point, does it make any difference?"

"It could make a great deal of difference to you."

As incredulous as it seemed in the circumstances, Gwen was sure he was trying to look benevolent.

"You see," he said magnanimously, "we're prepared to let you stay on for a few weeks, even a month. It will give you time to keep your eyes and ears open for something else and still collect your salary."

"And it will enable you to take your time finding the right person to fill my shoes, while not suffering any losses until then, because the magazine will still be in my very capable hands," Gwen said just as sweetly.

Smiling, he raised his hands in a gesture of amicable defeat. "All right—so you can see through to the other side of the coin. It will be a mutually beneficial arrangement. There's something to be said for that."

Gwen's gaze never left his eyes. "Yes," she said brightly, "three words: Go screw yourself."

She turned on her heel and left.

Downstairs, the door to Bill's office was open. Tapping it gently, Gwen stepped inside. "All right to close this?" she asked. "Or are you experimenting with air currents?"

Bill looked up from his work. "Close it. I kept it open only because I was afraid you'd try to sneak by again."

She sank down on a chair at the side of his desk.

"How did it go?" he asked.

She shrugged. "As I expected. I got the sack."

"Goddamn it to hell!" Bill jumped up from his chair.

"For heaven's sake, Bill! Calm down. I expected as much."

"Well, I didn't. Not when they put up with Cam's womanizing, Nolan West's guzzling, and the scrapes half the advertising guys are always getting themselves into. I thought they'd settle for a sharp rap on the knuckles."

"There's something you're overlooking. A woman has to be twice as good as a man—on the job and off—remember?"

"The hell she does!" He started across the room. "If you have to go, I'm going too."

"Bill, no!" Jumping up, she rushed over and grabbed his arm before he had a chance to open the door. "I told you before, it's my battle!"

"And this is my decision!" His hand was on the knob.

"No! It's not going to change anything for me, and you'll only make a pack of trouble for yourself."

He gestured impatiently, but she rushed on. "You're not entitled to such a decision—throwing over your job to protest someone else's unjust treatment. It's like trying to hold the tide back with one hand. You'd only be drowned. And you have too many people depending on you for bread and butter and a roof over their heads. Futile gestures are for the young and unencumbered."

Bill shook his head. "You don't understand. I've worked my way into being too valuable a property for them to let me go easily. My threat of resignation may well get them to reinstate you."

"And if it doesn't?"

"Then I wouldn't want to stay here any longer anyway."

"That's nonsense. You know as well as I do that anyplace else you go would be the same." She put her hand on his arm. "I know that it's as a friend that you want to do this, but I'm asking you—as a friend—not to. It's not sour grapes when I say I wouldn't come back here if they asked me; it's a simple statement of fact. It's my problem and my life, Bill, so lay off."

Putting his hand over hers, he smiled sadly. "All right. When it comes to your life, you should be the boss. I can't argue with that."

For a moment they stood looking at each other, as close as two friends can be. Then Bill dropped her hand and slammed his own against the door.

"Christ!" he said, his voice cracking a little as he turned his face away. "If only Doc were alive!"

"But he isn't," she said softly. Then remembering Paul's words, she added, "Let's not start with if onlys." She put her hand on the doorknob.

Bill turned back to her, his eyes sparkling, but not with mischief. "Where do you go from here?"

She shrugged. "I have lots of connections. I'll find something sooner or later."

"I have no doubt about that," he said. "I wasn't talking about a job."

Smiling sadly, she shook her head. "Right now, that's the only problem I have that I'm willing to talk about."

"Well, when you need to talk or want to talk, you know where Shari and I are. God knows, you've done enough for us. It's time we did something for you."

"Just knowing you're there is enough." Her eyes filling, she took his hand. "Right now, I have some loose ends to tie up, and you have work to do. I'll be seeing you."

"Scout's honor?"

"Scout's honor." She drew a breath, hoping her voice would sound normal when she said her usual parting words: "Love to Shari and the kids."

Bill nodded, but he could manage only a ghost of his cocky smile as he gave her his mock salute.

Quickly, she opened his door and closed it behind her.

Walking through the outer office toward her own cubicle, she pretended not to notice that all eyes were on her once again. She stopped at Betsy's desk, telling her to ask Laura to come into her office in about ten minutes.

At her door she paused, her eyes sweeping the room. All the curious stares that had been directed at her quickly faltered beneath her gaze—save one. Cam Eckhart, who until her appearance on the scene had distracted him, had been deep in conversation with a buxom new secretary, let his eyes meet hers for a full three seconds before flicking them away without a sign of recognition and abruptly turning his back on her. True to his tradition of deserting sinking ships, he had finally dropped all designs on her. Her lips curling in ironic amusement, Gwen swung her door open and she entered her office for the last time.

She had not occupied the office long enough to stamp her personality on it. There were only a few personal possessions to remove from her desktop and drawers, and none from the walls. By the time she had finished slipping her few ball-point pens, her ceramic pencil holder, her desk mirror, her emery board and her half-empty bottle of cologne into a large Manila envelope, there was a tap on the door, and Laura came in.

"Betsy said ten minutes, but I forgot my watch today. Am I too early?"

Gwen shook her head. "On the dot." She nodded toward the chair at the other side of her desk as she began winding the envelope's string around its fastener. Then she placed the envelope on her desk and gave it a little pat. Trying to keep her voice light, she said, "My worldly possessions."

Laura's eyes went from the envelope to Gwen's face. "You don't mean you're leaving!"

Gwen nodded.

"Don't do it, Gwen!" Shifting to the edge of the chair, she leaned toward Gwen, her face grave, her voice earnest. "Leaving would be running away, and no one who knows you could possibly believe that you have anything to run away from—no matter what the papers say."

Though they were less than a decade apart in age, Gwen suddenly felt centuries older than this lovely girl who was on the threshold of life. She smiled sadly. "It doesn't often happen, but this time I'm afraid your youth and innocence are showing, Laura. You'd be surprised at all the people who are prepared to believe the worst."

Laura frowned. "Then let them! People like that don't count."

"Around here, they count for a great deal." She sighed. "I'm not resigning, Laura. I've been fired."

For a second, Laura sat there in stunned silence. Then she jumped up, her eyes blazing. "The bastards! How could they do that to you after all you've done for this magazine?"

"I assure you, they found it very easy."

"Well, if you're through here, I'm through, too! I want no part of a company like this!" She whirled and started toward the door.

"Laura!" The name rushed from Gwen's lips like a command.

Obeying, Laura stopped and turned.

"There *is* no other kind of company." Gwen's voice was resigned. "Surely, you know that."

"I know it," Laura said softly, "but that doesn't excuse what Waterford has done to you, or make it any more acceptable to me."

"I didn't offer the observation as an excuse or as an exoneration. A person in my position would be the last to do that. All companies are the same, especially where women are concerned. If Waterford could dismiss me lightly, it would take your resignation lightly too. Bill wanted to do the same thing, and I insisted that he didn't—just as I'm going to insist that you don't. The gesture would be meaningless to everyone but me, and your staying here means more to me than your leaving."

Laura looked incredulous. "Surely, you're not talking about loyalty to the company!"

Smiling a little, Gwen shook her head. "I leave the propagation of that kind of nonsense to prigs like Cam Eckhart. The hell with Waterford! I'm talking about your loyalty to yourself and to the people you're directly responsible to—like David and the child you're carrying. I'm sure you have plans for the money you'll be earning during the last few months you'll be working. Don't screw them up. *I* don't want you to, and I'm the one you'd be doing it for." She nodded toward the chair. "Please. Come back and sit down."

Reluctantly, Laura crossed the room and perched on the chair. "I wish you'd try to see it my way."

"Believe me," Gwen insisted, "I *am* seeing it your way—far more than you are. You owe it to yourself, to David, and to the baby to stay." Spotting another pen that belonged to her, she opened the envelope and slipped it inside. "You know, I wouldn't be surprised if they offered you this." She made a little gesture that encompassed the room. "You really should think about it."

Laura shook her head emphatically. "No. I told you what my priorities are."

Gwen nodded. "Well, then," she said, her voice quivering a little, "I guess that's that." Vaguely, she looked around the room. "I think I have everything that's mine. If you should come across something..."

"I'll mail it," Laura picked up where she left off. She leaned forward. "Gwen, what are you going to do?"

Shrugging, Gwen rose from her chair and walked to the window where she stood looking out at the rain, watching a tug pull a garbage scow down river. "I'll find something. A new job will be the least of my problems."

Laura came over, her eyes brimming with tears. "I wish there were something I could say that would tell you all I feel about what's happened, and all I wish for you in what's to come."

Gwen took her hand. "Your eyes have said it all." She drew a deep breath, trying to steady her voice. "Do me a favor? Don't mention that I'm going until after I've left. Then say good-by for me. I know it's the coward's way out, but after facing the lion upstairs, I think I'm entitled to one cowardly act."

Laura's grip tightened on her hand. "There's a world of difference between cowardice and old-fashioned self-preservation. Don't worry. I'll take care of everything."

"Thanks." Despite her effort to control it, her voice cracked.

"Good luck, Gwen."

"You too. Take care of those priorities of yours." Gwen released her hand.

Her lips quivering slightly, Laura managed a smile. Then she turned and started toward the door.

Through eyes blurred with tears, Gwen watched Laura's exit, noting the thickening of her waist and broadening of her hips that hinted at her pregnancy through her loose-fitting clothes. She remembered how Laura had looked the evening she had revealed her condition—her face glowing, her eyes shining. She had been so sure then that she was making the right decision in giving up her career. Gwen closed her eyes, shaking her head. She hoped that Laura would always be sure, that she would not be destined to share Shari's fate and wake up one day feeling torn between two opposing worlds.

At the sound of the door gently closing, Gwen opened her eyes. She returned to her desk and sat down. Absently, she ran her fingertips along its edge, then wearily, she swiveled around in her chair and took one last look at her editorial domain. Sighing, she stood up and walked over to her coat

Love After Hours

tree, slipped on her trench coat, tied her scarf beneath her chin. She picked up her purse and her envelope and opened the door, relieved to see that Betsy was not at her desk.

As she started across the outer office, the volume of typing increased; the secretaries were determined to appear too busy to notice her final exit. Bill's door was closed now and she was glad; she could not bear any more good-bys. Over the top of his partition, the soft tan of his wailing wall stood out in stark relief against the surrounding institutional green. It was the last thing she glimpsed as she went through the door that led to the corridor and the elevators.

Because it was only a little after eleven, she had the elevator to herself. Crossing quickly through the lobby, she pushed open the heavy glass door that led to the street and ducked her head against the rain. Not until she was almost upon him did she notice a man huddled near the entrance. Her head still down, she saw only the skirt of his raincoat, raindrops making little rivulets to its edge then leaping onto his damp trousers and wet shoes.

"Paul!"

Her heart felt as though it were still in the elevator, and the blood rushed to her head so fast that it fogged her vision and dazed her senses. If he had not reached out and grabbed her arm, she might have fallen. For a moment she sagged against his damp shoulder, relaxing in the hard, strong circle of protection offered by his arms. Finally she pulled away and looked up at him, her face wet with tears and rain.

"Why did you come?" she asked, the ache in her throat audible in every word. "It will only make it harder for both of us."

"It can never be harder." His face was drawn and lined, his eyes and voice heavy with weariness.

How can one person age so much in so few days, Gwen wondered. But she knew how. The same way she had aged—both inside and out.

"If necessary, I was prepared to wait here all day for you to walk through those doors," he said, his hands firm on her arms. "We have to talk."

Tears crowding her eyes, she shook her head. "There's nothing left to talk about."

"Then we'll sit and stare at each other like Quakers until one of us has a revelation," he said. "But first let's get out of this rain."

His arm tight around her shoulders, as though he were afraid she might bolt, he led her in a quick-trot down the street. They turned off at Seventh Avenue and ducked into Nick's. Since it was still well before the lunch-hour rush, they had the place to themselves and managed to walk all the way to a table at the rear before Beauregard was aware of their presence.

"Good morning! Good morning!" he said, bobbing over and rubbing his hands together. His smile faded a little as he recognized them; in this modern age, even sacred grottoes are not immune to news of scandal. "Ah, Miss Hadley, Mr. Lockhart. An early lunch today?"

"No, just coffee," Gwen said, looking toward Paul, who nodded his agreement.

"Coffee. That's fine. Fine." Having given his approval to the order, Beauregard hurried off.

While Gwen removed her wet scarf and ran her fingers through her damp hair, Paul lit his pipe. "You *are* out early," he said. "How come?"

"I was fired."

He slammed the pipe down in the ashtray. "Those sons of bitches! I'll—"

"Don't," Gwen pleaded. "They're not worth your anger, and neither is the job. I expected as much. I don't really think I care—I'm too numb from everything else."

Beauregard brought their coffee and bobbed away.

"Everything else," Paul said, his eyes holding hers. "That's what we really have to talk about, isn't it? Why have you been running from me, Gwen?"

"I'm not running, Paul," she said softly. "I'm holding firm." There was an awful ache pushing at the back of her eyes. Her throat tried to close up and forbid passage to her next words, but somehow she forced them out. "It's over, Paul. It has to be."

Never had she seen such pain in another's eyes. "It doesn't have to be unless we let it. We've been to hell and back, but we're still the same two people, our love is the same." He ran

Love After Hours

his hand across his eyes. "God! That's the only thing that kept me going these past few days—the knowledge that no matter how upside down my world became, what we have together can never change. Are you trying to tell me now that your feelings have changed?"

Her heart had never been more full of love than at that moment, sitting across the table from the man who had become her whole world, the man she was convinced she must give up. She longed to reach over and smooth the lines that sorrow, worry and hurt were etching so deeply in his face, to kiss away the agony she read in his eyes. Instead, she clutched her hands tightly in front of her.

"It isn't my love that's changed, Paul," she managed to say at last. "It's our circumstances." She drew a shuddering breath. "Do you remember the night we realized we couldn't take the hotel route to love? Remember how you said that we couldn't go back to the way we were before that? Well, we can't go back now, either. Not after what's happened."

He reached across the table and took her hand. "I don't want to go back. I want to go on."

The warmth of his touch radiated throughout her body, until withdrawing her hand was like turning her back on the sun. "Paul, what's happened to you? You were always the one who could see things clearly. Why can't you see that we can't go on—not with Verna's death between us. Right now, we're blaming ourselves. How long would it be before we started blaming each other?"

"But we're *not* to blame!" He ran his hand over his tortured face, but it could not smooth away the lines of pain. "Oh, God! I know! I know!" he said in answer to the protest he realized was about to leave her lips. "That's reasoning, and it has no effect on the emotions. God knows all the nights I've lain awake, all the moments I've felt like tearing my hair out because I didn't make more of an effort to keep my word about picking her up for that goddam party. But two facts remain: The first is that she brought it all on herself; and the second is that, according to the doctor, she would have died even if I'd arrived at the proper time, because she had so much liquor in her before she took all those pills. Sooner or later, we'll learn to accept that."

"And what about Melanie?" Gwen asked quietly. "Will she learn to accept it?"

"What about Melanie?" Paul countered, his eyes searching hers. "Do you realize how much she needs you right now? She's completely withdrawn into herself since this happened. Can you imagine the guilt feelings of her own that that child must be trying to deal with? Verna was such a bitch to her that she probably wished her dead a thousand times—and now it's happened. I can see that she's tearing herself apart inside over it, but she won't let me get through to her." He leaned across the table, his eyes pleading. "You could do it, Gwen. You could help her through this awful time."

Her heart aching, Gwen shook her head. "She hardly knows me, Paul. If she's locked you out, she certainly wouldn't let me in."

"But she would!" he insisted. "You have no idea how much you mean to her. Ever since her birthday, you've been almost all she'd talk about when we were alone. She seemed to be longing for the day when she could see you again."

"That was before all this happened. Surely, after what's been in the papers, I'm the last person she'd want to see."

"I've kept all that ugliness from her." Paul dismissed the argument with an impatient wave of his hand. "As far as she knows, Verna died from an accidental overdose of sleeping pills. You don't think that the friends and relatives who have been helping take care of her are going to tell her anything different, do you?"

"She's not going to be surrounded by kind relatives and friends forever. Sooner or later, someone—either out of stupidity or maliciousness—is going to let the newspaper version of the truth slip. Then where will we be? She'll hate us both."

"Not if we're truthful with her and handle the situation right from the beginning."

"Don't you see that's exactly what I'm trying to do—handle it right by getting out of your lives?"

"Right for whom?" he demanded. "For yourself—so you can run and hide? Melanie and I need you now—and you need us." He reached for her hand again. "Gwen, I'm not asking you to run right out and marry me tomorrow. What I'm asking you to do is to help me through this terrible period and to let me help you through it—step by step, one day at a time, until the time comes when we feel strong enough to take the future in our hands and mold it. Right now, helping each other is all that matters."

Tears welled up in her eyes, and every beat of her heart sent a knifing pain through her chest. "That isn't all that matters," she whispered. "The future matters too—not only Melanie's but ours." She forced herself to withdraw her hand. "Whether we help Melanie now won't really matter in a few years, because she'll grow up and leave us one way or another. But Verna never will. What she has done will erode everything we have."

"My God!" he said, clenching his fists. "What do I have to do to make you realize that we're not responsible? Even the press has made that clear. Every man and woman who has been slavering over their copies of *The News* or *The Post* will tell you that Verna brought it all on herself. Why can't you accept that too? God knows, I hated what she was doing to me, to us, to Melanie, but I never wanted her dead. I'm appalled by her death and the surrounding circumstances. You are too. It's because we're the kind of people we are that we feel regret and even guilt. But the fact remains that she brought it on herself."

"One other fact remains, Paul." Her voice quivered with the effort of pushing it past the tears dammed up in her throat. "The fact that if it hadn't been for our love, for our affair, she could never have dreamed up such an awful scheme. We provided her excuse. That's what's fatal to us. That's what we have to live with for the rest of our lives. Apart, we might make it, but together, never."

"Dammit!" he hissed. "It's apart that we'll be destroyed. Only together can we help each other rise above the mess Verna created. She was her own victim. She was like a woman who bought a gun intending to kill her husband and his lover, but while laying a trap for them accidentally discharged the gun and killed herself instead. But she was worse than that kind of woman, because her motivation wasn't one of human passion—love or jealousy or even hate. Verna's motivation was cold, calculating ambition." He shook his head. "Sure, our affair provided her with the excuse she used.

But even if she hadn't known about us, Verna would have invented another excuse to put on the same macabre publicity show—and it would have backfired on her the same way. Verna didn't care about destroying us—all she cared about was using us as a means to create interest in her own career. And if she hadn't used us, she'd have used someone or something else. She was a cruel, conniving, twisted, neurotic woman. We can't let her destroy us."

"She already has." The pain in Gwen's chest was excruciating. "Do you think I want it this way?"

Paul opened his mouth to answer, then closed it abruptly. His eyes raked over her face, and anger suddenly replaced the grief and hurt that had been visible in their depths. He clenched his hands on the table until the knuckles showed white beneath the skin.

"God help us," he said, his voice ominously quiet, "I think you do."

Her head snapped back as though he'd slapped her, and tears sprang into her eyes. "Paul!"

"It's true." His nostrils dilated, and a nerve in his jaw began to jump. "You're as afraid of love's commitments now as you've always been, and you're using Verna's death as an excuse to run away from them."

She shook her head, hurt and unbelieving. "No, no! You're wrong!"

"I wish to God I were." He closed his eyes, and when he opened them again, they seemed dull and lifeless. "A year ago," he said wearily, "I had my daughter, I had my work. I thought I was set for life. So what if I never knew what real love was like? So what if there was a big empty hole somewhere in the center of my soul? I was managing. What the hell difference did it make?" He shook his head. "Then I met you, and I found out what the difference was—the difference between light and darkness, between being alive and numbering myself among the living dead."

"Do you think it was any different for me?" Her lips were trembling so much it was difficult to control them and make them form around her words.

"I think it was a damn sight different, or you wouldn't be ready to turn your back on all we had!"

Love After Hours

"But Paul! Don't you see—"

"I do see! That's the problem. I see so much, it makes me sick." He leaned across the table, coming so close that she could feel his breath hissing against her face. "I see the woman I love more than life itself running out on me because she's too damn scared to stand by me when the going gets rough." His eyes blazed. "I was stupid enough to believe you were over all your fears when you took that apartment, but I was wrong; you were only masking them. You were willing to play house—but that's all. Now that I really need your help and support, you're running scared." He held up a hand to ward off her protests. "Oh, you make a great show of basing our breakup on moral grounds, but the truth is that you're scared stiff of standing by me, because you know that eventually it will lead to a final and binding commitment." He stood up, his face livid with rage, his eyes deadened with disillusionment. "I only wonder what your excuse would have been if Verna had gone through with the divorce as planned."

All through Paul's accusations, Gwen had been shaking her head in denial, fighting desperately to keep down the silent scream that was rising inside her like a wail of mourning. "Paul, please!" she begged. "Don't say such terrible things. You're breaking my heart."

"Not any more than you've broken mine."

"Why won't you listen to reason? Why do you refuse to see that this is the way it has to be?"

"Because it isn't the way it has to be. It's the way you want it to be."

"No, *no!* I love you!"

"Not enough!" he grated. "Not enough to help me through this terrible time. You're as scared to death of love's commitments as you were when we first met. Well, I won't infringe on your precious independence any longer. I give you back to it—and to your fears. Maybe you'll find happiness with them. As for me—" His eyes clouded and his voice broke. "—all I can say is that the guy who said it's better to have loved and lost must have been demented."

Twice she opened her mouth, but no sound could penetrate her grief. When she finally managed to whisper his name, it was too late. He had already turned his back on her and begun to walk toward the exit. Closing her eyes over her tears, she listened to his footsteps, heard the cash register ring as he paid their bill, heard the front door close with a soft click that was like a switchblade opening and entering her heart. Tears pushed past her lashes and slipped down her cheeks as she opened her eyes.

"Miss Hadley, Miss Hadley! Are you all right?" Beauregard was standing over her.

She fished in her purse for a tissue and wiped her eyes. "Yes, yes. I'm fine," she said.

He gave a quick shake of his head. "You and Mr. Lockhart didn't drink your coffee, and now it's cold. Cold. I'll bring you another cup."

"No, please. I don't want any more." She wished he'd go.

His gaze went to the ashtray, and he clicked his tongue. "And Mr. Lockhart left his pipe." He looked toward the door.

She shrugged apathetically. What was a pipe compared to everything else they'd lost? "It makes no difference. He has others."

"As you say. As you say."

She stared straight ahead of her, but still he did not move away.

"You know," he said suddenly, "the people who come in here think I'm like a machine." He bobbed his head as she looked up at him. "That's what they think. That's what they think." Shrugging, he made a choppy gesture of dismissal with his hand. "Let them. As long as they keep coming back, I don't care. But I'm not a machine. I think and I feel like everybody else. And right now I think and feel that you are very sad."

She tried to respond, but he held up his hand.

"No. You don't have to deny it. I know you have trouble. I just want to say that I'm sorry. Really sorry."

She could tell from his eyes that he meant it. "Thank you, Beauregard."

"And I just want to remind you that life goes on. Life goes on."

"That, Beauregard," she said softly, "is the hell of it."

He looked puzzled by her remark, but did not have time to ponder it. The front door opened and he hurried off to greet his first customers for lunch.

Absently, Gwen watched him lead them to a table, but in her mind she was taking measure of the long, lonely stretch of life that lay ahead of her. It would have been so much easier to face if Paul had seen things as she did. But how could she bear to walk that road with the memory of his scorn?

Oh, Paul! she thought, slipping her purse onto her shoulder and picking up her envelope and scarf. *Why did you have to say such hurting things? Why did you have to make it end in bitterness?*

He was wrong. So wrong. After all they had meant to each other, how could he misjudge her love that way? Biting her lip to still its trembling, she rose to go. Why couldn't he see that she *did* love him enough, that it was just that . . . Her thoughts trailed off, and she felt a frightening confusion. Just that what? Frantically, she searched her mind for a comforting answer, but somehow the moral grounds she had been pleading earlier sounded as weak to her now as they had to Paul. How could it be right to allow an evil and malicious act to destroy something that was pure and good when they had the power to save it?

She clenched her fists and shook her head to clear it. She had to pull herself together. Now was no time to have doubts. Not now when everything was over.

Over. Her blood seemed to freeze in her veins at the thought, and the emptiness she had sensed waiting for her outside was suddenly within her. It was over. Finally and brutally. All along, she had seen herself as making a noble sacrifice of love, but Paul had robbed her of that illusion. And without that illusion, what was left? Only the truth. The truth that Paul had seen. The brutal truth that she would have to live with in the self-imposed vacuum that would be the rest of her life.

Idiot! a silent voice screamed inside her. *Stupid, frightened idiot!* She had held love in her hands and thrown it away.

Her eyes blurring with tears, she took a lingering look at

the untouched coffee cups on the table, at Paul's vacant chair, at his forgotten pipe. Gently, as though afraid it might shy away, she reached out and touched the pipe. How would she be able to stand life without Paul? Her fingers closed over the pipe, and she brought it up to her face, pressing it hard against her cheek. Then suddenly, as though the pipe had touched a vital hidden switch, her heart began to pound with a vigor she'd thought she'd never know again. The blood that had frozen in her veins melted, and as its life-giving warmth coursed through her body, she realized that in recognizing the last vestiges of her fears she had finally defeated them. She did not have to face the loneliness and the void after all.

Jamming the pipe into her pocket, she rushed out of Nick's.

The sky had cleared. The rain had left behind only little puddles that winked and sparkled in the bright sunlight. Frantically, she looked in both directions, finally spotting Paul down the street. His hands were in his pockets and his head bent. How old he looked. How broken. And it was her fault. All her fault.

She ran as she had never run before, flying past the early lunchers, dodging through traffic. Her legs ached with the effort, but still she pushed them on, her chest expanding to take in great gulps of air, her purse thwacking hard against her side.

"Paul!" she cried as she closed the gap between them. "Paul!"

At last he heard and turned, incredulous, just as she caught up with him.

Panting, her heart pounding, her nostrils quivering with the effort of breathing, she extended the pipe toward him with a trembling hand.

"You left this."

For a moment he didn't speak; his eyes probed deep into hers as he searched for answers that went beyond words.

"I left something else too," he said at last.

She shook her head. "I'm not giving back your love."

The words seemed suspended in the air between them,

Love After Hours

echoing off the cars and the buildings, reverberating through all the street noises that surrounded them.

His expression impassive, Paul stood there and continued to study her. Her heart began to pound with a new fear—the most awful fear of all—the fear that he would now reject her love.

Then, slowly, as if to assure himself that she was truly there before him, Paul reached out and touched her cheek. "It won't be easy." His eyes sparkled and his voice was husky with tears.

Her trembling lips curved into a smile. "Who," she asked, slipping her hand through the arm he held out to her, "ever said it should be?"

"One of the best books of the year."
The New York Times Book Review

endless love

By SCOTT SPENCER
author of LAST NIGHT AT THE BRAIN THIEVES BALL and PRESERVATION HALL

Praised unanimously by critics across the nation, ENDLESS LOVE is an astonishingly sensual story about the sheer agony and unbearable ecstasy of first love. It is about a young man who ventures beyond passion into exquisite madness. It is about the crime of loving too much.

"Satisfying and fully dramatized...a genuine love story. ...It reaffirms those fundamental truths of the human heart: Love is real, love is contagious, love hurts, love feels wonderful, love changes us, love is like the fire in its spark and appetite."
Tim O'Brien, *Saturday Review*

"Stunning, breathtaking....For a few hours of my life it broke my heart."
Jonathan Yardley—*Los Angeles Herald-Examiner*

"I devoured it....Reading Mr. Spencer's novel you remember for a while when it seemed possible to die of love."
Christopher Lehmann-Haupt, *The New York Times Book Review*

AVON Paperback　　　　　　　　50823/$2.75

Available wherever paperbacks are sold, or directly from the publisher. Include 50¢ per copy for postage and handling; allow 4-6 weeks for delivery. Avon Books, Mail Order Dept. 224 West 57th Street, New York, N.Y. 10019